Our Sweet
Violet

Rosie Goodwin is the four-million-copy bestselling author of more than forty novels. She is the first author in the world to be allowed to follow three of Catherine Cookson's trilogies with her own sequels. Having worked in the social services sector for many years, then fostered a number of children, she is now a full-time novelist. She is one of the top fifty most borrowed authors from UK libraries and has sold over four million copies across her career. Rosie lives in Nuneaton, the setting for many of her books, with her husband and their beloved dogs.

Rosie GOODWIN

Our Sweet Violet

ZAFFRE

First published in the UK in 2025 by
ZAFFRE
An imprint of Bonnier Books UK
5th Floor, HYLO, 103–105 Bunhill Row, London, EC1Y 8LZ
Owned by Bonnier Books
Sveavägen 56, Stockholm, Sweden

A CIP catalogue record for this book is
available from the British Library.

ISBN: 978-1-80418-306-9

Also available as an ebook and an audiobook

1 3 5 7 9 10 8 6 4 2

Typeset by IDSUK (Data Connection) Ltd
Printed and bound in Great Britain by Clays Ltd, Elcograf S.p.A.

MIX
Paper | Supporting
responsible forestry
FSC® C018072

Zaffre is an imprint of Bonnier Books UK
www.bonnierbooks.co.uk

This one is for each and every one of you who is reading this book, with all my love and thanks for your ongoing support.
Rosie xx

Prologue

Outside the snow was falling fast, and as the doctor joined his wife and his one-year-old son at the side of a roaring fire in their smart home in Swan Lane, he heaved a sigh of relief. As well as doing his regular morning surgery, he had been out on house calls all afternoon. Flu was sweeping through the town, and sadly the old and the very young were dropping like flies, despite his best efforts to save them. It was the same every winter.

'So you're finally back.' His wife sniffed her disapproval and laid her embroidery aside. 'And I suppose you're hungry now.'

William Stroud nodded as he peeped into his son's crib. 'Starving actually. I only had time for a sandwich before I left after surgery. I haven't stopped all day.'

'Then let's hope all those that you've visited pay up,' she answered sarcastically as she rose from her seat and went to pull the rope at the side of the fire. She knew her husband was inclined to do free visits for the poorer members of the community. 'I imagine Cook would have put your dinner in the oven to keep warm, although I'm sure it will be ruined by now.'

There was a tap at the door and the maid appeared.

'Nellie, did Cook save any dinner for the doctor?'

'Yes, ma'am. Shall I lay the table again in the dining room?'

'No, no, Nellie, there'll be no need for you to go to all that trouble,' the doctor assured her. 'I can have it on a tray or in the kitchen, if you and Cook don't mind?'

'Right you are, sir. I'll go an' get it out o' the oven for you if you'd like to come through.'

He followed her out of the room. Behind him, his wife lifted her embroidery and continued with what she had been doing. William Stroud knew his wife didn't approve of him eating in the kitchen with the servants, but tonight he was too tired to care.

As he entered the kitchen Cook, who was sitting to the side of the fire in a comfy chair with a pot of tea at the side of her, smiled.

'Hello, lad, come an' take the weight off your feet,' she urged kindly. 'You look fair worn out!'

Edie Thompson had been William's father's cook before William was born and when the old doctor had passed away and his son had taken over the surgery, she had stayed on. She could still remember clearly the day William had been born and she had loved him like a son ever since.

Edie was in her early fifties now and William often worried that the job might be too hard for her, but she wouldn't hear of retiring.

'I'm as fit as a fiddle,' she would tell him whenever he broached the subject and William was glad. He couldn't imagine his life without Edie in it.

Seconds later Nellie placed his dinner on the table and William's stomach rumbled with anticipation. Cook had made him one of his favourites: steak and ale pie with lashings of mashed potatoes and vegetables to go with it, and as he began to eat, he felt himself warming up.

'This is delicious, Cook,' he told her as he tucked in, and she preened with pleasure. William was always grateful, unlike that snooty wife of his.

'So, what's her ladyship doin'?' she asked caustically and William grinned.

'Now, Cook, there's no need for that,' he scolded gently. 'She was embroidering I believe.'

'Huh!' Cook poured herself another cup of tea as she stared at the piles of wooden crates spaced around the edge of the room. 'I'd have thought she'd be helpin' wi' all the packin' we've still to do. It's only a month now till we move.'

'It'll get done,' William assured her. 'The nanny is seeing to all of Oliver's things up in the nursery and it looks like you've made a good start in here.'

'It's a case of havin' to! I just hope we don't all live to regret leavin' here! It's a long way away is Hull!'

'I'm sure we'll be fine once we've settled in,' William said confidently.

Nellie instantly started to cry as she dabbed at her eyes with her handkerchief. Sadly, she wouldn't be going with them. She was engaged to be married and so had chosen to stay in Nuneaton, although she hadn't managed to get another position as yet. She had enjoyed working for young Doctor Stroud and would miss him, although she couldn't say the same about his wife. Anna made no secret of the fact that she felt she had married beneath herself. She had come from one of the wealthiest families in the town and they had all been shocked when she suddenly decided to marry the young doctor. There was no doubt that with her looks and breeding she could have had her pick of any of the suitors who had pursued her, but then Nellie supposed stranger things had happened. With his thick dark hair and deep brown eyes, William was a catch after all.

She had just poured the doctor a cup of tea when an urgent knocking sounded on the front door and the cook sighed.

'Eeh, I hope that ain't somebody needin' a visit,' she said. Then turning her attention to Nellie, she asked her, 'Go an' answer that would yer, lovie.'

Nellie hurried away only to return minutes later to tell the doctor, 'There's a lady at the door demandin' to see yer, Doctor Stroud. She has a baby wi' her.'

3

William sighed. So much for a peaceful evening by the fire with his newspaper.

'All right, Nellie. Show her into the surgery, would you, and tell her I'll be with her presently.'

He lifted his cup and quickly drained it. 'No peace for the wicked, eh?' He gave Cook a wry grin and quietly left the room.

He saw the door to his surgery was open and he entered with a smile on his face. But it quickly died away as he found himself staring into the eyes of a young woman who was clutching a baby to her chest. She had fair hair and blue eyes with nothing but a thin shawl about her shoulders over her shabby gown to keep the cold at bay.

'S . . . Sadie!' He hastily closed the door behind him before asking, 'What brings you here?'

'I had to come,' she told him in a wobbly voice. 'I just got thrown out of my digs because I'm behind with my rent and I've nowhere to go. So . . . the long and the short of it is, you'll have to take her.'

Now William's eyes almost popped out of his head as he stared at the tiny bundle in her arms. 'What do you mean I'll have to take her?'

'She's yours,' Sadie told him quietly as she stared down at the sleeping baby, who looked to be no more than two or three weeks old. 'I never told you I'd fallen for a child because we only ever lay together the once, and I wouldn't have done if I could have kept her. But things are impossible now, so I've no choice but to leave her with you.'

'B . . . but . . .' William was clearly in shock as she stepped forward and pressed the baby into his arms.

'Her name is Violet,' Sadie told him softly. 'Take good care of her.' And then stopping only long enough to kiss the infant's forehead, she left the room and seconds later he heard the front door shut behind her.

As he stared down at the baby she woke and stared up at him from eyes that were exactly the same colour as his own.

It was then that Nellie entered the room and she too looked shocked as she asked, 'Who's this then, sir?'

'She er . . .' William didn't know how to explain her away. 'The mother has left her here with us,' he said with a catch in his voice. 'It seems that she's been turned out of her room and she has nowhere to take the child.'

'Good grief!' Nellie looked almost as shocked as he felt. 'How long for? An' what is the missus goin' to say?' Nellie couldn't imagine that Anna would want another baby. She only had eyes for her own baby son, but certainly wasn't so keen on the practical side of caring for a child, hence the nanny.

'I'll have to go and tell her what's happened now,' William answered. 'And then you'd better ask the nanny if she'll come and fetch the baby for me.'

With his heart in his mouth, he set off for the drawing room. He dreaded what he was about to do but what choice did he have? He could hardly keep the baby hidden, so better to get it over with.

Anna blinked when her eyes settled on the baby and she scowled. The nanny had already been down to take Oliver and settle him in the nursery for the night. 'Who is this?'

'A young woman who has nowhere to go has just left her with us,' he told her as calmly as he could.

'*What?*' Anna looked horrified. 'Are we a home for waifs and strays now? Why didn't she leave her at the workhouse? The brat can't stay here!'

'You know as well as I do that most babies in the workhouse don't even survive until their first birthday! Would you *really* wish that on the child?'

There was something about the infant that was tugging at his heartstrings and suddenly he knew that Sadie had been telling the truth. This was *his* child; his own flesh and blood, and no way was he about to abandon her now.

Anna marched over to him, her pretty face a mask of fury, and as she flicked the shawl aside and examined the child, she gasped, looking from the baby to her husband.

'This is *your* child, isn't it?' Her eyes were flashing.

William's shoulders sagged; he might have known he couldn't fool her. She was as sharp as a knife. 'I'm afraid she is . . . but I can explain!'

'Explain? *Huh!* How do you explain a flyblow and the fact that you've been unfaithful to me?'

'It was only ever the one time . . .' he began, but she was in no mood to listen.

'What are we going to say to people? If I can see that she's yours, don't you think everyone else will? Why, we'll be a laughing stock! Or at least *I* will! How could you do this to me?' She started to pace the floor, her satin skirts swishing.

William's anger began to rise. All Anna cared about was what people would say. 'Well, you've hardly been an angel yourself, have you?'

She rounded on him. 'And just what is *that* supposed to mean?'

The child in his arms began to whimper at the raised voices. 'I fell in love with you the very first time I laid eyes on you.' His voice was as cold as the snow softly falling outside. 'But you weren't interested in a lowly doctor. Oh no, you had set your sights higher. On a certain young son of a wealthy mill owner you were dallying with at the time if I remember correctly. Then suddenly his parents sent him abroad and you finally had time for me. In fact, you were all over me like a rash and couldn't marry me quickly enough. Until we were wed that was, and then you didn't want to know me. Within no time after Oliver was born you insisted on separate rooms, that was why I . . . Well, let's just say the night I met Sadie again I was out on a reunion with some of the chaps I went to university with. I'd had too much to drink and when I saw Sadie, a young woman who actually had time for me, one thing led to another. I'm not proud of it! But had you been a proper wife to me this would never have happened. So, what we're going to do is bring this baby and Oliver up to believe they are brother and sister. Do you understand me?'

She looked dumbstruck. 'But what will we tell people?'

'There's no need to tell them anything. We'll be gone from here in a month's time and only Cook is coming with us and I would trust her with my life. In Hull people will just assume they are both our children. Her name is Violet, by the way.'

Anna's lip curled with distaste. 'How *very* working class. Can't we at least change it?'

'No, we cannot! I think it suits her.'

She wanted to argue but she had never seen William like this before and didn't dare.

'In that case I suppose I have no say in the matter,' she said peevishly. 'But don't expect me to ever love the brat. I'm not as stupid as you!'

She flounced from the room to call the nanny. As far as she was concerned the less she saw of the child the better.

Chapter One

'Oh Cook, where can he be?' Violet turned from the window and Cook smiled at her indulgently. Oliver was due home from school that day for the Christmas holidays and Violet had been like a cat on hot coals all morning. She adored her brother and missed him when he was gone, although she couldn't say the same for him. Violet and Oliver had been close as children but now he barely had time for her. Since starting boarding school he had become much like his mother – self-centred and cold – whereas Violet was a loving soul, much more like her father.

'He shouldn't be too much longer now, pet,' Cook told her. 'An' you peerin' out o' the window every two seconds ain't goin' to make him come any quicker. Now come an' sit down. You're makin' me feel dizzy wi' all your buzzin' about.'

With a sigh, Violet did as she was told, but she had no sooner done so than the front doorbell rang and she was up and off again.

She entered the hallway just in time to see their maid Lottie admit Oliver, and with a whoop of joy she flew down the hall and threw herself into his arms.

He laughed as she almost knocked him over. 'Steady on. We both nearly ended up in a heap then,' he teased. 'Anyone would think you had missed me.'

'I have.' She smiled up at him but at that moment Anna appeared in the doorway of the drawing room and Violet instantly stood back.

'Ah, Oliver, welcome home.' His mother greeted him with an outstretched hand as she gave him a kiss on the cheek. 'I trust you had a good journey.'

'It could have been better,' he answered as he peeled off his hat and coat and handed them to Lottie. 'The snow is coming down thick and fast now. How are you and Father? Is he in?'

'What? At this time of day!' She snorted. 'Of course he isn't. As soon as morning surgery was over, he was off doing his house calls as usual. I doubt we'll see him again until early evening.'

'Ah well, some things never change.'

'Lottie, bring a tray of tea to the drawing room,' Anna instructed, and turning around she headed back the way she had come with Violet and Oliver following closely behind.

'So, tell me, how are things at school?' Anna asked when they were all seated. 'And how are your exams going? It won't be long now before you're heading off to university. Have you decided what you want to study yet?'

Oliver looked vaguely uncomfortable as he ran his finger around the starched collar of his shirt. He could have told her that once more he had narrowly escaped being expelled that term, and that he detested the place. He could also have told her that he had no idea what he wanted to do with his future, but of course he didn't.

'I think the exams are going all right,' he hedged. 'Although I have to admit they are much more difficult than I thought they would be. And no, I haven't really given much thought as to what I want to study at university yet. I thought I'd just concentrate on the exams and get them out of the way first.'

Satisfied with his answer, Anna nodded her approval. 'That sounds sensible.'

Oliver turned to Violet. 'And I believe it will be your birthday in a few days. Have you anything special planned?'

'No, she hasn't,' Anna answered for the girl. 'I can't see the point in making any fuss for a seventeenth birthday. And don't you have a piano lesson in a few minutes, Violet?'

'Oh, er . . . yes, Mama.' Violet rose and after smiling at Oliver she headed for the day room where her piano teacher would no doubt be waiting for her.

He was and so with a sigh Violet sat down at the small baby grand in the corner of the room and her lesson began. She was very good, as her tutor had informed her father on more than one occasion, and William was proud of her, although Anna had constantly complained about what the lessons cost.

'Why waste all that money?' she had said nastily. 'When she's old enough we'll marry her off and then her husband can pay for lessons.'

'What Violet's piano lessons cost is a drop in the ocean compared to what I pay to keep Oliver in school,' her father had pointed out, but each time the subject arose Anna had simply flounced off.

William was surprised she had settled in Hull as well as she had. It was no doubt due to the circle of rich friends she had accrued since the move. Many of their husbands owned factories on the docks or businesses and he and Anna had many a row because William couldn't afford to keep Anna in the style she would have liked. He did his best but had been forced to accept long ago that theirs was a marriage in name only. Ever since the night Sadie had delivered Violet to their door, Anna had banned him from her bedroom completely. Even so, he was a wonderful father, although Oliver could sorely try his patience at times. He took after his mother in looks with fair hair and blue eyes. He was a good-looking chap with no shortage of young ladies throwing themselves at him, a fact that he took full advantage of.

Violet took after her father, with long, dark, wavy hair and dark brown eyes that could change to almost black depending on her mood. Oliver was tall whereas Violet was quite dainty and petite, and their natures were completely opposite – Oliver was extro-verted, but Violet was gentle-natured.

Anna had been true to her word and ever since the night Vio-let had come to them, as far as he knew, his wife had never once cuddled her or given her a kind word. It had troubled him deeply when Violet was a little girl, but thankfully Cook absolutely doted on her, as did he, and so, as she grew, it was to them that the child turned for affection, keeping out of her mother's way whenever possible. What did surprise William was the way Violet absolutely adored her big brother. On the day Oliver had left for boarding school when he was eight years old, Violet had sobbed for days. Anna, too, had been inconsolable, and had never forgiven him for sending her son away, although all he had hoped to do was give the boy the best education he could.

As soon as the lesson was over Violet hastily rose and rushed off to find Oliver only to be disappointed when Cook told her, 'Sorry, pet. Oliver has gone off to meet some schoolfriend off the train. He'll be stayin' here wi' us over Christmas apparently.'

'Oh! I could have gone with him.' Violet's face fell.

'Never mind. Come an' have one o' these mince pies. They're straight out o' the oven,' Cook encouraged.

Normally Violet would have obliged but today her eyes strayed to the window. 'Did he say how long he would be?'

Cook sighed. 'No. An' like I said before, you sat there starin' at the window won't make him come back any quicker. Anyway, I could do wi' you bein' here. Your father told me the Christmas tree is bein' delivered today an' I thought you could help Lottie decorate it.'

Violet perked up a little at that; she always loved decorating the tree. At that moment there was a knock at the front door and soon after, Lottie appeared. 'The tree is 'ere. The lad 'as it at the front door, Cook.'

'Well, he ain't doin' no good there, is he?' Cook grumbled. 'I'll be damned if I'll let him drag it all through the clean hall. Tell 'im to bring it round the back, would yer?'

Lottie, a fresh-faced girl of sixteen, raced off to do as she was told and soon a small boy with a runny nose and threadbare clothes appeared through the gate to the yard dragging a large tree behind him. He was painfully thin and looked frozen through. Cook fished in her purse and handed him a shiny sixpence.

'Here y'are, lad,' she said kindly. 'An' how would yer fancy a nice hot cup o' sweet tea an' a couple o' mince pies afore you leave?'

The boy's face lit up. 'Not 'alf, missus, thank yer kindly.'

'Then come in an' shut the door. You're lettin' all the cold air in,' she scolded.

Violet smiled at him and he smiled shyly back. She'd seen Cook do this many times before for those who looked hard done by, although she dreaded to think what her mother would have to say if she ever found out. Anna wasn't the most generous of souls with anyone apart from Oliver, and had little sympathy for those lower in class than she was.

Within minutes the boy was seated at the table gobbling down mince pies and sipping at his tea as if he hadn't eaten in months.

'Where do you live, lad?' Cook enquired.

'Down by docks, missus,' he said, spraying crumbs all over Cook's nice clean table, although she didn't mind.

She nodded. That was where William had been doing most of his house calls lately, much to Anna's disgust.

'Live wi' yer mam an' dad do yer?'

He nodded. 'Aye, and me eight brothers an' sisters. I'm the oldest,' he informed her proudly. 'So I earn what I can doin' odd jobs for anybody as needs 'em doin' an' then I give the money to me ma.'

'What a good lad you are,' Cook said approvingly. 'An' how would yer like to earn another sixpence?'

When he nodded, she pointed to the door. 'When you've finished eating you can go an' fill the bucket outside the back door wi' earth for me and carry it into the drawin' room. Then yer can stand the Christmas tree in it ready fer decoratin'. Are yer game for it?'

He nodded vigorously and as soon as he'd finished his tea, he vanished out into the snow again only to return shortly after, hefting the heavy bucket.

'Violet, go an' show the lad where yer want it puttin',' Cook told her.

Violet led him through the hallway and into the drawing room. 'Just over there to one side of the fireplace, please.' When he'd done as he was asked, she said, 'And now I'll come and help you carry the tree through. I don't think Cook would appreciate you dragging it across the hall floor, and it looks too heavy for you to carry on your own. My brother has just gone out otherwise he could have helped you. What's your name?'

'It's Jimmy, miss. Jimmy Clarke.'

'Right, Jimmy Clarke, shall we fetch the tree in?'

After a deal of grunting and groaning they finally managed to manoeuvre the tree into position and returned to the kitchen where Cook paid him his extra sixpence and gave him a large linen bag. 'There's some pie in there if you think your family might use it,' she told him. 'Oh, an' I've popped a few mince pies an' a bit of beef an' a fresh baked loaf in as well.'

Jimmy's eyes grew round. 'Cor ta, missus.' He almost snatched the bag from her, as if he was afraid she might change her mind. He could hardly wait to get home now. With a shilling in his pocket and a feast in the bag he knew his mam would be over the moon. He headed for the door where he paused to ask, 'Could I call in again, just in case you've any errands or any other little jobs yer might want doin'?'

'Yer certainly can, lad. Now get yerself home. The weather is worsenin' from what I can see of it.'

When he had gone Violet helped Lottie fetch the baubles down from the attic and they set to.

They had almost finished when Anna returned from her friend's sometime later. She studied it solemnly. 'I suppose it will do,' she said eventually. 'Although it isn't nearly as big as Mrs Cartwright's. Trust your father to skimp for the sake of a few shillings.'

Violet frowned as she too stood back to survey their efforts. It looked perfectly fine to her; she would even have said, lovely. But then she was used to her mother's negative attitude towards anything she did. But she had no time to comment for at that moment they heard the front door open and laughter in the hallway. It was Oliver returning from the station with his friend.

Violet rushed out to greet them. Oliver's friend was a tall, lanky youth and he eyed her appreciatively, instantly making Violet feel uncomfortable.

'Violet, this is George Martin, my friend from school. George, this is Violet, my sister,' Oliver introduced them.

'Very pleased to meet you, I'm sure,' George said, shaking Violet's hand. 'You never told me your sister was so pretty, Oliver.'

Oliver guffawed with laughter. 'Now, George, behave yourself.' He gave his friend a gentle punch on the arm while warning Violet, 'You'd best keep your eye on him. He likes a pretty face.'

Violet took an instant dislike to the youth. He was good-looking, admittedly, with brown hair and blue eyes, but he was obviously aware of the fact and Violet supposed he would expect every girl he looked at to fawn over him. Well, she certainly didn't intend to be one of them. Deep down she knew she was probably being unreasonable, but she had expected to have Oliver all to herself over the holidays and instead, he had turned up with a school pal in tow.

'Lottie and I have just finished decorating the tree,' she told Oliver, taking her hand from George's. 'Come and look at it.'

The two young men followed her back into the drawing room but it was soon clear that they had other things on their mind as they barely glanced at the tree.

'I'll get Lottie to take your things up to your room for you, then we could perhaps go out after lunch and I can show you around the town?' Oliver suggested to George.

Disappointment pierced Violet like a knife. She had so been looking forward to Oliver coming home but he barely seemed to have time for her. Lottie came into the room just then and the two young men followed her from the room, and with a sigh Violet made her way to the kitchen.

'What's wrong wi' your face?' Cook asked. 'You look like you've lost a bob an' found a tanner.'

'Oliver just wants to be with his friend, and from what I've seen of him I don't much like him.'

'Huh, you've hardly give him a chance 'ave you?' the cook pointed out. 'I reckon you're just put out that you won't 'ave Oliver all to yourself. But he's a young man now; it's normal for him to want to be out an' about with his friends.'

'I suppose you're right,' Violet answered, leaving the room.

When she was gone, Edie sighed. She loved Violet as if she were her own child and didn't like to see her sad. But she did worry about the attachment she had to Oliver. To all intents and purposes, they were brother and sister – although Edie knew differently – and Violet hero-worshipped him. Sadly, Oliver was only interested in himself, and the sooner Violet understood that, the better.

Chapter Two

Once the New Year was over, Oliver and his friend returned to school. The holiday had not gone at all the way Violet had hoped. She had spent very little time with Oliver and she was glad to see the back of George, who had become a nuisance. After the first couple of days of him being there, Violet had taken to staying in her room as much as she could just to avoid him – not that he and Oliver were in much. There had been an awful row one evening when Oliver and George had rolled in late roaring drunk. Anna had been incensed and told Oliver that he was never to invite George to stay again, so Violet supposed that was one good thing. Usually, Anna didn't much care what he was doing as long as he didn't bother her, but the thought that he might have made a spectacle of himself in the streets was more than she could bear.

As usual Violet's father had tried to defuse the situation.

'They're young men just finding their feet, my dear,' he had soothed.

But Anna had curled her lip. 'And what would *you* know?' she had sneered. 'All you ever care about is work, work, work! When do you ever take any time off to have fun?'

William had bowed his head. He did work hard, but she had known that before she married him. Even so he didn't argue. He had learnt a long time ago that it did no good.

Now as Violet sat in the kitchen staring glumly out of the window, Cook raised an eyebrow.

'Missin' him already are yer?'

Violet shrugged. 'Not really. For what time I spent with him he might as well not have been here. He didn't even stop in to celebrate my birthday.'

16

Since leaving school, Violet had spent a lot of time in the kitchen with Edie. She was the one who Violet had always turned to when her father wasn't there.

'What's going to become of me, Cook?' she said morosely. 'I'm not trained to do anything and I don't want to just sit about doing nothing forever. It's different for Oliver. He'll go on to further education and learn a trade and have a career but me ... Well, it doesn't seem fair that I have to just sit at home. Lots of women do jobs nowadays. But I think Mama wants to marry me off. She's invited the Powells and their son for dinner tomorrow evening and Adam is *so* boring!'

Edie chuckled. Violet wasn't far wrong there. The Powells owned a grocery shop in town and their son Adam made no secret of the fact that he was sweet on Violet. The problem was, Violet wasn't sweet on him.

'But no one's gonna hold a gun to your head an' *make* you get married,' she sensibly pointed out. 'Your father wouldn't allow that. An' anyway, you're only just seventeen.'

At that moment William entered the room. He often popped in to have a cup of tea with Edie, even though Anna didn't approve of him mixing with the servants.

'Hello, pet.' He smiled when he saw his daughter. After taking Oliver and George to the train station that morning he had decided to take a rare day off. He had thought perhaps he could take Anna out to lunch but as usual she had already made arrangements to lunch with a friend. She had lots of friends and William wasn't at all sure that all of them were female, not that it troubled him anymore. 'How would you fancy coming out with your old dad for a spot of lunch, Violet? Would that be all right with you, Edie, or have you already got it ready?'

'It's fine by me,' she assured him. 'Go on, you don't get enough time to spend together by half. Get off an' enjoy yourselves an' while you're gone me an' Lottie can 'ave an hour off.'

17

Looking slightly brighter, Violet skipped away to get ready as Edie poured William a cup of tea.

'Is Violet all right?' he asked when they were alone. 'She troubles me sometimes. She doesn't go out much since she finished school and she must get awfully bored.'

'She does.' Edie pushed the sugar bowl towards him. 'In fact, she were just sayin' as how she wished she could get a job.'

'Oh? What sort of job?'

Edie shrugged. 'I don't know. In a shop perhaps. Lots o' women work nowadays an' I reckon Violet would enjoy it, but she knows her mother wouldn't approve. What do you think o' the idea?'

'I hadn't really given it any thought,' he admitted. 'But I can't see what harm it could do, as long as she was working somewhere respectable. In a lady's gown shop or a milliner's or some such, perhaps? I'll put the idea to Anna and see what she thinks.'

Cook snorted. 'Huh! Good luck wi' that.'

Violet soon returned, looking very pretty in a becoming burgundy gown and a dark grey coat and matching hat.

'Will I do, Papa?' she asked, giving him a twirl.

'You most certainly will, my dear,' he said approvingly and after offering her his arm she pecked Cook on the cheek, and they set off.

That evening at dinner, William put Violet's idea to Anna. 'Violet was thinking of perhaps taking a little job now that she has so much spare time on her hands . . . In a gown shop or someplace like it. What do you think, my dear?' he asked.

Anna's lips set into a grim line and she stared frostily at Violet across the table. 'Do you *really* want to make a laughing stock of us? Really, what would people say? The doctor and his family are *so* poor that they have to send their daughter out to work! *No . . .* it's *quite* out of the question, I'm afraid! And as for your spare

18

time, I'm sure it would be better spent helping about the house, Violet. The laundry woman has just handed in her notice; you could take her place and save us a little money that way.'

Now it was William's turn to look angry. 'I will not have Violet doing the laundry!'

'Oh, but I wouldn't mind, Papa,' Violet told him, sensing a row brewing. It was very rare that her father went against her mama's wishes but when he did it usually resulted in a row.

'Enough said on the subject. You will *not* be doing the laundry,' he said grimly. 'Now may we just finish this lovely meal Cook has made in peace?'

The rest of the meal was eaten in an uncomfortable silence and Violet was relieved when it was over and she could escape to her room where she sat on the side of the bed and dropped her head into her hands. More than ever now she wondered why her own mother didn't love her – or even like her, for that matter. Admittedly she was civil to her in front of her father or if they had company, but the rest of the time she looked at her as if she was a bad smell under her nose. Looking back, she realised that even as a tiny girl it was Cook or Oliver who she had run to for affection. Oliver had had time for her back then, she thought sadly, but now he seemed more interested in his friends than her. It was Cook who had nursed her through the childhood illnesses and Cook who had kissed her better if she tumbled and hurt herself, never her mother. A tear slid down her cheek as she lay down and curled into a ball. And now she had the dreaded dinner party with the Powells to look forward to the following day. She shuddered as she thought of Adam. He was nice enough, but the idea of his thick, slobbery lips filled her with revulsion.

'Please don't be late this evening,' Anna told William as he was leaving to do his house calls after morning surgery the following day. 'Remember we have the Powells dining with us.'

'I'll do my best,' William promised, pecking Violet on the cheek and making a hasty exit.

'And you' – Anna turned her attention to Violet – 'do make an effort with your hair and how you dress this evening. I want you looking your best.' And with that she sailed from the room leaving Violet to glare after her.

Even so, when the time came, Violet took her best gown from the wardrobe, then releasing her hair from its clips, she let it fall down her back and brushed it until it shone. Their dinner guests were due in half an hour and her father still hadn't returned. Violet shuddered to think what would happen should he be late, but thankfully at that moment she heard him enter the hall. Violet stuck her head out of her bedroom door as he climbed the stairs on his way to get changed and grinned at him.

'Phew, that was cutting it fine,' she whispered.

'I know.' He glanced along the landing to make sure there was no sign of Anna. 'I don't know what all the fuss is about. Your mother usually likes to invite a wealthier class of people to her soirées and I just wonder what she's up to. Anyway, I'd best go and get into a decent suit or I'll never hear the end of it. I'll see you downstairs shortly.'

Fifteen minutes later, Violet went down to find Anna waiting for her in the drawing room. She eyed her up and down before saying, 'I dare say you'll do, although you could have done something with your hair. Put it up or something!'

'I'm afraid it'll have to do,' Violet answered. 'I don't have time to do anything else with it now.' And sure enough, just as her father entered, the doorbell rang heralding the arrival of their guests.

After taking their outer clothes from them Lottie showed their guests into the drawing room and Anna rose from her seat to greet them with a gracious smile. 'Mr and Mrs Powell, Adam, how lovely it is that you could make it. Do come in and get warm. Lottie, please pour our guests some drinks.'

Anna ushered the couple towards the chairs on either side of the fireplace while Adam made a beeline for Violet, an adoring smile on his face. Violet had been delivering Cook's grocery list to their shop each week for some time now if Lottie was too busy and he was the same every time she saw him. In fact, sometimes she felt that he lay in wait for her.

'M-may I say how pretty you look this evenin', Miss Violet,' he said, blushing violently and she stifled a sigh.

They took their seats at the table soon after and Lottie began to serve the food, which Cook had gone to considerable trouble over. There was a wild mushroom soup to begin, followed by a saddle of lamb that was cooked to perfection, but Violet could feel Adam's eyes boring into her and the food seemed to stick in her throat. He had seated himself right next to her and more than once their arms brushed, making her want to shudder. Adam was a kind enough young man but she didn't find anything about him attractive. He was very tall, well over six foot, she gauged, and had dark hair. He also had rather a large nose and very thick lips that he continuously licked; a habit that Violet found very off-putting.

Anna, however, was almost fawning over him. 'So, my dear, what are your plans for the future?' she purred sweetly.

Another blush from Adam but it was his father who answered.

'He'll take over the shop when I retire,' he said proudly. 'A right good little business it is an' all. When he chooses a wife, she an' any family they may have will not go short o' nowt. They'll have the flat above it to live in an' all, lock, stock an' barrel. Me an' the missus will get us a little cottage in the country.'

'How lovely.' Anna beamed at him.

Violet lowered her eyes. Her mother was making it more than obvious that she was trying to matchmake the pair of them, but worse still, Adam's parents seemed to be going along with it.

One glance at her father, however, showed that he wasn't so keen on the idea. 'But that will be some long time away in the future, surely? Adam is only a young man,' he commented.

21

'Not really. He'll be twenty-one in a couple o' months. Just the right time to be thinkin' o' settlin' down.'

At this Adam smiled at Violet and her heart sank. Thankfully, her father abruptly changed the subject and the meal continued.

After they'd finished the main course, Lottie served a strawberry trifle topped with whipped cream, then at last coffee was served, and Violet began to look at the clock, longing for the awful evening to be over.

William clearly wasn't enjoying it much more than she was. 'Goodness me, look at the snow,' he said suddenly as he looked towards the window. 'It's turning into a blizzard by the looks of it.'

'Oh dear.' Mrs Powell, who was a nervous little woman, followed his gaze. 'You're quite right. Perhaps we should think of going before it gets any worse.'

Violet breathed a sigh of relief as Mr Powell nodded in agreement. 'Aye, you're right, love, we'd best gerr off while the goin's good, otherwise we might end up havin' to stay here. Mind you, that wouldn't be such a bad thing for our Adam, would it, lad?' He guffawed with laughter and slapped his son on the back. 'I reckon he's taken a rare shine to your lass.'

Violet blushed, wishing she could just disappear.

'Any road, thanks for the lovely meal. It were well nice an' I'm sorry to eat an' run but as the missus said, it's gettin' worse by the minute out there.'

Soon they were all standing in the hallway saying their goodbyes, although Violet made sure she stood behind her father, as far away from Adam as she could get.

'We must return the favour an' have you round to ours for a meal,' Mr Powell said with a wide smile. 'Happen the two young 'uns would like that, eh?'

Once the door had closed on the Powells, Violet breathed a huge sigh of relief. The whole evening had been an embarrassment for her, and she had the feeling it hadn't been much better for her father.

'Whatever made you invite them?' William questioned Anna with a frown. 'I mean, I'm sure they're very nice people but we barely know them.'

'Oh, William, can't you see that young Adam is totally besotted with Violet.' Anna giggled. 'She could do a lot worse. As his father pointed out, he'll have his own little business and a place to live when they retire.'

'I'd rather *die* than marry him!' Violet said emphatically, and Anna stared at her coldly.

'Yes, and in case you'd forgotten, Violet is only just seventeen,' William added. 'So please in future refrain from inviting them here again. I'm sure when Violet feels ready for a young man, she'll choose one herself, but I hope it won't be for a long time to come.' With that he took his daughter's elbow and led her away, leaving Anna standing there with a sly grin on her face. It wasn't over yet, not by a long shot.

Chapter Three

'I don't want to marry Adam,' Violet sobbed as soon as she got to the kitchen with her father close behind her. 'I don't want to marry anyone at the moment. The Powells are nice enough, but not the sort Mama usually associates with so why is she pushing me on Adam?'

'Now, now, pet. Calm down,' Cook soothed as she came to put a comforting arm about her.

William ran his hand distractedly through his hair. 'Perhaps she was just trying to be kind,' he suggested awkwardly, although he secretly agreed with his daughter.

Violet snorted. 'Oh Papa, you *know* I'm right. Mother's friends are all business people. People with money. She'd normally have nothing to do with common shopkeepers, as she calls them!'

William spread his hands helplessly. Anna had never made a secret of the fact that she wanted rid of Violet, but what she had done that evening was unforgivable. Both he and Violet had been extremely uncomfortable. There were times over the years when he had wanted to just take Violet and leave, but he was an honourable man. He had made vows, and although theirs had been a marriage in name only for some time, he had stood by them. Even before Violet had arrived, he had hoped that moving to Hull would be a new start for the family, but Anna's demands were as bad here, if not worse, than they had been back in the Midlands. She had insisted they should have a home in the better part of the town, as well as servants to wait on her, and at times it had been a financial struggle for him. None of his doctor friends had servants, but as usual he had given way to her. But on this, he wasn't about to and turning about he stormed towards the drawing room where he found his wife drinking wine and reading the newspaper. She glanced up briefly before returning her attention to the paper.

'I think it's time you and I had a little talk,' he said sternly.

Something in his tone made Anna lay the paper down and give him her attention. It wasn't often that he raised his voice to her. In fact, it wasn't often that they spoke.

'What you did tonight was appalling,' he told her sternly. 'You made it more than obvious to the Powells that you would like their son to join our family. But I'll tell you now, it's not going to happen. I can't believe you would stoop so low as to try and palm Violet off on the first young man to pay her any attention.'

Anna raised her chin and stared at him with a sneer. 'And why ever not? She's a flyblow. She should be grateful that anyone is paying her attention.'

William's eyes narrowed to slits as angry colour flooded into his cheeks. 'Like your son, you mean?'

Now it was her turn to get angry. 'Oliver wasn't a flyblow. We were legally married when I gave birth to him!'

'But only because you tricked me into it.' He leant towards her, a menacing expression on his face, and for the first time she looked slightly worried. 'You forget that I'm a doctor! Oliver was born seven months after we married and you told me he was at least two months early. Huh! As if I wouldn't know a premature baby when I saw one. If anything, I would say he was a little overdue. You only married me because your fancy lover ran off and left you!'

Anna looked shocked, but then recovered herself. 'If you've known all this time, why didn't you ever say anything before?' she spat, not bothering to deny it.

'I didn't say anything because I loved you. But let me tell you something I never have before. Sadie Perkins, Violet's mother, was a sweet girl. I knew her as I was growing up. She always had a soft spot for me but like a fool I had my eye on you. Oh, it didn't take me long to realise how stupid I'd been once you had my ring on your finger. And on the night I met Sadie and we . . . Well, let's just say I'm not proud of what we did, but I'd had too much to drink and realised by that time that Sadie was worth ten of you. She was a good, hard-working girl who made no demands, and I'll never forgive myself for the position I put her in. Every time I look at Violet, I see her mother and I regret how I treated her. You've never made any attempt to be a mother to my girl, you've only ever had time for Oliver and you've ruined him! If it wasn't for me, Violet would walk around in rags. You begrudge every little thing I do for her, but one thing you can't say is that I haven't done right by your son. He's not the easiest, but I've always treated him as my own. So you'd better start making an effort to treat Violet better or I tell you now, things are going to change!'

'W-what do you mean?'

'For a start we could get rid of the maid. I'm not a rich man; you knew that when you married me. Most doctor's wives work with them, but what do you do? You do *nothing* apart from make demands and play the lady! Well, it stops now.'

Anna's eyes welled with tears. 'William . . . I can't believe you'd talk to me like this,' she protested weakly, but he wasn't finished.

'Oh, believe me, this is long overdue. So, make more of an effort with Violet or you're going to live to regret it.'

'I notice you don't mention getting rid of Edie,' Anna said sarcastically.

'Edie has been like a mother to me ever since my real mother died. She's also been more of a mother to Violet than you ever have, so just think on what I've said!'

And with that he turned and stormed from the room.

A couple of days later, Violet watched as Cook wrote out a shopping list. 'Couldn't Lottie deliver that to the Powells' shop today, Cook? After the other evening, I don't feel ready to face Adam again just yet.'

Cook smiled at her understandingly. 'I don't see why not, pet. An' how was your father this mornin'? I know he's still in his surgery but he looked a bit peaky to me at breakfast.'

'Yes, I thought he looked a bit pale,' Violet agreed. 'I worry that he does too much. It's always worse for him in the winter when everyone is getting poorly. He didn't come in until really late last night.'

'Aw well, we'll just 'ave to keep us eye on him.'

Lottie entered the room just then, and once Cook had sent her off with the list, Violet helped to prepare the lunch.

It was almost one' clock before William joined them in the kitchen and he looked tired. 'Phew, the waiting room was heaving this morning,' he said sadly. 'And I've a list of house calls to make as long as your arm. Goodness knows what time I'll finish this evening, but it can't be helped.'

Violet had recently taken on the task of writing down the names and addresses of people requesting visits and it had been a great help to him.

'I was just sayin' that I reckon you're doin' too much,' Cook scolded as she handed him a steaming mug of tea. 'So sit down an' drink that.' She held her hand up to silence him as he went to object. 'Come on, I won't take no for an answer. You're not leavin' this house till you've somethin' inside yer. There's some pork pie and bread an' cheese an' I'll 'ave you a nice hot dinner ready by the time yer get home tonight.'

Lottie came in just as the doctor was finishing his meal and, placing her basket on the table, she grinned. 'I just called into Powell's grocery shop to drop the list o' things that Cook needed and the son there were none too pleased that I wasn't you, Violet.'

Violet frowned as she and her father exchanged a glance but soon after he left to begin his house calls while Violet went to prepare for her piano lesson.

'I really don't think there's any more I can teach you,' Mr Partridge told her at the end of the lesson. 'You play beautifully and I fear I would just be taking your father's money for nothing if we continued. I believe you are at the stage that you could be giving lessons yourself.'

'Thank you. I shall miss you.' Violet rose from the piano stool and shook Mr Partridge's hand and after she had handed him the money her father had left, he departed.

Violet hurried into the kitchen to tell Cook what he had said. It didn't occur to her to go and tell her mother; she knew that she wouldn't be interested. The only reason she had allowed her to have the lessons in the first place was because she could brag to her friends about them.

'Well done, pet.' Cook at least was proud of her and she knew her father would be too.

'I was wondering if that might perhaps be something I could do,' Violet mused. 'I'm sure even Mother wouldn't object to me giving piano lessons.'

'Hmm, it's certainly worth thinkin' about,' Cook agreed. 'Why don't you 'ave a word to your father about it this evenin' when he comes in? It would get you out o' the house an' give you an interest an' you could earn a bob or two into the bargain.'

It was later that afternoon when a loud knock came to the front door and Lottie appeared in the kitchen, looking pale and afraid. 'Please, Miss Violet, there's a lad 'ere askin' to speak to the mistress. I reckon sommat's up, an' seein' as your ma ain't in I thought per'aps you could see him.'

Violet had been keeping Cook company in the kitchen – there was nothing else to do and the snow was falling so thickly now that she couldn't even venture out for a walk. 'Of course I will,' Violet said obligingly. She was used to seeing people at the door who had medical emergencies and needed to see her father. 'Although if they're after Papa I don't know what time he'll be able to get to them,' she added as she followed Lottie into the hall.

A young boy stood by the front door looking frozen and ragged. 'Please, miss, it's about your pa, Doctor Stroud,' he told her. 'He were payin' a visit to me sister; she's got whoopin' cough, see? Anyway, while he were there he had a funny turn an' passed out. Me ma sent for an ambulance an' she said I was to come an' tell you.'

Violet's hand flew to her mouth as she felt the colour drain from her cheeks. Cook had only commented that very day that he didn't look well and it seemed she had been right.

'Where did the ambulance take him?' Violet's heart was beating nineteen to the dozen as she tried to remain calm.

'They said they were takin' him to the Royal Infirmary on Prospect Street, miss.'

'Thank you for letting me know. I'll go to him straightaway.' Violet fished in the pocket of her gown and after extracting a sixpenny piece she pressed it into the boy's palm.

'Cor, thanks, miss. I hope yer pa's all right. He's a kind chap is Doctor Stroud.' And with that he shot off to be swallowed up by the fast-falling snow.

Without wasting a second Violet turned to Lottie and asked, 'Would you fetch me my boots and my hat and coat please, Lottie.'

'O' course, miss. Do you want me to come with yer?'

'No, no, I'll be fine. You stay here with Cook. There's no sense in us both going out – it's blowing a blizzard out there. And be sure to tell my mother what's happened and where I am the minute she's back.'

Seconds later she set off with her head down. Normally she would have hailed a cab but there seemed to be few about today, so she hurried on, slipping and sliding on the icy cobblestones.

By the time Violet reached Prospect Street, the light was fast fading from the day and she breathed a sigh of relief as the hospital came into view. The journey had taken twice as long as it should have because of the atrocious conditions, and she fairly flew through the doors and approached the reception desk.

'Could you tell me where my father is please? His name is Doctor Stroud and he was brought in by ambulance a short time ago,' she asked in a quavering voice.

'I'll go and find out for you. Take a seat, dear.' The kindly receptionist hurried away as Violet began to pace up and down.

'He's on the men's ward,' the woman informed Violet when she came back. 'One of the doctors is assessing him now, and as soon as he's finished, he says he'll be out to see you.'

'Thank you.' Violet continued to pace.

At last a small, portly man with a balding head and a bushy grey beard and wearing a white coat with a stethoscope hung about his neck approached her. 'Mrs Stroud?'

'No, I'm Miss Stroud, his daughter,' Violet told him anxiously. 'I'm afraid my mother was out visiting when we were informed my father had been taken ill. What's wrong with him and how is he?'

'Come into my office,' the doctor said. 'It's a bit quieter in there.'

She followed him down a long narrow corridor until he stopped at a door and ushered her inside.

'Right, Miss Stroud, I'm afraid there's no easy way to say this, so I'll just come out with it. Your father has suffered a massive heart attack.'

'Oh no.' The tears she had so bravely held back now began to course down her cheeks. 'But he will be all right . . . w-won't he?' she asked shakily.

'It's too soon to tell. But rest assured we are doing all we can,' he told her gently.

'I see.' Violet felt as if she was trapped in the grip of a nightmare. 'W-will I be allowed to see him?'

He nodded. 'Yes. But be warned, he hasn't come round properly yet and he may not know you're there. If you come with me, I'll take you to him now. But please don't stay for more than a few minutes. He needs rest right now more than anything.'

Numbly, she followed him from the room to the men's ward. Beds lined each side of the room and one had the curtains pulled about it. It was at that one that the doctor paused to tell her, 'Your father is in here, but remember what I said, just a few minutes, please.'

He pushed the curtains aside just wide enough to allow her entry and as her eyes rested on her father she felt as if her heart would break in two. His face was grey, his lips had a bluish tinge to them and he was lying so still she feared he was already dead. She dropped into the chair at the side of him and gently took his cold hand in hers.

'Oh Papa,' she said brokenly. '*Please* get better. I can't go on without you.' For the next few moments, she continued to speak to him, hoping that somehow, he could hear her. But soon a nurse in a starched white cap and apron appeared.

'I'm sorry but I'm afraid you'll have to leave now,' she said quietly. 'Mr Stroud needs his rest, but you may come back tomorrow. Visiting time is at one o'clock.'

'Oh, please let me stay,' Violet begged.

The nurse shook her head. 'I'm afraid I can't, it's doctor's orders. But don't worry, we're doing everything we possibly can for him.'

Reluctantly Violet rose and bent to kiss her father's forehead. 'I'll be back as soon as they'll allow me to,' she promised, and with tears in her eyes she slowly turned and left him there, wondering if she would ever see him alive again.

Thankfully on Prospect Road she was lucky to see an empty cab so after hailing it she gave the driver her address and hopped inside.

Once she arrived back at the house, she found Cook and Lottie anxiously waiting for her.

'How is he?' Cook looked almost as worried as Violet felt.

'He's not good.' Violet slowly took off her hat and coat and dropped them across the back of a chair. 'I'm afraid he's had a heart attack.'

'Oh, good Lord!' Cook looked appalled. 'Didn't I try to tell 'im he were doing too much?'

'Is my mother back?'

Lottie nodded. 'She's in the drawin' room waitin' for you.'

'In that case I'd better go and tell her what's happened.'

Violet crossed the hall and opened the door to the drawing room to find her mother calmly pouring herself a cup of tea.

'Ah, here you are. How is your father?' she asked. Violet didn't think she looked overly concerned.

'Not good. Father has had a massive heart attack. I thought you might come and join me at the hospital when you got home and heard what had happened.'

Anna shrugged as she added a sugar lump to the dainty cup. 'There didn't seem much point until I knew what was happening. Is he going to be all right?'

'It's too early to say. They're doing what they can for him, but they wouldn't let me stay any longer. They said he needed to rest.'

Anna sipped at her tea. 'There you are then. It would have been a waste of time me coming all that way. We'll go back tomorrow and see how he is.'

Violet stared at her mother coldly. 'I shall be back there first thing. You can go when you like,' she snapped, and turning about she left the room.

Mother must have a swinging brick in her chest instead of a heart, she thought as she slowly climbed the stairs. And then began one of the longest nights of her life as she tossed and turned and fretted about her father.

Chapter Four

By the following morning, Violet's eyes were red-rimmed from crying and lack of sleep. Every time she had closed her eyes a picture of her father's pale face had flashed before them. She had never felt so useless in her life. Eventually she gave up trying to rest and crept down to the kitchen in her robe. To her surprise she found Cook already up, although it was not yet five o'clock, and she looked almost as bad as Violet felt. She too was in her nightclothes with her grey hair in a long plait that hung over her shoulder.

She was sitting at the side of the fire drinking tea and when Violet entered, she nodded towards the teapot. 'You couldn't sleep, eh?'

Violet shook her head.

'Nor me.' Cook waited for Violet to pour herself a drink before asking, 'What time did the hospital say you could go back in?'

'They said visiting is at one o'clock, but I can't wait till then.'

'So what time are you going?'

'As soon as I've had this,' Violet said dully. 'The worst they can do is make me wait in the waiting room, isn't it?'

'An' what about your mother?'

Violet shrugged. 'I doubt she'll break her usual routine. She isn't normally up much before lunchtime and I'm certainly not going to wait for her. She can come and join me when it suits her.'

'In that case I'd best get you some breakfast. I don't want you goin' out on an empty stomach.' Cook made to rise from the chair but Violet gently pressed her back into it.

'No . . . thank you, but I can't eat a thing until I know Papa is going to be all right.'

Cook sighed. 'I can understand that. I feel much the same. The house feels empty wi'out him, don't it? Even if he weren't in half the time. But I'll tell you now, I'll be puttin' me foot down when he comes home. He's been workin' far too hard.'

'I agree,' Violet answered miserably.

They sat in silence until they had both finished their tea, then Violet rose and made for the door. 'I'm going to get dressed, then I'm setting off.'

Cook frowned. 'But the snow is still comin' down thick an' fast out there,' she warned. 'An' there won't be no cabs about this early in the mornin'.'

'I don't care. I'd crawl there if I had to.'

When Violet stepped out onto the street twenty minutes later, the bitterly cold air took her breath away. As Cook had said, the snow was falling so fast, she could barely see more than a few yards in front of her and it was so deep that before she had reached the end of the road her boots and the hem of her gown were sodden but she struggled on regardless. *He's sure to be a bit better this morning*, she told herself, trying to keep her spirits up.

Apart from the men hurrying towards the docks to start their day's work there wasn't another soul in sight and the journey seemed endless, but at last the hospital loomed ahead of her in the darkness. There was no one on the desk when she entered the reception area so after shaking the worst of the snow off, she hurried to the men's ward. Outside she paused to peer through the glass in the top half of the door, but the ward was gloomy and she couldn't see more than halfway down it.

As quietly as she could she pushed the door open, but she had barely set foot inside when a young nurse seated at a desk writing patients' notes rose to greet her.

'Excuse me, visiting time isn't until one o'clock,' the nurse said.

Violet nodded. 'I am aware of that, but my father was brought in yesterday. I came last night as soon as I heard and was told I could come back today. I was hoping you'd let me in early? That's my father's bed there.' She pointed down the ward. 'The one with the curtains drawn around it.'

'Oh . . . I see.' The nurse frowned. 'Would you mind waiting here a moment. I'll fetch the doctor to speak to you.'

'Why?' Violet started to panic. 'Isn't he any better?'

'Please, just wait here.' The nurse hurried away and returned a few minutes later with a tired-looking doctor beside her. It was a different doctor from the previous night.

'And you are?' The doctor frowned as he stared at her.

'I'm Miss Violet Stroud. Doctor Stroud's daughter.'

'I see, then perhaps you would come this way, Miss Stroud. We'll speak in my office.'

Violet's legs suddenly felt wobbly as she followed him back out of the ward, dread coursing through her. He led her into a small office with a large bookshelf in one corner full of what looked like medical text books, a desk with a chair behind it and another in front of it and little else. It was a cold, clinical room and Violet started to shiver.

'P-please tell me – how is my father this morning?'

The doctor licked his lips and lowered his eyes. This was a part of his job that he hated. 'I'm afraid your father passed away almost two hours ago, Miss Stroud,' he informed her solemnly. 'I'm so sorry. Believe me we did everything we possibly could, but he never regained consciousness. If it's any comfort to you, I can truthfully tell you his end was very peaceful.'

Violet stared at the doctor numbly as she felt her whole world crashing down around her. This doctor was telling her that her father was gone, that she would never see him again, but how could that be? Her father had been her whole world. The only one of her parents who had ever had any time for her.

There was an endless silence until the doctor asked gently, 'Would you like me to get Sister to fetch you a cup of tea, my dear? I'm afraid you've had a very nasty shock. Once again, my condolences. I assure you, if there had been anything more we could have done . . .'

'W-what?' Violet felt detached from everything. As if she was trapped in a world that was so painful that for now it was beyond tears. Even the doctor's words seemed to be coming from a long way away. 'Er . . . no, I don't want tea, thank you.' And then, 'May I see him?'

'Yes, of course. We wouldn't move him until his next of kin had been informed. Please wait there for a moment.' He quietly left the room to return shortly after with the young nurse Violet had seen in the ward. 'Nurse Jenkins will take you to him now.'

Violet rose, her face chalky white, and after nodding at the doctor, she followed the nurse back into the ward. When they reached her father's bed the nurse gently pushed the curtain to one side and told her softly, 'Please, if you need anything just ask.'

Violet stepped past her and heard the curtains close behind her and then she stood for a moment, steeling herself to look at her father, convinced that this must all be some ghastly mistake. They must have mixed him up with another patient. But no, as her eyes fell on him, it hit her like a ton of bricks that he really was gone, and her legs gave way, making her drop onto the chair that the nurse had placed at the side of the bed for her.

'Oh Papa.' The tears came at last, racing in a torrent down her pale cheeks. 'How can I go on without you?'

She gently took one of the hands that was crossed across his chest, shuddering as she felt how cold it was. But thankfully his face was serene. He looked just as if he was sleeping peacefully and could wake at any minute. 'Y-you were the best papa anyone could ever have wished for,' she told him brokenly. 'And I'll never ever forget you.' And then she lay her head on his chest as she thought of all the happy times they had spent together. There were so many of them.

At last, the young nurse reappeared and told her gently, 'I'm afraid the men are here to move your father now, Miss Stroud.'

Violet shuddered violently as she realised they had come to take him to the morgue.

'Could you let us know what funeral directors you will be using so they can come and fetch him? There's no rush if you don't feel up to it today.'

Violet staggered to her feet. 'Er . . . yes, yes of course.' Morgue, funeral directors . . . she was trapped in a nightmare, surely? But no, one more glance at her father assured her that she wasn't. She placed one last kiss on his cold cheek before turning about and stumbling blindly back up the ward.

Outside again, the snow was still thickly falling as she somehow made herself head for home. She had no idea how she got there but at last she stumbled into the kitchen.

After taking one glance at her face, Cook started to wail. 'Aw pet . . . *No!* Don't tell me he's gone.' She already had her arm about Violet's waist and was leading her to a chair.

Violet could only nod, but finally she asked, 'Where's Mother? I shall have to tell her. And we'll have to inform Oliver too. He'll have to come home for the funeral.'

'Huh! Where you'd expect her to be. Still abed, o' course. Do you want me to go an' tell 'er?'

'No, I'll go.'

Upstairs Violet tapped on her mother's door and after a few moments a voice mumbled irritably, 'Yes . . . what is it?'

'It's me, Mama.' Violet entered the bedroom, which was still in darkness, and crossed the room to open the curtains.

Anna frowned and pulled herself up against the pillows. 'What is it? And why are you dressed for outdoors at this time of the morning? It can't be much after nine o'clock.' Anna sounded annoyed at the disturbance, but Violet didn't care.

'I've been to the hospital.'

'What? Already?'

'I'm afraid Papa passed away early this morning.'

'Oh!' Anna looked shocked rather than upset, Violet noted.

'We have to let the hospital know which undertaker we wish to use so they can fetch him.'

With that Violet turned and hurried to her own bedroom where she dropped onto the bed and cried as if her heart would break.

Anna got up shortly afterwards, and after instructing Lottie which undertaker she wished to use, she sent the girl to ask them to call on her.

'What do we do now?' Cook sniffed.

Anna shrugged. 'I don't imagine we'll have to do anything, that's what the funeral director's job is,' Anna answered coldly. 'Now, is there any breakfast ready, Cook? I'll take it in the dining room. I hope the fire has been lit in there.'

'*Hard-hearted bitch*,' Cook muttered, scurrying away then to start frying some bacon.

The undertaker called later that morning, and Anna and Violet received him in the drawing room. The day room had been converted into William's surgery when they first moved in, and the small foyer outside it was used as a waiting room for his patients.

Mr Farrell the undertaker was a tall, thin man with a long nose, which reminded Violet of a ferret's, and he was fawningly consoling. He had brought with him some brochures of coffins that he spread out on the table for them. Anna stared down at them.

'I imagine madam will be wanting one of our very best for such a prestigious man,' Mr Farrell simpered. 'Perhaps this solid mahogany one with brass handles and a pure silk lining?'

Anna looked at the price of the coffin in question and scowled. 'I don't think that will be necessary,' she told him firmly without consulting Violet. 'What about this pine one here?'

Mr Farrell looked slightly taken aback. 'Er . . . Well, that is actually one of the cheapest we do,' he pointed out.

'They all do the same job; that one will do.' Anna was clearly not prepared to spend any more than was absolutely necessary. 'How soon can the funeral take place? I would prefer it to be sooner rather than later, and I don't want a fuss. I'm sure William wouldn't have wanted that,' she added hastily, seeing the look of disgust on Violet's face.

'Very well, madam.' The disappointed undertaker lifted the brochure. It was more than obvious that this widow wasn't prepared to spend even a penny if a ha'penny would do. 'Have you a preference about which church we use or where you would like your late husband to be buried?'

Anna waved her hand with a look of distaste on her face. 'Oh, just the nearest church will do, and as I said, the sooner the better.'

'Of course, madam. I'll be in touch.' He put his top hat back on and bowed before quietly leaving the room.

Minutes later Lottie appeared looking all of a fluster. 'Please, ma'am. Could we put a sign on the front door or somethin' explainin' that the doctor 'as passed away? I've turned away loads o' people wantin' to see him already this mornin', an' as many again requesting he does a house call.'

'Oh, just do whatever you have to,' Anna told her sharply, then lifted the newspaper and began to read it as if this was just any other day.

Violet could only stare at her in disbelief. She felt as if her whole world had fallen apart and yet Anna hadn't even shed a tear yet as far as she knew. She couldn't bear to be with her a minute longer, so she went to join Cook in the kitchen. She had always felt more at home there with her than she had in the drawing room with her mother.

'Is it all sorted, pet?' Edie was rolling pastry for a meat pie for their dinner, although she doubted any of them would have much of an appetite.

'Yes, the funeral director is going to organise everything,' Violet answered dully.

'And what about a do for after the funeral? Will your ma be wantin' it here? It's normal for the mourners to get together after the service for somethin' to eat an' drink, an' pay their respects. I shall need to know so as I can get on wi' some bakin'.'

'Mama hasn't mentioned that yet. I'll ask her for you.' Violet retraced her steps. Anna still had her nose stuck in the paper and when Violet told her what Cook had said she shrugged.

'I hadn't thought that far ahead. I suppose we shall have to do *something*.' She didn't look at all happy at the idea, but she realised that it wouldn't look very respectful if she didn't at least make a token effort. 'Very well, tell Cook to go ahead with whatever she has to do.'

Violet turned and left without a word.

'Don't worry, pet. I'll put on a spread for 'im that would do justice to a king,' Edie promised when Violet told her what her mother had said. 'It's the least he deserves if she's layin' 'im to rest on a shoestring!'

'Thank you, and I'll do all I can to help.' Violet went into the shelter of Cook's ample arms. It was more than clear that her mother would offer her no comfort.

Chapter Five

Two days before the funeral was to take place, Oliver arrived home.

'I didn't even know Papa was ill,' he said when Violet flew through the hall to welcome him back.

'Neither did we,' she admitted as she helped him off with his coat. 'Although he'd been pushing himself too hard for months with all these winter illnesses about. His surgery was full every morning and sometimes he wasn't getting home until late at night when he'd done all his house calls. You know what he was like; he wouldn't let anyone down if he could help it and I think he just pushed himself too hard.'

'And what's going to happen to us all now? Papa was the bread-winner so what will we live on without his income?'

Violet looked perplexed. She hadn't even thought of that. 'I don't know, but I do know that Mother has an appointment immediately following the funeral with Mr Chapman, Papa's solicitor. I dare say he'll tell us where we stand financially.'

Could Violet have known it, at that very moment, Anna was in her father's small office rifling through his drawers. He had informed her some months before that he had written a codicil which he intended to be added to his will, but she wasn't aware of him taking it to the solicitor. He had been far too busy. But now she was wondering if the clause might not be in her interest, and she was keen to find it before the reading of the will. The first two drawers she searched yielded nothing but in the third drawer she came across a sealed envelope addressed to Mr Chapman, c/o Chapman and Lloyds solicitors, Anlaby Street, Hull.

This must be it, she thought as she hastily slit the envelope and withdrew the sheet of paper. Her eyes flew across the page and she frowned.

I, William Morris Stroud, do on this day the 21st of October 1904, wish it to be known that should anything happen to me, any assets or money I leave behind not already stated in my original will, should go my daughter, Violet Stroud.
William Stroud

Anger distorted Anna's face and she crumpled the letter in her hand. She could distinctly remember the day he had written this; it had followed a heated dispute between them. William had wanted to ensure that Violet would be provided for, but Anna wasn't about to allow that to happen while she had breath in her body. As far as she was concerned, she had been trapped in a loveless marriage for far too long and now finally she would reap the rewards. It was she who would inherit the house and any monies William had left.

She smiled at the thought. It was a grand house in a good area and she was sure it would fetch a pretty penny. She intended to sell it then give Violet her marching orders. After all, the girl was quite old enough to fend for herself. As for Oliver . . . well, he was her son by birth, so naturally she would allow him to finish his education, by which time he too would be old enough to make his own way in the world, and he would hopefully help to look after her as well. And then finally she would be free to do as she pleased. She could hardly wait! Anna had never been particularly happy since marrying William but now, suddenly, the life she had always dreamed of was within her grasp and she intended to seize it with both hands.

Quietly she left the office and made her way back to the drawing room, where she threw the codicil into the fire and smiled as the flames hungrily devoured it. Now as William's grieving widow, everything he had owned would be hers.

The day of the funeral finally dawned and as Violet dressed in the sombre black gown Anna had insisted she should have, she felt numb. It was rare for Anna to buy her new clothes and Violet was sad to think that it was an occasion such as this that had prompted her this time.

When she was ready, she slowly made her way down to the hall where Anna and Oliver were waiting for the pall bearers to arrive to carry her father's body out to the waiting hearse.

The funeral director had brought him home three days before and since then he had lain in his surgery. As Anna had said, where else was there for him to go when he already used their day room to see his patients? Ever since he had come back, there had been a steady procession of people coming to pay their respects before the lid of his coffin was nailed down. Anna had said from the start that she didn't want this to be a much publicised affair, but word of the doctor's demise had spread quickly, and they had been inundated with floral tributes and people lamenting his passing. It made Violet proud to see just how well loved and respected her father had been, although it had annoyed Anna.

'I shall just be glad when the whole thing is over and we can get back to some sort of normality,' she had stated churlishly. 'I feel like I'm living in a goldfish bowl with all these people coming and going!'

Deep down Violet knew things could never return to normal. How could they now that her father was gone? But she wisely held her tongue, and now the day she had dreaded had arrived.

At twenty minutes to eleven on the dot the pall bearers entered wearing long black frock coats and black silk top hats. They reminded Violet of a flock of hungry crows as they lifted her father's coffin and solemnly carried it out to the glass-sided hearse.

It was pulled by two beautiful coal-black horses wearing feathered plumes, and their shiny coats stood out in stark contrast to the thick snow lying on the ground.

Violet, her mother and Oliver followed the hearse in another carriage to the nearby church, and finally the service began. They were surprised at quite how full the church was and Anna whispered, 'I hope they don't all come back to the house after the service. Cook will never have enough to feed them all!'

Violet was shocked that she could even think of that but then she supposed she should have expected it. Today, Anna looked beautiful in a black satin gown and a hat with a small black veil, and she was playing the part of a grieving widow to perfection, although Violet still hadn't seen her shed so much as a single tear.

The service and the interment seemed to go on forever but at last it was over and Oliver took her elbow and led her and their mother through the churchyard, under the lychgate and into the waiting carriage. Violet was numb with grief and heartache.

Once back at the house Anna removed her hat and greeted her guests graciously. Violet noticed that within minutes of being back Oliver was helping himself to the shorts that Lottie had poured out for the gentlemen. She herself helped Lottie to circulate amongst the ladies with trays of tea. As well as a number of Anna's wealthy friends there were also a great number of working-class people who her father had treated, and she could see the waves of disapproval coming off her mother every time they approached her.

'He were a good man, none better,' one old lady told Anna. 'He 'elped my Bert after he 'ad an accident on the docks, he did! I reckon if it 'adn't been fer Doctor Stroud my Bert would 'ave lost 'is leg, an' not a penny piece would 'e take off us till Bert were workin' again, bless 'is soul.'

'Yes, my husband could be very, er ... generous,' Anna responded coldly. 'But thank you for coming. I'm sure you'll be wanting to get home now, so don't let me keep you.'

The old woman eyed the buffet table and sighed regretfully. She'd had her eye on a slice of that lovely pork pie, but it sounded like the missus was showing her the door. In the nicest possible way, of course, so she said her goodbyes and took her leave.

Within an hour Oliver was glassy-eyed and swaying, looking more like he was attending a party than a wake.

'I think you should go up and have a lie-down, my dear.' Anna took the glass of whisky from his hand and propelled him towards the door. 'I fear the day has proved to be too much for you,' she said politely for the benefit of the guests.

Finally, the last guests took their leave and only the solicitor, Mr Chapman, and Violet remained.

'Shall I start the clearin' away, ma'am?' Lottie asked.

Anna waved her hand dismissively. 'No, not yet, Lottie. Go and make us a tray of tea.'

She was impatient to hear what the will said and smiled fawningly at the solicitor as she ushered him to a chair. 'So, Mr Chapman, shall we begin?'

Violet stood at the back of the room with her hands clasped in front of her.

The solicitor raised an eyebrow as he took William's will from his bag. This woman certainly wasn't acting as he would have expected a grieving widow to act so soon after her husband's demise. William had instructed him as his solicitor shortly after moving to Hull, and over the years the two men had become friends. Mr Chapman had got the impression that William's marriage wasn't a particularly happy one but decided to give Anna the benefit of the doubt. After all, she was probably just concerned about the future for herself and her children.

'Very well, ma'am.' He perched a pair of wire-framed spectacles precariously on the end of his nose and began, 'This is the last will and—'

'Oh, don't bother with all that.' Anna glared at him. 'Just get to the important bit please.'

'Ahem!' Mr Chapman cleared his throat, clearly embarrassed. 'Of course. To Edie Thompson, who has been like a mother to me and a loyal servant for many years, I leave the sum of twenty pounds.'

Anna looked none too happy about that but he went on, 'And to Lottie Benson, our maid, I leave the sum of five pounds. Any money and all the rest of my assets to my wife Anna Stroud with the understanding that she will ensure that our children's future is secure.'

Anna looked happy. 'I assume the house is included in the assets?'

The solicitor frowned. It appeared Mrs Stroud had not been aware of what he was about to tell her. 'I'm afraid the house never belonged to Mr Stroud,' he said quietly. 'The house was rented after you moved from the house that you first lived in when you came to Hull.'

Shock registered on Anna's face. 'B-but we had to move from there,' she said in a trembling voice. 'It was totally unsuitable and in a very poor area. William knew I wasn't happy there, which is why he bought this house.'

The solicitor shook his head. 'No, Mrs Stroud. This house was beyond your husband's means, which is why he had to rent it.'

'What happened to the money he got for the other house? I know he owned that.'

'It was put into the bank, but of course over the years your husband had to use it to cover expenses – school fees, etc.' He glanced down at the will again. 'I can tell you now that the sum remaining in the bank after paying out the legacy to your staff and my fees will be just short of a hundred and fifty pounds.'

'*A hundred and fifty pounds!*' Anna looked horrified. 'But that can't be right.'

He nodded solemnly. 'I assure you it is. I have the statement from the bank here, look. However, your husband did mention to me a short time ago that he was going to make a codicil to the will, leaving a set amount to his daughter. Would you happen to know if he did that?'

Anna flushed as she pictured the said codicil being eaten by flames. 'No, I, er . . . I haven't found anything like that. But what am I to do? If I don't own this house, how am I to buy another and how am I supposed to live?'

He glanced around at the expensive furniture. 'Well, maybe things aren't as bad as they may seem. Perhaps you could get an auction house in to sell the more expensive items for you, and then you could rent a more modest establishment. Both children are of an age where they could get jobs, and if you got one too, I believe you could all live quite comfortably.'

'*Me get a job!*' Anna was spitting with fury now as she sprang from her seat and began to pace. 'How could William do this to me? The trouble with him was he was too soft-hearted – always treating patients who couldn't afford to pay him! I told him it had to stop a million times, but would he listen? And now look at the dire straits he has left me in!'

The solicitor gulped as he tucked the will back into his bag and rose from his seat. It was the daughter he felt sorry for. The poor girl looked heartbroken at the loss of her father. Whereas the wife seemed to care only about herself.

'If that is all, ma'am, I shall take my leave now. Good day to you.' He smiled at Violet and hurried away just as Lottie appeared with the tray of tea and a plate of biscuits.

'Take them away, you stupid girl! Can't you see that you're too late?' Anna screeched and Lottie hastily reversed out of the door and flew back towards the kitchen with the pots on the tray rattling dangerously. 'And you get out as well!' Anna turned her wrath on Violet, who also made a speedy exit.

'What the *hell* is goin' on?' Cook asked as Violet stumbled into the kitchen. Lottie was sobbing uncontrollably and Cook had her arms about her.

'M-Mama is angry,' Violet stammered. 'She just found out that this house never belonged to us. Papa only rented it.'

'Huh! I could 'ave told 'er that years ago,' Cook snorted. 'An' serves her right an' all! Your father found you a perfectly nice house closer to the docks when we first came 'ere. But o' course it weren't right for 'er ladyship. She wanted somewhere posher, didn't she!'

'So what will happen now?' Lottie asked with a frown.

'Well, the solicitor suggested that Mama should auction all the expensive furniture we have and that we should rent a cheaper house.'

'Hmm, that'll mean that my job will be gone.' Lottie sighed. 'Still, I'll be wed soon so it won't much matter to me.'

'Actually, Papa left you and Cook a small inheritance,' Violet informed her. 'Five pounds for you and twenty pounds for Cook.'

'Ah, God bless 'is soul.' Cook sniffed loudly and wiped her eyes on the edge of her apron. 'All we can do now is wait an' see what your mother decides to do, then we'll 'ave to start thinkin' where we go from there, eh?'

The two young women nodded, neither relishing the thought of the changes ahead.

Chapter Six

The following morning Oliver looked, as Cook described him, 'like death warmed up'.

'And it's hardly surprisin' seein' the amount o' drink he poured down his throat yesterday,' Cook stated unsympathetically. Oliver was suffering from a severe hangover and couldn't face food or drink.

It was no surprise when they were all summoned to join Anna in the drawing room. 'Here we go,' Cook whispered to Violet as they went along the hallway with Lottie and Oliver trailing behind them.

Anna had been up for most of the night going through the accounts in William's study and she was in an even worse mood than she had been in the day before, if that was possible.

She was standing in front of the fireplace with her hands clasped at her waist, frowning, when they entered.

'I dare say Violet has informed you that my husband left you each a small legacy?' When Cook and Lottie nodded, she went on, 'Things are actually even worse than I feared. Having gone through our accounts I find that we owe quite a lot of money to various tradespeople as well as some fees to Oliver's school. Which will mean' – she looked pointedly at her son – 'that you will not be able to return to school.'

Oliver opened his mouth to protest but one glare from his mother made him think better of it and he clamped it shut again, folding his arms tightly across his chest and scowling.

'It also means that we will no longer be able to stay here. I'm afraid the rent will be too high for us without William's wages coming in. So, regretfully, I am going to have to let you both go,' she told Cook and Lottie.

Cook shrugged. 'Don't worry about us. We'll be all right. But what will you an' the young 'uns do?'

Just for a moment Anna looked vaguely uncomfortable but then drawing herself up to her full height, she said, 'I shall do as the solicitor advised and bring in an auction house to sell some of my more expensive pictures and furniture. Oliver and I will then move to a smaller house and Oliver will have to take a job to help meet our bills.'

'*What?*' Oliver looked appalled. 'But—'

'Be quiet!' Anna's eyes flashed as she turned on him and he looked shocked. His mother never spoke to him that way. 'It's either that or we'll find ourselves on the streets. Which do you prefer?'

Once again, he swallowed his objections.

'An' may I ask? Where does that leave Violet?' Cook asked boldly.

'I rather think that now she is seventeen Violet is quite old enough to go and make her own way in life,' Anna answered unfeelingly.

Hands on hips, Cook glared at her as Violet visibly wilted at her side, unable to speak. 'I allus thought somethin' like this might happen if owt ever happened to the master,' Cook ground out. 'You should be *ashamed* o' yourself. But don't worry, I'll see as she comes to no 'arm.' And with that she took Violet's arm and almost dragged her from the room.

Violet was crying by that time and when they reached the kitchen she said brokenly, 'I don't understand what's going on, Cook. What's to become of me now? Why would Mama suddenly desert me like that?'

'That's somethin' she'd 'ave to tell you 'erself if she had a mind to,' Cook said grimly. 'But don't you fret, pet. I've been makin' a few enquiries since your father passed an' I think I've found just the place fer us. You'll be comin' wi' me.'

When Violet raised an eyebrow, she lowered her voice and went on, 'Things ain't as bad as you think. I don't know if your dad feared somethin' like this happenin', but every week, he's given me a bit o' money to put by for you. You've got quite a few pounds stashed away now. An' me – well, I've been savin' an' all an' I've accrued quite a little nest egg. I've seen this little tea shop down by the docks wi' livin' quarters above it an' I happen to know that the old lady who runs it is thinkin' o' sellin' up an' retirin'. To be honest I don't think she's ever made much out of it, probably because she ain't been caterin' to the right customers, see? Tea an' cakes is all very well, but who uses the docks the most, eh? Why, it's the chaps that work there. Sailors an' dock hands, an' such. Now, were I to buy it an' alter the menu, start servin' more down-to-earth food – cooked breakfasts, dinners an' such – I reckon it could do really well. I could just about manage it, so what do you think? You could come an' work wi' me there an' you'd have a home for as long as you wanted one.'

Violet slowly nodded. The thought of leaving her home was daunting but she loved Cook like family.

'If it comes to that I'd be happy to come with you,' she said gratefully. 'But let's wait to see what Mama decides to do first, shall we? What I mean is, she's just had a nasty shock after discovering that Papa didn't leave her as well off as she'd thought, and she might have a change of heart.'

'Huh! I don't think you'll have to wait long,' Cook grunted as she went to put a piece of beef into the oven for their dinner.

Cook was proved right when there was a sharp rap on the front door the following morning. Lottie hurried to answer it and came back to the kitchen to tell them, 'It's someone from the auction house come to value the contents o' the house. He's in wi' the missus now.'

Two hours later, once the man had departed, Violet, Lottie and Cook were summoned to the drawing room again where

Anna told them unfeelingly, 'The furniture will be taken away in the morning and auctioned, so I'm afraid as of tomorrow you will have to find somewhere else to stay. I apologise for the short notice, but I have no choice. I am going to view a smaller property to rent for Oliver and myself this afternoon.'

Violet gasped with shock. She hadn't been able to believe that her mother would really do this. 'And does that include me, Mama?' There was a catch in her voice.

Anna scowled. 'Yes, it does include you, didn't I make that clear yesterday?'

'But I don't understand.' Violet was crying. 'Why would you take Oliver and not me? I'm your child too.'

'You are fortunate that Adam Powell is willing to marry you; it's not as if I'm turning you out with no options. And as for you being my child, that is where you are *very* wrong!' Anna's eyes were full of malice. There was no need to keep up the pretence now that William was dead. 'You have *never* been my child. You are the consequence of an affair that your father had and you were *foisted* upon me.'

Violet's head shook in denial. 'N-no . . . you're lying!'

'I think you will find I am not.' Anna's eyes were as cold as the snow that lay on the ground outside. 'You are a flyblow, and for all these years your father has forced me to put up with you. But he's gone now, so there is no need to hide the truth any longer. You are a bastard and the sooner you accept the fact the better it will be for all of us.'

'Why, you hard-hearted *cow*!' Cook was furious. Hurrying over to Violet she put her arms about her as the girl swayed with shock.

'I *won't* marry Adam!' Violet stated vehemently. 'And as for her not being my mama, she's lying, isn't she, Cook? Tell me she's lying!'

Cook sadly shook her head as she smoothed a damp dark curl from Violet's forehead. 'No, I'm afraid she ain't, pet. But don't think about it for now. You certainly ain't goin' to be palmed off on Adam Powell! We're goin', me, you an' Lottie. Why, I wouldn't stay 'ere for another day, not for a king's ransom. Let this bitch cook her own dinner for a change an' I hope it chokes her. Come on, we've got packin' to do.' And with that she led Violet from the room. They all went to their separate rooms and when Lottie and Cook had packed their own things, they went to Violet's room to help her finish packing hers.

'B-but where will we go?' Violet sobbed. 'You haven't managed to sort out buying the café yet and we need somewhere to sleep tonight.' She had thought nothing could possibly get worse when her father died but it just had. Now she was homeless.

'Don't you get worryin' about that,' Cook soothed. 'Lottie 'ere will go 'ome to her mam an' dad, an' you an' me will rent a room somewhere till the sale o' the café goes through. The old lady who owns it as good as told me that it was a case of the sooner the better. The poor old dear is riddled wi' arthritis an' can barely keep goin', so we could be in there wi'in a week or so.'

'But what about Oliver? I thought he was my brother. Will I ever see him again?'

Cook knew how much Violet idolised the young man, although personally she had never been able to see what the attraction was. As far as she was concerned, he was just as self-centred and selfish as his mother was.

'Let's worry about that another day,' Cook urged. 'For now, I just want to be out of 'ere. In fact, the further away the better. I'm done wi' takin' orders from that witch.'

Soon Violet's bags were piled by the door and Cook told Lottie, 'We're never goin' to be able to carry this lot. Could you go out an' hail a cab for us all, pet?'

Lottie obligingly set off to do as she was asked.

Twenty minutes later, she was back to tell them that a cab was outside, so they carried the bags downstairs and the driver stacked them in the back.

Oliver came out of the drawing room as the last of the bags were being carried through the door and Violet rushed over and grasped his hands. 'How shall I get in touch with you?'

He frowned. 'I don't know, do I? We don't know where we're going yet either.' He pushed her hands away in annoyance. He wasn't looking forward to the prospect of having to work at all.

Cook told him where the café she hoped to buy was and he shrugged. 'Fair enough. I dare say I'll pop in and see you sometime if I'm near there.'

Then Cook and Lottie each took one of Violet's arms and hauled her away. Oliver didn't attempt to stop them.

'But I haven't said goodbye to Mama,' Violet wailed as they unceremoniously bundled her into the cab.

Cook and Lottie shook their heads as they exchanged glances, and then Cook had a hasty word with the driver before joining them in the cab.

'He knows where there are some cheap rooms to rent,' she informed them as they pulled away. 'So he's takin' us there now. I doubt they'll be posh but beggars can't be choosers, eh? An' hopefully it ain't goin' to be for long.'

Violet was in shock. In a matter of days her whole world had turned upside down. She had lost her beloved father, the only home she had ever known, and discovered that the woman she had always thought was her mother wasn't at all. To make things worse, Anna had made it crystal clear that she had never had any love for her. It was just too much to take in and, as she sat staring sightlessly out of the window, Violet felt as if her mind had shut down.

A short time later the cab drew up outside a row of terraced houses close to the docks, and Cook and Lottie had to almost lift her down.

'Don't look much,' Cook commented once she had paid the cabbie and they stood with their bags around them. 'But never mind, 'opefully it'll only be for a short time.' She rapped on the door and presently an elderly woman with wispy grey hair tied in an untidy bun and wearing a grubby apron inched it open.

'We're lookin' for a room to rent for a few days,' Cook informed her. 'Me an' the young lady 'ere.'

'Only got the one double room empty at the minute an' it's up in the attic,' the woman informed her.

'Then we'll look at it, if we may.' Cook and Lottie began to lift their bags into a dark, unpleasant-smelling hallway, but Violet just stood there, unwilling or unable to move.

'Foller me,' the old woman said, and they started up a steep, narrow staircase that seemed to go on forever.

At the top, the old woman, who was huffing and puffing, flung a door open and Cook and Lottie stepped past her into the room.

'This is it.' The old woman spread her hands. 'Take it or leave it; you'll not find cheaper.'

Cook sniffed disapprovingly as she glanced around. A double bed with grubby pillows and blankets took up most of one wall. The roof was slanted and had a skylight that was so dirty it barely let any light in, and in places the faded wallpaper was hanging off the walls. Two old hard-backed chairs stood either side of a rickety table and there was an old chest of drawers coated in dust. It was bitterly cold in there too, but there was a small fireplace. Cook supposed she could buy some coal and light a fire in it, and after all, hopefully it was only going to be for a very short time, and it was better than being on the streets.

'We'll take it,' she said decisively.

'Then I'll want a week's rent up front.' The woman named her price and when Cook had taken out her purse and paid her, she left.

'It's a bit grotty, ain't it?' Lottie said uncertainly.

Edie shrugged. 'It'll do. Now come an' help me get the bags up an' then I'm goin' to go an' buy some coal. It'll look cheerier wi' a fire burnin'. I'm also goin' to see the lady with the café to see if we can agree on a price. Will you wait here wi' Violet till I get back?'

Lottie nodded. 'Of course.'

They trooped back downstairs and by the time they had got all the bags up and Violet was sitting quietly on the bed, Edie was red in the face.

'Right. I'll get off. I'll be as quick as I can an' I just hope we won't have to be here for too long. Them stairs would be the death o' me.'

She came back some time later bearing a bag of coal, some bread and cheese and wearing a jubilant expression on her face.

'The sale's all agreed an' the lady that owns the café 'as promised to be out for the weekend, so we'll only be 'ere for a few nights, thank goodness.' Cocking her head towards Violet she lowered her voice to ask Lottie, 'How's she been?'

'She ain't said a word since you left, poor little soul,' Lottie answered sadly. 'An' no wonder after the way the missus told 'er what she did.'

Edie scowled. 'Don't you worry, pet. You know what they say, "what goes around comes around". She'll get 'er comeuppance. Her sort allus do.'

After they'd said a tearful goodbye to Lottie, promising to keep in touch, Edie made sandwiches for herself and Violet, although Violet didn't even attempt to eat them.

Poor little bugger! Edie thought. But as she considered her new venture, she smiled. It would be a brand-new start for them, and hopefully, once Violet was over the shock of all that had happened, there would be better times ahead.

Chapter Seven

On the following Saturday morning Edie went out to hail a cab, and she and Violet loaded all their possessions into it and set off for what was to be their new home. Violet had been painfully quiet, but Edie had expected that. The girl had a lot to come to terms with.

'Be it ever so humble, here it is.' Edie grinned from ear to ear as the cab eventually drew up in front of a small shop.

The cabbie lifted their luggage down for them, and taking the key she had collected from the solicitor that morning, Edie opened the door and ushered Violet inside ahead of her.

'So, what do you think? I mean, I know it ain't much at the minute but we'll soon 'ave it shipshape!'

Violet looked around. There was a counter to one side with a door behind it that she assumed must lead into a kitchen, and spread about the room were a number of small tables and mismatched chairs.

'I'm sure it can be made very nice,' Violet answered quietly as Edie took her hand and led her through the door and behind the counter. As Violet had thought, they found themselves in a fair-sized kitchen with a large stove against one wall and an enormous pot sink and draining board on the other. A large number of shelves covered the walls and Edie was delighted to see that the previous owner had left all the pots, pans, dishes, mugs and cutlery for her. 'Hmm, that'll save us a few shillin's,' she said happily. At the back of the kitchen was a smaller room used for storing stock, and beyond that was a yard with an outside toilet and a tin bath hanging on the wall.

They went upstairs to explore their living quarters next, and were surprised to find it was bigger than they had expected. There was a small kitchen, a fair-sized sitting room and two decent-sized bedrooms. Here too, the old woman had left all her furniture, and although it was dated and a little shabby, they could at least be comfortable until she could afford to replace it.

'You an' me are goin' to be really happy 'ere, pet,' she promised Violet as she took her hand and squeezed it, hoping to cheer her up a little. 'This'll be the first time I've ever owned me own place in me whole life.'

'I'll help you clean it all and get the café up and running,' Violet promised and Edie didn't argue with her. The way she saw it, being busy would be a good way of keeping Violet's mind off all that had happened.

'I reckon if we work 'ard an' stick in together we could 'ave this place open in a week or so,' Edie mused. 'I think we'll start up 'ere an' get this place sorted so as we've got some place comfy to come to when we ain't workin', then we'll tackle the shop. A coat o' whitewash wouldn't go amiss down there an' goodness knows when the shop winders were last cleaned. But first, which bedroom would you like?'

'I really don't mind.'

'Right, then you 'ave the one that overlooks the road. There's more to see from that one,' Edie said generously. 'Perhaps you can start to unpack our things while I go out an' get a bit o' shoppin an' pick up some new beddin'. I don't mind settlin' for second-hand furniture but I do like me own beddin'.'

Once Edie had hurried away, Violet sank onto her bed. For days she had felt as if she was in a daze as her mind tried to process all that had happened to her, but now the fog was lifting and questions were forming. If Anna wasn't her birth mother, then who was? And why had her father never told her? The fact she and Oliver were merely half-brother and sister, explained why they looked nothing alike. It was as if the pieces of a jigsaw were fitting into place. Ever since she was a little girl, she had wondered why Anna had never shown her an ounce of love or affection, and yet had always had time for Oliver. Now she knew: she had clearly resented her since the day she had arrived on her doorstep. Perhaps that was why Anna and her father had always had separate bedrooms – because Anna hadn't been able to forgive him for his infidelity. But if Cook had known of it all these years, why had she never told her? There were so many questions, but it was too soon to ask them. Everything was still so raw.

Edie came back two hours later loaded down with bedding and a basket of shopping. 'First things first, we'll have us a nice cup o' tea then get crackin', shall we?'

Violet nodded and, while Edie made them scrambled eggs and tea, she put the food away in the kitchen cupboards.

'I'm ready for anythin' now,' Edie told her when they'd eaten. She was studiously avoiding mentioning what had happened, and forcing herself to be jolly for Violet's sake, despite Violet barely touching her food.

Together they scrubbed the living quarters from top to bottom, which took them the rest of that day. When they'd finished, Edie fried them some potatoes and chops, but again Violet merely picked at the food. There was a fire burning in the grate now and with the curtains closed against the bitterly cold snowy night the little living room was warm and cosy.

'We'll make a start on the café tomorrow.'

Violet stared at her. 'You don't have to keep me here, you know,' she said quietly. 'What I mean is, you're very kind, but as Mama . . . Anna . . . said, I'm old enough to manage on my own now. I don't want to be a burden on you.'

'*What?* Why, I've never heard such nonsense in me life!' Edie scowled at her. 'You're here for a reason, me girl. You don't think I could do this all on me own, do you? I need you to be in the café seein' to the customers while I'm in the kitchen cookin'. I can't be in two places at once, can I?'

'Well . . . no, I suppose not,' Violet admitted, feeling slightly better.

'An' another thing, I reckon it's time you started callin' me Edie. Cook were fine while I was workin' for your dad but it's just you and me now.' Seeing the flash of pain in Violet's eyes, she sighed. 'Sorry, pet. Me an' me big gob, eh? It'll get me hanged one o' these days.'

'It's all right . . . Edie.' It felt strange to be addressing her as anything other than Cook after all those years, but she supposed she would get used to it eventually.

'I don't know about you, but I'm jiggered.' Edie eased her boots off and rubbed her swollen feet. 'I think we've done our whack for today so we'll have us a nice quiet night by the fire, eh?'

The following week passed in a blur of painting, cleaning and getting the shop to Edie's high standards. Lottie called in a few times to help as she hadn't yet secured a new position, but at last, they were ready.

'I reckon all we've got to do now is work out the menus,' Edie said as she sat with a pad and pencil ready for ideas. 'As I said, I think we should be catering more for the dockworkers, and they like something more substantial than just tea and cake.'

'You can't go wrong with sausage or bacon batches,' Lottie suggested, and Edie wrote that down.

'And what about stew and dumplings to serve at lunchtime? We can cook big panfuls and keep it hot – that's always nice, especially in the winter.' This suggestion was from Violet.

It was added to the list and eventually Edie smiled. 'I think that's enough to be goin' on wi', till we've built up a bit o' trade anyway. We don't want to end up wi' loads of waste every evenin'. I could perhaps do some rice puddin's and apple pies an' all for them that are wantin' a puddin'.'

It was agreed that Violet and Edie would go shopping the following day to buy all the food and that they would open the day after that.

The next morning, they bought all the food they thought they would need and Edie set to making big pans of creamy rice pudding and apple pies. She also prepared the vegetables for an enormous pan of stew and dumplings. Everything else would be freshly cooked when it was ordered.

Violet was in the café writing out the menus – one to put in the window and one for on the counter – when Lottie popped in again.

'You'll never guess what I've heard,' she said, her cheeks rosy from the cold air outside and the gossip she had to impart. 'I saw Mrs Nelson, your old neighbour, Violet, an' it seems that not long after we left your ma's, your brother walked out an' all.'

'What?' Violet was shocked. 'But why would he do that?'

Lottie grinned – she had never had time for Oliver. 'From what Mrs Nelson could gather, he didn't like school but it seems he liked the thought of havin' to work to look after the missus even less, so he left her to it!'

'But where is he now?'

Lottie shrugged. 'Don't know and I don't much care to be honest.'

Violet chewed on her lip 'Oh dear, I hope he's all right.'

Edie, who had come in to listen to Lottie's news, frowned. She knew Violet had always adored the lad and considered him to be her big brother. Of course, Edie knew differently, she just hadn't thought it was her place to tell Violet. Just as she had never told her that Anna wasn't really her ma. And Violet had had so many revelations to deal with recently she didn't want to add to the burden now.

'So where is Mama – I mean Anna – now?'

Lottie shrugged. 'The last Mrs Nelson saw of her was when she went off in a cart with what was left of her things. But I shouldn't worry, people like her allus drop on their feet. No doubt she'll find some mug to take her in.'

'You're quite right, Lottie,' Edie agreed. 'But that's enough about the missus, we've got a café to open come mornin'. What do you think o' the place?'

Lottie looked around and nodded her approval. Everywhere was clean and fresh. 'It looks grand. I'll pop in some time durin' the day to see how you're doin. But I'd best get off else me mam will have me guts for garters. I only popped out to get some potatoes for us dinner. Ta-ra for now!' And with that she was off, leaving Violet and Edie to prepare for their new venture.

Chapter Eight

'All right, pet, you can turn the sign to open now,' Edie said with a smile early the next morning. The kettle was singing for anyone who wanted tea, and in the kitchen everything was prepared for breakfast.

The first hour passed and although people glanced curiously in through the newly washed windows as they hurried by, no one came in. Edie started to look a little worried. She had sunk her life savings into this place and she had to make it work.

At last, at just gone ten o'clock, two dockworkers paused to glance at the menu in the window and after a few moments they entered.

'Two fry-ups, if you please, ladies,' one of them said. 'An' some nice mugs o' hot tea.'

Edie skittered away to get the food cooked while Violet made their tea, and soon after the little bell on the counter rang and Violet popped into the kitchen to fetch the food. She had to admit it looked delicious and the two men seemed to think so too as they tucked in.

'That was grand,' the larger of the two men told her when they had cleared their plates. 'An' I see you do a lunchtime menu an' all.'

'We certainly do, so please spread the word,' Violet said with a smile. Just as they were leaving another man entered and ordered the same.

'Seems like the bacon an' eggs might prove to be popular,' Edie whispered when Violet placed the order.

Throughout the rest of the day a few more people ventured in, but when they finally turned the sign on the door to closed Violet was dismayed to see how much food was left.

'Never mind, it was only us first day,' Edie pointed out. 'An' on the plus side, we'll eat like kings tonight. At least them that came in went away happy wi' full bellies, an' word o' mouth is the best advertisin' you can get.'

Lottie had said the same thing when she called in during the afternoon and Violet hoped she was right. She knew how much this venture meant to Edie, who was finally her own boss.

Later that evening, as Edie sat knitting, Violet said quietly, 'I wonder where Oliver and Mama – Anna – are now. I can't help worrying about them; he's still my half-brother after all, and I thought she was my mother for my whole life. Do you think they'll be all right?'

'O' course they will,' Edie answered. She had always worried about the attachment Violet had to Oliver and knew that what she was about to tell her would break her heart, but she had agonised with herself and decided that Violet had a right to know. 'The thing is, though, there is sommat I should tell you.'

'Oh, yes?'

Edie laid her knitting in her lap and sighed. The poor girl had had so much to come to terms with lately and now she was about to tell her something else shocking. 'The thing is . . . you and Oliver ain't related at all. At least not by blood. You see, Anna was already havin' Oliver to another man when she tricked your dad into marrying her.'

Violet looked shocked. 'You mean, he's not even my half-brother?'

When Edie nodded, she screwed her eyes up and a tear slid down her cheek. 'So he probably won't even bother coming to see me now!'

Edie shook her head. 'No, he probably won't. I know you've allus hero-worshipped him, but I'll tell you now, as he's grown he's got more like his mother every day. I warn you, Oliver is a bad 'un. His father was a mill owner's son, a right tearaway an' a womaniser by all accounts, an' I reckon Oliver's inherited the worst o' both his parents.'

'I don't agree. Admittedly Oliver has been somewhat spoilt, but I think now that he'll have to stand on his own two feet he'll come into his own. I just hope he comes to find me. And *why* have you never told me this before?'

'Because I knew it'd upset yer an' I was obviously right!'

Violet glared at her and Edie suddenly wished that she hadn't told her. If anything, it had made things worse instead of better, but there could be no going back now. 'Anyway, we'll have to wait and see if he turns up, but chances are you won't ever see him again.' She sighed as she picked up her knitting. It had always been Violet seeking Oliver out. Since getting older he had never had time for her and had always considered her a nuisance, so the chances were that even if they did ever meet again, he wouldn't be in the least bit interested in what became of her. At least, that was what she hoped.

The next morning Edie drastically cut down on the food she prepared. She couldn't afford to have the amount of wastage they'd had the day before. Thankfully, over the course of the day a few more people drifted in and they were a little busier.

'How did we do today?' Violet asked when they closed up that evening.

'Better than yesterday but still not enough to cover the costs.' Edie hid her concerns. 'But in fairness I didn't expect to be rakin' the money in straightaway. I know that a business has to be built up. I notice that two of the blokes who came in yesterday were back, so fingers crossed we'll do better still again tomorrow.'

By the end of the first week, though, they were still not taking enough money to cover the costs, let alone make a little bit of profit, and Violet was concerned.

'Rome weren't built in a day,' Edie said with a false grin, hoping to keep the girl's spirits up. 'An' I'm more than happy wi' how things are goin'. We make a good team you an' me, an' you've certainly been a hit wi' the sailors from what I could see of it. It seems it helps to 'ave a pretty face takin' the orders.'

Violet blushed. It was true that more than one young man had tried his luck with her and asked her out, but she wasn't interested in any of them.

One evening the following week, as Violet was cleaning the kitchen ready for the next day, she thought she heard something in the yard. She glanced up nervously. Edie had gone upstairs early, suffering from a raging toothache, and suddenly Violet was very aware that she was all alone in the café. Thankfully the back door was locked, so crossing to it she peered out into the yard.

'Is anybody there?' she called out, her heart thumping painfully.

'It's me, Violet. I need to see you!'

'*Oliver!*' She unlocked the door and flung it open, and there he was – the answer to her prayers. She'd been so worried about him.

'Quickly, come in out of the cold.' Taking his elbow, she hauled him over the step, shutting the door behind him. His teeth were chattering with cold and his chin was covered in bristles, telling her he hadn't shaved for days. His clothes were damp and bedraggled, and began to steam in the heat from the oven.

'Have you eaten today?'

When he shook his head, she gestured for him to sit at the table, and filled a bowl with stew and dumplings that were still warm on the top of the range. Placing the bowl on the table, she pushed a loaf of bread and a pat of butter towards him before hurrying away to put the kettle on. Oliver had always been so self-conscious about his appearance and it was strange to see him looking so unkempt. There was so much she wanted to say to him, so many questions to ask, but she forced herself to remain silent as he attacked the food as if he hadn't eaten for months. As well as the stew he managed over half the loaf of bread before he sighed and sat back, sated.

'Where have you been?' she finally asked. 'I heard you didn't leave with Mam— Anna.' It was still hard to think of her as anything other than Mama.

'Here and there,' he answered cagily as he held his hands out to the dying fire. Violet hadn't bothered to make it up because she had intended to go upstairs once she had finished her cleaning. But now she crossed to the hearth and threw a shovel full of coal onto the flickering flames.

'Have you found somewhere to stay?'

He shrugged. 'Like I said, here and there.' And then with a sigh he admitted, 'Well, I was staying in a room just up the road but my money's run out.'

'Oh Oliver. Thank goodness you came here. How did you find me?'

'Edie told me where you would both be going as you left the house.'

'Where will you be sleeping tonight?' she asked worriedly.

He shrugged. If truth be told Violet had always been a thorn in his side as he had got older, clinging on to him every chance she got and being a nuisance, so it went against the grain to have to come to her for help, but what other options did he have? 'No idea. A shop doorway probably.'

Violet's eyes filled with tears. She couldn't bear to think of him homeless. Thankfully it hadn't snowed for a few days, but it was still bitterly cold and the snow that still lay on the ground had frozen solid.

'I, er . . . suppose I could ask Edie if you can stay here,' she ventured uncertainly.

He shook his head, his expression sullen. 'Huh! Why waste your breath? You were always her favourite.'

'But you can't stay out in this weather. Have you tried to get a job?'

He scowled at her. 'Only jobs going are casual work on the docks and from what I've heard it's back-breaking.'

'Then perhaps you'll have to swallow your pride and go back to Anna. Do you know where she is?'

'I heard she's rented a couple of rooms somewhere, though how she'll pay for them when the money she has runs out I don't know.'

Violet stared at him for a moment, wondering if he knew that he wasn't her real brother. Should she tell him? And then before she could stop herself, she blurted out, 'Did you know that my father wasn't yours?'

'*What?*' It was his turn to look astounded.

She nodded. 'It's true. Edie told me that your father was a mill owner's son who dumped your mother when he discovered she was with child. She married my father in haste by all accounts, so that you would have a name. So, all in all it seems that neither of us is who we thought we were, and we're not even blood related.'

Oliver stared at her in shock before saying callously, 'Ah well, at least your father did marry her, so I was born in wedlock, unlike you.'

Seeing the hurt cross her face, he realised he had made a grave mistake. She was the only one who might be able to help him so he would be foolish to upset her. 'Of course, that isn't your fault,' he added hurriedly. 'But I always thought Father liked you best. Now I know why. I wasn't really his at all.'

'And I was never your mother's,' she pointed out. Glancing at the clock she began to get worried. Edie would be down to see where she was if she didn't go upstairs soon, and she couldn't imagine she'd be very pleased to see Oliver here. 'Look, I've got some money,' she told him. 'I'll give you enough to get a room out of the cold for a couple of nights but soon you really do need to find yourself a job. I'm working here with Edie and believe it or not I'm actually quite enjoying it, although we could do with being a bit busier. Still, as Edie says, it's early days yet. Wait there while I go and fetch the money for you.' She hurried upstairs and when she came down, she found Oliver hovering by the door.

'Here, that should be enough for food and shelter for a few nights.' She pressed some coins into his hand and without a word of thanks he dropped them into his pocket and turned to the door.

'Will I ever see you again?'

He turned back to look at her and was shocked when he saw the love she felt for him in her eyes. He grinned at her. If she really did love him like that, maybe he'd be able to play her like a fiddle until he'd milked her dry. 'I'll be back,' he promised and leaning forward he gently kissed her cheek, amused to see her colour mount.

Violet watched him disappear into the cold night and her hand rose to touch the spot he had kissed, thrilled that he still cared about her even after learning they were not related. She locked the door and blew out the candles before climbing the stairs, a smile on her face.

'You're lookin' chirpy this mornin',' Edie observed as she began to prepare the food in the kitchen ahead of opening the café for the day.

'Am I?' Violet said coyly as she raked the ashes from the fireplace. Next, she made her way into the café and began to light the candles in the middle of each table. It was still dark but they had discovered that if they opened very early, they could catch a few of the dockers who enjoyed a cooked breakfast on their way to work. Seconds after turning the sign to open the first customer entered and the day began.

Violet spent the whole day watching the clock, desperate for the evening to come, certain that Oliver would visit again. But when evening arrived, even though she lingered for a long time in the kitchen after Edie had gone upstairs, there was no sign of him and she eventually went to bed disappointed.

By the end of that week Edie's Café, as it was now named, was still not making a profit and even Edie was becoming concerned.

'I think it's time we did sommat to attract a few more customers,' she told Violet that evening.

Violet raised an eyebrow 'Oh yes, what did you have in mind?'

'Well, I've given it a lot o' thought an' I reckon we should do an hour at lunchtime fer the next couple o' days wi' all the meals half price.'

'But won't we be working at a loss?'

Edie nodded. 'Aye, we will, love. But if it gets the customers in an' they like what they have, happen they'll come back an' it could pay dividends. I were wonderin' if you could perhaps do a sign fer the window advertisin' half-price meals between twelve an' one o' clock fer the next two days?'

'Very well,' Violet agreed tentatively. 'If you're sure it's worth the risk.'

'It will be,' Edie replied with a confidence she was far from feeling. 'We can't keep goin' on like this, so I reckon it'll be worth it.'

The following morning, after the sign had been hung in pride of place in the middle of the window, they opened the doors. As usual the trade was slow throughout the morning but then at the stroke of twelve four burly dockworkers entered, closely followed by two more and within half an hour the place was full. So much so that Edie could hardly keep up with the orders. To Edie's delight, the same thing happened the next day and the day after that, and many of the men who had taken advantage of the half-price offer returned. From then on they became busier by the day, and by the end of that week they were finally breaking even.

Edie was relieved. 'I reckon if it carries on like this I might add a few more things to the menu in a couple o' weeks or so, especially now there's more comin' in for their dinners,' she said thoughtfully. 'I thought perhaps cottage pie, an' sausage an' mash. Simple things that will keep the price down but be fillin'. What do you think?'

Violet nodded her approval. 'Good idea, and what about pie and mash, that always goes down well, and you make lovely pies.'

Edie agreed, and four weeks later Violet added the new items to the menus. It would mean more preparation work but they both thought it would be worth it.

They were proved to be right. On the first day of trying out the new dishes, they barely had time to sit down and when they finally did, Edie said, 'I reckon I might offer Lottie a job if she still ain't managed to find one. You an' me are runnin' around like headless chickens. An extra pair of hands would be more than handy. An' we could afford to pay another wage now we're makin' more money.'

Luckily Lottie popped in to see them the very next day. They were rushed off their feet, so she agreed to start there and then, and within minutes was up to her elbows in soapy water washing up the dirty pots as Violet returned them to the kitchen. It was nice to be all together again, but Violet was still edgy as she watched and waited for another sign of Oliver. It had been some weeks since she had first seen him and she was becoming increasingly worried about him.

It was mid-afternoon when the bell above the door tinkled to admit another customer and as Violet went to serve him, she saw that he looked to be very well dressed, nothing like the dockers who mainly frequented the place.

'Yes, sir, what can I get for you?' she enquired pleasantly. He was very good-looking with a square-cut chin, twinkling blue eyes and thick dark hair, and he looked vaguely familiar to her, although she couldn't recall where she had seen him before.

'Just a cup of tea and a slice of that rather nice-looking sponge cake please. To be honest I came in to see who the new owner was. I didn't expect to see someone quite so young.'

Violet flushed. 'Oh, I'm not the owner. I just live and work here.' He was eyeing her curiously and making her feel uncomfortable.

'I own an eating house in the town,' he informed her. 'Brabingers.'

'Oh!' Violet knew of it; her father had taken the family there for special occasions and now she recognised him. 'Ah, so you must be Toby Brabinger?'

'At your service.' There was that twinkle again and she flushed an even deeper shade of red.

She had never been formally introduced to him but now she judged he must be somewhere in his mid-twenties. She remembered her father telling her he had taken over running the eating house from his father when he retired, and by all accounts he was doing a very good job of it. It was one of the most popular eating establishments in Hull, and certainly one of the most expensive.

Although Toby was being pleasant, Violet was aware that people were now waiting to give their orders.

'If you'll excuse me, I have to get on,' she told him and after quickly taking his order she moved on to another customer.

When she took the orders into the kitchen and told Edie who was in the shop, Edie was impressed. 'Ooh, we've got the gentry comin' in now, 'ave we?' She laughed.

Violet was painfully aware that she was far from looking her best. Her hair was scraped up into a bun and she was wearing a plain gown in a dove grey, although she had no idea why she was particularly bothered.

'Well, go an' pour him 'is tea while I get on wi' these orders,' Edie said, and Violet did as she was told.

Once Toby's tea was poured, she placed it on a tray with the slice of sponge cake he had ordered and carried it towards his table. His back was to her and she saw that he was speaking to a lady who had come in for afternoon tea. They'd had quite a few ladies call in for morning coffee and afternoon tea since they had done their half-price event and word had spread of how good the food was.

'Come to judge the competition, have you?' Violet heard the lady ask.

'I'd hardly call this backstreet café competition,' he laughed. 'We get a much more upmarket clientele in my establishment.'

Violet felt angry colour flood into her cheeks. So, he'd come to gloat and look down on them, had he? Well, he could go to hell as far as she was concerned, and reaching the table she slapped his tray down in front of him.

He looked startled. 'Oh, er . . . thank you, Miss . . .?'

'Stroud!' she answered coldly and he looked startled.

'You're not Dr Stroud's daughter, are you?'

'Yes, I am, or I was.'

'Oh.' He looked shocked. 'I heard he had passed away and I was very sorry to hear it. Your father was a kind man.'

With a curt nod she turned away and studiously avoided him for the rest of his stay. When she next glanced at his table, he had left.

Good and I hope he doesn't come again, she thought as she began to serve the meals Edie had ready. He'd obviously only come to gloat over how much better his restaurant was than theirs, and now he could laugh at her change in circumstances as well.

And yet for some reason, for the rest of the day a picture of his handsome face stayed in her mind.

Chapter Nine

By the beginning of April the café was doing a roaring trade and every night Violet and Edie dropped into their beds exhausted.

'Crikey, I reckon we'll have to take on another pair of 'ands to help us at this rate.' Edie was delighted with the way things were going but she was also realising that she was getting no younger.

'Hmm, you could be right.' Violet had been sitting staring into the fire as they drank their cocoa before retiring that evening. She had still not asked her any of the questions that were buzzing around in her head, but tonight, she felt ready to.

'Edie, do you happen to know the name of my mother? My birth mother.'

Edie had been expecting this. 'I do as it happens,' she admitted cautiously. 'But what would be the point of worrying about that now? It's all in the past.'

'Even so, I'd like to know who she is.'

Edie sighed. 'Her name was Sadie, Sadie Perkins. She was a nice girl and had a crush on your dad for years. Trouble was by the time he realised, he had already met Anna and was besotted with her. They were married in no time. We know why now; she just latched on to William to give a name to her baby. Anyway, within months your dad realised he had made a grave mistake. The second his ring was on Anna's finger she had no time for him. After a while, he had a rare night out with his old pals from university and that was when he met up with Sadie again. I reckon they had too much to drink and . . . Well, the rest is obvious ain't it? Your dad admitted to me that he bitterly regretted what happened. He liked Sadie. An' then after nine months she turned up on the doorstep wi' you. Her parents had kicked her out an' she had nowhere to take you. That were the last we heard of her cos shortly after we moved to Hull.'

'I wonder if she still lives in Nuneaton?' Violet said thoughtfully.

Edie scowled. 'Now don't go gettin' no silly notions about goin' to find her,' she warned. 'The poor girl went through enough an' it couldn't have been easy for her lettin' you go. Chances are she's married wi' a family. Think how awful it would be for her an' them if you just turned up outta the blue!'

Violet nodded. 'I understand what you mean. But if I were to find her, she needn't know who I am. What I mean is, it would just be nice to see her; to know what she looks like. Do I look anything like her?'

'You do as it happens. But what do you have to gain by draggin' the past up? Your life 'as always been here in Hull.'

'I wasn't thinking of leaving for good,' Violet assured her. 'I was only thinking of visiting there and seeing if I can find her. My life is here with you and I don't know what I'd have done without you when Papa died.'

'You just promise me you'll do nothin' rash. Give yourself some time to think on it before you make a decision, eh? You've led a sheltered life an' the thought o' you travellin' all that way on your own worries me.'

Violet smiled and gave her hand an affectionate squeeze. 'I'm a big girl now, Edie.' Then seeing how much it was upsetting her, she changed the subject.

The following day, Toby Brabinger visited the café again. It was mid-afternoon, so the lunchtime rush was over, and they were preparing for the next busy time, when the men came home from work.

'Good afternoon, Miss Stroud.' Toby removed his hat and smiled sheepishly as he approached the counter.

Violet felt herself blush. He was a good-looking devil and she was sure he was aware of the fact and had women falling at his feet when he turned on the charm, but she didn't intend to be one of them.

'Good afternoon. What can I get you?' She stared at him coldly, but this seemed to amuse him, which annoyed her even more.

'One of your very nice cups of tea, if you please. I don't suppose you serve coffee here?'

'You may certainly have coffee if you prefer.'

'Then I'll have coffee please.'

She bustled away to the kitchen to fetch his coffee. 'That Toby Brabinger is here again,' she told Edie.

'Oh yes? You don't seem too pleased about it.' Edie looked slightly amused.

'The arrogant devil intimated that we wouldn't be upper class enough to serve coffee. He's too big for his own boots, that one. Just because he owns a posh eating house!'

'Now then, he's still a customer,' Edie pointed out.

Violet glared at her as she poured the coffee, then stormed back into the shop. 'Your coffee . . . sir!' She slammed it down onto the table.

He sighed. 'I was rather hoping you'd call me Toby.'

'And why would I do that?' Violet snapped. 'I don't even know you.' She was tempted to tell him that she didn't want to get to know him either. He was one of the most annoying men she had ever met, but she wisely held her tongue as she turned her back and began to clear the tables.

Toby watched her as he drank his coffee, and once he'd finished, he put his hat back on, gave her a little bow, and left.

'*Ooh*, there's something about that man that I can't *stand*,' Violet said when she returned his empty cup to the kitchen. 'He's just *so* full of himself!'

'He seems perfectly pleasant to me,' Edie said calmly. 'An' he'll be a rare catch for some lucky girl.'

'Huh!' Violet slammed the cup on the draining board and flounced away.

Her second visitor appeared much later that evening when she was cleaning the kitchen before going to join Edie upstairs, but she was happy to see this one. There came a tap at the door and opening it, Violet found Oliver standing there.

'Oh, where have you been? I haven't seen you for weeks and I've been so worried about you,' she scolded as she admitted him.

'Luckily I met up with an old schoolfriend who is letting me stay with him for a while,' Oliver told her.

'That's good, and have you had any luck finding a job yet?'

He shook his head, looking glum. 'I'm afraid not . . . which is why I'm here.' He gave her a charming smile. 'The thing is, I was wondering if you could loan me a little more cash – just to tide me over for a while longer. I'd like to give my friend a bit towards my board. I don't want him to think that I'm taking advantage of his good nature. I will pay you back, of course, when I do manage to get a job.'

'How much do you need?'

'Er . . . could you manage five pounds?'

Violet was shocked. It was a lot of money, but then she did have what her father had left her as well as the money he had entrusted to Edie, and she didn't want to appear mean.

'All right,' she said quietly. 'That should keep you going for at least another month. By then hopefully you'll have found a job.' Five pounds was more than she earned in a month, but she didn't want to refuse him. 'The thing is, though, you'll have to come back tomorrow for it. My money is upstairs and if I go up to get it, Edie will wonder why I need it tonight.'

For a moment a scowl crossed his handsome face but almost instantly the smile was back. He couldn't afford to upset her. 'Very well, I'll call back at the same time tomorrow.' He turned to go, annoyed because he'd had a good card game lined up for the evening.

'Are you going already? We've hardly time to chat!' Violet asked in dismay.

'I know, but knowing how Edie disapproves of me I don't want to get you in trouble.' He kissed her cheek and then he was gone, leaving her feeling strangely cheated. Still, she consoled herself, she would see him again tomorrow and hopefully then he would stay a little longer.

The following morning Lottie arrived at work with some gossip. 'You'll never guess what I've heard on the grapevine,' she said as they all sat together in the kitchen enjoying a cup of tea before they opened.

'Well, go on, spit it out,' Edie scolded. 'Don't keep us in suspense, we ain't got all day!'

'All right, all right!' Lottie grinned. 'My chap told me last night that Oliver has shacked up with a widow twice his age. She's rollin' in money, apparently, an' he's livin' the life o' Riley.' She chuckled. 'It don't take much of an imagination to guess what he's doin' for her in return, does it? She's spendin' money on 'im like it's goin' out o' fashion, by all accounts. Though I don't think it's goin' to last long. My Frank reckons he's gamblin' again. You'd think he'd keep 'is head down and know when he's on to a good thing, wouldn't you? But then, they do say leopards can't change their spots.'

Violet felt sick. What Lottie had told them would tie in with why Oliver had looked so much smarter the night before. It would also explain why he needed her money – to pay off his gambling debts. Perhaps his widow woman hadn't known about them, or refused to pay them off? One thing was for sure, she would certainly be having words with him when he came to collect the money.

That wasn't the only bit of gossip Lottie had to impart. 'One more thing you ought to know afore we start work.' Lottie looked worried now. 'My Frank were also sayin' that some shops in our area have been vandalised over the last couple o' days. Windows smashed an' things like that.'

Edie's ears pricked up. 'I'd noticed that,' she agreed. 'In fact, I heard one window break the other night. It were so loud that I got up to check it weren't mine. Who do you think is doin' it?'

'Apparently a lot o' the shop owners down this way pay protection money to a gang to prevent it happenin'. There're two gangs, it seems. The coppers are allus after 'em for stealin' from the docks an' whatever. Has anyone approached you about payin' 'em?'

Edie shook her head. 'No, they ain't, an' if they come 'ere they'll go away wi' a bloody flea in their ear, believe me. Why, it's disgustin' that honest, hard-workin' people don't feel safe when they're just tryin' to earn a livin'.'

'Well, just be on your guard,' Lottie advised. 'Now you've had time to settle in you're likely to get a visit.'

Violet shuddered at the thought, but they had no time to discuss it further because it was time to open the café.

Despite being busy, the day seemed to pass interminably slowly for Violet. On the one hand, she was looking forward to seeing Oliver again that evening. But on the other, the thought of Oliver fawning over an older woman made her feel sick, although she wondered if she should take the gossip with a pinch of salt. After all, neither Lottie nor Edie had ever made a secret of the fact they didn't have much time for Oliver.

At last, they turned the sign on the door to closed. As word had spread amongst the dockers about how tasty the food was, they seemed to be busier with every passing day. That day had been no exception and Edie was now making a fair profit, although it was hard work.

'There, that's me done,' Edie told Violet when they had cleared all the tables and locked up. Lottie had left for home a short time before. 'Do you mind sortin' the kitchen out?'

'Of course I don't.' Violet smiled at her. Edie wasn't a young woman anymore and she looked worn out. 'You go and put your feet up. I'll see to anything else that needs doing.'

Edie left her to it, and as Violet set about the cleaning she kept one eye on the gate in the yard through the window. At last, she saw it open and a shadowy shape approach the back door, so she hurried to open it.

'Come in.'

Oliver entered and rubbed his hands together. He was wearing what looked like a very expensive new overcoat and hat.

'Phew, it's cold out there.' He gave her a smile that would have charmed the birds out of the trees as he crossed to hold his hands out to the fire. 'Had a good day, have you?'

'Not as good as you, by the looks of it,' Violet answered sharply as jealousy reared its ugly head. 'It looks as if you've been shopping.'

'Oh, this, you mean.' Oliver glanced down at his coat. 'My new employer bought it for me. I took your advice and found a job.'

Violet frowned. 'Doing what?' she asked shortly.

'I'm working for a widow in one of the posh houses up on Lilac Hill. I'm sort of a handy-man-cum-chauffeur for her.'

'Oh! And do you live in?'

'Yes, I have a couple of rooms above the stables. They're quite comfortable, actually.'

'Why didn't you tell me this last night?'

He shrugged. 'I didn't move in properly until today. I was doing odd jobs for her but today she offered me living accommodation and made the job official, so I snapped her hand off. Hence the new clothes. I suppose she didn't want me wearing rags if I'm to be seen driving her all over the place.'

Violet chewed her lip uncertainly. The relationship he claimed he had with the woman sounded very different to the one Lottie had told them about, and certainly more respectable. And she did so want to believe him.

'So, what's this lady like?'

'Fat, middle-aged and loaded.' Oliver grinned. 'Her husband was a politician, and she has a house in London as well as the one she owns here.'

'I see, so why do you still need money from me?' Violet asked.

'I'm going to be paid monthly and I just need some to tide me over,' he told her.

'But if you've got board and lodgings thrown in with your job it seems an awful lot just to tide you over.'

Oliver scowled, looking hurt. 'Fine, you don't have to give it to me. Of course, I have every intention of paying you back when I get paid.'

Violet relented and took the money from her pocket. 'Here you are.' She handed it to him and he slipped it into his pocket. 'So what are you doing this evening?'

'Oh, I'll just go back and get properly settled into my new rooms.'

'Would you like a cup of tea before you go?' She was desperate to spend a little time with him, but now he had what he wanted he seemed eager to be gone.

'No, I'd best get back. We don't want Edie catching me here, do we?'

'When will I see you again?'

'Don't worry, I'll be back.' He planted a gentle kiss on her lips, and she looked startled.

'All right . . . look after yourself.' But he had already disappeared out into the yard, leaving Violet feeling confused.

Chapter Ten

Two nights later, Violet and Edie were woken abruptly by the sound of shattering glass. They both rushed out of bed, dragged their dressing robes on and almost collided as they charged into the lounge.

'What the hell were that?' Edie looked shaken and pale.

'It was downstairs. You stay here and I'll go down and have a look.'

'You will *not*, young lady,' Edie snapped indignantly. 'What if someone's in the café? No, we'll go together. Get that candle lit.'

Violet was trembling so much that it took two attempts, but at last they set off down the stairs with Edie insisting she went first.

After going through the kitchen Edie inched the door leading into the café open. There appeared to be no one there so they moved on, gasping when they saw that the glass in the door was shattered and spread across the floor around a large brick.

'What lousy bugger would do that?' Edie cursed, staring at the mess.

Violet hurried outside onto the cobblestones but there was no one in sight.

'Well, whoever it was has gone.' Seeing how upset she was Violet placed her arm around Edie's ample waist. 'It could have been worse. It could have been the big shop window.' She was hoping to lighten the mood but if Edie's face was anything to go by, she had failed dismally.

'Ooh, I'd like to get me hands around the lousy devils' throats,' Edie spat angrily.

Violet, meanwhile, went out to the yard to find something they could board the window up with until a glazier could be called. She managed to find some pieces of wood and an hour later, when they had mackled the door up, they swept the floor. The glass seemed to have got into every corner and by the time they'd finished the sky was lightening.

'Ain't much point me goin' back to bed now. I'd never rest knowin' someone might come back in,' Edie said tiredly. 'But you go back up an' try an' snatch a couple of hours, pet.'

Violet shook her head, flicking her long dark plait across her shoulder. 'I'm not leaving you down here alone. Come on, we'll go and make a hot drink and get the fire going, then as soon as the glazier's opens, I'll go round and get them to come and measure up. Do you think we should open tomorrow, or I should say today?'

'Yes, I do,' Edie said defiantly. 'I ain't goin' to let no bully rule me an' make me lose trade. We've worked too damned hard to build up this business.'

And so, after a hot drink they went to get dressed and started their work early.

By closing time late that afternoon, the glass in the door had been replaced at considerable expense and both Edie and Violet were tired. Lottie had asked if they would like her Frank to sleep at the café for a while in case whoever had smashed the glass came back, but Edie wouldn't hear of it. She was an independent soul.

'They'll bloody wish they 'adn't if they do,' she said angrily. The words had barely left her mouth when Toby Brabinger appeared.

'I heard of your trouble and came to see if there was anything I could do,' he said politely as Violet glared at him.

Edie on the other hand seemed pleased to see him. 'Thanks, lad, but we have everythin' sorted now. The glass has been replaced as you can see, an' it'll be God help 'em if they come back an' try it again.'

'Have you had a visit from the Dockers gang?'

Edie frowned. 'Who are they?'

'They're the gang that are going into shops demanding protection money. Ned Banks is their leader,' he explained.

Edie shook her head. 'No, there's no one like that been in.'

'Then I should prepare yourself. A visit from them usually follows something like this. I've seen it before. They tell you they're protecting you from another gang they're at war with, but personally I think it's them that do the damage if you don't pay up. Unfortunately, this is rather a rough area, and there tends to be a lack of police presence at night when it's most needed.'

'Thanks for warnin' me,' Edie answered. 'But don't worry, I can look after meself.'

'Then I'm sorry for disturbing you. Don't hesitate to call on me if you need assistance. Good day, ladies.' He doffed his hat and left.

'The big-headed oaf!' Violet fumed. 'Who does he think he is coming here gloating? Just because his place is in the fashionable part of town and we live close to the docks.'

Edie looked bemused. 'I think it were nice of 'im to check on us,' she answered. 'An' I can't think why you don't like him. He's a good-lookin' chap, wealthy an' all, an' I reckon he's got a soft spot for you.'

'Oh, don't be so ridiculous.' Violet scowled. 'You forget what I heard him telling that woman about us being no competition for his posh place. As if we're nothing!'

'I'm sure he didn't mean it the way it sounded. An' why ever he came, it ain't worth arguin' about,' Edie pointed out. 'So let's just get tidied up, eh?'

They began to clear the tables and were just carrying the last of the pots through to the kitchen when there was a knock on the door.

'Sorry, we're closed,' Edie shouted, but the knock came again, more insistent this time, so with a sigh she went to unlock it. The instant she had two large men pushed their way into the café.

'Here, what do you think you're doin'?' Edie protested angrily as the second one to enter slammed the door behind him.

'We've come to 'ave a little chat wi' you that might be to your advantage,' the first one said with a sly grin that revealed his brown, stained teeth.

'Oh yes, an' what would that be?' Edie said sceptically.

'Well, we 'eard you'd 'ad a bit o' trouble last night. Broken door, weren't it?'

Edie narrowed her eyes. She didn't like the look of these two, they seemed shifty and the younger one was staring at Violet with a dirty grin on his face that set her teeth on edge. They both looked like they could do with a damned good bath and their clothes were dirty.

'What about it?'

The man leant back against the counter and picked at his stained teeth with a grubby fingernail as he stared insolently back at her. 'It just so 'appens that we could stop that from ever happenin' again . . . For a price o' course. Nothin' comes free, does it, Gran'ma?'

'Why, you cheeky bugger you! From where I'm standin' you ain't no spring chicken yourself.'

He shrugged. 'Two quid a week I'm askin'. Now that ain't much to keep you an' your place safe, is it? I mean, you must be rakin' it in. Place is full o' customers every time I pass recently.'

'*Two quid a week!*' Edie was outraged. 'You can go an' whistle, me man! You'll not get a brass dime outta me!'

The man's expression turned ugly and he leant towards her menacingly. But Edie stood her ground and glared right back. Her heart was going nineteen to the dozen but there was no way she'd let him see that she was afraid.

'That's a shame,' he said. 'It just might be your *big* shop window as goes next time. Just imagine how much that would cost to fix, let alone the mess it'd make! Think on it, eh? We'll pop back an' see you again tomorrer.'

'You come near 'ere again an' you'll get the rollin' pin wrapped round your bloody ear,' Edie told him heatedly.

He laughed as he beckoned to the younger one, who was still openly ogling Violet. 'Come on, Billy boy. We've got money to collect off folks who ain't quite as daft as this old dear!'

As soon as they'd swaggered out of the door, Edie slammed it resoundingly and locked it behind them.

'Filthy blackmailin' scum,' she ground out.

'It's funny they should appear the same day Toby Brabinger warned us about them, isn't it?' Violet commented. 'You don't think he's connected with them, do you?'

'Of course he ain't! The chap were just tryin' to help us,' Edie retorted. 'Come on, forget about 'em. I think I've made it clear how I feel an' I doubt they'll be back.'

As they got on with the clearing up, Violet wasn't so sure.

Once again neither of them slept much that night, but thankfully it passed with no trouble and they both got up feeling as if they hadn't been to bed.

'It makes me wonder what the world is comin' to,' Edie said with a shake of her head as they sat together over breakfast the next morning. 'I was readin' in the paper about the underground railway in London. You wouldn't get me on that! Ugh, imagine bein' trapped down there if owt went wrong – it don't bear thinkin' about. An' those buggers comin' in 'ere tryin' to blackmail decent hard-workin' folk out o' their hard-earned money. Huh! They'll not get a penny piece out o' me an' that's a fact.'

Violet couldn't help but smile. Edie was a force to be reckoned with when she got the bit between her teeth and Violet almost pitied the men who had threatened her if she got her hands on them.

Two more days went by with no further incidents but on the third night, they were again woken by the sound of breaking glass.

'Oh, not *again*,' Edie groaned as they shot down the stairs. This time it was the kitchen window that had been smashed. Edie had brought the poker downstairs with her and she rushed out into the yard brandishing it, but there was no sign of anything apart from a large black cat who lay on the wall lazily washing his paws.

Edie was seething when she went back into the kitchen to survey the mess, and continued to rant while they cleared up the glass.

The next morning the glazier again called to measure and by lunchtime the glass had been replaced, again at considerable expense to Edie.

The man had just finished when Toby Brabinger strolled in. 'I hear you've had some more trouble,' he said to Violet, looking concerned.

Bristling, Violet raised her chin. 'We have, but don't worry we have everything under control.'

'It'll be Ned Banks and Billy Boy behind this,' Toby answered, ignoring his frosty reception. 'They've got a gang of thugs work-ing for them. The police have been after them for ages but haven't been able to pin anything on them.'

'As I said, we have everything under control, thank you,' Violet said primly.

Toby shook his head and sighed. 'Why don't you and Mrs Thompson come to my eating house this evening? It would do you both good to get away from here for a while and the meal will be on me. Anything you fancy.'

'We have everything we need here.'

'Is there anything I can do to help then?'

'Nothing at all, thank you.'

As the exchange was taking place, Lottie, who was wiping down the empty tables, almost felt sorry for the man. Violet was making it quite clear she had no time for him, although from where Lottie was standing, he was being perfectly nice.

'Was there anything you wished to order?'

Toby shook his head. 'No, I just called to make sure you were both all right. Good day, Violet.'

'Good day, Mr Brabinger . . . And I'm *Miss Stroud*, by the way.'

The door had barely closed behind him when Lottie said shortly, 'You were a bit hard on him, weren't you? The poor bloke 'ad only called in to see if you was all right.'

'We don't need people like him poking their noses into our business,' Violet said more sharply than she had intended to.

Lottie shrugged. 'Suit yourself, but I'd say he's got a soft spot for you.'

'I've said the same,' Edie echoed from the open kitchen doorway.

'More like he's come to gloat,' Violet snapped. 'He remembers me going to his eating house with my father and he's probably amused to see that I don't even have my own home now.'

Glancing up she saw the hurt flit across Edie's face and was instantly contrite. 'Oh Edie, I'm so sorry. I am grateful that you've taken me under your wing, really I am.'

Edie sniffed. 'I'd hardly call it that. Be it ever so humble I thought this was a home for both of us. Sayin' that, I know you won't be here forever. You're young wi' your whole life ahead o' you, an' soon no doubt you'll meet a young man who'll sweep you off your feet an' you'll go an' build a new home wi' him, which is how it should be.'

Violet thought that was highly unlikely. The only young man she had ever cared about was Oliver, and that was as a brother. But now he didn't seem remotely interested in her, apart from when he needed money. She hadn't seen him for days.

A customer entered at that moment and there was no more time for chatting as they started to get busy.

The day turned out to be particularly busy, and when Edie ran out of bread rolls, Violet wrapped her warm shawl about her shoulders and set off to the bakery. It was only a short distance up the road and she was almost there when she glanced down an alley and saw Oliver speaking to another man. She thought of calling to him but he was obviously deep in conversation and she didn't like to disturb him. The man took something from his pocket and passed it to Oliver, who quickly tucked it into the pocket of his overcoat and strode off in the opposite direction. Just for a moment the other man glanced towards her before scurrying away.

Violet frowned. There was something vaguely familiar about him, but for the life of her she couldn't think where she had seen him before. After buying the rolls, she was returning to the café when she remembered who the man was. He was the younger of the two men who had come into the café demanding money, the one the older of the two had referred to as Billy Boy. But what was Oliver doing associating with someone like that? One thing was for sure, she would make him tell her the next time she saw him!

With a grim expression on her face, she moved on. She would have to keep this to herself. If Edie were ever to find out that Oliver had anything to do with either of those men, she would dislike him even more, and that was the last thing that Violet wanted.

Chapter Eleven

'Delivery for Miss Violet Stroud.'

It was the next morning and Violet was serving a customer. Startled, she looked up. Delivery? But she couldn't think of anything she had ordered.

She blinked as she saw a young boy standing by the door carrying the biggest bouquet of flowers she had ever seen.

'Er ... I'm Violet Stroud,' she said uncertainly. 'But I think there must be some mistake. I can't think of anyone who would send me flowers.'

The man she was serving chuckled. 'Looks like you've got yourself an admirer, pet,' he teased.

Violet blushed furiously. 'Are you quite sure you have the right name? Who sent them?'

The boy shrugged as he thrust the flowers into her arms. 'Ain't got no idea, miss. I just do the deliveries for the florist. Ta-ra.' And with that he went off whistling merrily.

Violet carried the blooms through to the kitchen.

Edie raised an eyebrow and smiled. 'Crikey, looks like somebody's popular. Who are they from?'

'I have no idea.'

'There's usually a card tucked in wi' 'em,' Edie advised.

Violet gently searched amongst the flowers but there was nothing.

'Aw well, they'll brighten the upstairs no end,' Edie said cheerily. 'An' no doubt whoever sent 'em will let you know in their own good time. They must have cost a fortune, though. Look at 'em, they're all out-o'-season blooms, so whoever it was must be keen as mustard on you.'

An idea came to Violet then, and she smiled as she took the flowers to stand in a bucket of water in the yard until she had time to arrange them. They could only be from one person – Oliver. They were probably his way of thanking her for lending him money. Suddenly the day seemed a little brighter and she went back to work with a smile on her face. Until late afternoon, that was, when the door opened to admit the two men who had tried to blackmail them.

Thankfully, Edie had been keeping a watch for them through the kitchen door and before Violet could say a word, she came out clutching the rolling pin, her face a mask of fury.

'What do you two want? Didn't I make meself clear the last time that you ain't welcome in 'ere?'

'Now don't be like that, missus. We've just come in for a nice cup o' tea . . . an' then we'll talk business.' The older man glanced around and nodded his approval. 'Fair play to you, you've got this place real nice. It'd be a shame if it were to get smashed up, wouldn't it?'

'You just try it, son, an' you'll find out you've met your match,' Edie said threateningly.

'Ooh, I'm shakin' in me shoes, Gran'ma!' Ned Banks chuckled. Unfortunately, it was their quiet time so the shop was empty and there were no dockers in there to protect them, but Lottie and Violet came to stand beside Edie.

Glancing down at the pots that Violet had been loading onto a tray when they entered, Ned picked up a mug.

'Hmm, not bad quality for a backstreet café,' he remarked, before letting the mug fall from his hand to smash on the floor.

'Why, you bloody hooligan!' Edie was almost spitting with rage as he picked up yet another mug and did the same again.

'Oops, butter fingers me,' he smirked.

Lifting the rolling pin above her head Edie advanced on him, but he was a big man and catching her arm he twisted it, making her yelp with pain and drop it.

'Now listen 'ere, Gran'ma,' he ground out. 'You've 'ad your last warnin'. Two quid a week or I won't be responsible for any damage done to your property – understand me? I'll be back the same time tomorrer an' if you ain't ready to play ball . . . Well, let's just say on your own 'ead be it.' He cocked his head at Billy and they sauntered out, leaving Edie almost weeping with rage and frustration.

'Go an' fetch the coppers,' Edie ordered Lottie.

Lottie shook her head. 'It wouldn't do no good, Edie. The coppers won't 'ave nuthin' to do wi' Ned Banks an' 'is gang. They're a bloody law unto themselves. I reckon you're just goin' to have to cough up an' pay 'em.'

'Will I hell as like.' Edie glared at her as she rubbed her sore arm. She looked down at the broken pottery on the floor and barked, 'Now get that lot cleaned up. We'll have the teatime rush on in a minute.' Then she stamped off back to the kitchen.

Later that evening, as they sat together in their upstairs rooms, sharing a pot of tea, Edie said apologetically, 'I'm sorry I shouted at you earlier on.'

Violet smiled. 'Don't worry about it. You were upset.'

'Hmm, but it got me to thinkin'. You're a young woman an' you shouldn't be cooped up in here day after day wi' an old woman, workin' all the hours God sends!'

'No? So where else would I be? I don't have many friends – Anna always saw to that. She'd never let me invite any home so when I left school, we lost touch. The only real friend I had was Oliver. And anyway, I like being here with you.'

'Even so it ain't healthy.' Edie stared at her for a moment before saying tentatively, 'To be honest, it ain't much good for me either. I could do wi' a break, so perhaps it wouldn't be such a bad idea to take Toby Brabinger up on his offer of havin' a meal at his place. It would be nice for me to be waited on for a change.'

Violet shrugged. 'Accept his offer then.'

Edie shook her head. 'Not unless you agree to come along wi' me. I wouldn't feel right dinin' there alone. What do you think?'

It was the last thing Violet wanted to do, but she loved Edie and she had been so good to her that she didn't like to refuse.

'All right,' she said reluctantly. 'If he comes back and offers again, we'll accept.'

Edie gave her a smug little grin as she sipped at her tea.

Sure enough, the next day the bell above the door tinkled and Ned Banks and Billy Boy Mellor appeared yet again.

Edie was out of the kitchen like a shot to glare at them.

'So, Gran'ma, had time to think an' see sense, have you?' Ned sneered as he picked at his nose with a grubby fingernail.

'Oh, I've 'ad time to think all right, an' me answer is still the same,' Edie told him defiantly. 'So now you can go an' sling your hook an' threaten some other poor bugger cos you'll not get a penny piece outta me an' that's me final decision.'

Ned tutted as he approached the counter where Lottie had the mugs lined up ready for the next lot of customers.

'Bad decision that, Gran'ma.' With a single swipe he knocked all the crockery onto the floor where it smashed into a thousand pieces. 'But this ain't the end of it. Happen you'll see sense and in a few days' you'll be beggin' me to keep the place safe.'

The door opened at that moment and Toby Brabinger entered, frowning as he noted the shattered crockery on the floor.

'What's going on here?' His face was grim.

'Nowt for you to concern yourself wi', boss.' Ned beckoned to Billy and made for the door. He was a typical bully – happy to put the frighteners on someone smaller than himself, but Toby Brabinger was a big chap. 'Just 'ad a bit o' business to sort wi' the lady 'ere!'

As soon as they'd left, Edie burst into tears of frustration.

'Threats again?' Toby said grimly.

Edie nodded and despite her brave words to Ned Banks she was shaking like a leaf.

Toby scowled. 'Right, let's get this sorted for you. Do you have a broom?'

White-faced, Lottie hurried away to fetch it and when she returned, Toby helped her sweep up the mess.

'What do you think we should do now?' Edie asked when the floor was clean again. All three women were shaken and thankful that Toby had come in when he had.

'It's clear that it's Ned and his gang who cause the damage at night,' Toby answered. 'And I think we should catch them out.'

'An' just 'ow are we supposed to do that?'

He thought for a moment before saying, 'Leave it with me. In the meantime, I really think it would do you all good to get away from this place for a while so my offer of a night out at my restaurant still stands. What do you say? I could send my carriage for you tomorrow evening.'

'I shan't come. I'm seein' me chap,' Lottie said. 'But thanks for the offer, an' for what it's worth, I think you're right.' She looked towards Edie and Violet. 'Neither of you 'ave set foot out o' this place since you opened apart from to go shoppin', so I think you should take Mr Brabinger up on his kind offer.'

'In that case, we accept. Thank you,' Edie said, glancing at Violet, who didn't look too happy with the idea. 'Shall we say seven thirty? But will it be safe to leave this place unattended?'

'Don't worry about that. I shall be dealing with it,' Toby assured them.

That evening both Violet and Edie were on tenterhooks and kept glancing from the window to see if Ned Banks was about, but by the time they went to bed all had been quiet, although they

noticed someone standing back in the shadows in the alley opposite the café.

'Do you reckon that could be one of his cronies?' Edie asked
worriedly.

'I've no idea but even if it is, there's nothing we can do about it,'
Violet pointed out.

They had a restless night but were relieved to rise in the morning
to find everything intact.

It was another busy day, and when the café closed, Violet
dragged the tin bath from the wall in the yard into the kitchen to
fill with hot water from the copper. They'd discovered that it was
far easier to bathe in there than drag the bath upstairs.

Once they'd bathed and washed their hair, they hurried upstairs
to get ready.

'It feels strange to be wearing one of my nice gowns,' Violet said
when they were back in the sitting room doing their hair in the
mirror that hung above the small fireplace.

'You look beautiful,' Edie assured her, and she did. She was
wearing a pale blue shot silk gown trimmed with guipure lace that
showed off her slim figure, and her thick dark hair was piled into
curls on the top of her head.

'You look very nice yourself,' Violet said with a smile.

Edie chuckled as she patted the skirt of the two-piece lilac costume she was wearing. 'I dare say I ain't scrubbed up too bad for
an old 'un. Come along now, Mr Brabinger's carriage should be
here any time now.'

Within minutes the smart carriage arrived and as they climbed
into it, Edie beamed. 'Crikey, I feel like a toff,' she chuckled as she
sank back against the leather squabs and settled the skirt of her
costume about her.

Despite the fact she didn't want to go, Violet was pleased to see
Edie looking so happy and relaxed, and she determined that she
would do her best to enjoy herself as well.

Soon they were trotting through the high street in the centre of Hull and eventually the carriage drew up in front of a very smart restaurant with 'Brabinger's', emblazoned in gold letters above the door.

Toby must have been looking out for them because he hurried out to meet them, looking very smart in a dark pinstriped suit and a gaily coloured waistcoat.

'Ladies, it's lovely to see you,' he greeted them with a broad smile as he helped them down from the carriage. 'Welcome to my establishment. Please come inside, I have a table all prepared for you.'

When they entered, Edie blinked with surprise at the luxurious décor. The walls were papered with a velvet flock paper in a rich red colour, and a deep gold carpet covered the floor. Crisp white cloths covered the tables, which were laid with gleaming silver cutlery and crystal glasses. Two waiters in dark suits with white cloths across their arms hovered around a table by the window.

'I thought you might like to sit here where you can watch the world go by,' Toby told them. 'And I hope you don't mind but I've had the table laid for three. I was hoping I might join you?'

'The more the merrier,' Edie told him cheerily, although she was feeling rather like a fish out of water. This place was certainly a far cry from her small café.

The waiters pulled the chairs out for the ladies and once they were seated the wine waiter handed Edie the wine list.

'Ooh, I er . . . I'm afraid I don't know much about wine,' Edie faltered.

'Not a problem, may I suggest the Madeira? It's very palatable,' Toby said quickly to save her embarrassment.

Edie nodded and the second waiter handed them the food menu.

They each decided on the prawn and avocado for a starter, then Edie and Toby chose the tenderloin of pork with mustard brandy sauce, while Violet decided on the sea bass for their main courses.

'This is delicious. A bit different to the stuff I serve in the café, eh?' Edie laughed.

'There's absolutely nothing wrong with your menu. You just cater for a different clientele that's all. But how well you're doing in such a short time speaks for itself.'

Edie beamed at Toby. He really was such an obliging young man, she just wished Violet could see it, but she had been very quiet since they'd arrived.

'Didn't you say you'd been here before?' Edie asked Violet, hoping to draw her into a conversation. Edie had had two glasses of wine by that time and was feeling quite merry.

'Yes, I came here with Papa on a few occasions.' There was a catch in Violet's voice as she remembered happier times.

'Let's just hope this will be the first of many more visits,' Toby said softly, his eyes openly admiring as he smiled at her.

'I'll drink to that,' Edie chuckled and raising her glass she drained it, only for Toby to immediately refill it.

Despite herself, Violet was warming towards him a little. After all, he had been very kind to them and it was nice to see Edie letting her hair down and enjoying herself for a change.

'Right, what do you two lovely ladies fancy for a dessert?'

Violet held her hand up. 'Oh, not for me, thank you. I'm quite full.'

'Well, I'll have one if you'll join me?' Edie looked at Toby hopefully.

'Of course. I'll have the crème brûlée.' He grinned. 'It's my favourite, but what can I tempt you with, Mrs Thompson?'

'I reckon I'll try the fresh fruit trifle.' Edie snapped the menu shut and handed it to the waiter.

This really was turning out to be a brilliant night! Edie's happy mood disappeared the moment they drew up outside the café late that evening. In the light from the street lamp, she could see the pavement was covered in shattered glass and the large front window had been smashed. Her heart sank as she realised it was going to cost a fortune to replace. It was a terrible ending to what had been a very pleasant evening.

Chapter Twelve

There were men milling about everywhere and as Edie alighted the carriage one of them rushed up to her.

'Don't worry, Mrs Thompson, everythin's in hand,' he told her. 'An' we caught a couple o' the buggers that did it red-handed. Let's just say I don't reckon you'll get any more trouble from them. We'll sweep the mess up, and then board the window up for you.'

'Ned Banks was it?' Edie asked dully.

The man nodded. 'Aye, it was 'is gang though we didn't manage to catch 'im, more's the pity.'

'How come you were here an' why are you doin' all this for me?'

'Someone 'as had me an' me men watchin' the shop for the last couple o' nights,' the man told her.

'Oh yes, an' who's that then?' Edie questioned.

'Couldn't say, missus, it weren't me as dealt wi' him personally.'

'That must be who we saw loitering in the alley,' Violet said.

'It was, but now you ladies go on in. Don't worry, we won't leave till everythin' is secure so you can sleep easy.'

'Huh! I doubt that.' Edie was worried. 'Lord knows how much this window is goin' to cost to replace. Still, thanks for what you've done.'

The man doffed his cap and returned to sweeping up as Violet and Edie picked their way through the glass to the door.

Very early the following morning, they were woken from an uneasy sleep by the sound of banging and hammering downstairs and they both grabbed their dressing robes and flew downstairs, dreading what they might find.

'What's going on here?' Edie snapped at the two men who were removing the temporary boards from the window.

'Don't ask me, missus.' The larger of the two respectfully removed his cap. 'We've had instructions to come an' get this window ready for the new glass to go in. Hopefully it'll be here by mid-mornin'.'

Edie looked shocked. 'But how can that be? I haven't even ordered it yet.'

The man shrugged. 'No idea, missus. I'm just paid to do as I'm told.'

'Come on, Edie, let's go and get the kettle on,' Violet suggested. 'We'll know what's going on soon enough.'

They hurried into the kitchen and lit the fire. They'd agreed there was no way they could be open that day. But then if what the man had told them was right and the glass was replaced that morning there was every chance they'd be able to open that afternoon.

'I just wonder how much it's goin' to cost?' Edie said glumly as they sat sipping their tea. 'An' I wonder who had it measured an' ordered it?'

Violet had her own thoughts on that. It could only be Oliver keeping his eye on them; the thought made her smile. Who else could it be?

Sure enough, shortly after ten thirty the large pane of glass was delivered and within an hour no one would ever have known what had happened the night before.

'So 'ow much do I owe you?' Edie asked as the men tidied their tools away.

'No charge,' one of them informed her. 'It's all been taken care of.'

Edie really was shocked now. 'By *who*?'

The man shook his head. 'You'd have to ask me gaffer, missus. My job is just to fit the glass. I've no idea who orders an' pays for it. Now if you'll just sign this to say you're 'appy wi' the job we'll be on us way.'

Edie's hand was trembling as she signed her name. 'Any idea who'd do that for us?' she asked Violet once the men had left and they were admiring the new window.

Violet smiled. 'The only one I can think of who'd go to all that trouble for us is Oliver.'

'*Oliver!*' Edie snorted disdainfully. 'Why, I reckon there's as much chance o' him doin' that as hell freezin' over. The only person that young man thinks about is 'iself!'

'But who else could it be?'

Edie shrugged. 'I've no idea but they do say as you shouldn't look a gift 'orse in the mouth so let's start to get ready to open, shall we? We've already lost a mornin's trade an' there's no point in losin' any more.'

They had little time to speak of it for the rest of the day, for from the moment they opened, they were rushed off their feet.

'Phew.' Once they'd turned the sign on the door to closed, Lottie sank down onto one of the chairs and kicked her shoes off. 'Me poor bloody feet are on fire,' she groaned.

'I know what you mean,' Edie agreed. 'Happen it's time I advertised for another person to come in an' help us. It's takin' all me time to keep up wi' the amount o' food that needs cookin' now.'

'By the way,' Lottie said, 'word 'as it that the old couple who own the hardware shop next door are thinkin' o' closin' down.'

'Is that right?' Edie said thoughtfully as she played with an idea she'd had recently. 'Funny you should say that cos I've been thinkin' that we could do wi' bigger premises as well as more staff. I wonder how much they'd be askin' an' how much it would cost to knock it through into 'ere?'

'Why don't you go and see them to ask if the rumours are true,' Violet suggested. 'I could help you out if need be, because I still have the money my father left me put by. Thanks to you giving me a home, I've hardly spent a penny of it. And perhaps the bank would lend us the rest of the money if we need it.' She could have added, 'Apart from what I've lent to Oliver,' but thought it wise not to.

'Aw, bless you.' Edie beamed at her. She was a good girl was Violet. 'I might just do that. But not tonight. I'm too jiggered.'

Lottie left shortly after and Edie said, 'It's only a few weeks to Lottie's weddin' an' I were thinkin' we could perhaps close the café for the day an' lay a little spread on 'ere for 'er. What do you think?'

'I think that's a lovely idea,' Violet agreed enthusiastically. 'We could lay a buffet style meal on for everyone to help themselves, perhaps?'

'Good idea.' Edie helped herself to another cup of tea before heaving herself up out of the chair. 'Do you reckon we could leave the tidyin' up till the mornin'. I'm fair worn out.'

'You go on up,' Violet encouraged. 'I can see to whatever needs doing down here.'

'Are you sure?'

'Quite – now be off with you.' Violet pecked her on the cheek and once she had gone, she started to clear the tables and wipe them down ready for the breakfast rush the next morning.

She had almost finished when there was a tap on the door and she found Oliver standing on the doorstep. It was the first time she had seen him since the night he'd come to borrow money and she assumed he'd come to pay it back.

'Come in,' she urged, ushering him into the kitchen with a broad smile. 'How are you?' He certainly looked very smart.

'I'm very well, and yourself?'

'I'm fine. Oh, and thank you for the lovely flowers. No one has ever sent me flowers before.'

'Flowers?' He looked slightly confused before saying quickly, 'Ah yes, the flowers. I'm glad you liked them.'

She looked at him expectantly, waiting for him to offer her the money he had borrowed but instead he looked mildly uncomfortable.

'Actually . . . I, er, have another little favour to ask you. I wondered if you could lend me a bit more money? Just until I get paid, of course.'

'Oh!' Violet looked concerned. 'How much do you need this time?'

'Another five pounds should do it.'

She shook her head. 'Ah, if you need that much again it could be a problem because I've put nearly all of my money into the bank now. Edie didn't think it was safe to have money around here, just in case. You've probably heard we've had a few problems with Ned Banks.' As she said this, she suddenly remembered seeing Oliver speaking to one of Ned's cronies. 'I saw you talking to the chap that's usually with him a while back, as a matter of fact,' she went on. 'What on earth were you doing mixing with the likes of him?'

Oliver looked flustered for a moment before answering, 'Actually, I only met him to get back some money he owed me.'

'Why would he owe you money?' Violet frowned.

He had the good grace to look embarrassed. 'He lost to me in a card game.'

'Oh, Oliver, you're not still gambling, are you?' She looked genuinely concerned. 'Surely you've learnt by now that it's a mug's game? Especially if it means you're mixing with the likes of Ned Banks!'

Oliver scowled at her. 'That's easy for you to say, sitting pretty here with Edie to look after you.'

'It isn't quite like that, I assure you,' she responded. 'I work from early morning till evening to earn my keep. Perhaps you'd do better if you got a proper job! Are you still working for that widow?'

'I am as it happens, not that it's any of your business,' he answered sullenly.

Suddenly Violet felt ashamed. Perhaps she had been a little hard on him? But another five pounds! Her money would be gone in no time if she kept handing over that amount each time he came to see her.

'So how much could you let me have?' he asked.

'I think I've got about a pound upstairs.'

'A measly *pound*? That isn't going to get me far, is it?'

'It's the best I can do for now,' she told him apologetically.

'In that case I suppose it will have to do. Would you go and get it?'

Violet raised an eyebrow. 'Why? Are you in a rush to be off? You've only just got here. I was going to make us a cup of tea so we could sit and have a chat.'

In the blink of an eye, he was his usual smarmy self again. 'There's nothing I'd like more, but I have to take the widow to visit her friend. But don't worry, I shall be back soon and perhaps we can spend a little more time together then. In fact, we could perhaps meet up one Sunday when you're not working?'

Violet blushed with pleasure. 'Oh yes, I'd like that. Wait here and I'll go and see how much I can get together for you.'

Luckily, Edie was in her bedroom when she got upstairs, so she was able to grab her purse and shoot downstairs again without Edie seeing her.

Back in the kitchen she counted out just over a pound in coins onto the table. 'There you are, there's one pound two and three-pence there,' she said.

Almost before the words had left her mouth Oliver had quickly lifted it and dropped it into his pocket. 'Thanks.' He flashed her a smile. 'I'll be back soon and we'll arrange to meet up.' Then he pecked her on the cheek and was gone, leaving Violet feeling disappointed and upset. She had looked at Oliver through rose-coloured glasses ever since she was a little girl. He had been her big brother, her hero, but suddenly she was seeing a side of him that she didn't like.

The following morning, during the quieter spell between break-fast and lunch, Edie slipped next door to see the old couple who owned the hardware shop and when she came back Violet and Lottie were waiting for her.

'How did you get on?' Lottie asked.

'Well, we had a good chat and this is what they're wantin' for the place,' Edie said glumly as she laid a piece of paper with the price written on it on the table.

'That sounds reasonable enough,' Violet commented.

Edie nodded. 'I reckon it is. They'd leave all the contents for that an' all. Not that they'd be much good to us but I dare say we could always sell 'em on. I could just about manage that with the rest o' me savin's. Trouble is I'd have nothin' left to knock it through an' get it set up for openin'.'

'You would if you used the money my father left me, and if we got a small loan from the bank. I'm sure they'd give you one now that you can show them the café is making a profit,' Violet pointed out.

Edie shook her head. 'Bless you for offerin', but even if the bank would, I wouldn't feel right takin' your money from you.'

'Why not?' Violet gave her hand a gentle squeeze. 'It's only sitting in the bank doing nothing at present.'

'Even so . . .' Edie dithered. She had always been fiercely independent.

'All right. How about if we said it was a loan?' Violet suggested. 'You'd pay that back and be in profit in no time if we had room for twice as many tables. As it is I barely get time to clean one down before someone else is sitting waiting to be served.'

'She's right,' Lottie agreed. 'Though we would 'ave to take more staff on. Us three can 'ardly manage now let alone wi' twice as many tables.'

'I'll think about it. I've told Mr and Mrs Miller that I'll get back to 'em wi' an answer afore tomorrow so I don't want to go makin' any rash decisions.'

Much later that evening, as they were sitting together drinking their cocoa upstairs, Violet asked, 'Have you given any more thought to what you want to do about next door yet?'

'I've thought o' little else all day,' Edie admitted. 'Though I still ain't 'appy about takin' money from you an' havin' a bank loan. But I have thought o' one way we could do it.'

'Oh yes?'

'Yes.' Edie smiled at her. 'I'd take you up on your kind offer on one condition: that we become partners in the business. We'd be equal owners.'

'What *me* . . . own part of the café?' Violet was astounded.

'Why not? It would be comin' to you when owt happened to me anyway. I've no one else to leave it to 'ave I?'

'Oh Edie.' Tears stung the back of Violet's eyes. Edie had been more of a mother to her over the years than Anna ever had and now here she was proving how much she loved her. Violet had often wondered how she would have coped with the death of her father and the wicked way Anna had thrown her out without this dear woman.

'Well . . .' she said uncertainly. 'Only if you're sure? The offer of the money is still there with no strings if you want it.'

'I know that, pet, an' I appreciate it. I also know that you won't allus be 'ere to help me run things. You'll meet some nice chap one o' these days an' move away to 'ave a family of your own, an' that's just how it should be. When that 'appens I'll bring in extra staff but at least you'll know you've allus got security and an income. So . . . what do you say?'

With tears in her eyes Violet grinned and held her hand out. 'I say deal, partner.'

Chapter Thirteen

The next day, Edie closed the café for one hour while she went to speak to the bank manager. Then with her loan secured she went with Mr and Mrs Miller to see the solicitor to arrange the purchase of the hardware shop.

When she came back, she was smiling. 'It'll be all done by the end o' the week,' she told Violet and Lottie. It had all happened so quickly she could hardly believe it and she just hoped she hadn't taken on more than she could chew.

Violet and Lottie were both pleased, although Violet did have a few reservations. She still hadn't decided whether she wanted to begin a search for her birth mother, as the pain of losing her father was still too raw. But now that she would be part-owner of the café, she realised it wouldn't be quite so simple to get away; she couldn't just leave Edie to do all the work. Still, that was a bridge she could cross when she came to it and for now it was nice to see Edie so excited.

'They reckon they'll be gone by Saturday,' Edie rushed on. 'Then the real work will begin.'

'I'll go to the bank and have my money transferred into your account,' Violet offered. 'Then as soon as you have the keys, we can start looking round for tradesmen to come in and begin the work. We'll need a door put through from the café into the shop for a start.'

'Yes, an' we'll have to sell the stock they're leavin' behind,' Edie said sensibly. 'Happen that'll raise a few quid if we price it right.'

'Once any structural work is done, we can all chip in an' do the paintin' ourselves. That'll save a bit.' Lottie was almost as excited about the new venture as Edie was.

'Don't you think you've got enough to do wi' workin' here nearly every day an' plannin' your weddin?' Edie didn't want to take advantage of the girl's good nature, but Lottie simply laughed.

'That's all arranged, an' I know Frank an' some of his chums will come along to help if he asks 'em to.'

'Do you think we'll have it all up and running before Lottie's wedding?' Violet asked.

'I reckon there's a fair chance if we pull our fingers out.' Edie had already told Lottie that she was going to hold a small reception for her and Lottie had been touched. It would have been just a pint at the inn after the service if it hadn't been for the kind offer.

'So there you are. It'll be in our interest to get it done in time, won't it? We need to start advertisin' for extra staff an' all. We'll certainly need another cook to help you in the kitchen. An' we'll also need at least another two people workin' in that part o' the café.'

As the week progressed, they were full of plans and when Toby Brabinger paid them a visit on Friday afternoon Edie was bursting to tell him the good news.

'Congratulations, Mrs Thompson,' he said with a smile when she had blurted it out. 'And to you too, Miss Stroud. I believe you and Mrs Thompson will be partners in the new business.'

She stared at him. Was he looking down on her again? Since hearing his cryptic remark on his first visit to the café she always had that feeling but she merely nodded. 'Yes, we will. But of course, we won't be any threat to you. We cater to a completely different type of customer.'

Toby had the good grace to blush. 'What does it matter who your customers are if you provide a good service? There's room in this trade for many different types of eating houses and I wish you every success.'

At that moment the door opened and the same young boy who had delivered the last bouquet of flowers appeared with an even bigger one.

'Miss Stroud?' Violet flushed with pleasure as she hurried to take them. They must be from Oliver again. It was clearly his way of showing his appreciation each time she lent him money.

'Ooh, the secret admirer strikes again,' Edie teased as Violet headed for the kitchen with the flowers.

'Nobody ever sends *me* flowers,' Lottie sighed enviously. Turning to Toby she asked with a smile, 'An' what can I get for you today, sir?'

'Just a pot of tea if you please, Lottie.'

Once Toby had left Lottie asked Violet, 'Why don't you like Mr Brabinger? I reckon he's really nice an' he clearly likes you.'

Violet frowned at her. 'I never said I didn't like him!'

'You don't 'ave to, it's written all over your face the minute the poor bloke sets foot through the door.'

'He's a snob enjoying the fact that I've come down in the world,' Violet said heatedly.

'He's posh, admittedly, but I wouldn't 'ave said he's a snob,' Lottie answered. Her eyes strayed to the flowers Violet was arranging in a vase and she grinned. 'Do you think they could be off 'im?'

'No, I do not. Why would he send me flowers?' Violet snapped, keen to change the subject. Luckily the café got busy again, so Lottie didn't get a chance to answer as they both bustled away to serve the customers.

The Millers brought the keys to the hardware shop round to Edie on Saturday morning, but the café was so busy, they didn't get a chance to view it until the evening.

The shelves were still covered in hardware – everything from buckets and bowls, nails and screws to hammers and gardening tools, and Edie scratched her head as she eyed it all.

'I think we should 'ave a sale an' get rid o' this lot afore we even start to think o' makin' any alterations,' Lottie said sensibly.

'I reckon you're right but who'd be in 'ere to sell everythin'? We're all rushed off us feet next door.' Edie said anxiously.

'My sister would come an' help for a small wage,' Lottie suggested. 'An' she'd be glad of a job in the new part o' the café when it's done. She's a good little worker. She's been a maid in one o' the big houses up on Lilac Hill since she left school, but the family 'ave moved to London so she's out o' work at the minute. We could price everythin' up then she could come in an' sell the stuff.'

'Sounds good to me, what do you think, Violet?' Edie asked.

'Sounds good to me too,' Violet agreed. 'Why don't you bring her in to meet us?'

'I'll do that tomorrer,' Lottie promised.

They trooped upstairs to look at the living quarters. They were almost identical to the ones next door and Edie stared around thoughtfully.

'We could do this place up for you, Violet, so you had your own space?' she suggested.

Violet was quite taken with the idea, although the place would need some work.

They had talked in depth about how the partnership would work, and Edie had insisted that once the new part of the café was open, they should split any profits between them. Violet was reluctant as Edie had put in much more money than she had, but Edie was insistent.

'It'll all be yours one day anyway,' she had pointed out.

Violet knew it would be pointless to argue; Edie could be very stubborn when she'd made her mind up about something.

'Sorry to leave you to it but I'm seein' Frank tonight so I'd best be off,' Lottie said after a time.

'You get off, pet,' Edie encouraged her. 'I'm goin' to have a cuppa and a bite to eat and then start pricin' some o' this stuff up.'

'I'll help too,' Violet volunteered.

By bedtime they had priced the majority of the stock and were covered in dust from head to foot.

'Just look at the state of us,' Edie chuckled. 'It's a good job we ain't open tomorrer cos I'm too tired for a bath tonight.'

More than happy with what they had achieved they set off next door and fell into their beds exhausted.

They were busily pricing the remains of the stock the following morning when Lottie and Frank appeared with a younger girl who had a look of Lottie about her. She had long, light brown hair, blue eyes and a ready smile and both Violet and Edie took to her immediately.

'This is me sister, Maisie,' Lottie introduced her, and Edie and Violet greeted her warmly.

'As you can see,' Edie said, spreading her hands wide, 'we've plenty to keep you busy, pet. We've priced everything low to get rid of it, are you up for it?'

'Oh yes.' Maisie nodded enthusiastically. 'I don't mind what I do.'

Violet and Edie exchanged satisfied glances.

Frank, meanwhile, was walking about having a good look around. 'And when all this stuff is sold, I could knock this wall down for you,' he offered. 'I've already spoken to a few of me mates an' they'll be happy to come along an' help wi' any jobs that need doin'.'

Edie looked slightly worried. 'That's wonderful lad, but don't forget I ain't got much left to pay 'em at present. All mine an' Violet's money has gone into buyin' the place.'

Frank chuckled. 'All we'll cost you is as many sausage an' bacon batches as we can eat an' as much tea as we can drink.'

Edie beamed. 'In that case I'll be grateful to take you up on your offer. I'm sure we can manage that,' she told him. 'Though most o' the work on the knockin' through will 'ave to be done at night when the café is empty. Folks don't want dust flyin' around when they're eatin' their meals.'

'That's the only time we could come anyway, we're all at work durin' the day.' And it was agreed.

Over the next two weeks Edie and Violet worked in the café each day and next door every evening. Everything was really starting to take shape. Maisie had proved herself to be a good salesperson and almost all of the stock was now sold. Frank and his friends had also been working hard taking down any shelves that weren't needed and painting the walls.

'I reckon we'll be ready to knock the wall through to next door this Sunday,' Frank told them one evening.

'I'd best look at gettin' some more tables an' chairs in that case,' Edie said excitedly. 'An' think about gettin' someone else in to help wi' the cookin' an' all. If it goes as I hope it will, there'll be too much for me to manage on me own. We've already asked Maisie if she'll stay on to help serve.'

As promised Frank and his friends arrived early the following Sunday and began the last job of getting the wall down. Unfortunately, it proved to be a dirty, dusty job and Edie made the decision to close the café for a couple of days to get everything back to rights. Once the main wall was down the men began to plaster what remained and by bedtime they were finished. The women's work began the following morning as they scrubbed and cleaned everything while Edie prepared to go out to order some more tables and chairs.

'I've heard that Fred Harper's got some in 'is second-hand shop,' she told them as she pulled her coat on. 'Apparently one o' the pubs in the town 'as just 'ad all new ones so I'm goin' to 'ave a look at 'em. I dare say the chairs will all need a coat o' paint but so long as they're sturdy we'll just give 'em a good clean for now an' they'll have to do. It don't matter so much about the tables cos nobody will ever see 'em once we put cloths on.'

She made for the door only to blink with surprise when a cart pulled up outside with some rather smart tables and chairs on the back.

'What the . . .?'

'Mrs Edie Thompson?' The young man sitting next to the driver enquired.

Edie nodded.

The man nodded to the driver, and they jumped down from the cart and started to unload the new furniture and carry it inside.

'Now 'old fire,' Edie demanded in a panic. 'I ain't ordered these, lad. I can't afford new stuff.'

'It's all right, missus. They're all paid for. We was just told to deliver 'em.'

Edie's mouth gaped open. 'But I don't understand! Who ordered 'em an' who paid for 'em? Are you *quite* sure you're bringin' 'em to the right place?'

He nodded as he placed the first of the tables in the new part of the café. By that time Violet, Lottie and Maisie had come to stand with her.

'Sure as eggs is eggs,' the man said cheerily. 'But as for who paid for 'em I've no idea. We was just told to pick 'em up an' deliver 'em.'

When the rest of the tables and chairs had been carried in, the women stood staring at them.

'First the glass for the winder an' now this,' Edie murmured. 'But who'd help us like this?'

Lottie giggled. 'Who cares, God bless 'em, that's what I say. Now let's get 'em all set out. Eeh, they're lovely quality. Almost too good for a dockers' café.'

By Tuesday afternoon they had almost finished but there was one more thing to come that Edie hadn't mentioned.

'There's a cart just pulled up outside,' Violet told Edie. 'Have you ordered anything?'

'I 'ave as it happens.' Edie winked at Maisie and Lottie. 'It's a surprise, so get out the back till I call you.'

112

With a frown Violet went off to tackle the pile of dirty pots in the large stone sink, wondering what on earth it could be.

Half an hour later Edie came to fetch her and led her outside.

Lottie, Maisie and Edie had broad smiles on their faces as they waited for her.

'What am I supposed to be looking at?'

Edie pointed up and Violet's mouth gaped open as she saw the new sign above the door which read *Violet's Café*, in red letters.

'*Oh!*' She was speechless as a smart carriage pulled up and Toby Brabinger climbed out.

'I'm not too late for the unveiling, am I?' he laughed.

'You're just in time,' Edie told him as Violet pointedly ignored him.

'But shouldn't we have called it "Edie's café"?' Violet queried.

Edie shrugged. 'What would be the point? As I've told you, it'll be all yours one day, so it might as well be your name above the door from the start. I hope you like it?'

'I-it's lovely.' Violet didn't wish to appear ungrateful but was squirming with embarrassment, for she had no doubt that Toby had come to laugh at her. As nice as she and Edie had tried to make the place, she was painfully aware that Toby's smart eating house was in a different league.

'You'll be giving me a run for my money at this rate,' Toby commented light-heartedly.

Violet glared at him. 'I think we both know that that is highly unlikely,' she retorted, and with her nose in the air she went back to get on with the washing-up. Inside she was fuming. How dare that arrogant prig come here looking down on them? But she'd show him if it was the last thing she did.

Chapter Fourteen

'What was all that about?' Edie asked after Toby had left.

Violet sniffed. 'I just don't like him,' she said bluntly. 'I always get the feeling he's looking down on me. Don't forget he first knew me when we lived on Lilac Hill, not far from his house. Father used to take me to his establishment for meals from time to time as a treat and now here we are living in Dockside Road in a café serving the dockers.'

The minute the words had left her mouth she regretted them as she saw the hurt on Edie's face.

'Well, I'm sorry you feel like that. From where I'm standin', we've made the best of a bad situation. We've got ourselves our own little business an' somewhere to live into the bargain, an' I'm sorry if it ain't good enough for your ladyship!'

'Oh Edie, I didn't mean it like that,' Violet said hastily but the damage was done and with a shrug Edie turned and walked away.

Thankfully, as the day wore on Edie returned to her normal cheery self and by late afternoon, she had forgiven Violet. She'd had a lot to come to terms with lately, Edie reasoned, and loving her as she did, she could never stay mad at her for long. And now at last they were ready to reopen the next morning and Edie was looking forward to it. She stared around the extended café with satisfaction. After all their hard work, the place was gleaming. All that was left to do was to sort out Violet's new living quarters, but for now she and Edie would continue to share the small rooms above the first shop.

'Right, I reckon we can all knock off now,' Edie told them. 'Get yourselves home an' get a good night's sleep. Hopefully we'll be busy tomorrow. An', Lottie, don't forget to put that advert for an assistant cook in the post office winder for me, will you? If things go to plan, I'm goin' to need one.'

Lottie and Maisie left promising to be back early the next morning and Violet put the kettle on to make tea for Edie. She'd been feeling guilty for her selfish outburst all day.

'Ah that's better,' Edie sighed and placed her swollen feet up on one of the kitchen chairs. 'Me feet feel as if they're goin' to drop off. It's been bloody 'ard work, ain't it? Now let's just 'ope it pays off an' it's been worth it.'

'I'm sure it will be, and, Edie . . .' Violet placed a steaming mug of tea in front of her and cleared her throat. 'I am *really* sorry about being so horrible earlier. I wasn't getting at you, I promise. I don't know what I'd have done without you after Father died. It's just that Toby Brabinger always seems to be smirking at me.'

Edie shook her head. 'I dare say you're entitled to your opinion but if you're interested in mine, I reckon you're far off the mark. Mr Brabinger is a gentleman. I reckon he's quite taken wi' you.' Seeing the prim expression on Violet's face she quickly changed the subject. It seemed that Toby Brabinger and his motives towards them was something they were never going to agree on.

'These tables an' chairs are lovely,' Lottie commented the next morning just before they opened. 'Any idea yet who sent 'em?'

Edie shook her head. 'Not a clue, but I dare say it's the same person who paid for the window. But when I do find out who it were, I'll pay 'em back every last penny.' Secretly, she had her own thoughts on who their benefactor might be.

There was no more time for talk then as they noticed customers outside hungry for their breakfast, so with a smile Lottie rushed to turn the sign on the door and admit the first customers into Violet's Café.

From that moment the little business proved to be a resounding success, and by the end of the first week they were rushed off their feet.

Edie had already interviewed three women for the job as assistant cook but she had turned them all down. The first had smelled like an old bag lady and had looked little better, the second admitted that she couldn't even boil an egg, and the third was a woman who wanted to bring her six children to work with her each day. As much as Edie sympathised with her position, she knew it could never have worked with little ones racing round under their feet.

'The right person will turn up,' Edie said optimistically.

Sure enough, a couple of days later the bell above the door tinkled and a tidily dressed, gentle-faced woman, who appeared to be in her late thirties to early forties, appeared. She had dark hair and dark eyes and was softly spoken, and Edie rushed her away into the kitchen to speak to her.

'She looked all right, didn't she?' Lottie whispered to Violet as they prepared the tables for the lunchtime rush. 'Can't say as I've seen her around here before though.'

Violet grinned. 'Hull is quite a large place; I should imagine there are lots of people you haven't seen before.'

Minutes later Edie appeared with the woman. 'This is Mrs Bridges, girls. She's going to be helpin' me in the kitchen as from tomorrow.' Then turning to the woman, she introduced them. 'This is Maisie, this is Lottie an' this is Violet, my business partner.'

'It's very nice to meet you all,' Mrs Bridges said, shaking their hands in turn.

'An' you,' Lottie said enthusiastically. 'It's goin' to be so much easier wi' another pair o' hands on board. But what shall we call you? Mrs Bridges is a bit formal.'

The woman smiled. 'You can call me Sally.'

'Right you are,' Lottie said. 'Welcome aboard.'

Sally started the next morning and in no time at all it was clear Edie had made a good choice. She was a hard worker and willing to lend a hand to anything that needed doing when she wasn't cooking, although they soon discovered that she was quite a private person.

'So, are you from round 'ere?' Lottie asked one day as they were wiping the tables down.

'Er, yes, I rent a room not far from here,' Sally said cautiously.

Lottie had noticed she wore a wedding ring and asked next, 'An' is there a Mr Bridges?'

Sally flushed. 'Not anymore.' She looked uncomfortable. 'My husband and son died from scarlet fever last year.'

'Oh, I'm so sorry to 'ear that.' Lottie wished she hadn't asked, and wisely didn't ask any more questions. It was obvious that Sally found it hard to talk about and she had no wish to upset her.

In no time at all they were into July and the business was doing a roaring trade. Now all their thoughts were on Lottie's wedding, which would take place the following weekend. Edie had bought her a beautiful length of white satin that Lottie and her mother had been busy making into a wedding gown, and Edie was planning the food for the reception.

'It wouldn't hurt for you to treat yourself to a new gown an' all,' Edie commented to Violet one day. 'I can't remember when you last had one. Why don't you take a couple of hours off tomorrow an' go shoppin'? You can afford it now that we're doin' so well. Same goes for you, Sally. You could go together. There's a lovely ladies shop up on the high street. I'm sure you'd both find something you'd like there.'

'I, er . . . I'd like that, so long as Violet wouldn't mind me tagging along,' Sally said shyly with a gentle smile at Violet.

117

'I'd be glad of the company,' Violet answered. She and Sally had taken to each other.

'That's decided then.' Edie looked pleased as she returned to frying the sausages.

The next afternoon Violet and Sally set off for the shops. It was a beautiful day with the sun shining in a cloudless blue sky and Violet enjoyed being out in the fresh air.

'I hope the weather is like this for Lottie's big day on Saturday,' Violet said to Sally as they arrived at the ladies' shop.

Inside, the shopkeeper showed them the ready-made gowns she had in their sizes and the two women enjoyed trying them on.

'Oh, that's the one,' Sally told her when Violet came out of the fitting room in a pale green dress that showed off her slim figure to perfection. 'It fits you like a glove. Perhaps we could find you a new bonnet to go with it?' She had already chosen a more reserved gown in a pale lemon colour, so the next stop was the milliner's where they spent a happy hour trying on hats. Violet eventually chose a wide-brimmed hat trimmed with silk roses that perfectly matched her gown.

'It's so lovely,' she sighed. 'But it's rather expensive. I don't know if I'd ever get to wear it again. I don't go to many places where I could since . . .' As her voice trailed away and her eyes watered Sally hurried forward to give her a hug. It was the first physical contact they'd had but it felt comforting.

'Why don't you let me buy it for you? You'll regret it if you don't have it because it could have been made to go with your new gown,' she said kindly.

'Ah, that's really nice of you but I wouldn't dream of letting you do that,' Violet said hastily. 'But you're quite right. It is perfect so I'll have it!'

They left the shop in a happy mood but the smile died on Violet's face when she was suddenly confronted with a face from the past she had never expected to see again.

'Mam— Anna.' It was still hard to think of her as anything other than Mama. It was the first time she had set eyes on her since the day she had left their lovely home on Lilac Hill and Violet was shocked at the change in her. Anna had always been so glamorous, but now she looked tired and a little shabby.

'Violet.' Anna stared back at her as Sally discreetly turned away to study something in a shop window. 'How are you? Oliver tells me you have a business now and are doing well.'

'You've seen him?' Violet said eagerly. She hadn't set eyes on him since the last time he had come to borrow money, and she had been worrying about him. 'And, er, yes. Edie and I do have a café, although she owns far more of it than I do.'

'Oliver is living with me at present,' Anna said. 'He had a job but it didn't, er . . . work out, unfortunately, so he's looking for another position at present.'

Unsure what to say to her, Violet squirmed uncomfortably. They had parted on bad terms, so she was surprised Anna was giving her the time of day. She wasn't even sure she wanted her to if truth be told, not after the way Anna had treated her.

'So where are you living now?' Violet asked eventually when Anna showed no sign of moving away.

'I have some rooms in a house in Back Street.'

Violet nodded. She knew the area enough to know that it was a far cry from Lilac Hill, certainly not the sort of place she would ever have expected Anna to choose, but she supposed that she hadn't had much choice.

'I hope everything goes well for you.' Violet was keen to get away now, but as she made to move on Anna suddenly reached over and caught her arm.

'Will you come and see me? I have things I need to say to you.'

Violet was shocked. She had thought Anna had said all she wanted to say on the day they had parted. Seeing her hesitation, Anna rushed on, '*Please* . . . I know how badly I've behaved towards you and I want to make it up to you.'

'There's really no need.'

'Oh, but there is. We live at number seven, the top floor. Please say you'll come . . . your father would have wanted you to.'

It was her final words that swayed Violet. She supposed Anna was right. He would have been very unhappy about the way they had parted, so as much as she didn't relish the idea, she would go.

'Very well. Shall we say this Sunday afternoon about three o'clock?'

'I shall look forward to it.' Anna released her arm and walked away.

Sally turned back to her and scowled. She looked almost as unhappy about the idea of Violet visiting Anna as Violet felt.

'Your, er . . . mother?'

'My stepmother, actually, although I didn't know that until after my father died. I'm afraid we didn't part on good terms.'

Sally chewed on her lip. 'Look, I know it's none of my business,' she said quietly. 'But just be careful. There was something about her that I didn't take to.'

Violet nodded. 'Don't worry, I will. Although there's not much she could do to hurt me now, is there? I'm only going because I think it's what Papa would have wanted. But thanks for your concern.'

'Perhaps Edie could go with you?'

Violet shook her head. 'I shall be quite all right. And I shan't be staying for long, I assure you.'

Her words didn't seem to reassure Sally, who still looked worried, and the journey home was made in silence.

When they got back, Edie was horrified when Violet told her of the meeting with Anna, and what had been said, and even more horrified when she found out that Violet had agreed to visit her.

'How could you even *think* o' goin' after the way she's treated you?' Edie fumed.

Violet bowed her head. 'I think Papa would want me to,' she answered in a small voice, tears stinging at the back of her eyes.

Edie put her arm about her shoulders. 'I suppose it can't do no 'arm,' she mumbled. 'Just so long as you don't make a habit of it. That woman never does nowt wi'out it benefits 'er, so just be careful an' be on yer guard.'

'I know why Oliver's last job didn't work out,' Lottie informed them the next morning when Edie relayed what had happened the day before. 'I 'eard that he's heavily into gamblin' an' the widow he'd latched on to got sick of 'im holdin' his hand out, so she showed him the door. I've also 'eard that he's in wi' that gang that steal from the docks an' sell the stuff on. The coppers 'ave been tryin' to catch 'em for months now, an' when they do, they'll lock 'em up an' throw away the keys wi' a bit o' luck. One of our neighbours is a night watchman down in one o' the warehouses an' they nearly brained 'im last week when they broke in an' stole a load of silk from China. Worth a fortune it was apparently.'

Violet listened but said nothing. It was hard to believe that Oliver could be involved in anything like that, and deep down she was hoping she would see him when she visited Anna. But first they had Lottie's wedding to look forward to, so she tried to put the meeting to the back of her mind.

Chapter Fifteen

The day of the wedding dawned bright and sunny and from early in the morning, Violet and Edie were busy putting the finishing touches to the food Edie had prepared for the reception. She had even found time to bake her a two-tiered wedding cake, which stood in pride of place in the middle of the buffet table that stretched all along one wall.

'It looks wonderful, Edie. Well done,' Violet praised as they finally stood back to survey the finished results. 'Now we really ought to go and get changed or we're going to be late for the service.'

They hurried upstairs and half an hour later, dressed in their finery, they rushed to the church and watched Lottie walk down the aisle on the arm of her proud father.

The bride was radiant, and Edie sniffed back a tear as Lottie and Frank exchanged their vows. 'Eeh, I don't think I've ever seen a more beautiful bride,' Edie whispered as Frank slipped a slim gold band onto Lottie's finger. And then the happy couple were walking out into the sunshine to be showered in rose petals and rice before setting off back to the café.

The reception went without a hitch, although Violet was surprised when Toby Brabinger walked in shortly after they arrived at the café.

Seeing Violet frown, Edie hissed, 'I invited him. You don't mind, do you?'

Violet shrugged, surprised to see that he had come bearing a large, colourfully wrapped box, which he handed to the blushing bride.

'I hope you'll be very happy together,' Toby told her.

Lottie opened the parcel and gasped with delight to find a stunning bone-china dinner and tea set inside.

'Oh!' She was clearly taken aback at such an expensive present. 'It's beautiful. The trouble is, I don't know if I'll ever dare to use it. Thank you so much.'

'Aye, thank you.' Frank shook Toby's hand. 'It's very much appreciated. Come and have a drink. There's a barrel of ale over there, or wine if you'd prefer.'

Toby thanked him and went to get a jug of ale before sidling over to Violet. 'The buffet looks beautiful,' he praised. 'Well done to you and Edie. You've done the bride and groom proud.'

Violet stared at him. 'I suppose what you mean is it's all right for a backstreet café,' she retorted. 'And nowhere near as posh as what you would have provided.'

Toby frowned. 'Why do you always take everything I say the wrong way, as if you think I'm trying to make fun of you all the time?' Then before she could reply he hurried on. 'As well as responding to Edie's very kind invitation, I also came hoping you'd agree to come out to dinner with me one evening. We needn't go to my place; we could go anywhere you like.'

Violet sniffed, taken aback. 'Thank you very much for the offer but I'm afraid I'm far too busy to be gallivanting off leaving the others to do all the work. Some of us can't afford to have managers to do work for us, you see!' With a rustle of silken skirts, she moved away with her chin in the air as Toby shook his head, thinking how pretty she looked when she was angry.

Very soon the tables and chairs were pushed to the edges of the rooms and the party really began as the ale flowed. Lottie's father was playing a harmonica and soon couples were jigging around the floor in the confined space. Laughter was bouncing off the walls and Violet was happy to see that Frank and Lottie had eyes only for each other, just as it should be. It was clear they were perfectly suited and she somehow knew they were going to be happy together. More than one of Frank's young friends came forward asking her for a dance but Violet declined them all and instead started to clear some of the dirty pots into the kitchen. She had just placed one trayful down on the large wooden draining board when Toby followed her in carrying another one.

'There's no need for you to be doing that,' she snapped more sharply than she had intended to. 'You're a guest here.'

His face suddenly hardened. 'And do you *really* think I don't get my hands dirty at my own place when we're short-staffed, Miss Hoity-Toity?'

Violet blinked in surprise.

'Then let me tell you, my father started his business from a barrow in the market place selling mushy peas and jacket potatoes. He worked every hour God sent until he could afford a little café, nowhere near as big as this, may I add!' He was clearly annoyed. 'He worked his way up from nothing until eventually he bought the eating house. When I left school, I started working there with him. My father believed in starting at the bottom, so I began by sweeping floors and peeling potatoes! It didn't matter that I was the boss's son.' Seeing the look of surprise on her face he went on. 'Father believed I should know every job it takes to run a business, so believe me, I've done everything that you do and more. Your trouble is you feel belittled because you've come from a privileged upbringing and now have to work for a living, but as far as I'm concerned there's absolutely nothing wrong with that. In fact, I admire you for working so hard with Edie, but your problem is, Miss Stroud, that you're a terrible snob! Now, if you'll excuse me, I'll wish you good day! I certainly won't trouble you again.'

And with that he turned on his heel and stormed away with a face like thunder.

Violet chewed her lip as she watched him go, feeling slightly guilty. She had been rather abrupt and rude to him, and in truth he

124

hadn't really done anything to warrant it. It was just that he always managed to make her feel inferior.

With a sigh she went back to the party, but somehow, she didn't feel quite in the mood for it now and she was relieved when the night was finally over.

'Couldn't have gone better, could it?' Edie said with satisfaction when they had closed the door on the last guest late that evening. The newly-weds had left early in the evening to spend their first night in the little house they had rented close to Lottie's mother, and Edie had told her not to come into work until mid-week.

'It went really well,' Violet agreed.

Edie glanced at her thoughtfully. 'Toby Brabinger left rather suddenly, didn't he?' she said quietly.

Violet flushed. 'I, er . . . didn't notice. Did he?'

'Hmm, I saw him follow you into the kitchen wi' a tray o' pots an' the next thing I looked up an' he were goin'.'

'I dare say he had things to do.' Violet avoided her eyes as she put some dirty pots to soak in the sink. They were both too tired to deal with them that evening. As lovely as it had been it had been a long day.

'Ah well, let's get usselves upstairs, eh? Me poor old feet are on fire. There's nowt down here as can't wait till mornin'.'

'All right, you go on up. I'll just check everywhere is locked up safely and I'll be up shortly.'

Once alone, Violet sank onto a kitchen chair and stared thoughtfully into space for a time before rising to follow her.

The following day Sally and Maisie came in to help with the cleaning up and by late morning everything had been put to rights.

'Isn't it today that you're going to see your stepmother?' Sally asked just before she left.

Violet sighed. 'Yes, it is.'

'You don't sound too enamoured with the idea?'

'I'm not, but at least I'll get to see Oliver and if things don't go well, I shan't stay for long.'

'Well, just be careful,' Sally warned as she put on her bonnet to leave.

Edie was no happier with the idea of the visit than Sally, and voiced her opinion. Violet was looking smart in one of the outfits she hadn't worn since leaving Lilac Hill. 'You must want your 'ead examinin',' Edie grumbled. 'No good'll come o' this, just you mark me words. Anna never does anythin' wi'out sommat in it for her!'

'I think she's just sorry for the way we parted,' Violet answered.

Edie pursed her lips and shook her head. 'It ain't the sort of area for a young lady to be in on her own,' she persisted. 'You know your father would never 'ave allowed you to go there. Some o' them that live there would cut your throat for sixpence.'

'I'm sure they're not all the same,' Violet said, giving Edie's hand a reassuring pat. 'And it's not as if I'm going there in the dark. It's broad daylight. I shall be back before you know it.'

'Just make sure as you are.' Edie clamped her lips shut and refused to say another word.

Violet knew Edie was still slightly nervous when on her own in case the gang came back to do more damage, but thankfully all had been quiet on that front since the night they had smashed the front window. Still, she didn't intend to be gone for long.

Despite her brave words, though, soon after setting off, Violet started to feel nervous as she turned into the warren of depressing little alleys that led to Back Street. On either side of them were terraced houses so tall that they allowed no sunlight to shine down between them. Barefoot children in ragged clothes were playing in the gutters, their arms and legs were stick thin and their sunken eyes watched her curiously as she passed. At one point Violet had to side-step a mongrel dog that was devouring a dead rat and her stomach revolted at the sight. And to think that, out of the goodness of his heart, her father used to come here regularly to treat patients who were unable to pay for his time or the medicine he gave them. He really had had a heart of pure gold. It had always been a bone of contention between him and Anna. Little could she have known when she was living a life of luxury that soon she would be living amongst the poor souls.

Eventually Violet turned into Back Street and walked until she came to number seven. The door to the house was wide open and even from outside Violet could smell the stench issuing from it: stale cabbage, urine and other smells that were so vile she didn't even want to think about what they might be. A young woman was sitting on the front doorstep with a scrawny baby sucking at her breast and she stared from dull eyes as Violet stepped past her. Inside, the sounds of people shouting and children crying followed her along a hallway where the wallpaper was peeling from the walls.

'Spare a penny, missus?' A small, emaciated boy with the face of an old man suddenly appeared from nowhere holding his hand out towards her. Without thinking Violet immediately dug into her purse and pressed a few pennies into his hand. His eyes lit up and he was off out of the door like a rocket as Violet began to climb the narrow staircase. In places the stairs were so rotten she could feel them giving way beneath her weight, and her heart began to thud. What had she let herself in for? But it was too late to turn back now so she moved on. On the first-floor landing was another staircase that led up again and she started to climb. Finally, she reached the top floor where there were two doors on either side of a small landing. She hesitated, wondering which one to knock on, and approached the first.

The door was opened by a woman in a gown cut so low that her sagging breasts looked in danger of falling out of it. She smelled strongly of body odour and cheap perfume and her face was heavily rouged, giving her the appearance of a macabre china doll.

'What d'yer want? I thought you was me next customer,' she said suspiciously as she eyed Violet up and down.

'I, er . . . I'm so sorry to trouble you. I was looking for Mrs Stroud.' Violet was so nervous that the words came out as a squeak.

'That door there,' the woman said ungraciously as a ruddy-faced seaman appeared behind her. 'Ah, here you are, me darlin',' the woman crooned, forgetting all about Violet as she greeted her visitor. 'Come on in. You'll not regret it. Old Ruby knows 'ow to please a chap, you just see if she don't.' She grabbed the man's arm and almost hauled him into her room, slamming the door shut behind her.

Violet stood there for a moment until her heart slowed to a steadier rhythm wondering what sort of place she had come to. Then plucking up every ounce of courage she had left, she crossed the small landing and knocked on the other door.

'Violet, we're so pleased you could come,' Oliver greeted her as the door creaked open. 'Come on in.'

The smell in the room was as bad as in the rest of the house and as Violet took in the elegant curtains hanging at the grimy windows, she couldn't help but think how out of place they looked. They were the same ones that had graced the living room in their home on Lilac Hill. Anna's expensive Persian carpets were thrown across the shabby floorboards and on a small table was the dainty china tea set that Anna had used to entertain visitors.

'Violet, how good of you to come. Do sit down.' Anna rose and ushered her to a leather wing chair that she recognised as another piece from their old home. A lump formed in her throat. It had been a particular favourite of her father's and she could picture him sitting there with a newspaper on his lap.

'Thank you.' As Violet sat down her eyes strayed to a cheap truckle bed with a straw mattress and a folded blanket beneath the window. She supposed this was where Oliver slept. Anna probably used the only bedroom, which led from this room.

Anna, meanwhile, was straining tea into the delicate cups and saucers on the table. 'Is it still one sugar?' she asked sweetly, and

Violet nodded. 'As you can see, I managed to keep a few pieces of furniture. Unfortunately, the rest had to go to the auction house.'

'Or the pawn shop,' Oliver quipped drily.

His mother glared at him before plastering a smile back on her face and returning her attention to Violet. 'So how have you been keeping, my dear?'

Violet could never remember Anna addressing her as such before, and as she took the cup and saucer she was being offered, she was aware that her hands were trembling. Suddenly she wondered why she had come. Perhaps Edie had been right, some people were best left in the past.

And then, as if Anna could read her mind, she went on, 'I dare say you are wondering why I asked you to come here today? The answer is simple. I wanted to make my peace with you and apologise for the way we parted. I'm afraid your father's death was a terrible shock for all of us, and I realise now that I didn't handle it at all well.'

'It's in the past now,' Violet said quietly as she sipped at her tea.

'Yes, you're quite right.' Anna gave her a charming smile – the one she usually reserved for special visitors. 'But I hope that won't stop us being friends again? After all, I was the only mother you ever knew. And I have to say, I – in fact both of us – are delighted to see how well you are doing for yourself. Your father would have been proud of you.'

Violet said nothing. She was finding the whole visit very surreal but then she wondered if she wasn't perhaps being a little hard on the woman. Could it be that she had really changed, and for the better?

'Oliver tells me that you and Edie have extended your café?'

When Violet nodded, she rushed on. 'And would I be right in thinking there are vacant rooms above the shop you have just acquired?' She sighed as she glanced around the dismal surroundings. 'How lucky you are not to have to live somewhere like this.'

Now Violet had an inkling as to why she had been summoned but she wasn't going to fall for Anna's hard-luck story.

'As soon as I've had time to get them ready, I intend to move in so that Edie and I have our own places,' she informed her.

'Oh . . . I see.' Anna looked disappointed but after glancing at Oliver she went on, 'We were hoping that you might allow us to rent them from you, but I quite understand if you intend to live there yourself, of course. But until that comes about, I wonder if we might ask a favour? The thing is, Oliver has started a little business, buying and selling.'

'Buying and selling what?'

'Almost anything he can sell on that will make a little profit. He's doing very well at present, but the problem we're up against is where to store the things he buys. As you can see, there's hardly room to swing a cat in here so I was wondering – do you think you could allow us to use those empty rooms to store things? Just until you move in, of course. By then, hopefully Oliver will have saved enough to buy a little shop of his own.'

Violet bit down on her lip. 'I, er . . . I'm not sure that would be such a good idea,' she answered cautiously. 'You see, Edie still officially owns more of the business than I do and I'm not sure she'd be happy with that.' This, she thought, was an understatement. Edie had no time for either Oliver or Anna. But then she looked up and Oliver was staring at her so sadly that her heart skipped a beat.

'I, um, I suppose I could help temporarily, just until you can find somewhere else,' she said uncertainly. 'But Oliver would have to deliver the things he wants storing at night after the shop is shut. I'm not so sure Edie would approve of him coming in and out during the day while the café is open. Would that be a problem?'

'Not at all,' Oliver declared with a broad smile.

'And these things you're buying. They are, er . . . legal, aren't they?' Violet had heard stories of things going missing from the warehouses, not that she wanted to believe that Oliver would be involved in anything like that.

Oliver looked so hurt that she instantly wished she could take the words back. 'Of course they're legal. I'm not a criminal, Violet! We pawned Mother's jewellery to buy most of the goods. I have the pawn tickets if you want to see them.'

'No, no, of course I don't. I believe you,' she told him hastily. She was feeling more uncomfortable by the minute but it was too late to go back on her word now. 'So do you have anything you'd like to store there at present?'

'All being well, I will have after tonight.' He looked pleased with himself. 'I'm hoping to take delivery of some crates of wine. You can always sell spirits.'

'Then perhaps you could get word to me and I'll let you in through the back yard,' Violet suggested as she placed her cup and saucer down.

'That's most generous of you.' Anna inclined her head and Violet rose, keen to be away. She hadn't felt at all comfortable the whole time she had been there. 'Thank you for the tea,' she said politely and minutes later she was clattering down the stairs and out into the reeking alleys. The same little boy she had given some pennies to was waiting for her and held his hand out hopefully but Violet was in too much of a hurry to notice, and lifting her skirts in a most unladylike manner, she scooted away as fast as her legs would carry her.

While Violet put as much distance as she could between herself and the house she had just visited, Anna was purring with satisfaction.

'That girl still idolises you,' she told her son with a smirk of satisfaction. 'She always has, ever since she was a little girl, so if you play your cards right, she'll be putty in your hands.'

'Do you think so?' Oliver grinned. He hoped his mother was right.

Chapter Sixteen

'How did it go?' Edie queried when Violet arrived back. She was sitting in their cosy little sitting room with a book in her lap and a pot of tea at the side of her.

Violet took off her bonnet and smiled falsely. 'Oh, much as I expected,' she said vaguely. 'I think Anna just wanted to apologise for how she'd treated me and ease her conscience. But you needn't worry, I shan't be going there again.'

'Was it bad?'

Violet nodded. 'Very. The house they're living in is packed to the rafters and it smells awful. There are whole families there, all crowded into one room.'

'Huh! How the mighty are fallen, eh?' Edie retorted with not a scrap of sympathy. 'An' when I think of how your poor dad worked 'is fingers to the bone to keep 'er like a lady. But I still reckon she had an ulterior motive for gettin' you there.'

Violet didn't dare tell Edie about agreeing to store Oliver's goods or the fact that Anna had all but suggested that she and Oliver move into the rooms above the new shop, so she quickly changed the subject.

On Wednesday morning Lottie returned to work. She was glowing and it was clear that married life was suiting her. She also had some gossip to impart. 'There's been ructions down at the docks again,' she told them as she and Maisie began to lay the tables for the breakfast customers. 'Another warehouse break-in, but this time the night watchman were badly injured, poor soul. They knocked 'im nearly senseless by all accounts. He's in hospital.'

'An' what did they get away wi' this time?' Edie was busy frying bacon and sausages, but she always made time for a bit of gossip.

'Barrels o' rum come in from Jamaica and crates of wine from Italy.'

'Crikey.' Edie raised an eyebrow. 'There must 'ave been a few of 'em to get away wi' that lot. I bet that Ned Banks an' his gang are behind it.'

'Just so long as they leave us alone,' Lottie answered.

The following night Violet was woken by the sound of something tapping on her bedroom window. Dragging herself from her bed she crossed the room and twitched the curtains aside and once her eyes had become accustomed to the gloom, she saw Oliver standing in the yard. He had been throwing pebbles at the glass to waken her. She opened the window and leant out.

'Can you come down with the keys for next door?' he hissed.

With a sigh Violet hurried away to get them, praying that she wouldn't wake Edie.

'What are you doing here at this time? It must be after midnight,' she said when she opened the door to him.

'Sorry.' He gave her an apologetic smile. 'I didn't mean to be so late and I'm sorry for disturbing you. Just give me the key and I'll get the stuff upstairs in no time. You don't need to stay with me.'

Violet wasn't too happy about this but she had agreed so she reluctantly handed the key over. 'Just leave it here under this plant pot when you've finished, and for goodness' sake, be quiet. If you wake Edie my head will be on the block.'

'No problem.' He gave her a peck on the cheek and disappeared off into the shadows while Violet let herself back in and crept up the stairs again.

'Did you 'ear anything outside last night?' Edie asked the next morning at breakfast.

Violet felt so guilty that she almost choked on the slice of toast she was eating. She hated to lie to Edie. 'N-no, I don't think so. Why . . . did you?'

'I thought I did but then it all went quiet again.' Edie shook her head. 'Still, not to worry. It were probably just a stray cat goin' through the bins.'

Someone rapped on the café door and, glad of a chance to escape, Violet hurried through the shop to let Maisie, Sally and Lottie in.

Later that morning Toby Brabinger appeared and seated himself at a table. To Violet's surprise he didn't even look her way, and for some reason that she couldn't explain it irked her.

'Morning, Sally. A pot of tea, please.'

'Right away, Mr Brabinger.'

Sally was back with his order within minutes, closely followed by Edie, who was clearly pleased to see him. He hadn't been near the café since the day of the wedding.

'How are you, lad?' she greeted him.

'I'm very well and I must say you're looking well too.' Toby glanced around at the tables, which nearly all had customers sitting at them. 'And it looks as if business is still booming. I'm pleased for you.'

'Aye it is, thanks to a kindly anonymous benefactor who supplied us wi' the new tables an' chairs.' There was a twinkle in her eye as she smiled at him, but he merely lowered his eyes and didn't comment.

Lottie raced over and said shyly, 'Thanks again for the lovely weddin' present, Mr Brabinger. It looks a fair treat on me dresser.'

'Look, couldn't you all just call me Toby?' He smiled at them but still pointedly avoided glancing towards Violet. 'I think we all know each other well enough by now to be on first-name terms.'

'Edie, are those sausage batches for table seven done yet?' Maisie called and with an apologetic smile at Toby, Edie hurried away.

Toby started to drink his tea, watching the passers-by through the window, while Violet tried her best not to look at him, which proved to be difficult. He had obviously taken the words they'd had on the day of Lottie's wedding to heart. *So what do I care?* Violet asked herself. *Let him sulk if he wants to.* She went through to the kitchen to fetch an order and when she came back, she was just in time to see Toby disappearing through the door.

Violet felt miffed, although she had no idea why she should. After all, he was just a snob and she didn't care if she never saw him again.

With a sniff she went about her work and put him from her mind.

A few days later, in the dead of night, Violet woke to the sound of activity in the upstairs rooms next door. Creeping out of bed, she peeped out of the window and down into the yard just in time to see three dark figures emerge from the back door and hurry towards the gate. It was obviously Oliver and whoever he was working with putting some more things into store. Suddenly curiosity overcame her and flicking her long dark plait across her shoulder, Violet slipped on her night robe and crept out.

Next door, she climbed upstairs and inched the door open. It was pitch black outside so lifting the box of matches she kept on the windowsill, she lit a candle and held it high. Almost immediately her eyes fell on a number of large wooden barrels and crates and she gasped. They were barrels of rum and bottles of wine. Hadn't Lottie told them that that was what had been stolen on the night the night watchman had been injured? There were two more long parcels on the floor next to them and flicking the material that covered them aside she saw three bolts of pure silk. Further investigation uncovered large quantities of tea, coffee beans and sugar, all things that had recently been reported stolen from the warehouses.

With a thump she sat down on the nearest rickety chair with tears in her eyes. Surely Oliver couldn't be responsible for the thefts? And if he was how could he involve her like this? Surely, he knew that if these were stolen goods and they were discovered here it would be her and Edie who would be held responsible for them. There was only one thing she could do; she would have to find him the next morning and order him to remove everything immediately. What choice did she have? And yet the thought of it filled her with shame. Oliver and Anna were obviously down on their luck, but even that couldn't excuse Oliver turning to crime. He had always been her hero, the one she adored and looked up to, but now suddenly she was wondering if he was as wonderful as she had always believed. The minutes ticked away as she sat there trying to work out what to do, until eventually she blew out the candle and crept away, feeling like a criminal herself.

She slept very little for the rest of that night and when she got up in the morning to join Edie in the kitchen the woman looked at her with concern.

'Eeh, you don't look too well, pet. Have you had a bad night?'

Violet nodded, studiously avoiding looking at her. Edie could always read her like a book and she didn't want to give anything away.

'I did actually, and I have a raging headache. Do you think I could slip out to the apothecary when the breakfast rush is over? He might be able to give me something for it.'

'You can slip out as soon as his shop is open,' Edie told her kindly. 'We can manage well enough here. Just go and get something to put you right.'

Shortly after nine o'clock, Violet set out and headed for Back Street. She had hoped she would never have to go there again but she knew this had to be sorted as soon as possible. If the things in the rooms had been stolen, as she feared, and if someone discovered them, then goodness knew what might happen. The premises were in Edie's name, and Violet wouldn't be able to bear it if anything happened to her because of what she'd allowed Oliver to do.

After passing the same pitifully thin children playing in the gutters, she climbed the stairs and rapped sharply on Anna's door. A voice shouted irritably, 'All right, all right, I'm coming!'

The door flew open and there was Anna tightening the belt of her dressing robe with her hair loose about her shoulders. She had clearly just tumbled out of bed – there was no change there then. Violet remembered all too well that she had never risen much before lunchtime.

She looked surprised. 'Oh . . . Violet. What brings you here at this time of the morning?'

'I need to see Oliver . . . *now*!' Violet's eyes flashed with anger as she pushed past Anna, but the truckle bed was empty.

'Where is he?'

Anna looked bemused. 'I have no idea. He probably stayed at a friend's house last night. I didn't even know he hadn't come home until you woke me. Why, what's the matter?'

Violet clenched and unclenched her fists as she wondered whether to tell Anna. She decided to give her the benefit of the doubt. After all, Anna would surely never condone him stealing.

'It's the things he's been storing in the empty rooms above our shop,' she began. 'I popped up there yesterday and discovered . . .' She licked her suddenly dry lips. This wasn't proving easy. 'The thing is, there have been a number of robberies from the warehouses on the docks recently and it appears that some of the things that were stolen are in those rooms.'

Anna narrowed her eyes. 'Oh yes, what sort of things?'

'Rum, wine, tea, coffee beans, just to begin.' Violet wrung her hands.

'And so you immediately assumed Oliver was the one who stole them?' Anna was looking none too pleased, but Violet was determined to plough on.

'You must admit it looks odd. I just want Oliver to assure me that he came by these goods legitimately, that's all.'

'I'm sure he'll be able to do that when he returns. Was there anything else you wanted?'

Before Violet could reply the door behind her opened and Oliver appeared looking dishevelled and grubby.

'Oh . . . Violet!' He looked surprised to see her and ran a hand through his hair, trying to flatten it.

'I came to see you actually.' Despite the fact she was annoyed with him and concerned about the goods at the shop, her heart did a little flutter at the sight of him.

'Yes, it seems Violet has some concerns about the stock you are storing at her premises.' Anna's eyes were as cold as ice as she stared at her son, but he merely smiled.

'Concerned. What about?'

Once again Anna cut in and repeated what Violet had told her.

When she had finished, Oliver smiled at Violet. 'You silly goose.' He leant forward and gently chucked her beneath her chin. 'How could you even think I would do anything like that? I can assure you everything stored there is completely legal. All bought and paid for.'

Violet desperately wanted to believe him but still the niggling doubt remained. 'I'm sure it is,' she said falteringly. 'But even so, I think it might be better if you found somewhere else to store it. Edie is keen to make a start on the rooms, and I did say it could only be temporary.'

The smile slid from Oliver's face and his jaw set. 'Very well, if that's what you want. How much time do I have before I have to move it?'

'Well, er . . . I'd appreciate it if you did it as soon as possible.' Violet felt dreadful but common sense told her she was right to stand her ground – just in case. She would never forgive herself if Edie were to get into trouble because of something she had allowed to happen.

'Leave it with me.' He turned away dismissively.

Feeling awful, Violet nodded towards Anna and headed for the door. Once outside she took a great gulp of air, tears stinging the back of her eyes as she remembered the way Oliver had looked at her. She had clearly upset him, but what choice did she have?

At that moment the same skinny child she had given the pennies to the last time she had been there crept up to her and held out his hand, his eyes hopeful, so with a sigh Violet rummaged in her bag, pressed another few coins into his grubby hand and left.

'Got what you needed, did you?' Edie asked when she arrived back at the café.

Violet flushed. She hated lying to her. 'Yes thanks, I'll just go and take my bonnet and coat off, and I'll be with you.'

'Have a day off if you're not feelin' well, pet. We can manage,' Sally said kindly.

Violet felt even worse. 'Thank you but I'm feeling much better now,' she assured her, hurrying away to get changed into her work clothes.

Chapter Seventeen

For the next two nights Violet barely slept as she lay listening for the sound of Oliver taking away his stock, but he didn't come. By Friday morning she was pale and drawn.

'I hope you ain't comin' down wi' nothin',' Edie fretted as she pushed a cup of tea across the table towards her. 'You ain't lookin' well at all.'

'I'm fine,' Violet answered shortly.

At mid-morning when she was busily clearing tables, the door opened and Toby Brabinger appeared with a very attractive young woman at his side.

'Hello, pet. It's nice to see you.' Sally greeted him as she hurried over to take their orders. Violet felt colour flame into her cheeks.

So much for Edie thinking he had a soft spot for me, she thought as she tried to avoid looking over at them. But somehow her eyes were drawn to the young lady, and she felt miffed for no reason that she could explain. The woman was dainty and petite, with fair hair and lavender-blue eyes, and there was no denying she was very pretty. She was also very smartly and fashionably dressed, and Violet was suddenly aware of the drab gown she wore to work in. She shuffled away with the tray of dirty pots to the kitchen and peeping past her into the café Edie commented, 'Oh, Toby is in. I must just go an' say hello to 'im. Pretty girl he's got wi' 'im, ain't she?'

'Can't say as I've noticed,' Violet answered shortly, failing to see Edie's grin as she passed her.

Eventually Violet had no choice but to go back into the café but again Toby didn't even look her way. *He can suit himself*, she thought, going about her business with her nose in the air.

After a time, Toby and the young woman left and when Violet next went into the kitchen, Edie grinned. 'Looks like you've missed your chance wi' Toby,' she commented.

Violet scowled. 'Good! I hope they'll be very happy,' she answered shortly before turning and flouncing out again, ignoring Edie's chuckle.

Two days later the boxes were still there and Violet was getting annoyed. Surely Oliver could have found somewhere else by now? The watchman who had been attacked at the docks was still in a critical condition and Violet trembled when she heard Sally and Edie talking about him.

'Poor bloke,' Edie said as she rolled out the pastry for some steak and kidney pies. They were growing the menu and doing a roaring trade, and Edie was saying they might have to employ yet another helper to cope with demand. 'A wife an' four little kids he's got. Lord knows how she's managin' wi' no money comin' in. I reckon I might start takin' any leftovers round to 'er at the end of each day till he comes home – *if* he comes home that is. No doubt the poor woman will be glad of 'em.'

'I could drop them in to her,' Sally offered. 'I know where they live and I pass it every evening on me way home.'

She and Edie were getting on like a house on fire but Edie's next words struck terror into Violet's heart.

'I've been thinkin'.' She smiled at Sally. 'All this toin' an' froin' to work seems a bit pointless when we've got rooms sat empty above the new shop. We was thinkin' that we could do 'em up for Violet to live in but she seems in no rush an' neither of us minds sharin' the rooms we 'ave, so 'ow would you like to move in? I can get Violet to take you up to 'ave a look after work one evenin' if you like?'

Sally's eyes lit up. 'Oh, that would save a lot of time, so long as you're sure?' She was obviously happy with the idea.

Violet's heart began to thud and she had to think quickly. 'Er . . . yes I'd be happy to but not this evening. I, er . . . have to go out.'

'Do you now?' Edie grinned. 'Got a date, 'ave you?'

Thankfully Violet was saved from answering as she had to rush away to serve a customer. She would have to go to Anna's again and demand that Oliver remove the goods immediately. How could she ever explain to Edie what they were doing there if he didn't?

As soon as the tidying up was done that evening, Violet got changed and set off for Back Street. She cringed as she made her way through the labyrinth of filthy alleys but at last, she reached the house and began to climb the steep, rotten staircase, carefully choosing where she stepped.

On the top floor she rapped on the door and when there was no answer, she rapped again, louder this time. The door opposite opened and the woman in the low-cut gown with her heavily rouged face opened her door to scowl at her.

'What's all the bleedin' racket about?' she snapped. 'I'm entertainin' in 'ere an' I can 'ardly 'ear meself think wi' all your bangin' an' 'ammering!'

'Sorry, I'm looking for Mrs Stroud,' Violet answered falteringly.

The woman snorted. 'Well, ain't no point in lookin' there, gel. They done a moonlight the night afore last. Loaded all their stuff up onto a cart an' pissed off in the dead o' night owin' rent, they did.'

'Oh . . .' Violet looked shocked. 'Do you have any idea where they might have gone?'

The woman shook her head. 'Ain't got the foggiest idea an' I ain't much bleedin' bothered! A right snooty pair they were.'

Violet opened her mouth to thank her but the door had already slammed shut.

Outside she stood for a moment chewing her lip as she tried to think what to do next. Then an idea occurred to her, and she addressed the little urchins who were playing in the gutter.

'Do any of you children know where Mrs Stroud went? She lived on the top floor with her son. If any of you can tell me where they went there's sixpence in it for you.'

The same little boy who had squirrelled pennies out of her before rose from a conker fight he was engaged in, and stared at her thoughtfully. 'I could 'appen find out fer you but it'd cost more'n a tanner. How's about a shillin'?'

Violet didn't even have to think about it and nodded. 'Deal! What's your name?'

He stared at her suspiciously for a moment before answering, 'I's Ricky, why'd yer wanna know? An' where can I find yer to tell yer where they are?'

'If you're going to be working for me, in a manner of speaking, I just thought it would be nice if I knew your name.' Then reluctantly Violet told him where the café was. 'But don't come in when you find them,' she warned. 'Just stand outside until you catch my attention and I'll come out to you. How long do you think it will take you to trace them?'

He shrugged. ''Ow long is a piece o' string? But I'll gerr on to it straightaway so keep yer eyes peeled fer me.'

Violet nodded. 'Very well.' She paused then to ask, 'Do you live round here, Ricky?'

Again, he stared at her before answering cautiously, 'I used to but me ma died an' since then I just doss about wherever I can.'

'You mean you don't have a proper home?' Violet was appalled.

The child shrugged. 'It ain't so bad really, the folks round 'ere is good to me an' in the winter one or another of 'em usually lets me kip down in their place.'

Violet's heart went out to the poor little scrap, but the ripe smell of the place was beginning to make her feel sick and she couldn't wait to be away from it.

'All right, Ricky, do your best,' she told him with a smile, and after slipping him a few pennies in advance, she hurried away.

'I'm beginnin' to think you've got a feller,' Edie teased when she got back. 'Keep disappearin' off all the time.'

'Oh, it's nothing like that I assure you.' Violet gave her a weak smile as she removed her shawl and bonnet. 'It's just nice to get out in the fresh air and take a walk after being cooped up inside all day.'

Edie frowned. 'I know it ain't much of a life fer a young woman,' she said dolefully. 'I worry sometimes that you don't get out enough wi' folks your own age.'

'Well don't.' Violet crossed the room to kiss Edie's wrinkled cheek. 'I'm quite happy here.'

'Hmm.' Edie didn't look so sure as Violet disappeared off into her bedroom.

Once there she began to pace. What would she do if Ricky couldn't find Oliver and Anna? She was beginning to panic now. She wouldn't be able to put off showing Sally the rooms for much longer and then the cat would well and truly be out of the bag. In the end she realised that worrying was going to change nothing so she wearily changed into her nightclothes and crept into bed.

It was the early hours of the morning when a sound made her startle awake and stare at the wall that divided the two premises. There was someone moving about in the empty rooms and it could only be Oliver. He was the only person other than her and Edie who had access to a key.

Swinging her legs out of bed she draped a shawl around her shoulders before creeping through the small sitting room and down the stairs. Crossing the yard she saw the back door swinging open. Breathing a sigh of relief, she started up the stairs almost jumping out of her skin when Oliver appeared at the top of them.

'Oliver . . . you made me jump!'

He glared at her. 'Shouldn't be nosying about then, should you?'

Violet sniffed indignantly. 'This is our property. I'm just relieved you've come to move everything out.'

'Ah, about that.' He glanced over his shoulder at a huge bear of a man who had come to stand behind him. 'The thing is . . . we're not actually taking anything out just yet; we're bringing some more in.'

'What do you mean?' Violet was horrified. 'Didn't I explain that Edie wants to let those rooms to a member of staff? I can't stop her coming up here forever and if she sees that stuff all hell will break loose. How can I explain everything that's stored here?'

Oliver's face turned ugly and his lips curled back from his teeth. 'That's *your* worry not mine. *You* were the one who said I could use the rooms.'

'Yes, but that was before . . .' Violet's voice trailed away. She had been about to say before she was aware the goods might be stolen, but Oliver looked so fierce she didn't dare. 'And where have you moved to? Why didn't you give me a forwarding address?'

'Asks a lot o' questions this wench, don't she?' The large, ugly man behind Oliver snarled, and Violet noticed a large angry scar that ran from one eye down to his chin. 'Happen she needs a bloke to keep 'er in line.' He licked his lips lasciviously as he eyed Violet's shape through her thin cotton nightgown, making her heart thump with fear.

'Get back to what you were doing, Vinny, I'll handle her,' Oliver ordered, and meek as a lamb the huge man lumbered away.

'Please, Oliver . . .' Violet was beside herself with worry now and prepared to appeal to his better nature. 'Please get these things moved out for me before—'

She stopped speaking abruptly as they both heard a ruckus on the stairs and the next moment Edie appeared, holding a candle in front of her. Her grey hair was confined in a cotton night cap and a shawl was wrapped around a voluminous white nightgown.

'So, what's to do 'ere?' Her eyes narrowed at she stared at the piles of boxes stacked around the walls. 'I heard a noise an'—' She stopped talking as her eyes settled on Oliver and she scowled. 'An' what the bloody 'ell are *you* doin' 'ere. Just what's goin' on?'

'Oh Edie . . . I'm so sorry,' Violet mumbled as tears started in her eyes. This was just what she had feared. 'It's all my fault. Oliver asked me if he could store a few things up here and I agreed to it. But then you mentioned you were thinking of letting Sally have the rooms so I've just come to ask him to move them.'

Edie continued to stare around, her lips pursed. 'Hmm, I suggest you do that right now, me lad, before I call the coppers.'

Oliver's face darkened. 'I wouldn't do that if I were you,' he snarled. 'I can be gone from here in seconds and what will you tell them when they arrive? If questioned I shall tell them that I have no idea what you're on about, and then it will be you and your precious Violet who are in trouble!'

'Huh!' Edie snorted. 'An' do you really think the police would believe that me an' Violet would be capable o' cartin' all this stuff up 'ere? From what I can see of it this is some o' the stuff that's been stolen from the docks, an' I want it out of 'ere *right* now, do you 'ear me?'

Oliver's fists clenched and unclenched as he tried to control his rage. 'You've always favoured her above me, haven't you, even when we were children!'

'Oh, grow up!' Edie spat back at him, her rage matching his. 'If I have it's per'aps because I discovered early on that you were a bad 'un. Now get off my premises an' take all your stolen loot wi' you otherwise I'll chuck the lot down the stairs meself. An' don't think I won't, me lad!'

'All right, all right, I'll move it.' Oliver glowered back at her. 'Just give me one day to find somewhere else to put it, that's not so much to ask, is it?'

Edie seemed to consider this for a moment before nodding. 'All right . . . one day – but that's it. If this stuff ain't out o' here afore tomorrow night's over I'm goin' to the police.'

Oliver turned to Violet and she shrank from the look in his eyes. It was one of pure hatred. 'You're going to be *sorry* for this, you

146

little bitch!' he hissed, then turning on his heel he disappeared down the dark staircase after Vinny. Violet leant heavily against the wall. The rose-tinted glasses she had always worn when it came to Oliver had finally slipped away and now at last she saw him for what he really was: a waster and a criminal with no thought for anyone but himself.

'You silly young bugger, you,' Edie scolded. 'He could allus play you like a fiddle. I just 'ope now you can see 'im for what he is. Oliver Stroud only loves one person, an' that's 'imself!'

Tears were rolling down Violet's cheeks and her heart broke even further as she realised Edie spoke the truth.

Holding her candle high, Edie ushered Violet ahead of her and down the stairs, and once the door was again securely locked they went back to their own rooms where Edie threw some coal onto the fire and pointed to the chair. 'Sit there. We need to talk.'

Violet meekly did as she was told and Edie sat down opposite her. 'I'm so sorry for getting you into this, Edie,' she said. 'I had no idea that the stuff he was planning to bring here was stolen. He told me he'd started his own little business.'

'An' like the innocent you are you believed 'im!' Edie shook her head. He might have been able to pull the wool over Violet's eyes but he couldn't fool her, and she had a horrible feeling that this was far from over. 'I want you to pack a bag an' get away for a few days,' she told Violet.

Violet's eyes almost popped out of her head. 'What d-do you mean?' she faltered.

'Exactly what I said. I wouldn't trust that young villain as far as I could throw 'im, an' if there's to be any trouble, I want you out o' here.'

Violet shook her head. 'But it's me who caused all this. If there is going to be any bother, I should be here to deal with it.'

'I want you gone afore anyone gets 'ere in the mornin'.' Edie's voice brooked no argument. 'I shall tell the rest o' the girls that I've sent you off for a little 'oliday an' that's what I want you to 'ave. It'll do you good.'

'B-but I don't want to leave you, and where would I go?' Violet said in a choky voice. She had led a sheltered life and had never ventured anywhere on her own before. Edie had been her backbone ever since the death of her father and she didn't know how she would have coped without her, especially after the way Anna had turned her back on her.

Edie chewed on her lip for a moment before saying, 'You can go an' stay in Nuneaton wi' an old friend o' mine, Flossie Barrett. She lives in Fife Street an' we kept in touch after we left. She'll look out fer you fer a while. I'll write you a letter this evenin' to give to 'er. Don't look so worried, it won't be forever. Just a week or two, eh?' Edie leant over and patted her hand.

Violet nodded reluctantly and although she hated the thought of leaving, the decision was made.

Chapter Eighteen

With her bags packed and waiting by the door, suddenly it all felt very real, and Violet was afraid. She had never travelled anywhere on her own before.

'Right, now get yourself off to the train station,' Edie ordered. 'Look what trains are due in an' don't forget to give Flossie the letter I gave you . . . and look after yourself, d'yer hear me?'

Violet nodded, too full of emotion to speak as she and Edie hugged. The older woman was almost as upset as Violet, but she knew this was for the best, so lifting one of the bags she pressed it into Violet's hand. 'Come on now,' she urged. 'The streets will be quiet at the moment, so get yourself gone an' don't come back fer at least a week!'

Violet lifted the other bag and blinded by tears she fumbled her way down the stairs and let herself out through the yard into the ginnel that ran behind it. Just as Edie had said, the streets were quiet save for the odd person making for the docks, their hobnail boots ringing on the cobbles. A few of them looked at her curiously – it was odd to see a young woman out and about so early – but none of them troubled her as she made for the train station.

As she walked, an idea came to her. Ever since Anna had told her about her birth mother, Violet had considered trying to find her. Perhaps this would be the ideal opportunity. She knew they had moved to Hull from Nuneaton when she was a baby, so it was more than likely that her birth mother would be from there. She started to feel a stirring of excitement as she made her way to the station.

Once she had purchased her tickets she went to stand on the platform. It was now early in August and despite the heat of the days the early mornings could be nippy, so she pulled the collar of her coat up as she shivered in the breeze. The train was due in half an hour and she wished there was somewhere she could get a cup of tea, but the small tearoom on the station wasn't open yet so she found herself a bench overlooking the track and settled down to wait.

Right on time the train roared into the station in a hiss of steam and smoke and Violet hurried aboard and found herself a window seat in one of the carriages.

It was mid-afternoon when the train pulled into Trent Valley railway station in Nuneaton, and as Violet lugged her bags out onto the streets, she suddenly felt nervous again. She had never been completely on her own before and she was missing Edie already.

Taking Mrs Barrett's address from her pocket she studied it before hailing a cab and giving the address. She hoped she wouldn't be imposing on Mrs Barrett too much; thankfully she had saved quite a bit of money, so she could more than afford to pay her way if necessary, especially as she hoped it wouldn't be that long before she could return home.

Soon the cab pulled up outside a row of terraced houses. They all looked the same, with front doors that opened directly onto the road, but they seemed to be neat and tidy. She paid the cabbie, then taking a deep breath she tapped on Mrs Barrett's door.

It was opened by a small, elderly woman in a large wraparound apron, her grey hair tied into a bun on the back of her head.

'Yes, luvvie, can I help yer?' She had a kindly smile, which reassured Violet somewhat as she told her who she was and handed her Edie's letter.

'Hmm, you'd best come in then while I reads it,' the woman told her.

Violet found herself in a small room with a horsehair sofa and a huge aspidistra standing on a stand in one corner. She noted that the lace curtains were sparkling white and everywhere was so clean she was sure she could have eaten off the floor.

'So, you're little Violet. Crikey, yer were only a tiny baby when I last saw yer,' Mrs Barrett said with a smile. 'An' yer right welcome, luvvie. Any friend o' Edie's is a friend o' mine. Come on through to the back room an' I'll get yer sommat to eat.'

Violet smiled gratefully and followed her into the back room, which again was spotlessly clean. There was a small fire burning in the grate and a large tabby cat was curled up in a chair to one side of it.

'Take yer hat an' coat off an' make yerself at home while I go an' put the kettle on,' Mrs Barrett suggested, before pottering into the kitchen.

'Are you quite sure you don't mind me staying here?' Violet questioned when the little woman returned with a tray on which stood a cup of tea and a plateful of cheese sandwiches. 'I know it's awfully short notice but I can always find a hotel if—'

'I wouldn't 'ear of it,' Mrs Barrett told her firmly. 'All my brood have grown an' long since flown the nest. There's only me an' old Puss 'ere now so I'll be glad o' the company, an' yer welcome to stay as long as yer like. Now get that down yer, it'll keep yer goin' till I cook the evenin' meal an' then I'll go an' make yer a bed up. I dare say you'll be tired tonight after all the travellin'.'

'I probably will be,' Violet admitted.

That evening Mrs Barrett prepared them a tasty cottage pie and soon after, when Violet smothered a yawn, she showed her upstairs to a small room with crisp white sheets and a colourful quilted eiderdown on the bed.

The journey and the upset of the night before had tired Violet more than she had realised, so she quickly changed into her nightdress and hopped into bed. But despite her exhaustion, sleep eluded her as she fretted about what might be happening back in Hull.

The next morning Violet still had dark circles beneath her eyes when she joined Mrs Barrett in the kitchen.

'You didn't sleep so well then?' the woman asked as she poured Violet some tea. She hadn't questioned why Violet had turned up so unexpectedly, figuring the girl would tell her in her own good time if she wished to.

'No, I, er . . . it was probably because I was in a strange place. Although the bed was very comfortable,' Violet assured her hurriedly. 'Would you happen to know a lady by the name of Sadie Perkins, or at least that was her maiden name, she could well be married by now.'

The woman shook her head. 'Can't say as I do, pet. How old would she be?'

'Oh, I should think somewhere in her early forties.'

'It don't ring any bells but I'll ask me neighbour. She knows most folks around 'ere.'

'Thank you. In the meantime, I thought I might have a look around town.'

'Well, you'll find the town busy today. It's market day,' Mrs Barrett told her as she placed some scrambled eggs and slices of toast in front of her. 'Eat that up afore you go. I don't want Edie sayin' I didn't take good enough care o' yer.'

After breakfast Violet put on her bonnet and with Mrs Barrett's directions into town ringing in her ears she set off for the market place. She was surprised to find that large pens had been erected and suddenly remembered Edie telling her that a cattle market was held there twice a week. Ruddy-faced farmers were cramming sheep, cows, pigs and goats into the pens, and there were also crates full of indignantly squawking chickens. Feeling sorry for them, Violet lifted her skirts and picked her way past, wondering where they would all end up. Further on were stalls selling everything she could think of, and she tried to take her mind off her worries by meandering amongst them, admiring the goods. But it was no use. Try as she might, she couldn't get the way Oliver had treated her or her concerns for Edie out of her mind.

After a while she decided she should really focus on trying to find her birth mother, so she began to stop shoppers at random asking if they'd heard of her. By lunchtime she'd had no success so she returned to Mrs Barrett's feeling disheartened.

It was the same in the afternoon when she returned after a short rest, and she soon realised that this mission was like looking for a needle in a haystack. Sadie Perkins could have married and changed her name or moved away, in which case she would be wasting her time. Despite the exertions of the day, once again when she retired that night she tossed and turned.

Four days later, when Violet returned to Mrs Barrett's after another day trying to track down her mother, the old lady told her, 'Jess next door didn't recall yer mam, but old lady Fallows down the road a bit did.'

'Really, Mrs Barrett?'

The woman flapped her hand at her. 'Oh, fer goodness sake, call me Flossie – everyone else does. An' yes she remembers a young woman o' that name. Poor lass had a baby out o' wedlock apparently an' got chucked out by her family. They lived in Bentley Road, but I don't know which number. Might be worth askin' about a bit.'

'Oh, I will, and thank you . . . Flossie.'

The kindly woman smiled at her. 'But not tonight, eh? You've been trampin' about fer days, so have a rest this evenin' an' start again fresh tomorrow.'

Bright and early the next morning Violet set off. Flossie had told her how to get to Bentley Road, and once she had found it she stood at the end wondering where she should start. It was highly unlikely she would find her mother here, but she hoped that perhaps her grandparents might still be there, and her heart beat faster at the thought.

She began systematically knocking on doors. Some people weren't in but by the time she'd walked halfway along the street, none of the people she'd spoken to had recalled a family called

153

Perkins, and she was starting to become dispirited. She had set out that morning with such high hopes but now she was beginning to feel as if she was wasting her time again. Even so, she went doggedly on until at one of the last houses on the road, a very old woman leaning heavily on a walking stick answered the door.

'Excuse me, but would you happen to know a family called Perkins?' Violet asked politely. 'I was told they lived along here. They had a daughter called Sadie.'

'Who wants to know?' The old woman stared at her suspiciously.

'Well, I, er . . . I believe I might be related to them,' Violet said uncertainly. 'But it's actually Sadie, their daughter, that I'm trying to trace.'

'Huh! I doubt you'll manage that,' the old woman said, pulling her old shawl more tightly about her.

'Why's that? Could you just tell me where they live if you know?'

The old woman nodded. 'I can tell yer where they did live. Three doors along – but they've both been dead fer some years now an' Sadie were chucked out long before. From what I 'eard she had a baby an' they turned their backs on 'er. Then next I 'eard she'd married a local chap an' moved away, but I don't know where they went an' I've never 'eard of 'er since.'

'Oh!' Violet was devastated. She had come so close to meeting her birth family but now she was back to square one. 'Well, thank you for your help.'

She turned away despondently, and as she retraced her steps back to Flossie's house there were tears in her eyes. She was also still desperately worried about what was happening to Edie back at the café and now, after days of searching, she realised that the chances of ever discovering where her real mother was were slim. It was then that she made a decision: she was going home. She should never have let Edie persuade her to leave in the first place. It was her fault that there were stolen goods stored in the rooms above the café and if they should be discovered she couldn't allow Edie to take the blame for them.

She told Flossie of her decision immediately she got back, and after breakfast the following morning she said her goodbyes, thanking her profusely for having her, and headed for the train station. Soon she was winging her way back to Hull. But as the train chugged along a sense of foreboding overtook her. What if the goods had been discovered and Edie had been blamed for them? Even now she could be languishing in a cell and the thought was almost more than Violet could bear. She would never forgive herself if anything happened to Edie.

Every minute began to feel like an hour and by the time the train finally pulled into Hull Violet was in a terrible state. As soon as she got out of the station, she took a cab to the café, and when it drew up outside, she was relieved to find that everything appeared to be as it should be. It was nearly closing time and through the window she could see customers still seated at the tables.

When she stepped through the door Sally rushed to greet her. 'Eeh, love, what are you doin' back so soon?' she questioned.

Edie popped her head round the kitchen door and she too looked surprised to see her, and beckoned her into the kitchen.

'Are you all right, Edie?' Violet asked before the woman could get a word in.

Edie nodded. 'O' course I am. Now shut that door, we don't want no nosy parkers listenin' in on us.'

Violet did as she was told and Edie went on, 'The panic's over. The stuff's all gone.'

'Gone? Gone where?'

Edie grinned. 'Soon as you were out of the way I got Lottie's Frank an' some of his cronies round 'ere to shift the stuff. Toby Brabinger came to help an' all. They carried it all down an' dumped it in the ginnel. Far as I know Oliver must 'ave 'ad it collected cos within a few hours the whole lot were gone.'

'But what if Oliver *didn't* collect it?' Violet looked worried and a little put out to hear that Toby Brabinger had poked his nose in again. 'If anyone else made off with it he's going to be very angry.'

Edie shrugged. 'Then happen it'll teach 'im a lesson,' she said unperturbed. 'But why are you back so soon? I thought we agreed you'd stay a week.'

'I couldn't stay away any longer; I was too worried about you,' Violet admitted. 'Flossie was amazing, she made me so welcome, and she sends you her love. I spent the time there trying to track down my birth family, but I had no luck. I found out where Sadie's parents used to live, but that's as far as I got. They died years ago and Sadie moved away. No one seems to know where she went.'

Edie looked vaguely uncomfortable as she turned back to washing the dishes in the sink. 'Aw well, you're back now so hopefully we'll get back to some sort o' normality. Just promise me you won't let Oliver talk you into doin' anythin' like that again. Now that the rooms are empty Sally's made a start on getting' 'em ready to move into. You can give 'er a hand if you like. But only if yer sure you don't want 'em?'

'I'm quite happy upstairs with you. And of course I'll help her,' Violet conceded.

'Oh, and by the way, a letter arrived for you while you were gone,' Edie informed her. 'It's upstairs on the mantelpiece an' it looks important. It's got the solicitor's address on the back.'

Violet frowned. Why would a solicitor be writing to her? With her curiosity aroused, she went up to the sitting room and took the letter from the shelf. From the address, she knew it was from her father's solicitor. She remembered Mr Chapman from when he'd read her father's will. He and her father had been quite good friends, sometimes enjoying a game of golf together and Violet liked the man.

Slitting the envelope open she removed the sheet of paper inside.

Dear Miss Stroud,

I would appreciate it if you could make an appointment to visit me at your earliest convenience at the address attached where I hope to inform you of something to your advantage.

Yours sincerely
Mr C. Chapman.

Violet was puzzled. Something to her advantage? But what could it be? The solicitor's office was in Anlaby Street off the High Street so she wouldn't have far to go, but when she glanced at the clock she realised it would be too late to visit him today, so she would have to do it the following morning.

'What was it about?' Edie asked when she joined her upstairs shortly after.

'I have no idea but I'll pop round and make an appointment first thing in the morning. The letter said there might be something to my advantage I should know about.'

'I think you should,' Edie agreed. 'Sounds to me like you might have some money comin' your way.'

'Money? But who from?' Violet was baffled. She couldn't think of anyone who might leave her anything.

'Well, you'll find out soon enough, won't yer?' Edie said matter-of-factly.

The next morning, as soon as the breakfast rush was over, Edie called Violet into the kitchen. 'Go an' make that appointment at the solicitor's now. They should be open. We can manage 'ere till yer get back.'

'Are you sure?'

Edie rolled her eyes. 'We managed well enough while you were away, didn't we? Now go an' do as you're told an' be sure to get changed first. You'll want to look smart.'

With a sigh Violet did as she was ordered.

Chapter Nineteen

Outside the offices of Chapman and Lloyd Solicitors, Violet paused to smooth down the skirt of her blue gown, then taking a deep breath she entered. A middle-aged woman was seated at a desk in the reception area, and she smiled as Violet approached her.

'Good morning, may I help you? Do you have an appointment?'

'Er . . . no, I don't, I came to make one. I received this.' Violet handed the woman the letter and after reading it the woman nodded towards a row of chairs.

'Do take a seat, Miss Stroud. I'll go through and have a word with Mr Chapman.'

Violet self-consciously did as she was told and soon after the woman reappeared. 'Mr Chapman will see you now, Miss Stroud. You're lucky, he doesn't have an appointment for another half an hour.'

'Oh!' Violet gulped. She hadn't expected to be able to see him so soon.

Rising, she followed the woman to a door and after opening it for her the woman encouraged, 'Do go in, my dear.' Then in a softer tone. 'And don't look so nervous. Mr Chapman doesn't bite, I assure you.'

Violet stepped past her into a bright office where the elderly man sat at a highly polished desk covered in papers. He had grey hair that matched his beard and moustache, and he rose to hold his hand out to greet her.

'Ah, Miss Stroud. How nice it is to see you again. Do take a seat while I get the file.'

He crossed to a large filing cabinet and after searching through it for a few minutes he returned with a hefty file. 'I suppose you are wondering what this is all about?'

'I, er . . . yes, I am rather.'

He nodded. 'Then I hope you will be happy with what I'm about to tell you.' He steepled his fingers and stared at her for a moment before asking, 'Were you aware that you had an aunt?'

Violet nodded. 'Yes, she was my father's sister I believe, but I understand they became estranged shortly before I was born. I know my father deeply regretted it, and unfortunately, I've never met her.'

'I'm sorry to tell you that you never will now. Mrs Fairhurst died shortly after your father, but I'm delighted to tell you that she has left you a very substantial legacy.'

Violet looked stunned. 'B-but why would she do that? She didn't even know me.'

'No, she didn't, but she knew of you, and because she and her husband sadly never had any children you are her last living relative, so everything she owned passes to you. She requested it in her will. Look, I have it here.'

Violet looked stunned as the solicitor handed her the will so she could see it for herself. 'So is my uncle dead too?' she asked eventually in a shaky voice.

He nodded solemnly. 'Yes, he died about four years ago. You've probably heard of Fairhurst's Boatyard?'

Violet nodded. It was one of the largest boatyards in Hull.

'Your uncle owned it, along with many fishing trawlers. It's a very healthy business,' he told her. 'And when he died everyone thought your aunt would sell it, but she didn't. Instead, she appointed a manager and with his help she kept it running admirably. Of course, it will be up to you now whether you wish to sell or not.'

Violet's eyes popped. '*What?* You mean that *I* own a boatyard now?'

He smiled. 'You most certainly do, as well as a very beautiful house, all its contents and any monies in the bank, which are quite substantial. In fact, my dear, you are now a very wealthy young woman.'

For one of the very few times in her life, Violet was speechless and could only stare at him open-mouthed. Never in her wildest dreams could she have imagined being in this position and it was more than she could take in. 'Did you know my aunt personally, Mr Chapman?' Violet realised her voice was trembling.

'Yes, I had that honour. Your Aunt Amelia was a charming woman. As you know, I also knew your father very well. Not only was I his solicitor, we met often at a gentleman's club we attended and played the occasional game of golf together. He confided to me that he and your aunt were very close when they were younger.'

'So, what happened to make them estranged?'

'Well . . .' He stared at her uncertainly for a moment, wondering whether it would be professional for him to comment, but the poor young lady looked so confused that eventually he went on, 'Your grandparents died when your father was just sixteen years old and Amelia became like a mother to him. They were very close but when he met your stepmother Amelia didn't approve of her. They had numerous rows about Anna but your father was smitten and so he and Amelia ended up parting company. Even so Amelia made it her mission to watch from afar and soon discovered that your brother, or who she thought was your brother, was no relation to her. Then you came along, and word reached your aunt that Anna wasn't your real mother. I hope you were already aware of that?'

Violet nodded. 'Yes, but I wasn't until shortly after my father died when my stepmother threw me out. It was quite a shock to discover that Anna wasn't my birth mother and Oliver wasn't my brother.'

'I can quite believe that. I also believe that your father moved you all here from the Midlands when you were a baby in the hope of reconciling with your aunt, as she moved to Hull when she married your uncle, but sadly it didn't happen.'

When Violet remained silent, he said kindly, 'Would you like me to take you to look at the house?'

She nodded numbly. A house! She had her own house, and a business, it was all so hard to believe, and she kept thinking she was going to wake up from a dream.

'I, er . . . yes, that would be most kind of you.'

'How would this evening suit? I could perhaps bring my wife along. She and Amelia were great friends and you might feel a little more comfortable with a woman present. I could collect you from the café at, shall we say seven o'clock this evening?'

Violet stood up but her legs seemed to have developed a life of their own and she wobbled dangerously, steadying herself on the edge of the desk. 'Th-thank you.'

Again, he shook her hand and she left the office with her mind spinning. She could remember her father speaking of his sister occasionally but never in front of Anna and now she knew why. It seemed that she had been the cause of the rift between them.

Somehow, she made it back to the café in a daze and the second she walked through the door Sally and Edie rushed to her to ask in unison, 'Well?'

'I . . .' She continued walking until she got to the kitchen, with both following close behind her.

'Spit it out then! Has the cat got your tongue, girl?' Edie said in her forthright way.

'It seems my aunt has died and left me a house . . . and a business . . . and some money.'

Edie's face broke into a smile. 'Why, that's wonderful! She was a lovely lass, though I'm sad to hear she's passed. But never mind that for now, where is the house?'

Violet stared at her blankly. 'I-I never thought to ask.'

'You never *thought* to ask?' Edie was flabbergasted. 'Why ever not? Why, do you realise what this means? You'll be set for life. You'll never 'ave to work again.'

'I didn't ask because it all came as such a shock. And if you knew my aunt, why didn't you ever tell me about her, Edie?'

Edie shook her head. 'It weren't my place to. Just the mention of 'er name would send yer stepmam into a towerin' rage. Her an' Amelia never did get on, but at one time Amelia an' your dad were inseparable. I stayed on wi' 'em to cook for 'em after your grandparents died an' we were all as happy as Larry till Anna came on the scene, then it were family at war. Round about that time Amelia met her 'usband, who were visitin' the town, an' when they got married, they moved 'ere. I allus felt that were part o' the reason your dad wanted to come to Hull, in the hope they could become reconciled, but Anna weren't havin' a bar of it an' allus stood in their way.'

'But how did my aunt know that I wasn't Anna's child?' Violet questioned. Even she hadn't known until after her father's death.

Edie had the grace to look uncomfortable. 'I dare say I may 'ave told 'er,' she admitted guiltily. 'We still wrote to each other from time to time, see? Not that I ever let on to your dad, it would 'ave opened up too many wounds for him, God rest 'is soul.'

'And was it you who told her that Oliver wasn't my father's child as well?'

As Edie bowed her head, Violet had her answer. 'How sad it is that I never got to know her,' Violet said softly. 'I would have loved to have had an aunt as I was growing up.'

'Hmm, an' as things were you only 'ad me,' Edie said glumly.

Violet hurried forward to give her a hug. 'Don't ever say that. You were my everything. I don't know what I would have done without you. It was always you I turned to and not Anna. She never had time for me but you were always there, and I know why, don't I?'

Sally had watched this scene silently and Violet was touched to see the tears on her cheeks. They had grown close in the time she had been working there and she thought herself very lucky to have such good friends, even if Oliver had let her down. She was still stinging from the way he had tricked her into allowing stolen goods to come into the café and yet she found she still couldn't hate him. Some feelings just ran too deep, she supposed. But for now, despite the exciting news, there was work to be done. There would be plenty of time to speak about it later, so she hurried upstairs to change.

Toby Brabinger appeared mid-morning, with the same young lady Violet had seen before at his side. She supposed she should thank him for the way he had helped Edie and Sally get the stolen goods out of the place, so she reluctantly crossed to them and after a curt nod to the young lady, who she saw was very pretty indeed, she said quietly, 'Thanks for helping Edie out.'

'Always happy to help.' He gave her a charming smile, just as Edie bustled out of the kitchen.

'Has she told you 'er good news?' she asked him excitedly.

He frowned. 'What good news would that be?'

Edie lowered her voice and told him of the inheritance, and Violet flushed. She would rather have kept it to herself for now, at least until she'd had time to take it all in.

Toby beamed and shook her hand. 'Congratulations, Violet. I couldn't be happier for you. I dare say you'll be leaving here now.'

Violet blinked. She hadn't even had time to think that far ahead yet. To hide her confusion, she left to attend another customer, wondering why her hand was tingling.

Both Sally and Edie spent a fair amount of time chatting to Toby and the young lady, and once again Violet felt peeved. Why he had to keep flaunting the girl in here she had no idea – although deep down she knew that she had no fair reason to care. He was entitled to see who he liked, and it wasn't as if she even liked Toby.

The rest of the day passed painfully slowly and as soon as they closed Violet hurried upstairs to get changed, ready for Mr Chapman to pick her up.

'Won't you come with us, Edie?' she pleaded. 'I'd feel so much better if I had someone I know with me.'

Edie had secretly been hoping she'd ask and didn't take much persuading, so they were both ready and waiting when a smart carriage pulled up outside.

'That'll be Mr Chapman,' Violet said as she fastened the ribbons of her bonnet beneath her chin. 'Let's go and have a look at this house, shall we? I can't imagine it will be that big if only my aunt and uncle lived there.'

Mr Chapman's wife was a charming woman and she soon put them at their ease.

'You're in for a pleasant surprise when you see the house, my dear,' she told Violet. 'I often visited Amelia there for morning coffee or afternoon tea. I must admit, I miss her dreadfully. We were great friends. The house overlooks Victoria Docks and has wonderful views.'

Violet was surprised. Victoria Docks was one of the posher residential areas of the town where the gentry lived. 'Does the house have a name?' she asked.

Mrs Chapman nodded. 'It does indeed. Seagull's Roost. It's nice, isn't it?'

While Mrs Chapman and Edie chatted away like old friends, Violet studied her surroundings through the carriage window. Eventually they turned into the road facing the docks and Violet peered at the houses. They all looked very grand. Soon the carriage drew to a halt and as Mr Chapman helped the ladies out of the cab, Violet stared open-mouthed at the tall three-storey building. It was surrounded by a small metal fence with steps to one side of the entrance that she guessed must lead down to the kitchen. Tall sash cord windows sat on either side of the door, which was painted a bright cheery red with a gleaming brass knocker in the middle of it. As they mounted the three marble steps leading up to it, Violet was sure that there must be some mistake. This huge house couldn't be all hers?

'Here we are then, my dear. Here's the key to Seagull's Roost. I'm sure you'd like to be the first to enter, seeing as you are the new owner,' said Mr Chapman jovially.

Violet took the key from him feeling as if she was caught up in a dream and inserted it into the lock.

Chapter Twenty

As they entered a large hallway, a young girl in a maid's outfit rushed forward to greet them and Violet was so startled that she almost dropped the key.

'Ah, Dora, I've brought your new mistress to meet you,' Mr Chapman told the girl. Turning to Violet he added apologetically, 'I'm so sorry, I should have told you, your aunt asked in her will if the three staff could be kept on until you took over. Of course, should you decide to sell the place they will have to be given notice, but as I know your aunt was more than a little fond of them all, I rather hope that won't be the case.'

He looked back to Dora and told her gently, 'Dora, this is Miss Stroud, the new owner of the house.'

Violet blushed as the girl bobbed her knee respectfully. She was about the same height as Violet and looked to be about sixteen or seventeen with a fresh face and blonde hair.

'Pleased to meet you, miss,' the girl said cheerily. 'I'm Dora, the maid 'ere an' there's also Mrs Cannon the cook an' Stan the gardener-cum-groom-cum-odd-job-man. I'll introduce you to 'em whenever you like.'

'Th-thank you, Dora, it's very nice to meet you,' Violet croaked, feeling totally out of her depth. She couldn't imagine having her own staff.

'I was hoping you might show Miss Stroud around, seeing as you know the house so well, Dora,' Mr Chapman coaxed.

The girl nodded obligingly. 'Course I will, sir. Shall we start in 'ere? This is the drawin' room. It were one o' the mistress's favourite rooms. She liked to 'ave tea in 'ere of a mornin' because there's such a nice view of the docks from this window.' Dora opened a door and ushered them into a room that took Violet's breath away. The furniture was solid and very old but years of polish had brought it to a mirror-like shine. Two comfortable wing chairs stood either side of the fireplace and squashy sofas and small occasional tables were dotted about. Lovely oil paintings hung on the walls and heavy velvet drapes framed the windows. It was a warm, welcoming room and Violet loved it at first sight. Next, Dora took them to the day room, which again was comfortably furnished, then they moved on to a library that again took Violet's breath away. Shelves stocked with books reached from floor to ceiling and she could imagine how wonderful it would be to be locked away in there. There was also a large office boasting a huge mahogany desk and a leather captain's chair. A separate dining room revealed an enormous table with twelve chairs around it, and the biggest sideboard Violet had ever seen. Further along the hallway a door opened on to stairs that led down to an enormous kitchen where Violet met Mrs Cannon, a stout elderly lady with steel-grey hair drawn into a bun on the back of her head and a kindly smile. Beyond that was a garden full of flowers and trees and to the side of that was a stable and a yard for the horse that had pulled her aunt's trap. Next, they began the tour of the upstairs, which revealed four very good-sized bedrooms, two of which had amazing views of the docks, and an indoor bathroom. A further staircase led up to what Dora informed her were the servants' rooms.

'It's huge,' Violet said as she tried to take it all in. She was still having to pinch herself to believe this was real.

'I'm sure you'll get used to it,' Mr Chapman told her, but Violet wasn't so sure. The place felt far too large for just one person and if she didn't need to work anymore, what would she do with herself all day? 'And if you find that you don't settle you could always sell it,' he pointed out.

'Oh, but I do hope you won't do that,' his wife added quickly. 'I'm sure Amelia would have been heartbroken if it were to be sold out of the family. She and her husband were so happy here and she loved every brick of it.'

They were back in the drawing room by this time and Mr Chapman withdrew some papers from a large file he had brought with him and handed them to Violet.

'This is the sum of money that your aunt had in the bank,' he told her solemnly.

Violet stared at the amount and gasped. Never in her wildest dreams had she thought of having this sort of cash.

'I shall be visiting the bank in the morning and will have everything signed over to you, my dear, and from then on you will be able to withdraw what you need whenever you wish.'

Violet plonked down heavily on the nearest chair. 'I can't believe that someone I never knew would leave all this to me,' she said wonderingly.

Mrs Chapman chuckled. 'Oh, you may not have known her, but she always kept an eye on you,' she informed her. 'She even knew what schools you attended and I truly believe that if it hadn't been for your stepmother, she and your father would have made their peace a long time ago.'

'But why did Anna hate her so much?'

Mrs Chapman sighed. 'From what she confided to me I gather Amelia had a suspicion that Anna was already pregnant when she wooed your father into marrying her and she accused her of being a fortune hunter. Of course, she was proved to be right, but Anna never forgave her.'

'If you remember I told you we kept in touch when she came to live 'ere an' it were me as told 'er about your real mam leavin' you wi' us. That's why she were so keen that all this should come to you one day. She knew that you were blood related whereas she and Oliver weren't,' said Edie.

'Oh . . . I see!' Violet's head was in a whirl.

Mr Chapman went on, 'Would you like some time to think about things before you move in? I do realise that all this must have come as a shock to you.'

Edie frowned as a thought occurred to her. 'But Violet ain't twenty-one yet. Her stepmam wouldn't be her legal guardian, would she? If she is, she could take control of everythin' till Violet comes of age, an' knowin' her an' Oliver like I do I can promise you that there won't be a lot left by then.'

The kindly gentleman smiled. 'You need have no fears on that score,' he assured them. 'Violet's aunt instructed me to act as her guardian until she comes of age, so all is well. Although I will admit I wouldn't be surprised if Mrs Stroud tried to claim something when word reaches her. But have no fear, should that situation arise, I'll deal with it.' Turning to Violet he asked, 'Have you any questions, my dear?'

Violet shook her head. It was all too much to take in and she just wanted to get back to the cosy little rooms above the café to try and digest everything.

'In that case we'll be on our way. Perhaps you would like me to give you the keys to the house now and then you are free to move in and decide what you want to do with it in your own time.' He placed a set of keys into Violet's hand and again she felt as if she must be caught up in a dream.

The cook and Dora waved her off after telling her to be sure to let them know when she wanted to join them so that they could have everything ready for her, and on the way home in the carriage the solicitor told her gently, 'We should also arrange a meeting with Mr Pope, the manager at the boatyard, so he can explain what running the business entails. Your aunt tended to leave much of the running of the place to him, which I have to say he has done admirably, but again it is up to you whether you want to keep the business on or sell it. Either way I can instruct you if you require my services. Oh, and by the way, I took the liberty of taking some money out of the bank for you so that you might purchase anything you feel you might need until the account has been signed into your name. There's forty pounds here. I trust that will be enough.'

Violet took the money and thanked him, and soon after she and Edie were dropped off at the café where Violet made them both a welcome cup of tea.

'Well, my love, seems to me you're set up for life now,' Edie commented as they sat drinking their tea. 'There'll be no more sloggin' away downstairs for you; you're a very wealthy young woman.'

Violet sighed. 'I just can't imagine having nothing to do all day,' she confided. 'And anyway, I wouldn't dream of going until you've found a replacement for me.'

Edie chuckled. 'No need to worry about me, pet. Sally will be movin' into the rooms next door any day now, so I'll not be on me own, an' there's never a shortage o' women who'll be glad of a job. An' as for doin' nothin' all day, there's lots you could be doin'. I happen to know that Amelia helped out wi' loads o' different charities. You could carry on where she left off an' do some good.'

'It sounds like you'll be glad to get rid of me,' Violet said peevishly.

Edie laughed. 'Don't talk so daft. This is a wonderful opportunity for you an' you should grab it wi' both hands. It's what your aunt wanted.'

An idea suddenly occurred to Violet. 'Why don't you come with me? I'll have more than enough money to keep us both and you could retire.'

Edie shook her head stubbornly. 'I'm grateful for the offer but I'd not want to leave this place. I've worked hard to build it up to what it is now an' I like bein' me own boss. Anyway, you'll be meetin' a young man an' gettin' wed one o' these days an' then you won't want an old crone like me livin' wi' you.'

'I would,' Violet said heatedly. 'You've been more of a mother to me than Anna ever was and seeing as I can't find my real mother, you'd be the next best thing to have close to me. In fact, even if I had found her, I'd still want you with me. But there is one thing I shall insist on, I want you to have my shares in the café so that you're the sole owner again. I won't need them now, will I?'

Edie was silent for a moment and at one point opened her mouth as if there was something she wanted to say, but then obviously thinking better of it she clamped it shut again. Eventually she smiled, saying, 'Very well, if you're sure that's what yer want. But first thing in the morning you're going to go shopping for some clothes that befit yer new station, me girl. Admittedly you're turned out better than most, yer dad saw to that, but even so, Anna were always careful how much you spent. You can use some o' the money Mr Chapman gave you last night. We can't have you takin' up residency in your new 'ome dressed like one o' the servants.'

'There's nothing wrong with my clothes,' Violet stated indignantly, but deep down she knew Edie was right. She had never had the means to spend on anything extravagant before and it felt strange to know that she could now.

As soon as the shops were open the next morning Edie made her go and get changed. 'Go on,' she ordered, 'me an' the others can manage here till you get back an' don't dare come back wi' nuthin', do you 'ear me?'

Violet set off for the shops, staring at the displays in the windows until eventually she entered one of the more expensive ones that Anna had favoured, where a middle-aged woman approached her with a smarmy smile. 'May I help you, miss?'

'Er . . . yes please.' Edie had made her a list of the things she thought she would need and when the woman read it, she beamed. It looked like it was going to be a good morning for sales.

'Right, miss, if you'd like to come this way, I'll show you our day gowns. Of course, if there are any that you like they can be altered to fit you.'

Violet chose two and the petticoats and underwear to go with them, then she was taken up to the next floor to look at the bonnets where she chose two to match her new gowns. 'And perhaps miss would like a cloak to go with them?' the assistant purred.

Before Violet knew it, it was almost lunchtime and she realised there was no way she would be able to carry all her purchases home. As well as the gowns and bonnets she had bought new nightwear and shoes, and now she was feeling shocked at the amount she had spent on herself all in one go.

'Don't worry, miss, we offer a delivery service,' the shop assistant told her. 'Just give me your address and your purchases will be delivered within the hour.'

And so Violet left the shop and made her way back to the café in a trance.

That evening, when the café closed, Edie, Sally, Lottie and Maisie stayed behind to examine Violet's new wardrobe, chattering excitedly as she laid everything out for their approval.

'I suppose now you've got the clothes to look the part, the next question is, when are you goin' to move into your house?' Edie questioned and when Violet didn't immediately answer she went on, 'I reckon this weekend would be a good time; Sunday perhaps? That would give your staff time to get everythin' ready for you.'

The others nodded in agreement, and it hit Violet like a ton of bricks just how different her life was about to become.

'Come on now, pet, there's no point in delayin',' Edie urged when she saw Violet's hesitation.

Before she could answer, however, Sally started to cough violently. She hadn't been too well for the last couple of weeks and Edie was growing worried about her. 'An' it's a trip to the doctor's for you tomorrer,' she told Sally sternly. 'This 'as gone on quite long enough. Maisie, run an' fetch 'er a glass o' water, pet.'

They all looked on with concern until the coughing had stopped and Sally smiled at them sheepishly. 'I'm all right, really I am,' she assured them. 'I've always 'ad a weak chest but it's nothin' to be worried about. I'll be right as ninepence in a couple o' days.'

Edie wasn't so sure, but she let it go for now, although she was determined that from now on, she'd keep a closer eye on her.

The rest of the week passed in a blur for Violet. She instructed Mr Chapman to sign her shares in the café over to Edie and he introduced her to Mr Pope, the manager of the boatyard, who seemed to be a very capable, trustworthy man.

'Have you decided what you want to do with the business yet, Miss Stroud?' he asked, and when she shook her head uncertainly, he smiled at her kindly. 'It's quite all right, my dear. I'm happy to continue running the business for as long as you like, and I will of course make sure that you have access to all the books.'

Mr Chapman also gave her a bank book in her name, which meant that from then on, she would have access to all her late aunt's money whenever she wanted it.

Violet was still struggling to get used to her new status but eventually agreed to do as Edie suggested and move into her new home that weekend. So, looking every inch the fashionable young lady in a soft-green day dress with a high neck, fitted waist and small bustle, and wearing a matching bonnet, she set off one bright sunny morning to inform her new staff, who gave her a warm greeting.

'You'll have to tell me when and how much you are paid,' she told them. 'And because I've never run a house on my own before I'll be very grateful for any help you can give me.'

'Don't you worry about nothin', me dear,' Mrs Cannon, or Cook as she preferred to be known, told her kindly. 'I've allus had housekeepin' money an' seen to the orderin' of groceries an' coal, an' anythin' else we need, though of course if you'd prefer to do it yourself . . .?'

'Oh no,' Violet answered hastily. 'I don't want to upset your routine and obviously my aunt was happy with whatever you were doing so I'm sure I will be too.' It had felt strange when she first arrived to unlock the door with her own key and she couldn't help but feel that she should have knocked. She still couldn't quite believe that this beautiful house was really hers. 'I, er, came to ask you if it would be all right if I moved in on Sunday?'

'Why, bless me soul, it's your house you can move in whenever you like,' Cook told her warmly. 'An' it's right welcome you'll be, ain't it?' she said to the rest of the staff, who nodded in agreement.

After this meeting, Mr Chapman arranged for her possessions and clothes to be moved to Seagull's Roost in his carriage on the Saturday, and suddenly it was Sunday morning and time for her to go to her new home.

'Oh Edie, I'm going to miss you so much,' she said in a quavering voice as she hugged her.

'Oh, get off wi' you. It ain't as if you're never goin' to see me again, is it?' Edie said brusquely, although her own eyes were teary. 'You'll be sick o' me poppin' in an' you know you'll allus be welcome 'ere. Now get off wi' you an' 'ave a good life. Your dad would be so proud if he could see you now.'

And so, at last Violet left the little café she had come to know as home, and with very mixed feelings set off for her new one.

Chapter Twenty-One

Two weeks after Violet had moved into her new home, Mr Chapman's secretary entered his office to tell him, 'There's a lady and gentleman here to see you, if you have time?'

He raised an eyebrow. 'And could they not make an appointment?'

'They said it's urgent and seeing as your next appointment isn't for an hour, I told them I'd ask if you have time to see them now, sir.'

'And their names?'

'Mrs and Mr Stroud.'

'Ah!' Mr Chapman had been half expecting a visit, so laying his pen down he told the woman, 'Show them in, Miss Hemshaw, but tell them I can only spare a few minutes.'

A few moments later, she ushered Anna and Oliver into the room. Anna had taken great pains over her appearance and was dressed in a smart two-piece costume with a matching bonnet, and she flashed the solicitor a dazzling smile as she extended her gloved hand.

'Mr Chapman, how good of you to see us. It's wonderful to see you again,' she purred.

He shook her hand and gestured to the two seats in front of his desk. Once they were seated, he asked, 'And how may I help you, Mrs Stroud?'

'Well . . .' Another dazzling smile. 'I think it might be more of a case of me helping you – or rather one of your clients. It has come to our attention that my stepdaughter has come into quite a sizeable inheritance, but as you know she has not yet come of age. I believe that, since the death of my husband, I am her legal

175

guardian, and I have no doubt that she will need me to help her manage her finances and the running of the house she now owns until she turns twenty-one. She is so very young to have to cope on her own, don't you think?'

Mr Chapman stifled a smile. From what he'd heard Anna hadn't been too concerned about that when she had kicked poor Violet out into the street following her father's death.

'That's most kind of you, Mrs Stroud, but rest assured your help will not be needed.'

The smile slipped and Anna scowled at him. 'What do you mean?'

'I mean that your late husband's sister appointed myself as Violet's guardian in her will,' he informed her. 'And I can assure you that she is managing very well. She has a very supportive staff to look after her and I keep an eye on her business interests.'

Anna looked shocked and angry. 'But why would she do that? It should be *my* place to look after her.'

He shook his head. 'I have no idea why she chose to do it, Mrs Stroud, but as I said, you can rest assured that Violet is being well taken care of. Now, is there anything else I can help you with?' He was keen to end the meeting. He could hardly bear to look at the woman or her sullen-faced son.

Anna bounced to her feet, her cheeks flushed with indignation. 'No . . . that will be all for now. But I warn you, you haven't heard the last of this. I shall be seeking legal advice from another solicitor. It should have been me that was appointed as her guardian.' And with that she flounced from the room leaving Mr Chapman with a very unprofessional glow of satisfaction. After the way she had treated Violet, as far as he was concerned it served her right if she didn't have two ha'pennies to rub together. He should warn Violet to expect a visit, though. He had a feeling Anna wasn't a woman to give up without a fight if there was something in it for her.

He wouldn't have smiled could he have overheard the conversation Anna and Oliver were having outside, however.

'Right, I think it's time for desperate measures if we're going to get our hands on that little bitch's money,' Anna stormed as she marched along with Oliver almost running to keep up with her.

'What do you mean, Mama?'

'What I mean is, we have to change tack. The stupid girl has always hero-worshipped you, so now it's time we used that to our advantage.' When Oliver still looked bemused, she sighed. He could be incredibly slow at times. 'She knows that you aren't blood related, doesn't she? So what's to stop you coming together? As man and wife, I mean! Think of the advantages it would bring us.'

As Oliver realised the implications of her words a slow smile spread across his face.

One blustery October morning, Violet was in the day room reading the newspaper when Dora tapped on the door and poked her head around it to tell her, 'Please, miss, there's a gentleman 'ere askin' to see you.'

'Did he give his name?'

Dora nodded. 'He said it's Mr Stroud.'

Violet's heart began to thump painfully. Oliver! She hadn't set eyes on him for months, not since the awful business with the stolen goods, but Mr Chapman had warned her that this could happen.

'Show him in please, Dora, and perhaps you could bring us some coffee?'

When Oliver appeared in the doorway, her heart gave a little leap. Even after the way he had treated her she couldn't deny that she still had strong feelings for him. He had been her adored older brother for many years, after all.

Oliver was holding his hat in his hands and he smiled sheepishly. 'Violet . . . why, you look absolutely stunning. Quite the lady of the manor now. Mother and I heard about your good fortune and I thought I'd come to say how pleased we are for you. I also wanted to make my peace with you over what happened between us over the goods I stored at Edie's. I promise you I had no idea they were stolen. I was working for Ned Banks at the time and I thought everything was legal and above board. Can you forgive me? I've missed you so much.'

Before Violet knew what was happening, he strode across the room and raising her hand he kissed it gently. It was time to turn on the charm and begin to woo her. But it would have to be done slowly, he didn't want to frighten her.

Violet felt colour flood into her cheeks. Oliver could charm the birds off the trees when he had a mind to, and despite the fact that she had promised herself he was part of her past, she felt herself weakening.

'I, er . . . won't you take a seat?'

He sat down on the sofa and patted the space next to him. 'Won't you come and join me? It will make my neck ache if I have to keep looking up at you.'

Violet chose to sit in a wing chair opposite him instead, and she was relieved when Dora appeared soon after with a tray of coffee.

The girl placed it down on a small table and asked, 'Would you like me to pour, miss?'

'No . . . no thank you, Dora, I'll do it.'

Violet could feel Oliver's eyes fixed on her as, with shaking hands, she poured the coffee into the delicate china cups.

'Two sugars, is it?'

He chuckled. 'You should know, we lived together for long enough.'

She made no comment but passed the cup and saucer to him, then lifting her own she asked, 'So, was there anything else you wanted, Oliver?'

'Just to see you.' He put his cup down with a deep sigh and ran his hand through his hair, looking upset. 'I didn't realise how much I was going to miss you until we parted on bad terms.'

'Let's put that behind us now.' Violet was keen to change the subject. 'And how is your mother?'

Another sigh. 'Actually, she's not at all well. We're living in a rather . . . shall I say humble apartment? No . . . I won't lie to you; we have one room in a slum dwelling, which is even worse than where we were before. The walls are running with damp, and cockroaches and rats come out of the skirting boards every night. It's like being trapped in a nightmare. I'm doing the best I can to find work so that I can move us to somewhere slightly better, but it isn't easy at this time of the year.'

'I see. I'm sorry to hear that,' Violet muttered.

'I, er, was wondering . . . Well, I know it's taking a liberty, but I was hoping you could have Mother to live here with you for a time, just until our circumstances improve? I can stay there; it doesn't matter about me.'

Violet was horrified at the thought. 'I'm afraid I'd have to take advice from Mr Chapman about that,' she said guardedly. 'He is my guardian, you see, until I come of age. The house is actually in trust for me until then, and any changes to who lives here have to be approved by him.'

Just for a moment the pleasant smile slipped. 'So, you don't actually own the house yet?' he queried.

'Not officially until I'm twenty-one.'

'I see.' He stared thoughtfully towards the window for a time as the uncomfortable silence stretched between them, but suddenly he was all smiles again.

'Well, I won't keep you any longer.' He lifted his cup and drained it before standing. 'I'll leave it to you to put my suggestion to Mr Chapman, but if he refuses the request, I'd still like us to see more of each other.'

Violet didn't know what to say. Her heart was saying that this was what she wanted too but her head was telling her that it wasn't a good idea.

When Oliver had left Violet crossed to the window to watch him striding away down the street. She was still standing there when Dora came to take the tea tray away.

'Who were that then?' she asked.

'He was my brother, or at least I thought he was until my father died and I discovered that Oliver and I aren't blood related.'

Dora wrinkled her nose as she piled the empty cups onto the tray. 'I'd watch 'im if I were you, miss. There were somethin' about 'im I didn't take to.'

Violet grinned. 'Don't worry, Dora, I will.'

By chance Mr Chapman called in to see Violet that very evening and when she told him of Oliver's visit and his suggestion that Anna should move in with her, he nodded.

'I rather expected something like this. Did you agree to it?'

When Violet shook her head, he sighed with relief. 'Thank goodness for that. I really think it would be a mistake.'

'So do I,' she admitted. 'Anna never had time for me when I was growing up and she couldn't wait to get rid of me when Papa died, so I don't know why she would want to live with me again now.'

Mr Chapman raised his eyebrows and spread his hands. 'I should think that's rather obvious. Somewhere to live rent-free and have servants to wait on her again. No, my dear, I would strongly advise against it. Blame me if you like. But tell me, how are you settling in now?'

'Well . . .' Violet felt guilty. 'It's a beautiful house and the staff are so lovely to me. I'm truly grateful to my aunt but . . .'

'But?'

She sighed. 'I'm finding it quite hard having nothing to do. I'm not used to sitting about. Some days I go to the café to give Edie a hand, especially as Sally still isn't too well. And it's good company for me.'

'Ah yes, Edie did mention she was concerned about Sally,' Mr Chapman said. 'She's a delightful woman.' An idea occurred to him, and he suggested cautiously, 'Why don't you ask her to come here to stay with you for a time to give her a rest, and maybe Edie could get someone else in to help at the café for a while? Now Sally is a woman who I would trust implicitly not to take advantage of you, and she'd be good company too.'

Violet thought about this for a moment and smiled. 'Yes, you could be right. It would do us both good. I'll ask her if she likes the idea when I go round there later. Thank you, Mr Chapman.'

Since moving into the house both Mr Chapman and his wife had been regular visitors and Violet had grown fond of them. Mr Chapman had gone far beyond the role of her solicitor and guardian and had become almost like a father figure – no doubt because he had been such good friends with her father and aunt – and Violet was more than grateful to him. Mr Pope was still doing a sterling job of keeping the trawlers and the boatyard running like clockwork, too, and with Cook keeping the household accounts it left little for Violet to do. She knew most girls her age would have been grateful for this, but she still felt guilty for having so much while others had so little.

'Perhaps you could become involved in some sort of charity work?' Mr Chapman went on. 'I know they're always crying out for volunteers to work at the orphanage and the workhouse for a start. Toby Brabinger does a lot for them.'

'Doing what?' Despite the fact that she didn't like the man she was curious.

'I believe he organises clothes collections from the larger houses to dress the orphans, and he's always arranging fundraising events. Why don't you have a word with him? I'm sure he'd be glad of your help.'

'I shouldn't think he'd need me if he has his young lady to help him,' Violet said surlily as she thought of the pretty young woman who'd been with him at the café.

Mr Chapman frowned. 'Young lady? I wasn't aware that he had one.'

They went on to speak of other things then, until it was time for him to go, leaving Violet with another long, lonely night stretching ahead of her.

Chapter Twenty-Two

The following day, Violet visited the café. There was no sign of Sally and she noticed that Edie had already taken on another woman to help out.

'She's upstairs in bed full of a cold an' that cough ain't no better either, I'm worried it could be turnin' to pneumonia,' Edie told her as Violet tied an apron over her pretty day dress. As always, she was more than happy to pitch in and help. It was then that she put Mr Chapman's suggestion to Edie, who chewed on her lip as she thought of it.

'It's a good idea if you can persuade her to go,' she admitted. 'A good rest an' bein' waited on is just what she needs, an' she'd be company for you an' all. The two o' you 'ave got on like a house on fire since the second you met. Why don't you pop upstairs when we have a quiet minute an' see what she thinks about the idea?'

'I will, but first there's something else I'd like to discuss with you.'

'Oh yes, an' what would that be?' Edie asked curiously.

'Well, I just wanted to make sure you knew that Mr Chapman has now turned my shares in the café over to you so you are now the sole owner.'

Edie looked embarrassed. 'I appreciate it, but there were no need to do that. You put your money into the place to get us up an' runnin', not to speak of how hard yer worked to help me get it off the ground.'

'Maybe I did, but the lion's share of it is yours,' Violet pointed out. 'And I also intend to pay off the rest of the loan we took out to cover the expenses.'

Edie opened her mouth to object but Violet held her hand up.

'*Please*, Edie, I intend to do this whether you like it or not. It's little enough for all you've done for me over the years.'

Edie gulped and sniffed. She was a good girl was Violet, there was no doubt about it.

Later Violet made her way upstairs, where she found Sally huddled in a blanket in a chair at the side of the fire. Sally's face lit up at the sight of her.

'Ah, Violet. Hello, love.'

'Hello, Sally, how are you feeling?'

'Oh, I'm not so bad, pet, just a bit of a cold.' Sally never complained but from the little of her past Violet had managed to get her to talk about she had not had an easy life and now she looked awful.

'Come to help out a bit again, have you?'

'I have but I've come for something else as well. I want to ask you something.'

'Oh yes, then ask away.'

Violet wondered how she should put this idea to her. Sally was a fiercely proud woman, and she didn't want to offend her by appearing to offer charity.

'Erm . . . actually, I've had an idea that might benefit us both. You see, Edie is concerned about your health. Now don't argue, just hear me out please.'

Sally frowned but obediently clamped her lips together.

'The thing is . . . I, er . . . To be honest, I'm finding it rather difficult living in that big house all by myself, so I got to thinking, if you were to move in with me for a while it would give you a good rest and I'd feel easier there. Of course, you'd be under no obligation to stay for longer than you wanted to. Just until you feel better and I'm a bit more at ease there. You could come back here whenever you like. What do you think? You'd be doing me a huge favour.'

'But what about Edie? How would she manage here?'

Violet smiled. 'I've already spoken to Edie about it and she thinks it's a great idea but it's up to you. No one wants to force you to do anything you don't feel comfortable with.'

Sally stared into the fire for a moment before smiling. 'In that case I'd love to take you up on your offer. But only till you feel more settled and I'm over this cold, mind!'

Violet clapped her hands with delight. She had taken to Sally since the minute she had clapped eyes on her, and it was nice to think she would have some company of an evening.

'I'll get Stan to come round and pick you up in the trap this evening, if that's not too soon. And don't worry about packing too much, I can always pop back here to get you anything you need.'

'Oh, you don't need to go to all that trouble,' Sally protested. 'I can walk.'

Violet shook her head. 'No, you will not walk. The weather has really turned and it's cold out there so be ready for seven.'

When Stan set off to collect Sally that evening Violet went with him. Anything was better than rattling around the house on her own. As they arrived at the café, they were just in time to meet Toby Brabinger leaving through the front door with a large basket in his hand.

'Good evening,' he greeted Violet.

Knowing that it would be churlish not to answer him, Violet nodded. 'Good evening.' It was the first time she had seen him since moving into her house and as she dropped her gaze to the laden basket, he smiled.

'Edie has kindly started to give me any food left over from the café at the end of the day so that I can distribute it amongst families where it's most needed. I do the same with any left-over food from the restaurant. Congratulations on your inheritance, Violet.'

Violet bristled with embarrassment. Even when Toby said something nice to her, she still got the feeling he was looking down on her, although she couldn't help but be impressed by what he was doing for the poor. It wasn't something she would have expected, with him being so arrogant.

Edie bustled out behind him then so thankfully Violet was saved from having to reply.

'Ah, here you are, pet,' she greeted her. 'Sally's all ready to go but it's goin' to be very quiet 'ere wi'out her.'

'So come with us,' Violet urged. 'I've asked you often enough and you know you'd be welcome.'

Edie shook her head, as Violet knew she would. She could be as stubborn as a mule.

'Thanks, pet, but as I've told you I've waited too long for me own little business an' me own fireside so I'm quite happy to stay 'ere.'

When Violet sighed, Toby grinned at her, just as Sally came to join them.

'I shan't be gone long, Edie,' she promised her with a catch in her voice. 'Soon as I can get rid o' this damned cough I'll be back.'

'You just stay as long as you like.' Edie gave her a hug. 'An' don't go gettin' upset now. I'm comin' to have dinner wi' you both on Sunday. It's nice to be waited on for a change.'

Without being asked, Toby placed the basket down and lifted Sally's case onto the trap before helping her up onto the seat. He turned and held his hand out to do the same for Violet, but she ignored him and clambered up beside Sally and Stan.

'I'll see you on Sunday, Edie,' she said as Stan urged the horse on.

When they arrived at the house Dora and Violet took Sally to look at the room they had prepared for her, and she got quite emotional.

'Why, it's just beautiful,' Sally sniffed as she gazed around. It was one of the front bedrooms that overlooked the sea and was decorated in shades of pink. 'I've never slept in a room like this in me whole life. I shan't be wantin' to go home.'

Violet chuckled. 'Then don't. You're welcome to stay for as long as you like – forever if you want to. I'll be glad of the company. It gets very boring being here on my own day after day.' She thought back to something Edie had said and asked cautiously, 'Do you know anything about all these charitable things Toby Brabinger is involved in?'

'Well, as you know he lost his father recently, and he and his sister were left the house. But I believe she'll be gettin' wed soon – I think she's marryin' a lord – an' much like you, Toby is sayin' that the house will be too big for him on his own and he likes to keep busy. I know he does a lot o' fundraisin' for the workhouse an' I heard he's just opened a soup kitchen for the homeless.'

'Really? I wouldn't have thought he was the type.'

Sally grinned. 'Oh, you'd be surprised. He's a smashin' young man. I reckon he'll make some woman a good husband one of these days.'

Violet put her nose in the air. 'Rather her than me,' she said primly.

Sally was staring from the window at the view and she frowned. 'There's a young man standing out there.'

Violet went to stand with her and seeing Oliver hovering about a few houses along she nodded. 'Ah, that's Oliver Stroud. He must be coming here. I'll leave you to unpack. Come down whenever you're ready and I'll get Dora to make us some tea.'

She hurried away with a sinking feeling in her stomach. No doubt Oliver was coming to see if she'd made a decision about his mother coming to live with her and she wasn't looking forward to telling him that it wasn't going to happen. Sure enough, as she reached the bottom of the stairs there was a knock on the door and when Dora opened it Oliver stood there.

'Come in,' Violet invited, as she came up behind Dora, and led him into the drawing room where a cheery fire was roaring in the grate.

'How are you?'

'I'm very well, and yourself?'

'Oh, I'm all right, but I can't say the same for my mother,' he told her sadly. 'Now the weather has turned, she's struggling in that damp room and I fear for her health.'

'I'm sorry to hear that.'

'Did you manage to have a word with the solicitor about her coming to stay here?'

Violet licked her lips. 'Yes, I did but, er . . . to be honest he wasn't keen on the idea.'

Oliver's face darkened. 'But surely, it's your decision in the end. It is your house after all.'

She sighed. There could be no avoiding what needed to be said. 'Oliver, I'm not so sure that we'd get on. What I mean is, Anna never had time for me when I was growing up, so I doubt she'd be happy in my company now. I can understand why now that I know she wasn't my mother.'

'But there's an easy way for us to put everything right.' Suddenly he was all smiles again and Violet was confused. 'You and I could get married and then we would be a proper family.'

Violet looked shocked as her hand flew to her throat. 'You and I . . . *married*?'

'Why not?' Before she could stop him, he took her hands and shook them up and down. 'Look, I know there were bad feelings between us over that misunderstanding, but I promise you I had no way of knowing the goods weren't legitimate. And now . . . the thing is I have feelings for you. As soon as I realised we weren't blood related I started to look at you in a different way. Can you honestly say that you have none for me?'

'O-of course I have feelings for you. But I've always thought of you as my brother,' she stuttered.

At that moment there was a tap at the door and Sally entered. Instantly Oliver dropped Violet's hands and scowled. 'Oh . . . I didn't realise Violet had visitors.'

'Actually, I'm not a visitor, I'm staying here,' Sally told him with no trace of a smile.

'*You're* staying here!' Oliver looked dumbfounded. 'But I thought you said Mr Chapman didn't want you having people moving in?' he said to Violet.

'Sally hasn't moved in. She's just staying here until she feels better, she's been ill,' Violet tried to apologise, feeling guilty.

Snatching up his hat Oliver rammed it on his head and turned for the door. 'I think I'd best leave now,' he muttered in a surly voice. 'It would be better to continue this conversation when we can get some privacy.' And with that he stamped from the room leaving Violet visibly upset.

'Now don't take on,' Sally soothed, putting her arm about Violet's shaking shoulders. 'I confess I heard what he was saying to you before I came in and I was horrified. Surely you can see that it's not you that he wants but all this!' She spread her hands and looked around the room.

'B-but he said he had feelings for me,' Violet said shakily.

'Of course he did. Think about it, if you marry him all that your aunt left you becomes his. I'm not saying that you're not a very beautiful young woman, Violet. Any man would be proud to have you as his wife, but I beg you to think carefully before you make any decisions. I've heard such dreadful things about him and the people he mixes with from Edie. She believes he's far more involved with Ned Banks's gang than he lets on. Why do you think Edie sent you away after the trouble at the café? She knows he's bad knews and she loves you like a daughter. Please don't go rushing into anything. Will you at least promise me that?'

Violet nodded, feeling wretched. Deep down she knew Sally was right, so why did she feel so confused? It was a question she would ask herself many times before she finally came up with an answer.

Chapter Twenty-Three

Two days following Oliver's visit, Violet and Sally were having morning tea together, when there was a knock at the door, and soon after, Dora entered the room bearing a beautiful bouquet of stunning red roses.

'These were just delivered for you, miss.'

'Ooh, someone 'as an admirer,' Sally teased.

Violet took the flowers from Dora and blushed. 'Thank you, Dora. They'll be from Oliver,' she told Sally. 'He sent me two bouquets shortly after Edie and I moved into the café.'

She failed to see Sally's frown as she buried her nose in the blooms before extracting a card pushed down amongst them.

But then she too was frowning as she saw what was written on the card.

Dear Violet,

After seeing you at Edie's I realised I had failed to send you a house-warming gift, so please instead accept these roses with wishes that you will be very happy in your new home.

Warmest wishes,

Toby Brabinger

'Is something wrong?' As Sally's voice sliced into her thoughts, she shook her head. She was feeling confused. She had been sure the flowers were from Oliver because they were identical to the ones that had been delivered to her at the café, and Oliver had sent those . . . hadn't he? Or could it be that those had been from Toby as well?

As the thought occurred to her, she sucked in a breath and suddenly everything Sally and Edie had said about Oliver made sense. He didn't have feelings for her at all. He only wanted her inheritance. She cringed as she remembered the money she had 'lent' him, and how she'd let him use the space above the café, even though she knew it was a terrible idea and it would upset Edie. Why had it taken her so long to see it? He hadn't sent her flowers and didn't care about her at all.

'Are you all right, pet?'

'What?' Violet dragged her eyes away from the card and looked at Sally, saying woodenly, 'The flowers are from Toby Brabinger.'

'But I thought you said—'

'That they were from Oliver? Yes, I thought they were, but I was wrong.'

'Let me take them through to the kitchen an' put them in water.' Sally took the flowers from her arms and walked out of the room, leaving Violet alone with her thoughts.

Suddenly she was seeing Oliver for what he really was. A spoilt, arrogant young man who would use anyone to get what he wanted, and with that realisation all her former feelings for him crumbled to dust. For years she had seen him through rose-tinted glasses, and when they'd first left their parents' house she had thought he still cared about her and was sending flowers to demonstrate this, but now she knew him for exactly what he was, and she determined to tell him that the very next time she saw him.

Her chance came much sooner than she expected. When she set off to help Edie in the café the next morning, she saw him striding along the road towards her.

'Ah, Violet, I was just coming to see if you'd care to come for a walk with me. We can't really talk with that nosy parker Sally back at your house listening to every word we say.'

He made to tuck her hand through his arm, but she jerked it away and carried on walking with her eyes straight ahead.

He trotted along at the side of her. 'Is there something wrong, darling?'

Her head whipped towards him. '*Darling?* I'm *not* your darling nor will I ever be. I don't know where this idea of us living happily ever after came from, Oliver, but I do know that it would never work.'

'But why not?' He caught her arm again and this time he dragged her to a halt. 'I told you I cared about you, didn't I? Doesn't that mean anything to you?'

'No, it doesn't, because you don't mean it,' she snapped as she dragged her arm away again. 'What you really care about is getting your hands on my money and my house. I'm not a complete fool, Oliver.'

He still wasn't ready to give up. He didn't usually have any trouble getting women to fall at his feet so Violet would be no different, he was sure. 'Look, sweetheart, we've both been through a lot lately, what with losing your father and then the house and all the upheaval.'

But this time when she stared levelly back at him, he could see he was flogging a dead horse. Violet had made up her mind. No doubt helped by that old busybody Edie and her sidekick Sally.

'It would be nice if we could be civil but other than that I see no reason for us to be in touch again.'

Suddenly Oliver's lips curled back from his teeth and his face became ugly as he grabbed her arm and gave it a painful twist. 'You stupid fucking little *bitch*,' he spat. 'You'd better watch your step from now on because I'll tell you now, I won't stand back an' see some other chap take what should have been mine.' It was strange that now he knew she didn't want him he realised that he really *did* want her, and Oliver was used to getting what he wanted by fair means or foul.

Violet had a terrible feeling that he was about to hit her as he raised his hand but at that moment, a number of dockers walked towards them and he roughly pushed her away. She fell against a wall as he disappeared up one of the many ginnels leading into the town.

As the dockers drew level one of them asked, 'Are you all right there, miss?'

'Yes . . . yes I'm fine, thank you.' He helped her to straighten up and with her face glowing with embarrassment she hurried away, praying that she wouldn't have to see Oliver again for a very long time.

'What's happened to you?' Edie asked the moment Violet entered the café, looking shaken.

'I, er . . . Oliver asked me to marry him and I just told him no. It didn't go down very well,' Violet muttered as tears threatened at the corners of her eyes.

'Well, thank goodness you 'ad the sense to do that.' Edie put her hands on her hips and glared at Violet. 'Finally realised that him an' his ma only want you for what they can get, 'ave you?'

Violet nodded miserably and Edie gave her a cuddle. 'I don't know, pet. You should be on top o' the world right now instead o' lookin' so glum. You've got everything you could possibly need. What's wrong wi' you?'

'I just feel so . . . so useless,' Violet told her quietly.

'Then do sommat about it, girl. Instead o' feelin' sorry for yourself get out there an' 'elp them as ain't so fortunate as you. I know you don't like the chap, though goodness knows why, but Toby Brabinger runs a business an' still finds time to 'elp folks as ain't as fortunate as 'imself. An' speak o' the devil, look who's just turned up.'

Glancing over her shoulder, Violet saw Toby entering the café and her heart sank. She was very aware that after the scuffle with Oliver she wasn't looking her best, although why she should care she had no idea. She was also aware that she should thank him for the flowers she had received that morning.

As he approached them, he glanced at Violet warily. 'Good morning, ladies. Is everything all right, Miss Stroud?'

She flushed as she quickly raised her hand to check if her bonnet was on straight. 'Yes, I'm very well, thank you. And thank you for the flowers.'

'You're very welcome.'

'She ain't all right really,' Edie told him in her forthright way. 'She just 'ad a run-in wi' that Oliver Stroud.'

His smile died. 'Did he hurt you?'

Violet glared at Edie before assuring him, 'No, he didn't but he wasn't very pleasant.'

'I'm aware it isn't my place to give you advice but I'd be careful when it comes to him if I were you. He's getting quite a bad reputation. And are you aware that the night watchman who was attacked in the warehouses died last night?'

'Oh no!' Edie looked upset. 'How will his poor wife manage now wi' all them little 'uns to look after? Will they 'ave to go into the work'ouse?'

'Not if I can help it.' Toby was solemn. 'I already have an appointment with my solicitor to see if he can get the widow some compensation from the man's employers, and I have some fund-raising events lined up too. I believe her mother has told her that she can look after the children during the day so I'm going to offer her some work in the kitchens at my restaurant.'

'Bless their souls.' Edie sighed. 'I could allus find her an hour or two in the evenin' an' all, cleanin' up when we've closed, if that'd be a help to the poor woman. I could use some extra help while Sally's not well.'

'And is . . . is there anything I could do?' Violet asked in a small voice.

Toby stared at her thoughtfully. 'There is, actually. You must have some very wealthy friends now and some other ladies I know in your position take clothes donations from the better off that can then be sold on to help people like this family. I could also do with someone to help with my new project, the soup kitchen, although it's not a particularly glamorous job and does involve early evening work.'

'I could do that,' Violet told him with her chin in the air. 'Where is the soup kitchen?'

'It's in the market place every evening from six o'clock till seven. It's a relatively new thing so not too many people know about it yet, but we do seem to get more people turning up each day.'

'Then I shall come along each evening,' Violet told him, rising to the challenge.

'Well . . . only if you're sure,' he answered uncertainly. 'I should warn you that the people who come are not the class of people you are used to mixing with.'

'I'm not a snob, Mr Brabinger,' she informed him coldly. 'And in actual fact, I'd welcome something to keep me occupied. I've never been afraid of hard work.'

'I wasn't trying to insinuate that you were.' His tone was as cold as hers now and Edie sighed. Why was it, she wondered, that these two always seemed to rub each other up the wrong way?

'All right,' she intervened. 'Who's for a cup o' tea?'

When Violet and Toby nodded in unison, she hurried away to ask Lottie to serve them and left them to it.

'I'd advise that you wear something warm when you come along tonight,' Toby said. 'Oh, and probably nothing too smart.'

'I'm sure I shall be quite able to dress for the occasion, Mr Brabinger.'

He opened his mouth to retaliate but seemed to think better of it and so they sat in an awkward silence until Lottie reappeared with their drinks.

When Violet got home and told Sally what she intended to do, Sally thought it was a splendid idea. 'It's good that you'll be gettin'

out an' about. I know Edie's been worried about the way you've stayed in since losin' your dad. In fact, I reckon I'll come along to help. I ain't so keen on you roamin' the streets when the nights are drawin' in. You never know who might be about.'

That evening, suitably wrapped up, Sally and Violet set off for the market place, but they had only gone a short distance when the cold evening air began to make Sally cough.

Violet drew to a halt and stared at her with concern. 'I think you should go back,' she advised. 'I know you want to help but the whole point of you coming to stay with me was to get better, and you're not going to if you're out in this cold. In fact, you'll be back to square one in no time. Go on, you go back,' she encouraged. 'I'll tell you how it goes when I get home.'

Sally sighed and nodded reluctantly. 'All right. But you just be careful. I'm not happy about you walking the streets alone at this time.'

'It isn't late,' Violet pointed out as she gently took Sally's arm and turned her about. 'Go on, I'll see you in a while. I shouldn't be too late.'

When Violet arrived at the market place, all the stalls were closed, apart from one that she glimpsed on the other side of the square. Toby was already there loading steaming tureens from his carriage onto a trestle table and when she approached, he smiled at her. 'Ah, so you decided to come?'

'I said I would, didn't I? And I'm not in the habit of breaking my word. What can I do to help?'

'You could get the bread baskets and the dishes and spoons out.'

With a nod she went to do as she was asked and very soon the stall was set up. A thick mist had floated in from the sea and Violet shivered as she pulled her warm shawl closer about her. How awful it must be for the poor homeless people who had to stay out all night in such weather. She had never really given it much thought before. Suddenly a figure appeared from the mist, an old woman dressed in rags with a mangy dog on a piece of string at the side of her, drawn by the enticing smell of the soup.

''Ow much is it?' she asked suspiciously.

Violet smiled at her. 'Absolutely nothing. Would you prefer chicken or vegetable?'

'I'll 'ave veg but can me dog 'ave a dish o' the chicken?'

When Violet glanced at Toby, he gave a little nod, so she quickly dished up two bowls of soup and handed them to the old woman, who immediately placed one down for the dog. Within seconds they had both cleared the dishes and Violet asked, 'Would you like some more, and perhaps you'd like some bread with it this time?'

'Ta very much.'

As she served the soup the old woman began to cram chunks of bread into her old coat pockets, but Violet pretended not to notice. By the time the dog and the woman had finished their seconds, another two people had approached and from then on there was a steady stream of hungry people to serve.

Just over an hour later, Toby whispered, 'I'm afraid that's about it for tonight. I'll just tell the people that are still here to take the rest of the bread if they want it.'

Violet nodded, too full of emotion to speak. The evening had been a real eye-opener for her. She had never realised there were so many hungry and often homeless people in Hull. What a sheltered life she had led.

While Toby's driver began to pack the empty soup tureens and dishes back into the carriage, Toby turned to Violet. 'Thanks for your help,' he said. 'That was the most I've served. I might bring an extra tureen tomorrow; word must be spreading. Would you like a lift home?'

'Thank you, but no, I shall be fine,' she assured him, then with a last wave, she set off for home with her mind whirling and her heart aching from the sights she had seen that evening. Hollow-eyed mothers with tiny ragamuffin children clinging to their skirts.

Men on crude crutches with limbs missing. Children who didn't look old enough to be out alone but were forced through circumstances to try and survive on the streets. Old women with nothing to their name but the rags they stood up in. It had been distressing to see, yet it had made her feel good to know that she was doing something to help them, and already she knew this was going to be the first of many nights she would help Toby. She even felt a little more kindly towards him After all, she reasoned, he couldn't be all bad if he was prepared to help the poor.

Chapter Twenty-Four

As they entered November the days turned even colder but Violet continued to help at the soup kitchen each evening and had soon got to know some of the people who visited. It was the only hot meal most of them would have each day and Violet recognised the importance of that more than ever. She had got to know some of her neighbours and had started to collect the clothes they no longer needed. Sally would then wash and iron them and Violet would take them with her of an evening and distribute them amongst the most needy, which Toby was most grateful for. Thanks to the rest and the loving care she had received, Sally was much better and felt ready to return to the café, but Violet had got used to her company and didn't want her to go.

'But I'll miss you,' she said every time Sally suggested it.

'You'll still see me when you come to the café,' she would point out with a smile.

Eventually they decided she would stay until after Christmas. It had already been agreed that Edie would join them for Christmas Day and Boxing Day and Violet was looking forward to it. She had agreed that the cook and the staff could join their own families, so they were going to prepare their meals themselves.

As well as keeping herself busy with the soup kitchen and collecting clothes, Violet was also showing an active interest in the boatyard. When she had first discussed it, Mr Pope the manager had been none too keen on the idea. After all, who had ever heard of a young woman being involved in what was obviously such a male business. But after going through the books with her each week, he soon realised that Violet had a sharp mind and some very good ideas.

All in all, things were going well, apart from the fact that many times on her way home from helping Toby in the evening, Violet had felt she was being followed, and it was rather unnerving. She'd had no further contact with Oliver, but she strongly suspected that he was tailing her, although she had never actually seen him.

'I think it's high time you took Toby up on his offer of bringing you home each night,' Sally told her worriedly. 'That Oliver is a slippery character an' I'm worried about what he might do.'

Could she have heard the conversation that was taking place that very minute between Oliver and his mother she would have known she was right.

'So, she was there again this evening, was she?'

Oliver nodded glumly as he took the weak, lukewarm tea his mother was holding out to him. They were having to eke out the small amount of coal they had left until he managed to bring some money in again. Hopefully it would be that evening as he was attending a card game. Unfortunately, he had been banned from most of them because he had been caught cheating so now his reputation preceded him, and he was having to go further afield.

'She's there nearly every night,' he responded, grimacing at the drink. But at least it was wet and warm.

'Then it's time you brought things to a head.'

'And how am I supposed to do that? I've asked her to marry me and she turned me down flat.'

'So you'll have to *make* her marry you, won't you?'

'Oh yes, and how do you propose I do that? I can hardly drag her to the altar kicking and screaming, can I?'

'You wouldn't have to if she had your child growing in her belly. She'd be only too glad to get a ring on her finger then.'

As he thought about this, he smiled. 'I hadn't thought of that. But what if she reported me for forcing her?'

'It would be your word against hers. You would just say that she'd been willing. But it won't come to that. She has a reputation to uphold, especially now she lives in that nice posh house. Can you really see her wanting people to know that she had been raped?'

'I suppose not,' he said uncertainly.

'Think about it,' his mother urged. 'It's dark when she sets off for home after the soup kitchen and there aren't that many people about in this weather. You'd just have to choose your moment.'

'I wouldn't be surprised if we have snow soon,' Toby commented as he and Violet stood together behind the trestle table serving their regulars one evening. As well as the soup and bread, Toby was now also providing tea, which was brought in a large tea urn on the floor of the carriage, and it was going down a treat, although it did tend to get cool as they neared the end of the night.

The only evenings they didn't serve were Saturday and Sunday but even then, Toby had two of his restaurant staff take their places. Neither of them liked to think of anyone going without food even for a couple of nights.

Just then, a small carriage drew up on the other side of the square and a very pretty young woman alighted. Violet instantly recognised her as the young woman she had seen in the café with Toby and she felt a pang of jealousy.

'Hello,' the woman said as she approached them, looking stunning in a thick cape with a fur-trimmed hood. She moved towards Toby and stood on tiptoe to kiss his cheek before smiling at Violet.

'You must be Miss Stroud. Or may I call you Violet? Toby has told me such a lot about you and what a great help you are to him.' She held her hand out in a friendly fashion and knowing it would be churlish to ignore it, Violet solemnly shook it before the young woman returned her attention to Toby.

'I've just been to see the vicar to discuss the flower arrangements for the church,' she told him happily. 'I can't believe the wedding is so close now. I'm getting quite excited, but I keep thinking I might have forgotten something.'

Violet's heart turned over. So they were getting married, and soon by the sounds of it.

'Er . . . when is the wedding?' she asked, feeling that she should say something and the girl smiled again making Violet feel positively dowdy. She really was extremely pretty.

'It's the last Monday before Christmas,' the girl answered and, scowling at Toby, she scolded him. 'And you still haven't introduced us properly, Toby. How remiss of you.'

'Oh, I'm sorry.' He slid his arm affectionately about her slender waist. 'Violet, may I introduce Annabel.'

'It's very nice to meet you,' Violet said primly but at that moment a man approached the stall eyeing the food greedily and she had a good excuse to leave the two to chat while she served him.

'I had no idea there were quite so many things to organise for a wedding,' Violet heard Annabel say, and again her heart did a little flutter.

Annabel left soon after and for the first time Violet pleaded a headache and set off home slightly early, leaving Toby to man the fort on his own.

'Please let my driver run you back in the carriage if you're not feeling well,' he pleaded.

Violet shook her head. 'No, he's needed here. I shall be quite all right. I'll see you tomorrow. Goodnight.' And with that she left hurriedly, her thoughts confused. She had no idea why she should be feeling as she did about Toby getting married. After all, she had known for some time he had a young lady, and it wasn't as if she was interested in him, was it?

She had just passed the warehouses on the docks and was heading for the better part of town and home when a dark figure suddenly stepped out of the shadows in front of her and she started. There were no streetlamps and her heart began to thump painfully.

'I . . . have no money on me if that's what you're after,' she faltered and then the hairs on the back of her neck stood to attention as a voice she recognised reached her.

'It's not money I'm after, Violet . . . it's *you*.'

'Oliver . . . is that you?' As he stepped closer his face came into focus and she scowled at him. 'Have you been following me?' she asked sharply.

He grinned. 'Why wouldn't I? I don't like you working with that posh so-and-so every night. I consider you to be *my* girl!'

'Oh Oliver, not that again,' Violet sighed. 'I've already told you that it would never work between us. Why don't you just leave me alone?'

He narrowed his eyes as he stepped even closer and Violet was suddenly afraid. 'Look . . . I must be going. Sally will be getting worried if I'm not back soon.'

But as she turned to move on, he lunged at her and smacked her cheek so hard that she lost her footing and hit the ground with a thud that knocked the air from her lungs.

Panic set in as he dropped down beside her and started to drag her skirt up. She felt sick as she realised what he was trying to do and opened her mouth to scream, but no sound came out as she struggled to breathe. And then suddenly she was flat on her back and although she tried to fight him, her strength was no match for his. Tears coursed down her cheeks as her bonnet came off and was snatched by the wind and she felt the cold air on the skin of her thighs.

'P-please . . . No!'

He was panting heavily now as he held her down with one hand while struggling with his flies with the other.

'It's your own fault. I offered to do it the right way and put a ring on your finger,' he ground out. And then there was nothing but pain as he pushed himself inside her and she wished she could just curl up and die. He was pounding away at her and she was helpless to stop him. At one point she lifted her hand and raked her fingernails down his cheek but it did nothing to stop him. Then just as she thought she could stand it no more he suddenly went rigid and groaned before flopping heavily down on top of her. She was sobbing uncontrollably by that time and finding it hard to breathe. Suddenly he rolled away from her and after standing up began to adjust his clothes.

'There, you're mine now whether you like it or not,' he spat, then he walked away into the swirling mist.

Violet curled herself into a ball as it came to her that no man would ever want her now. She was soiled goods and she felt ashamed and humiliated. Eventually she dragged herself into a sitting position and shortly after she managed to stand, although her legs seemed to have turned to jelly. Somehow, she made it the rest of the way home praying that she would be able to get to her room without being seen. She didn't think she could bear it if Sally or the others realised what had happened. But her prayer went unanswered for as she quietly let herself in, Dora appeared.

'Oh! My good God! Whatever 'as happened to you, miss?' She rushed forward just as Sally appeared in the doorway of the drawing room and she too looked horrified as she saw the state Violet was in.

'My poor girl.' She rushed forward and led Violet to the nearest chair where she sat with her head bowed. Her skirt was torn, her bonnet was missing and her lovely hair had escaped its pins and hung loose about her shoulders. Her cheek was swelling too and there was already the beginning of a black eye forming.

'Dora, run and fetch her a glass of brandy,' Sally ordered as she dropped to her knees beside her. Then softly she took her shaking hand and asked, 'Who did this to you, my love?'

Violet began to sob and shook her head as Dora appeared with a crystal goblet which Sally held to her lips and made her sip. As the fiery liquid slid down Violet's throat she gulped and coughed and suddenly she was in Sally's arms, sobbing as if her heart would break.

'Dora, run for the doctor,' Sally said as calmly as she could but at that Violet became even more distressed.

'No, no please don't! I couldn't bear anyone else to see me like this.'

Sally scowled. 'Did they . . .'

When Violet hung her head and cried even harder Sally had her answer and she too began to cry. 'Oh sweetheart, did you see who it was?'

Violet remained tight-lipped and when it became apparent she wasn't going to answer, Sally told Dora, 'Come on, we need to get her upstairs. We need to look at that cheek as well. My goodness she's going to have a right shiner on her tomorrow, if I'm not much mistaken.'

Between them they managed to get Violet up to her room and while Sally helped her to get undressed, Dora rushed away to get some water to bathe her face. By this time shock had set in and Violet was shaking violently. Even so, Sally somehow managed to get her into her nightgown and her torn clothes lay in a pile on the floor at the side of the bed. When Dora returned Sally gently bathed Violet's face and patted it dry. 'Try and get some rest now, pet. And don't worry, I shan't be leaving you all night. I shall be right here in this chair so you've nothing to fear.'

Violet was sure she would never sleep again. But soon shock and exhaustion took their toll and she slipped into an uneasy doze as Sally and Dora watched over her, feeling broken-hearted.

'If I could get my hands on who did this, I'd strangle him myself with my bare hands,' Sally said angrily. 'I have an idea this has something to do with Oliver!'

'Aye, an' if it is I'll hold him for you while you do it,' Dora agreed. 'Do you think she's goin' to be all right?'

'Well, if she's no better in the morning I shall be sending for the doctor whether she likes it or not,' Sally answered. 'And I think the police should be told as well, but I won't do that without her permission. She has enough to cope with as it is. First thing you could perhaps run and let Edie know what's happened. She'd never forgive me if I didn't tell her.'

'I could go now if you like?' Dora volunteered.

Sally shook her head as she gentled a stray lock of hair from Violet's forehead. 'No, pet, tomorrow will be soon enough. The animal who did this is still out there somewhere and we don't want to risk the same thing happening to you.'

Dora hadn't thought of that and she paled. After a time, Sally sent her to bed and her vigil at the side of Violet began as she silently cursed the man who had done this to her.

The next morning, bright and early, Dora set off for the café and soon returned with Edie, who was panting breathlessly.

Sally had gone down to make a tray of tea and met them in the hall on their return.

'How is she?'

'A little better this morning, I think. At least she isn't shaking now,' Sally responded.

Edie scowled. 'And she's still not said who it was?'

'Not a word.'

'Hmm, well I've got me own thoughts on that score,' Edie muttered as she took off her cape and threw it over the banister. 'But now you go an' get some shut-eye, pet. You've been up all night and you're as white as a ghost. Go on, I'll take that up to Violet. I've left Lottie an' the others in charge o' the café so I don't 'ave to rush back; they'll manage just fine.'

Sally reluctantly did as she was told, and Edie entered Violet's bedroom, holding back tears at the sight of the poor girl. One side of her face was horribly swollen and one eye was black and completely closed.

'Oh, Edie.' Fresh tears spurted from Violet's eyes when she saw the dear woman who had been like a mother to her and within seconds she was enfolded in her arms.

'Eeh, what a thing to 'appen,' Edie said in a choked voice. 'But you've got to try an' put it behind you now, pet. You ain't the first girl to be taken down by some lousy bastard an' I dare say you won't be the last. If you dwell on it, it could ruin your life an' I couldn't bear that.'

'But I'm *dirty* now, Edie,' Violet sobbed.

Edie bristled. 'No, you are bloody *not*, my girl! It's the filthy bastard scum that did this to you that's dirty! It was Oliver, weren't it?'

Violet lowered her head. She was about to deny it but knew Edie could read her like a book and would know she was lying, so she nodded miserably.

Edie held her close and let her cry it all out. There was nothing much more she could do for now other than let Violet know how very much they all cared for her.

Chapter Twenty-Five

For three days Violet didn't venture out of her room. Sally sent word to Toby that she was ill with a bad case of influenza, and the following day yet another beautiful bouquet of red roses was delivered to her with a card wishing her well.

Violet sobbed when the flowers arrived, wondering what he would think of her if he knew what was really wrong. But she concluded that he probably wouldn't care. He would be married to Annabel in a few short weeks. It was only when she acknowledged to herself how much the thought of that hurt that it came to her in a blinding flash: she cared for him – more than cared for him, for what good it would do her. He would soon be someone else's husband and even if he wasn't, he would never want her now. No decent man would.

'I think you should come downstairs today and sit in the drawing room for a while,' Sally encouraged her on the fourth morning after the attack. 'It isn't doing you any good locking yourself away in here day after day.'

'And what if someone were to call and saw me like this?' Violet snapped more sharply than she should have. 'It would take some explaining, wouldn't it?' She instantly felt guilty, for Sally had been running around like a headless chicken looking after her. 'I'm sorry, Sally,' she said humbly. 'I shouldn't have snapped at you like that. You didn't deserve it.'

'Oh, I've got a broad back, pet. Now let me go and put these beautiful flowers in water. They must have cost an arm and a leg at this time of year with them being out of season. I'll bring them back up here and leave them in your room. They might cheer you up.'

She bustled away leaving Violet to stare miserably out of the window. The water in the docks was grey and choppy today, much like her mood, and just for a moment she allowed herself to think how lovely it would be to just sink beneath the surface of the waves so she didn't have to remember what Oliver had done to her. She knew she was being selfish but she couldn't seem to help it. As she sat there a carriage pulled up outside, and the person she had been thinking about stepped out of it. It was Toby. She panicked. He mustn't see her like this, she wouldn't be able to bear it. She saw him climb the steps leading to the front door and minutes later walk down them again before climbing back into the carriage and being driven away.

Sally came back with the roses in a vase. 'You just had a visitor who came to see how you are, but don't worry, I told him you weren't well enough to see anyone and sent him away. It was Toby Brabinger and he was very concerned about you. He said to tell you that if you need anything, anything at all, to be sure to get in touch with him.'

'Huh! That surprises me. I would have thought he'd be too taken up with his forthcoming wedding plans to worry about *me*,' Violet responded ungraciously.

'*His* forthcoming wedding plans?' Sally frowned. 'As far as I'm aware Toby doesn't even have a young lady. Do you mean his sister's wedding plans? I know his sister, Miss Annabel, is set to marry her lord shortly before Christmas.'

'Annabel is his *sister*?' Violet's mouth gaped with shock. She had assumed Annabel was Toby's young lady; how wrong she'd been.

'Oh . . . I thought it was Toby getting married,' she said in a small voice.

Sally chuckled as she fetched a gown from Violet's armoire. 'You were wrong then, weren't you, miss? Now come on, I want you to get dressed today. You can't hide out in here forever. There's only me and the staff to see the bruises and none of them will talk outside these four walls. What happened to you was awful but you have to try and put it behind you now, although, for what it's worth, I still think you should have told the police.'

Half an hour later Violet was tucked up beneath a blanket in a chair by the window in the drawing room where she could watch the ships and the world pass by, but her thoughts were far away.

By the time they moved into December, Violet's bruises had faded to almost nothing but still she felt reluctant to go outside. Then one morning Sally told her cheerfully, 'I thought we could go into the market today and choose a Christmas tree. What do you think?'

Violet knew she was trying to entice her out of the house and stared at her warily. 'Isn't it a bit soon? It's only the second week in December.'

'So? It's never too soon to get the trimmings up. When my little boy was alive we used to—' She stopped talking abruptly and her eyes filled with tears.

Violet felt sorry for her. She knew very little of Sally's past for she barely spoke about it, and it was obvious that remembering the child who had died still hurt her deeply. It was that that decided her, so after taking a deep breath she nodded. 'Very well, but let's go later this afternoon when there aren't so many people about.' Sally had been so good to her that she felt it was her place to go along with this one wish of hers at least. 'But I don't think we have any baubles to decorate a tree with.'

'Oh yes we have.' Sally sniffed away her tears and smiled again. 'Me and Dora went up to have a rummage around in the attic and found a whole box full of them. They must have been your aunt's and they're quite beautiful. If we get the tree delivered by this evening, we could decorate it together tonight. Unless you intend to go back to the soup kitchen, that is?' she ended hopefully.

Violet shook her head and Sally didn't push it. Just getting her out and about again would be the first step and hopefully the rest would come in time.

They set off shortly after three o'clock and Violet found herself nervously peering down every ginnel they passed for a sight of Oliver.

'Stop being so nervous; no one is going to hurt you when there's two of us,' Sally scolded in a soft voice.

As Violet had hoped, most of the shoppers had gone by the time they reached the market and they made their way to the stall that sold Christmas trees. They selected one that Sally declared would be the perfect size.

'I thought we could put it beside the fireplace in the drawing room,' she suggested, and Violet nodded, not much caring where it went. She had stopped looking forward to Christmas on the night of her attack – stopped looking forward to anything if it came to that – and had only come to appease Sally. They arranged for the tree to be delivered then did a little more shopping for some bits Cook had asked for before setting off for home. They had just reached the edge of the market place when a tall figure stepped in front of them, and glancing up Violet found herself staring into Toby's bright-blue eyes.

'Violet!' He looked delighted to see her, a fact that was not lost on Sally, who stood back with a smile on her face. 'How lovely to see you out and about again. Are you feeling better?'

'Er . . . yes, thank you.' Violet felt colour seep into her cheeks and she lowered her eyes. 'I shall be back to help you soon.'

'Oh, don't worry about that. I just want you to be well again. We're managing fine. Not that we don't miss you, of course. Some of our regulars have been asking after you, especially Cleggy.' Cleggy was a particular favourite of Violet's. Then with a smile he told her, 'It's Annabel's wedding soon and I shall be giving her away. To be honest I shall be glad when it's all over. She's talked of nothing else for months. In fact, if you're feeling well enough, we'd love you to come.'

Violet shook her head. 'Thank you but I'm not sure I'm up to that just yet, but I might come to the church to see her come out. I hope she and her new husband will be very happy,' she responded primly, and again he smiled.

'Oh, I'm pretty sure they will be. They're mad about each other, otherwise I wouldn't let her marry him. There's only her and myself left now that our parents have passed. I don't mind admitting it's going to be very strange in the house without her.' He told her the time, date and which church the wedding would be at.

Sally stepped in to ask, 'So what will you be doing for Christmas Day if you're going to be on your own?'

He shrugged. 'Oh, I'll be all right. I've given the servants some time off to be with their families, so I'll just spend it quietly.'

Sally frowned. 'That doesn't sound very nice. Why don't you come to dinner with us on Christmas Day? Edie's coming too. That would be all right, wouldn't it, Violet?'

'O-of course.' Violet had little choice but to agree but inside she was seething. Whatever had made Sally invite him of all people? She was finding it hard enough just to face him after what Oliver had done to her, let alone to have to spend Christmas with him.

'Well . . . if you're sure I won't be imposing?'

'We'd love to have you,' Sally told him heartily. 'But we'd best get back and get this one out of the cold. I don't want her being ill again. Dinner will be at one o'clock on Christmas Day but feel free to come whenever you like.'

He doffed his hat as they said their goodbyes and watched them move on and when they were out of earshot Violet hissed, 'Whatever did you have to invite him to dinner for?'

'I invited him because it's as clear as the nose on your face that he's smitten with you, pet. And I have an inkling that you like him too.'

'Don't be so *ridiculous*.' Violet was angry now. 'And even if I did what good would it do? Once he knows what happened to me, he'd run a mile – as any decent man would.'

Sally caught her arm, dragged her to a halt and glared at her. 'Now you just listen to me, young lady. What happened to you was terrible, despicable, but it's done now. It's time you put it behind you and moved on; you've your whole life ahead of you. Just remember that what happened wasn't of your choosing. Oliver forced himself on you so who could blame you for that?'

Violet sniffed and put her nose in the air. The invite had been issued, there could be no taking it back, so they would just have to get on with things now.

Over breakfast on Annabel's wedding day, Sally enquired casually, 'Shall we take a walk to the church to see Toby's sister come out?'

Violet hadn't mentioned going again since the day they'd met Toby in the market but Sally was still trying to tempt Violet out of the house any way she could.

'I'm not sure,' Violet said uncertainly. Half of her wanted to go but the other half still felt afraid to step out of the front door in case they bumped into Oliver. Thankfully there had been no sign of him since the night he had attacked her, but she feared he was still out there somewhere waiting for a chance to get her on her own again.

'I think we should,' Sally went on as she buttered a slice of toast. 'And looking out of that window I wouldn't be surprised if we didn't have a white wedding in the true sense of the word. Look at the sky, it's full of it.' They'd had a flurry of snow in November that had barely settled before it had begun to thaw again, but now the sky was grey and heavy. 'Oh, come on, the fresh air will do you good and there's loads of last-minute things we need to get for Cook for Christmas Day. She's going to prepare as much of the dinner as she can before she leaves for her sister's on Christmas Eve, so what do you say? I could do with the help to carry it all.'

Violet nodded reluctantly. 'Very well, but we'll just watch them come out of the church from outside if you don't mind.'

Sally shrugged. 'Fair enough.'

And so half an hour before the wedding was about to take place they set off in their warmest clothes. By the time they reached the pretty church they could hear the wedding service already in progress inside and as they waited beneath a tall yew tree for the happy couple to appear, the first flakes of snow began to flutter down.

'Ah, how magical is that?' The words had barely left Sally's lips when they heard the sound of the organ followed by the pealing of bells and the bride and groom appeared arm in arm in the church doorway. They had eyes only for each other and barely seemed to notice the snow as their happy guests flooded out behind them and began to throw rice.

'Eeh, doesn't she look beautiful,' Sally sighed dreamily and Violet had to agree that she did indeed. Toby joined the couple then and gave his sister a hug before she and her groom made their way down the path and through the lychgate to a waiting carriage decorated with silk flowers and ribbons.

He spotted Sally and Violet and instantly left the wedding party to come and greet them. He was looking very dapper in a grey silk top hat and a matching suit with tails.

'Oh, I'm so glad you came,' he told them, and Violet noticed that his eyes looked teary as they followed the bride. 'That's it now. My baby sister is all grown up and married. I wish our parents could have been here to see her today.'

'I'm sure they'd have been proud of the way you've looked after her,' Sally told him.

He looked touched. 'Thank you. Can I convince you both to come and join the reception?'

'No, it's very kind of you but we have shopping to do,' Violet told him firmly. She had a few small gifts she wanted to get as well as the things Cook had asked for.

'Very well. I shall see you on Christmas Day then?'

Both women nodded and after doffing his hat he hurried away to his own carriage.

Almost before they knew it it was Christmas Day and Sally got up early to light the fires and put the goose in the oven. Cook had prepared almost everything for them before leaving the day before and there was very little to do apart from cook everything.

Violet joined her shortly after in her night robe looking pale.

Sally frowned. 'Are you feeling unwell, pet?'

'Not really, it's just . . .' Violet gulped before forcing herself to go on. 'It's just that my course was due a few days ago and it hasn't started. Usually, I'm as regular as clockwork.'

Sally's heart sank, but she pasted on a smile as she crossed to the teapot. 'Oh I shouldn't get fretting about that. Don't forget you've had a terrible shock. No doubt it'll come when it's ready.' But despite her words a sense of foreboding had sprung to life in her. 'Now get this hot drink inside you and go and get one of your prettiest gowns on, then when Edie gets up, we'll open our presents before we have breakfast, eh?'

Once Violet had gone, Sally leant heavily on the draining board and offered up a silent prayer, 'Oh please dear Lord, don't let him have planted his seed in her!' But all she could do was wait to see.

She had no doubt that the same terrible thought had occurred to Violet. She had led a somewhat sheltered life but she knew enough to know that one of the consequences of a late course could mean a baby was on the way, and she shuddered to think what would happen if her fears were proven to be true. But it was Christmas Day so she pushed her concerns to the back of her mind and determined that she would make the day as good as it could be for all of them.

Edie came downstairs soon after, all spruced up in her Sunday best, and they exchanged the presents they had bought for each other. For Edie Violet had bought a lovely warm shawl with a deep fringe in autumn colours that Edie decided she must wear straight-away. And for Sally there was a hat that Violet knew she had had her eye on in the milliner's window for some time.

Sally and Edie had bought Violet a gown between them that Violet was sure was so grand she would never go anywhere to wear it. It was cut quite fashionably low at the front with a small train at the back and was in a lovely sea-green shot silk trimmed with lace.

'It doesn't hurt to have one that's a bit special,' they both told her. 'You're a wealthy young woman now and you're bound to be invited to balls an' parties an' whatnot when you get to know a few more people.'

Violet doubted that would happen but she loved the gown all the same and counted herself lucky to have two such wonderful kind women in her life. It was almost like having two mothers and she couldn't picture herself without either of them now.

Chapter Twenty-Six

Toby Brabinger arrived shortly before twelve o'clock, by which time the dinner was cooking and delicious smells were wafting from the kitchen.

'Oh, my goodness, it makes my stomach rumble just smelling it,' he chuckled. 'With my cook and the maids away for a couple of days, I discovered this morning that I'm a dreadful cook. I even managed to burn a slice of toast. I was never any good at cooking even when I worked in the restaurant when I was younger. The chef used to say I could burn water! It's a good thing they're coming back the day after tomorrow or I might well starve as the restaurant is closed as well.'

'There's no need for you to do that,' Edie assured him. 'You can stay here till they come back if you like, can't he, Violet? I'm stayin' tonight an' there's still a spare bedroom. Are you not goin' to your sister's over the holiday?'

He shook his head. 'Annabel and Charles are still on their honeymoon. They're in the South of France and I bet they're not under layers of snow.'

As he handed them each a brightly packed present, Violet flushed. She hadn't thought to buy him anything. For Edie there was some lavender perfume that she immediately sprayed so lavishly she made them all cough. For Sally there was a beautiful gift box of scented soaps, which she loved.

'Go on, open yours now,' Edie ordered bossily, and Violet carefully removed the pretty paper to reveal a long slender box. When she opened the lid, she gasped. Inside was a delicate chain bracelet from which hung a tiny diamond heart.

'Oh . . . but it's beautiful . . . but far too much. I can't accept this . . .' she faltered.

'Of course you can.' Before she could say another word Toby took the bracelet from the box and fastened it around her wrist where the diamond twinkled in the firelight. 'You do like it, don't you?' he asked anxiously. 'We can take it back to the jeweller's and exchange it for something else if you don't, and I won't be in the least offended.'

'I-I love it,' Violet said shyly. 'But I'm afraid it must have been very expensive.'

Toby shrugged. 'I can afford it. Just wear it in the spirit it was given.'

Edie and Sally exchanged knowing winks.

'Right, who's for a nice glass o' sherry?' Edie piped up to break the awkward silence that had fallen on the room. 'Dinner will be ready in less than an hour.' She and Sally pottered away to get the drinks and check on the dinner leaving the two young people alone and, smiling, Toby told Violet, 'You're looking very pretty today, if you don't mind me saying. That gown suits you. Is it new?'

She nodded. 'Edie and Sally insisted I should have some clothes that befit my new status. They've actually bought me a ball gown too, although I doubt I'll ever get to wear it.'

'Ah, as it happens, I might just be able to help you there.' He gave her a smile that made her go weak at the knees. 'I was invited to a ball on New Year's Eve and I don't have anyone to go with now that Annabel is married. So, I was wondering . . . would you do me the honour of accompanying me?'

Edie had just entered the room with their drinks on a tray and caught what he was saying, and before Violet could reply, she chipped in, 'O' course she will. It'll do her the world o' good to get out an' about a bit.' Violet glared at her as Edie went on, 'So where is this ball?'

'It's at Redwood Manor on the edge of town.'

'Ooh posh!' Edie handed him his drink and, grinning at Violet, she told her, 'Didn't I tell you that gown would come in useful, eh? You can wear it wi' that nice cape me an' Sally bought you for your birthday a few weeks ago. So tell the poor chap you'll go with him an' put 'im out of his misery.'

'I . . . I . . . er . . .'

'She says yes,' Edie said smugly as she took a long swallow of her sherry and Violet sighed. It didn't seem like she had much choice in the matter.

Surprisingly the day went far better than Violet had expected. Toby was good company, and they were soon all chatting away. The meal was delicious. There was chicken soup or pâté to start, followed by the goose that was cooked to perfection, along with a dish of crispy roast potatoes, some of Cook's lovely sage and onion stuffing and a variety of vegetables. By the time it came to the pudding, which Cook had had standing in brandy for weeks, Toby was saying that he couldn't possibly eat another thing, but he still managed to put away a sizeable dishful and declared that the chef in his restaurant couldn't have done any better. It was a compliment to the cook and when they had finished, Violet insisted on doing the washing-up – Edie and Sally had done all the cooking, so it seemed only fair.

'I'll come and help you,' Toby offered as she loaded the dirty pots onto a tray, and although Violet felt slightly uncomfortable about it, she didn't refuse. It would have seemed churlish.

'In that case me an' Sally'll go an' put our feet up in front o' the fire an' let us dinner go down,' Edie said happily. It was nice to have a day off.

Throughout the meal Violet's eyes had been drawn to the bracelet on her wrist and once she and Toby were alone, she told him, 'I'm so sorry I didn't get you a present. I didn't think.'

'No need to apologise.' He carried some pots to the sink for her. 'If you could but know it you gave me the best present you could have by inviting me here today. I would have been on my own if you hadn't.'

He sighed regretfully and for the first time Violet glimpsed a side of him that she hadn't seen before. 'It's funny, isn't it? How you think of the people you miss at Christmas. It doesn't seem so very long ago that Annabel and I were sitting down to Christmas dinner with our parents as a family. And now suddenly my parents have both passed away and Annabel is a married woman. I think it's just hit me that I'm completely alone in the world. I shall be rattling around in that big house like a pea in a pod. I suppose it would make sense for me to sell it and buy something smaller, but it's been the only home I've ever known and my mother and father loved it so much that I'd feel I was letting them down if I let it go.'

Violet couldn't help but feel sorry for him. At least she still had Edie and Sally, she thought, realising again how lucky she was.

'It is hard,' she admitted. 'I still miss Papa every single day and I don't know what I would have done when he died if it hadn't been for Edie.'

'Well, from things I've heard you certainly didn't get much support from your stepmother,' Toby said sadly.

Violet nodded in agreement as she tipped hot water from the kettle into the sink. Suddenly they were speaking to each other as if they had been friends for years and it felt strangely right. They had never really discussed their families or anything personal before, but Toby was so easy to talk to and not at all arrogant as she had first thought. As Violet washed the pots, he dried them and when they had finished and everything was put away, Violet made them all a tray of tea and mince pies and carried it into the drawing room to rejoin Edie and Sally. They were both dozing contentedly in chairs at either side of the fireplace, while outside the window the snow continued to softly fall.

'I, er . . . suppose I should be going now,' Toby said when the tea was drunk and the afternoon was fast darkening. 'I don't want to overstay my welcome but thank you so much for inviting me today. It's been grand.'

'You're goin' nowhere, me lad,' Edie told him bossily. 'What's the rush anyway? Fed up of our company already, are you? Or is it that you're just keen to go back to an empty house?'

'No, no it's neither of those things,' he blustered.

Sally chuckled. 'Stop bullying him, Edie,' she scolded. 'Of course he'll stay. There are still cold cuts of meat, pork pie, pickles, Christmas cake, mince pies and all manner of food waiting to be eaten in that kitchen and we'll never get through it by ourselves.'

'In that case I'd be delighted to stay, although I can't promise I'll be able to eat much after that enormous dinner.'

'You'll find room for sommat an' what's more we'll expect you at the same time tomorrow for dinner,' Edie told him. 'Like I said earlier, you're more than welcome to stay the night if you've a mind to. Can't see the point in goin' all that way only to come back again tomorrer,' she grumbled.

But on that Toby would not be swayed. 'I will come back tomorrow if you're quite sure it's no inconvenience, but I won't stay overnight, if you don't mind. I'd just like to go back and check that all is well at the house.'

Despite what he'd said, Toby enjoyed a very large meal at teatime and didn't leave until almost eight o'clock that evening, by which time they were all so comfortably full that they were sleepy. It wasn't until he had gone that Violet suddenly realised she hadn't thought of Oliver once for the whole afternoon, which she found strange.

'Lovely young chap he is,' Edie said casually with a sly wink at Sally after he'd left.

Violet flushed as she collected the dirty glasses and plates onto a tray and sailed away to the kitchen leaving Sally and Edie looking smug.

Just as he'd promised, Toby was back the next morning, this time bearing two bottles of wine.

'I don't like to come empty-handed,' he told them as Edie ushered him into the drawing room. Violet was in the kitchen preparing lunch with Sally. Once again Violet had made an effort with her appearance and Edie and Sally were relieved. It was the first time she seemed to have cared what she looked like since the night of the attack, and they were both hoping she would start to try and put it behind her now.

The day passed pleasantly and they were all sad when it came to an end and darkness drew in. It was so warm and cosy with the tiny candles twinkling on the Christmas tree and the fire roaring up the chimney that Toby wished he could have stayed there forever. He had been pleased to see that Violet was still wearing the bracelet he had bought for her and hoped she might be a little friendlier towards him from now on. She had held him at arm's length before, but he had always felt attracted to her and had grown to like her even more as he got to know her. In fact, he had come to realise that he more than liked her.

Violet was unlike any other young woman he had ever met. Most of the girls he had known had been spoilt and pampered their whole lives but Violet was kind and seemed to be completely unaware of just how attractive she was. But that was only one of the things he liked about her and now he dared to hope they might finally start to grow a little closer. Only time would tell but he was prepared to take it slowly and move at her pace.

'Eeh, I can't believe it's back to the grindstone tomorrer. This holiday seems to 'ave passed in the blink of an eye,' Edie said dejectedly as she sat toasting her toes by the fire. She had started to feel her age recently and although she loved her café, she was beginning to wonder how much longer she would be able to keep up the long hours.

'We could always employ someone to come in to do the cooking,' Violet had pointed out when Edie had said as much earlier in the day, but for now Edie was adamant that she could manage.

'You could come and live here with me and pop round there just to make sure that everything is running smoothly.'

'I could see to the running of the place,' Sally had offered. 'I did say that I'd be going back there after Christmas was over, didn't I? There's no reason for me to be here any longer. I'm so much better after a rest and ready to go back to work now.'

Violet had found the idea of being alone again quite depressing, but now here was Edie bringing it up again.

'I, er . . . I suppose I should be coming back to help you with the soup kitchen as well,' Violet ventured, looking towards Toby.

He grinned. 'Actually, I have some good news to tell you on that score. As you know we've had to manage with a stall in the market place up to now, so the food is going cold before we've finished serving it in this weather. But thankfully I had a word with the local vicar of St Martin's church on the North Road and he's agreed that as from tomorrow we can use the church hall each evening to serve the food. Better still, he's said that while the weather is so bad some of the homeless people can shelter there through the night rather than be out on the streets.'

Violet's face lit up. She hated to think of the poor souls she had met sleeping out in the snow in shop doorways or wherever they could find shelter, especially Cleggy. 'Why, that's wonderful. I could bring some of the clothes I've been collecting and distribute them amongst those that need them most.'

'Yes, and I'll be sure to send along any food I have left over at the end of the day too,' Edie offered kindly.

And so, it was agreed that Violet would go back to helping the next day. Edie and Sally were delighted; it would surely be better for her than rattling around in a big house with nothing to do.

'There's only one thing,' Toby said, becoming serious. 'If you do come back tomorrow it will mean a longer walk for you and so I'd like you to let the carriage bring you to the church hall and take you home each night. There are still robberies going on in the warehouses along the waterfront and who knows what sort of villains you could bump into. Is it a deal?'

One glance at Edie and Sally's faces made Violet nod reluctantly. She knew she would never hear the end of it if she didn't.

Soon after, she saw Toby to the door and he stepped out into a white world with the snow still swirling down.

'Thank you again for having me.' He took her hand in his. 'I admit I wasn't looking forward to being on my own, but I've had a lovely time with all of you.'

'We've enjoyed having you.' There were little shocks rippling up her arm from his touch and she hastily withdrew her hand from his as she backed into the hallway. 'Have a safe journey home. Goodnight.'

He smiled and disappeared into the swirling snow.

Chapter Twenty-Seven

The following morning Edie and Sally returned to their rooms above the café. Suddenly the house felt enormous, and loneliness settled around Violet like a cloak. Thankfully, Cook, Dora and Stan returned shortly before lunchtime, which made her feel slightly better.

Even so the day passed slowly without Sally to keep her company, so Violet was glad when the day began to darken and she could get ready to go and help Toby.

The carriage arrived exactly on time and as Violet settled against the leather squabs and pulled a blanket over her knees, she realised she was looking forward to being useful and busy again. It would help keep her mind off what Oliver had done to her. She had found she'd missed the people she'd got to know when she'd served soup in the market place.

When she arrived at the church hall, she was thrilled with the set-up. Instead of the trestle table they had been using in the market place there were real tables lined up against one wall and a cheery fire was burning in the grate at one end of the room. Word of the new venue had quickly spread and already there were people warming themselves by the fire as they waited for what would probably be the only meal they would have that day. The vicar's wife – a small, homely-looking woman with grey hair piled into a bun on the back of her head – was there too, armed with old blankets and pillows that could be used by any of those that wanted to spend the night there.

Toby hurried forward to greet her. 'What do you think of it? It's a bit of an improvement to the market place, isn't it?'

'Just a bit.' Violet took off her bonnet and positioned herself behind the serving tables, fastening a large apron across her plain gown.

Soon the homeless people were queuing up and she was ladling thick soup into dishes and encouraging them to help themselves to bread while Toby poured cups of hot tea. It was so much easier to keep it warm inside and everyone was smiling. A familiar figure shuffled forward, and Violet smiled at him.

'Hello, Cleggy, had a decent Christmas, did you?'

'Oh, mustn't grumble, miss. An' yerself?'

'It was very nice, Cleggy, thank you.'

'We missed seein' you,' he said, blushing. 'I 'opes you're all better now?'

'Yes, I am, and I missed you too.'

Violet had a huge soft spot for old Cleggy. Very little was known about him apart from the fact that he had fought in the Boer War before returning with a severe limp in his left leg. The old coat he wore was tied at the waist with a piece of string and an old woolly hat covered his mop of long grey hair. It was rumoured that on returning from the war he had discovered that his wife had disappeared with his two children and he had found someone else living in what had been his home. When he had finally managed to track her down it was only to discover that she had left him for another man and from that day on he had lived on the streets, finding work where he could. Some said that the shock of it had turned his mind and they were wary of him, but Violet had always found him to be an affable soul.

'Will you be staying here for the night, Cleggy? There are some blankets and pillows over there and if you hurry you might bag a place by the fire. Better than being out on the streets, eh?'

'I might just do that.' He took the dish of soup she offered and shuffled away as she turned to the next in the queue.

'I'm on the last tureen of soup now,' Violet told Toby a little while later as she drained the last from the bottom of it.

Almost all the food had gone now – including the left-over sausages and bacon that Edie had sent. Thankfully everyone had eaten, some had even had seconds, and now most of them were sitting about feeling decidedly better for getting something warm inside them. Poor souls. Violet could only imagine how dreadful it must be to be homeless. Had it not been for Edie she was well aware that she could have found herself in the same position after her father died, had it been left to Anna. Thoughts of her step-mother made her think of Oliver and suddenly the smile slid from her face as she relived what he had done to her in her mind.

'Violet . . . Violet . . . are you all right? You've gone awfully pale.'

Toby's voice jerked her back to the present and she flushed. 'Er . . . sorry. I was miles away. What were you saying?'

'I was saying I think you should let the carriage take you home now. We don't want you overdoing it on your first night back.'

'Are you sure you can manage the clearing up?' she said, taking off her apron.

He grinned. 'Not a problem. When the carriage comes back from taking you home, I shall just throw all the dirties inside and they can be washed back at the restaurant. I have to get back there anyway – we have a party of thirty in tonight holding a twenty-first birthday so I suppose I should show my face.'

After putting on her bonnet and coat she wished him goodnight, smiled and waved at Cleggy, and hurried out to the waiting carriage.

When she entered the house, the loneliness closed in once more. Dora and the cook were sitting beside the fireplace in the kitchen and she didn't like to disturb them so she made her way to the bedroom and had an early night.

The next morning at breakfast Dora looked concerned when she entered the dining room to find that Violet had hardly eaten anything.

'Are you not feelin' well again, miss?' she enquired.

'Oh, I'm fine.' Violet flashed her a smile. 'Just a bit of a dicky tummy, that's all.'

'Let's hope you ain't comin' down wi' somethin'.' Dora gathered the pots onto a tray and left Violet to read the newspaper.

After a while, though, Violet decided to visit the café. Anything was better than sitting by herself day after day. She was missing Sally more than she had thought she would. She had taken to her the first time she met her, but during the time Sally had convalesced with her they had grown even closer.

'Will you be in for lunch, miss?' Dora enquired as Violet was getting ready to leave

Violet shook her head. 'No, I think I'll spend the day at the café and go straight on from there to help Mr Brabinger in the church hall, so don't bother with any dinner this evening. I can grab something at the café. I won't be needing the carriage to pick me up so you and Cook can have a nice easy day.'

She had only gone a short distance from the house when she got the feeling that someone was following her. She turned abruptly but there was no one there so she plodded on through the snow, although the feeling of unease remained and she was glad when the café came into sight.

Thankfully by the time she arrived the feeling of sickness had passed. Edie raised an eyebrow when she walked in through the door. 'What are you doin' comin' out on a day like this?' She tutted and shook her head. 'I'd have thought you'd be better off sittin' at the side of the fire wi' a good book. T'ain't fit for man nor beast to be out in this weather if they don't have to be.'

'I'd rather brave the weather than spend another day on my own,' Violet responded as she stamped the snow from her boots near the kitchen door. The bottom of her skirt was sodden, and Edie frowned.

'You'd best go up an' change into one o' my skirts afore you catch your death o' cold,' she ordered. 'It'll be too big for you but your apron will hold it up when you tie it round the waist.'

Knowing Edie wouldn't stop fretting until she did as she as told, she went upstairs. Once she'd hung her own skirt over the clothes guard to dry and slipped into one of Edie's, she glanced around the small rooms and sighed. The whole place wasn't as big as the hallway in the house she had inherited and yet she missed Edie's company and the cosiness of living here. Crossing to the window she gazed down into the street and her breath caught as she spotted a figure standing in a shop doorway over the road. It was a man with his hat pulled low over his face but even so she instantly recognised Oliver. Could it have been him following her earlier? Why else would he be hanging about? Was he planning on attacking her again? The thought made her tremble, but pulling herself together with an effort she dragged herself away from the window and went downstairs to help. At least while she was at the café she would be safe. He wouldn't dare approach her when there were so many people about.

They were kept busy all day. People were keen to come in out of the cold for a warm drink and the time passed quickly. Every now and again Violet found herself glancing towards the window for a sign of Oliver, but he had left the shop doorway shortly after she had spotted him and there had been no sign of him since. Even so, as it came towards the time to go, she grew nervous. She was tempted to ask Sally to walk with her, but it seemed unfair to drag anyone out on such a bitterly cold evening. And anyway, she convinced herself, as long as she stuck to the main roads where people were present, he wouldn't dare do anything, surely.

After saying her goodbyes Violet stepped out onto the pavement and glanced up and down the road. The lamplighter had been some time before and the streetlamps cast a yellow glow across the snowy road. With her heart in her mouth, she set off, frequently glancing over her shoulder, but thankfully she reached the church hall without incident. Toby was already there and his face lit up when he saw her, making her stomach do somersaults. He really was extremely handsome!

Cleggy was there too, and he shuffled across to greet her. 'Evenin', miss.'

'Hello, Cleggy. Did you have a good night last night?'

'I did that.' He grinned, displaying a set of stained teeth. 'I got down by the fire wi' a blanket an' I were snug as a bug in a rug all night long. The vicar's missus 'as already told me I can sleep 'ere tonight an' all if I've a mind to.'

'And have you? A mind to I mean?'

'Not 'alf!'

She smiled as she went to help Toby. Apart from feeling unwell first thing and glimpsing Oliver it hadn't turned out to be such a bad day after all.

Chapter Twenty-Eight

It was New Year's Eve and the day of the ball had arrived and she was so nervous that she hadn't eaten a bite of her lunch, much to Cook's disgust.

She was regretting her decision to go for a number of reasons. The first being that she had never attended a ball before, and she feared she would feel like a fish out of water. Toby moved in very different social circles and she was worried about letting him down. The second reason was Toby himself. She could no longer deny that she was drawn to him, but what could ever come of it? Always presuming he felt the same about her, which she had no idea if he did or not. And, she reasoned, even if he did his feelings wouldn't last long once he discovered what Oliver had done to her. The third reason was that she still wasn't feeling well. Strangely, though, whatever illness she had, it seemed to pass as the day wore on and by lunchtime she usually felt as fit as a fiddle again. At the back of her mind was the terror of what might be wrong with her if she wasn't ill, but the alternative was so awful that she tried not to think of it. Even so, when living at home with her father she had seen enough pregnant women to know of their symptoms and every day she prayed fervently for her late course to come.

However, when she voiced her concerns about the ball to Edie and Sally, who had come to help her get ready and would be staying the night, they scoffed at her. They had taken the afternoon off to help her get ready – they had more than enough staff at the café to keep it running smoothly now that it was doing so well.

'Whatever are you thinkin' of?' Edie snorted when Violet told her how worried she was about showing Toby up in public. 'You're as good as anyone who'll be there so just go an' hold your head high, me girl. I've no doubt you'll be the prettiest there.'

Her new gown was hanging on the wardrobe door and Violet eyed it uncertainly, still not convinced that the night would go well.

'Anyway, it's too late to let Toby down now,' Sally pointed out. 'Poor chap would be insulted, so let's have no more talk about you not being good enough. Go along now and get your bath. We want plenty of time to let your hair dry before I dress it for you.'

Violet did as she was told. There was no point arguing when there were two against one. Once she had bathed, she went back to her bedroom and went to stand at the window for a while as she brushed her hair. Thankfully it had stopped snowing for the first time in days and she hoped it would hold off. Some streets were impassable already. It was growing dark and everywhere looked new and fresh beneath the crisp blanket of pure white snow. She was just about to turn away when something on the other side of the street caught her attention and her heart missed a beat.

Someone was standing staring at the house, but they were too far away from the glow of the streetlight for her to see their face. Even so she knew instantly it was Oliver and it wasn't the first time she had seen him there over the last few days. Her hand flew to her mouth and she dropped her hairbrush. But then anger took over and she snatched the curtains shut. If she let him see that she was afraid of him he was only going to stalk her more. Perhaps she should confront him and have done with it? Now that the idea had occurred to her it wouldn't go away and she began to pace as she tried to decide what to do. Eventually she pushed her feet into her boots and after snatching up her cloak she cautiously made her way down the stairs. As she crossed the hallway, she could hear Edie and Sally chatting in the drawing room. Good, the last thing she wanted was for them to hear her leaving the house. One or both would want to go with her if they did, but if she was to know any peace at all, this was something she must do alone.

She had almost reached the front door when Dora appeared bearing a tray of tea, and seeing Violet with her wet hair and wearing her cape, she paused and frowned.

'Shh!' Violet held her finger to her lips. 'I'm just popping out. I shall only be a few minutes but I don't want Edie and Sally to know I've gone, so please don't say anything.'

Dora didn't look too happy about it but Violet was the boss so she nodded reluctantly. 'Right you are, miss. But make sure you ain't long. The cold's enough to cut you in two out there!'

Violet quietly slipped out of the front door, closing it softly behind her. The street was deserted apart from the solitary figure standing some way along. Her feet made no sound on the snow, so she was almost upon him before he realised she was there.

'What do you want?' she demanded, and his head snapped up. He was huddled in a shabby greatcoat with his hat pulled low over his ears and a thick scarf wound about his neck. Before he could reply she rushed on, 'I don't know how you've got the brass nerve to show your face around here after what you did to me!'

'Ah, well that's why I wanted to see you,' he said, his voice cajoling. 'I know I shouldn't have done what I did but I got carried away because I think so much of you.'

'Don't talk such *rubbish*!' she spat, her eyes flashing fire. 'Just think yourself lucky that I didn't report you to the police. There's still time to, so if I were you, I'd get yourself as far away from here as you can get.'

'Aw, don't be like that, sweetheart. I came to tell you that I want to make an honest woman of you. I meant what I said when I told you I wanted to marry you, Violet.'

'*Marry me!*' Violet's eyes stretched wide. 'Why, Oliver Stroud, I wouldn't marry you if you were the *last* man on earth.'

The smile slid from his face. 'If I were you, I wouldn't say things like that. After all, if it turns out that I've planted my seed in you you'll be glad to take me up on the offer. Nobody else is going to want you, are they?'

Violet felt sick, and wondered how she could ever have been so infatuated with him. Not so long ago he had been her hero, the only young man she had ever admired but now . . . Now she could see him for what he was: an idle, self-centred person who really believed the world owed him a good living. Even so, what he said had shaken her to the core and suddenly she wanted to be as far away from him as she could. He had taken her virginity; she had never even kissed, let alone lain with a man before, so surely she couldn't have got with child after just the one encounter? But the sickness every day and her missed course did have her worried.

The anger left her, and her shoulders sagged as she turned away. 'Just go away, Oliver,' she said wearily, her breath hanging like lace in front of her. 'And do me the favour of never coming back. I don't ever want to see you again.'

He rushed forward and caught her arm so abruptly that she almost overbalanced and went her length in the snow.

'Look – I've said I'm sorry, haven't I? What else can I do? Me and Mother are barely scraping by, and we are family after all. Surely you could spare us a few bob, at least?'

Violet snatched her arm away and glared at him with contempt. Then without another word she set off for home leaving him standing in the snow. She had just got to the top of the steps when the front door opened and Edie appeared.

'And where have you been, me girl, on your own an' out in the dark an' all? I wouldn't 'ave known if I hadn't gone to your room to fetch you for some tea. Dora had to tell me you'd popped out!'

Reaching out she almost dragged Violet into the warmth of the hallway and seeing no point in lying Violet shrugged. 'I saw Oliver standing along the street, so I went out to him. But you needn't worry, I've told him in no uncertain terms to keep away. I doubt he'll show up again.'

'He'd better not!' Edie puffed her chest out. 'Otherwise the dirty young bugger will 'ave *me* to contend wi'. What did he want?

234

I can't believe he'd 'ave the brass neck to show 'is face around 'ere again after what he did!'

'Actually, he said he'd come to apologise and he asked me to marry him again.'

'*Marry him!*' Edie was appalled. 'Well, I hope you told 'im where to go!'

'Oh, I did, don't worry,' Violet assured her glumly.

Edie forced a smile. Why did this have to go and happen today of all days! It should have been a special day for Violet, and she had every intention of making sure that it would be. Violet had never attended a ball before and Edie wanted it to be a day she would never forget.

'Well he's gone now so forget about 'im. Come into the drawin' room an' have this tea then we'll start to get you ready, eh? I can 'ardly wait to see you in your new gown.'

At six thirty Sally turned Violet around to look at herself in the cheval mirror in her bedroom. Violet gasped. She hardly recognised herself. Sally had teased her hair into curls and piled it on top of her head, holding it in place with jewelled combs that caught and reflected the light and leaving a few ringlets to fall across her slim shoulders. Her new gown made her waist look even tinier, although Violet was concerned that it might be a little bit too low-cut. She wore the bracelet Toby had bought her for Christmas, and she was amused to see that both Sally and Edie had tears in their eyes.

'Eeh, you look just like a princess. You'll be the prettiest girl there,' Edie sniffed proudly.

Violet enfolded her and Sally in her arms. 'Thank you both so much for going to all this trouble for me.'

'And why wouldn't we? You're the nearest thing to a daughter either of us 'ave ever 'ad,' Edie told her, which made Sally cry all the harder and made Violet realise just how lucky she was to have two people who cared so much for her in her life.

Dora entered the room then and she too gasped at the sight of her young mistress. 'Eeh . . . you look just . . . just *stunning*!' she croaked.

'Oh, stop it all of you, please, or you'll have me blubbing too and I won't look so nice with red eyes, will I?' Violet giggled.

Lifting the full skirt of the beautiful green gown she made her way downstairs with Sally and Edie hot on her heels and Dora following them with her cloak over her arm.

'So, what's this Judge Warrington who owns Redwood Manor like?' Violet asked.

'Well, he's middle-aged an' he's been a widow for a couple o' years now, I believe,' Edie told her. 'From what I've 'eard he's a bit of a ladies' man wi' an eye for a pretty girl, so lookin' like that you'd best stay close to Toby,' she teased. 'I think he spends weekdays in his townhouse in London to be close to the high court, but I believe he comes 'ome most weekends. Especially when the shootin' season is on. But you just go an' don't think of anythin' but enjoyin' every minute.'

'I'll try,' Violet promised just as the doorbell sounded. She was feeling nervous now, and when Dora admitted Toby, she gulped. He was in a dark evening suit with tails and a brightly coloured waistcoat that matched his cravat, and he looked so handsome that he almost took her breath away. It seemed that she had had the same effect on him, for when he saw her, he stopped dead in his tracks and blinked as if he couldn't believe his eyes.

'Why, Violet . . . you look absolutely *beautiful*.' As he came forward to take her two small hands in his large ones, they might have been the only two people in the room.

Edie broke the spell when she snapped, 'Come along the pair of youse! Don't stand there gawpin' at each other. You don't want to be late.'

Dora came forward and draped Violet's cloak across her shoulders and as Toby held his arm out, she slipped hers into it.

Edie, Sally and Dora stood on the snowy step and watched as Toby helped Violet into the carriage. Even Cook came through from the kitchen to see her go. It had just started to snow again and as Violet peeped out of the carriage window the night suddenly took on a magical quality. She felt like a fairy-tale princess from the books Edie used to read to her when she was a little girl.

Once the carriage was out of sight Edie sniffed and dabbed at her eyes. 'Eeh, they make a lovely couple, don't they?'

'They certainly do.' Sally took her arm and led her back into the house.

'I just hope Violet opens her eyes to what a good catch Toby is.' She paused then, before confiding, 'Some time ago a little bird whispered to me as it were Toby who paid for me new window at the café that time Banks's gang smashed it. They also said it were 'im that had the tables an' chairs ordered for us, bless 'im.'

'I guessed as much. But you know we can't make her love him,' Sally said sensibly. 'All we can do is keep our fingers crossed that things work out as we hope.'

'Amen to that.' Edie grinned as the two women settled down to have a friendly game of cards while they waited for Violet to come home.

'I, er . . . I'm feeling a little nervous,' Violet confessed as the carriage swayed along the road.

Toby took her hand and squeezed it gently. 'I can guarantee you'll be the belle of the ball so just try to relax and enjoy it. Just be yourself.'

Her first sight of Redwood Manor took her breath away. It blazed with light at the end of a long tree-lined drive with a large turning circle in front of it where people were descending from carriages.

'It's *huge*,' Violet gasped.

Toby chuckled. 'It certainly is. Hugh Warrington is one of the richest men in the county and Redwood Manor has been in his family for centuries apparently.'

The carriage drew up at the bottom of the enormous circular steps that led to the front doors, and Toby courteously held his arm out. 'Here we are then. Shall we go in?'

Chapter Twenty-Nine

As they entered a spacious hallway lit by glittering chandeliers, maids rushed forward to take their cloaks and bonnets, and Hugh Warrington, who was waiting to greet his guests, stepped forward.

'Toby, how lovely to see you, young man.' He shook Toby's hand and gave Violet a little bow. 'And pray tell me who your delightful companion is.'

'This is Miss Violet Stroud, sir.'

The gentleman took her hand and chivalrously raised it to his lips. 'You honour us with your presence, my dear.'

Violet smiled and blushed. Now she knew what Edie had meant when she said the judge was something of a ladies' man.

'Would you by any chance be related to the late Doctor Stroud?'

'Yes, sir, he was my father.'

He nodded, still keeping a grip on her hand. 'He was an excellent doctor and a fine man,' he said solemnly.

She nodded in agreement, wondering when she was ever going to get her hand back. Thankfully, other guests were arriving so he moved on, and Toby led her into an enormous sitting room where maids in starched lace caps were waiting to serve them glasses of the finest champagne in crystal goblets, and tiny canapés on silver trays.

'It's very grand, isn't it?' Violet whispered as they each took a drink.

It soon became clear that Toby knew a lot of the people there and they all came to shake his hand and bow to Violet. She sipped at her drink and blinked as the bubbles went up her nose. She had never tasted champagne before but she liked it. Everywhere she looked were women in beautiful gowns in all the colours of the rainbow and wearing jewels that glittered in the candlelight. Eventually they moved into the dining room, where there was a table that Violet was sure could have comfortably seated at least thirty people. But tonight it was covered in a sumptuous buffet and waiters were busily filling plates with food of the guests' choice. Next Toby led her into the ballroom where an orchestra was tuning up on the stage and again, she had to pinch herself to believe she was really here. It was like another world to the one she had known, although she was very aware that she had been fortunate compared to most. Toby led her to one of the small tables scattered around the dance floor and pulled out a chair for her. 'May I get you something to eat – some smoked salmon or caviar, perhaps? – and another drink?'

'I think I'm too excited to eat at present,' she admitted. 'But I'd like another drink.' Strangely enough, after the first one she found she was beginning to relax just a little.

Soon after the ball began and from the time Toby led her onto the dance floor she felt as if she was caught up in a dream. He was a wonderful dancer and gazing up at him, their eyes locked and she felt as if they were the only two people in the room. They danced almost the whole night, stopping only for refreshments, until finally she had to stop for a rest. 'My feet feel like they're on fire,' she told him, laughing, and he instantly led her out of the ballroom and onto a sheltered balcony where they stood and watched the snow falling. It was cold so they had it to themselves, but the cold was a blessing after the heat of the ballroom. Lanterns had been strung in the trees, and the candlelight flickering on the snow looked magical. As she stared out at the snowy vista, Violet sighed with contentment wishing the night could go on forever.

'I've had a *wonderful* time,' she told Toby softly and she meant it.

'So have I, and I hope it's the first of many nights we'll spend in each other's company.' He gently turned her towards him and kissed her, his heart beating against her own. She had tried to deny how she felt about him for so long, but now she knew without doubt that this was the man she loved, and she gave herself up to the pleasure of the kiss. Suddenly, though, reality came back to her with a sickening jolt and she gently disentangled herself from his arms. 'I, er . . . think we should go in now,' she said in a shaky voice.

Toby frowned. 'Violet, I'm so sorry if I've offended you. I never meant to—'

'It doesn't matter.' She turned and quickly made her way inside where the first person they saw was Hugh Warrington.

'Right, young man, I think it's high time you let me claim this lovely young lady of yours for a dance,' he laughed, and before Violet could object, he had taken her elbow and whisked her away back onto the dance floor.

'I have to tell you, sir,' she said falteringly. 'Mr Brabinger isn't my young man. We're just, er . . . friends.'

'Really?' There was an amused twinkle in his eye. 'Well, by the way you two were staring at each other when you were dancing you could certainly have fooled me. Still, it's none of my business. Now, would you like a drink, my dear; you look rather flushed.'

Mr Warrington led her to a chair and went off to get her yet another glass of champagne. Across the room, she saw Toby speaking to a very attractive young lady. The girl was staring up at him admiringly from behind her fan, batting her eyelashes, and Violet felt a pang of jealousy.

Mr Warrington returned shortly and handed her a glass. This would be her fourth and she thought she had better make it her last. She was actually feeling quite tiddly. Toby joined them soon after, and Mr Warrington strode away and up onto the stage.

'Ladies and gentlemen. We will be welcoming the New Year in in less than a minute, but before we do, I'd like to thank you all for coming and tell you that I hope the year ahead will be a good one for all of us. And now join me in the countdown. Ten, nine, eight, seven, six, five, four, three, two, one! *Happy New Year!*'

Once again, she found herself in Toby's arms and this time when he kissed her, she melted into him and didn't attempt to pull away. People were laughing and cheering and the atmosphere was merry as they finally broke apart. 'Happy New Year, Violet,' he whispered.

'And a Happy New Year to you too.' She smiled. Soon, though, they were caught up in a huge circle of people who were slapping each other on the back, kissing cheeks and wishing each other a Happy New Year.

'I suppose I should think of getting you home,' Toby said reluctantly after a time. 'Otherwise, I'll have Edie on at me for keeping you out too late.'

They went to collect Violet's cloak and Toby's coat and while a footman rushed off to tell one of the grooms to bring the carriage round, they sought out Mr Warrington to thank him for such a lovely evening.

'It was my pleasure to have you,' the man told them warmly. 'I hope we shall see you both here again. Goodnight, have a safe journey home.' And much to their amusement he was off like a greyhound to find the very attractive widow he had been chasing for most of the evening.

They were still chuckling as they settled back into the carriage.

'What did you think of your first ball?'

Violet's eyes sparkled. 'It was wonderful. Thank you for inviting me.'

Very gently he took her hand and no more was said until the carriage pulled up outside Violet's house. The lights were still on in the hallway and the drawing room and she laughed.

'It looks like Edie and Sally are waiting up for me.'

He nodded. 'It must be nice to have people like them to love you. I'm afraid I only have Annabel now that our parents are gone, and obviously her new husband is her priority now.'

'Oh, I'm sure at least one of the maids will wait up for you to take your coat and see that you have everything you need,' she said.

He shook his head. 'I told them not to wait up. Anyway, let's get you in out of the cold.'

He helped her down from the carriage and up the steps, but before they reached the door it was opened by Edie with Sally close behind her.

'So . . . did you have a good time?'

'We had a *wonderful* time.' Violet turned to Toby with stars in her eyes. 'Thank you again, Toby . . . Goodnight.'

He took her hand and kissed it, much to the delight of both Edie and Sally, then turned and went back to the carriage as the women ushered Violet inside.

'Come on, tell us all about it,' Edie pressed as Violet stifled a yawn.

'I will and happily, but can we talk in the morning? I'm really tired.'

'Get yourself off to bed then and I'll bring you up a cup of hot milk,' Sally said kindly.

But when Sally entered Violet's room shortly after it was to find her lovely gown hanging on the wardrobe door and Violet fast asleep, her beautiful dark hair fanned out on the pillow around her.

Sally smiled as she placed the cup down and tenderly stroked Violet's cheek, then quiet as a mouse she crept from the room and went to her own bed.

Violet's happy mood disappeared within seconds of her waking the next morning as a wave of sickness made her lean across the bed and retch into the chamber pot.

Sally was just entering the room with a cup of tea for her and she chewed her lip in concern as she saw what was happening.

She sat on the side of the bed, holding Violet's hair back until she had finished heaving, before asking with concern, 'Is this still happening every morning, love?'

Violet nodded miserably as she ran the back of her hand across her mouth and flopped back on the pillows.

'And have you had any other unusual things you've noticed?'

Violet thought for a minute before nodding. 'Yes . . . my, er . . . breasts are very tender,' she admitted in a small voice.

'I see, and have you missed any more courses?'

Violet frowned. 'Yes, I've missed two now.'

'Hmm, in that case I think it's time we got the doctor to have a look at you.'

'Why? What do you think may be wrong?' Violet looked seriously worried now. Were Sally's suspicions the same as her own?

'Well . . . I hate to say it but I have a horrible suspicion you could be carrying a child.'

Violet sat bolt upright. 'I've been fearing that too but surely it couldn't happen after just that one time?'

Sally took her hand and stroked it tenderly. 'I'm afraid it can, pet. And it looks suspiciously like it has.'

Edie entered the room at that moment and seeing that Violet was in a state she frowned. 'What's goin' on?'

Slowly Sally told her what she suspected and by the time she'd finished there were tears in Edie's eyes. 'Why, that dirty little bugger. I tell you if he were 'ere now I'd gladly throttle 'im wi' me own hands. But what do we do now?'

'I think the first thing is to get Violet to see the doctor and we'll take it from there.'

'But I *can't* have a baby . . . I just *can't*. Especially not Oliver's!' Violet sobbed, and their hearts went out to her. This was no fault of her own, and yet she was the one who'd have to bear the consequences.

'Do you think this is what Oliver was hoping for?' she asked brokenly.

'I've no doubt that's what he'd want,' Edie snorted angrily. 'He'd get his feet under the table good an' proper then, wouldn't 'e cos he'd think you'd have no choice but to marry him? An' I've no doubt he'd move his mother in an' all. But look, don't go gettin' yourself into a tizzy. We could be worryin' for nothin' an' it could be a false alarm. The doctor's surgery will be open tomorrow so we'll get you there first thing. We won't disturb 'im today, it bein' New Year's Day.'

Violet nodded, but the next day felt like a lifetime away.

Chapter Thirty

'Are you ready?' Edie asked the next morning after breakfast. She had agreed to go with Violet to the doctor while Sally went to open the café.

'As I'll ever be.' Once again Violet hadn't been able to face a thing at breakfast. Just the smell of food made her feel nauseous and now she just wanted to get this visit over with.

It had stopped snowing during the night but the snow that lay on the ground was frozen solid and as slippery as a skating rink. They clung on to each other for dear life as they skidded along, and Violet prayed as she had never prayed before that Sally and Edie might be wrong. The thought of having Oliver's child growing inside her after the way he had behaved sickened her. When they reached the surgery, they gave the doctor's wife Violet's name and took a seat in the small waiting room. As usual at that time of year it was crammed with people suffering from flu and coughs and colds. *If only that was all I was here for,* Violet thought.

At last it was her turn and gripping Edie's hand they entered the doctor's small surgery. Dr Grant was her father's successor and recognised her immediately, which somehow made it worse. *What would he think of her?*

'Ah, Miss Stroud. It's good to see you,' he greeted her affably. 'May I congratulate you? I heard that you had come into an inheritance. I'm sure your father would have been delighted for you. My patients tell me he was a wonderful man. What can I do for you on this cold and frosty morning?'

Violet opened her mouth to speak but try as she might no words would come out, so Edie took over.

'Back in November she were, er . . . attacked on her way home,' she told him with a catch in her voice. 'An' now the poor lass 'as missed two courses, so we fear the worst!'

'Oh goodness!' The doctor scowled. 'And was this incident reported to the police?'

'No, it weren't, cos Violet didn't want it known.' Edie sighed. 'It were Oliver Stroud who did it to her, see?'

'Her *brother*?' The doctor looked shocked.

Edie quickly explained that Violet and Oliver weren't blood related and how they had only discovered it following her father's death.

The doctor looked stunned. But after a moment he took a deep breath and said gently, 'Perhaps we should have a look at you, eh? Could you go behind that screen there and undress down to your underwear? Mrs Thompson is quite welcome to stay with you.'

Shaking like a leaf, Violet did as she was asked and soon after the doctor joined her and the examination began.

'All right, you can get dressed again,' he said eventually, and Violet shuffled back into her clothes feeling mortified.

Once they were seated in front of his desk again, Edie asked bluntly, '*Well?*'

The doctor steepled his fingers and peered over the top of them. 'I'm afraid in this case you were right to be concerned. I would say Miss Stroud is approximately two months pregnant. I imagine the child will be born sometime in July. I'm so sorry to have to be the bearer of bad news.'

Violet sat there, momentarily too stunned to speak as the colour drained out of her face.

Edie started to cry angry tears. 'I *told you* we should've told the police about the attack,' she snivelled.

Pulling herself together with a great effort, Violet shook her head. 'It's a bit late to think of that now and it wouldn't help the situation anyway. Come on, we must go. Thank you, Doctor.'

Outside on the frosty pavement Edie put her arm about Violet's shoulders. 'Eeh, pet, I don't know what to say. Let's go an' ask Mr Chapman for some advice, eh?'

In a daze they made their way to Mr and Mrs Chapman's house. They had been extremely good to Violet, and Edie valued the solicitor's opinion.

'I suppose I shall have no choice but to marry Oliver now,' Violet said glumly when they were almost there.

'What? An' let him get his 'ands on your house an' all your inheritance?'

'But at least the baby would have a father and be born in wedlock,' Violet pointed out, although the thought of Oliver ever touching her again made her cringe inside.

When they arrived at the house, Mrs Chapman's young maid showed them into the bright day room where Mr and Mrs Chapman joined them.

'This is a nice surprise,' Mr Chapman greeted them. 'Happy New Year to you both. I thought you'd be back at work today, Edie?'

She nodded. 'Aye, I should 'ave been but somethin' cropped up an' we need your advice.'

'Oh yes?' He went to stand in front of the fire and motioned them to the sofa while his wife took a chair at the side of him. 'So, what can I do for you? I should have been back at work myself today but Enid persuaded me to take an extra couple of days off.'

Edie licked her lips before blurting out the whole sorry story and when she was finished the Chapmans looked shocked.

'Oh my dear, how utterly dreadful. What will you do now?'

'Well, I suppose I don't have a lot of choice. I shall have to marry Oliver.'

The maid entered with a tray of coffee just then, and, scowling, Mr Chapman waited until she had left the room before saying, 'I'm afraid we may have a problem if that's the course of action you decide to take. You see, as I explained, it was Anna who caused the breach between your late aunt and your father, and she left a codicil in her will stating that should you ever offer shelter to either Anna or her son in your new home then you would forfeit both the house and all monies and businesses left to you. The estate would revert back to me to distribute between whichever charities I saw fit. I didn't want to mention this before as I knew you would find it upsetting.'

'But if I don't marry him, I shall be a single woman when I give birth and my child will be branded a bastard!'

The solicitor sighed. He had never thought the codicil would be a problem after the way Oliver and his mother had abandoned Violet, but then he could never have foreseen this happening.

'I'm so sorry, my dear.'

In the stunned silence that followed, his wife poured the coffee and handed the delicate bone china cups and saucers around.

When they'd finished their drinks, it seemed there was nothing more to be said, so Edie and Violet rose to leave. 'I'm so very sorry.' Mr Chapman was genuinely upset for her, as was his wife. They had grown very fond of her since her father's death.

'It's not your fault. You're only following my late aunt's instructions,' Violet told him with a watery smile. She was so muddled that she could barely think straight. In one way she was relieved that that option was no longer open to her, for the thought of marrying Oliver made her stomach lurch.

As she and Edie made their way home, they were silent, each locked in their own thoughts. It wasn't until they were seated in the drawing room getting warm by the fire that Violet said dolefully, 'What am I going to do, Edie? Once word gets out my reputation will be in tatters.'

'There's no rush to do anythin' just yet, pet. You won't be showin' for some months,' Edie pointed out.

'I suppose . . . I've heard there are people you can go to who can help girls in my situation,' Violet said quietly.

Edie was immediately incensed. 'Don't even *think* o' goin' down that path,' she warned. 'Do you 'ave any idea 'ow many young girls 'ave died after goin' to them butchers? No, we'll think o' somethin'. Now I really ought to be gettin' back to help Sally. Just promise me you won't go doin' anythin' daft. We'll both come back this evenin' after the café 'as closed.'

She gave Violet a kiss on the cheek and left, and only then did Violet give vent to the torrent of tears that had been building inside her. She had been floating on a cloud of happiness on New Year's Eve, and now here she was in the depths of despair.

Eventually she pulled herself together and went to stand at the window. In one way what Mr Chapman had told her had come as a relief. She couldn't picture herself married to Oliver, and anyway, she had a sneaky suspicion that when he learnt about the codicil, he wouldn't want to marry her anyway – she wasn't fool enough to think that he would have married her for love. She could see Oliver clearly for what he was now. He would only have married her for an easy life and a ready-made home for himself and his mother.

Dora pottered in to collect the tea tray and pausing she asked, 'Is everythin' all right, miss? You look a bit upset, if you don't mind me sayin'.'

Just for a second Violet was tempted to tell her about the baby but then thought better of it. Until she had reached a decision about what she was going to do, the fewer people who knew the better, although she wasn't foolish enough to think she could hide it forever.

As she thought back to New Year's Eve and how it had felt to be held in Toby's arms as they glided around the dance floor, the tears came once more. One thing was for certain, she must never encourage him again. She knew she wouldn't be able to bear the look of disgust that would surely show on his face when he found out she was with child. This thought presented another problem. She was still helping out at the soup kitchen each evening, but would it be sensible to continue? As Edie had pointed out, in the not-too-distant future she would no longer be able to hide her condition. No, she would send Stan with a message to say she was feeling unwell again. That would at least buy her a little time to come up with a plan for what she should do next.

There was no time like the present, so she sat down at the small escritoire next to the window and penned a note to Toby before hurrying out to the stables to ask Stan to deliver it. He set off immediately and as she went back into the house her heart was heavy as she thought of what might have been.

Chapter Thirty-One

February 1906

As they entered February, the violent morning sickness began to abate and Violet felt much better. Physically, at least. But inside she was an emotional wreck. Toby had called around on a number of occasions to see her but each time she had told Dora to tell him she wasn't well enough to receive visitors, and that she must not admit him at any cost. It hadn't prevented him from returning and sending flowers every few days and this made Violet feel even worse. He was such a kind person and she hated deceiving him, although in her heart she felt she was doing it for his own good.

She was now four months pregnant and although no one else would have guessed it by looking at her, she had noticed that the waistlines of her skirts were getting a little tighter. Very soon she would no longer be able to hide the fact, so she had finally made a decision: she would go away until after the baby's birth. She had no idea what she would do with the baby when it did arrive, but she reasoned that she could cross that bridge when she came to it. One thing she was sure of, though, there was no way she wanted to keep it. It would be a constant reminder of what Oliver had done to her and all she felt for the life growing inside her was disgust.

She had barely ventured out of the house since the pregnancy was confirmed, apart from to occasionally take a short stroll along the road when it was dark. And it was on one such evening that she bumped into Oliver again. He had been hovering in the shadows a few doors down from her house and as she approached, he stepped into the light of the streetlamp and smiled at her.

'What do you want? We have nothing to say to each other,' she told him icily. She'd known she'd see him eventually.

'Don't be like that.' His smile would have charmed the hardest heart, but it did nothing for her now.

'I've come to ask if you've given my offer any more thought? About marrying me, I mean.'

Violet decided to play him at his own game. 'I have as it happens, and the answer is yes, I'll marry you.'

His eyes lit up and he rushed forward to place his arms about her, but she remained rigid. 'I thought you'd see sense in the end,' he said, clearly pleased with himself. 'And I suggest we do it as soon as possible, what do you think?'

She shrugged nonchalantly. 'Fine, although there is something I think I should tell you before you rush off to book the church.'

'Oh yes?' He was smiling from ear to ear as he contemplated the easy life that lay ahead of him.

'The thing is, Mr Chapman, my solicitor, told me something very interesting.'

He was staring down at her, the smile still firmly in place. 'He told me that my aunt had a codicil added to her will.'

'And what was that?'

'She stated that should I ever give shelter to you or your mother in my house, every penny I have, the business and the house would all revert back to Mr Chapman, who could then sell everything and distribute the monies amongst charities of his choice.'

Seeing the look of confusion on Oliver's face it was her that was smiling now. 'So basically, I shall come to you with very little. But still, if you care for me so very much that won't trouble you in the least, will it?'

A look of horror crossed his face and he stepped away as if he had been burned. Violet was enjoying herself now and went on, 'I suppose I shall have to come and live with you and your mother. You won't mind that, will you?'

He shook his head, struggling to take in what she had said. 'You mean you'll forfeit everything?'

She nodded solemnly. 'Everything: the house . . . the money . . . the businesses.'

'Well . . . I, er, wouldn't like to make you do that,' he said, his face suddenly ashen. 'Perhaps we could come to some other arrangement?'

'Such as what?'

'Um . . . well, we could still be close. What I mean is, we could still see each other and if you have all that money, you could perhaps find me somewhere a little more salubrious to live and see your way clear to helping me out now and again.'

'You mean instead of me being your kept woman you'd be my kept man?' Violet was trying not to laugh at how quickly he had gone off the idea of marriage once he knew that she'd be penniless.

But then her face hardened and leaning towards him she spat, 'Even if there wasn't that clause in the will, I wouldn't have married you if you were the last man left on earth!'

His face turned ugly. 'No, but I bet you'll marry that bloody snob Brabinger! Just because he owns a fancy restaurant and can spend money on you!'

'In case you hadn't noticed, I don't need anyone to buy me anything anymore. I'm a wealthy woman and I certainly won't let an idle, no-good fortune hunter like you have a penny! So why don't you go now and leave me alone? I don't think we have anything more to say to each other!'

She turned to go back, but Oliver grabbed her arm and swung her about so abruptly she almost lost her footing.

'Let me tell *you*,' he snarled. 'I'm going to get my own back on you if it's the last thing I ever do. When I've finished with you *no man* will want you!'

He lifted his arm and Violet braced herself for the blow that was to come but thankfully the front door of one of the houses

254

opened and an elderly gentleman in a top hat and a heavy coat appeared.

'*Here, you!* What do you think you're doing!'

As he started down the steps Oliver turned and fled.

Hurrying to Violet's side the man put his hand out to steady her. 'Are you all right, my dear? Aren't you the young lady that moved into Amelia's house a while ago?'

'Y-yes I am, and I'm fine, thank you,' she answered in a wobbly voice. She dreaded to think what would have happened if he hadn't appeared. She knew all too well what Oliver was capable of.

'Then let's get you back to your home and out of the cold.' He gently led her back to the house, refusing to leave her until Dora opened the door. 'If you have any idea who that thug was, I suggest you report him to the police,' he suggested, then after giving her a little bow he went on his way.

Dora led Violet to the drawing room. 'Eeh, whatever's happened, miss? Why, you're as white as a ghost. Sit yourself down while I go an' make you a nice cup o' hot, sweet tea, or perhaps you'd like somethin' a little stronger?'

'No, no, I'm fine!'

Edie and Sally appeared just then – Sally still had a key to the house and they often let themselves in so as not to bother Dora.

Edie frowned as she noticed Violet's pale face. 'What's happened?'

Violet told them about her confrontation with Oliver.

While Sally wrung her hands, Edie began to pace. 'That's it! It's time we got the police involved! That bugger has got to be stopped one way or another.'

'No!' Violet bounced to her feet, and in that instant she knew there was only one thing she could do. 'I-I've decided to go away.'

'Away? Away where?' Edie looked appalled. Violet had always led such a sheltered life; how would she survive on her own? Especially now she was carrying a child.

'I'm not going to get any peace if I stay around here, am I?' Now that the decision was made, Violet felt surprisingly calm about it. 'So I think it will be for the best if I move away until after the baby is born.'

'Oh yes, an' then what?'

Violet shrugged. 'I haven't thought that far ahead yet,' she admitted. 'But you must see it makes sense?'

'I think she may be right.' Sally surprised Edie by agreeing. 'But I'd feel a lot happier about it if you let me come with you.'

Violet looked shocked. 'But how will Edie manage at the café without you?'

'I'll manage just fine. There's allus folks are glad of a job,' Edie told her. 'An' for what my opinion's worth I'd feel a lot better about it if you 'ad someone you know with you. The staff 'ere are more than capable o' keepin' the house runnin' smoothly till you come back.'

'I'll give it some thought,' Violet answered quietly. 'And I appreciate the offer, Sally. Just give me a little time to get things straight in my mind. I haven't even decided where I'm going yet. I just know it needs to be somewhere far enough away from here that Oliver won't be able to find me.'

Edie sighed. It sounded like Violet had made up her mind. 'Why don't you go to London? Ain't much chance of anyone findin' you there if you don't want to be found. It'd be like lookin' for a needle in a haystack.'

'Hmm.' Violet quite liked the sound of that. Her father had taken her to London once for a sightseeing tour and she had loved it. It looked like she had a lot of plans to make.

Chapter Thirty-Two

Three days later Dora entered the day room. 'Miss, there's a man at the door askin' to see you.'

'A man?' Violet's heart started to thump. 'It isn't Mr Brabinger, is it?'

Dora shook her head and lowering her voice she went on, 'He says is name is Mr Bernard Clegg. He says you know him, but . . . well, I reckon he's a tramp. He certainly looks an' smells like one!'

'Oh!' Violet smiled. What could Cleggy be doing here? 'Show him in, please, and then could you bring us some tea and biscuits.'

'Bring him in here?' Dora looked shocked. But seeing her mistress meant what she said, she went to do as she was told with a disapproving look on her face.

When Dora showed Cleggy into the room, he was clutching his old hat in both hands, his wiry hair standing out around his head like a wild grey halo.

'Cleggy, how nice it is to see you. Come on in.' Violet was genuinely happy to see him. She had missed the people she had come to know at the soup kitchen, especially Cleggy.

'I's sorry to disturb yer, miss. But I were worried about you. Mr Brabinger said as yer were ill an' I just wanted to see how you were.'

'Oh, bless you. Come and sit down and get warm,' Violet invited.

Cleggy eyed the velvet upholstery of the small sofa uncertainly but limped forward to do as she asked. She noted that his old coat was still tied at the waist with string and the soles of his boots were flapping off his feet. His beard hung down to his chest, wild and untamed, and he looked frozen. It was no wonder, she thought, it was still bitterly cold outside.

'I'm fine, thank you, Cleggy,' she told him. 'Just taking precautions, but how about you? Are you still staying in the church hall?'

He shook his head. 'Not fer the last few nights, miss. It were booked up for a weddin' reception a few days ago and various things since.'

'So where are you sleeping now?'

He shrugged his thin shoulders. 'Oh, here an' there, yer know. Shop doorways or anywhere where there's a bit o' shelter, really.' Then seeing the look of dismay on her face he hurried on, 'But it ain't so bad. At least the snow's goin' now, an' I'm used to it.'

Dora appeared with a loaded tray and after another disapproving glance towards the visitor she placed it down next to Violet and left the room, leaving the door ajar behind her. After all, she had reasoned, you never knew what a vagabond like that might try to do to the miss and at least if the door was open, she would hear her if she cried out.

Violet poured Cleggy a cup of tea and he took it nervously. He wasn't used to such dainty cups and saucers.

'Did Mr Brabinger know you were coming to see me?' Violet enquired as she offered him a plate of shortbread fresh from the oven.

'No, miss. But I know he's worried about you. I heard him talkin' to the vicar's wife an' sayin' how much he missed your help.'

Violet bit her lip as she glanced towards the window. It was raining cats and dogs outside and now that Cleggy had come into a warm room his clothes were starting to steam, poor thing. It was then that she made a hasty decision that she hoped she wouldn't live to regret.

'Are you any good at painting and doing jobs around the house, Cleggy?'

He looked slightly confused as he nodded. 'I'm a dab hand at a bit o' decoratin' an' I can turn me hand to most things. But why do you ask, miss?'

'How would you fancy coming here to live with me as my odd-job man?'

He looked so shocked that he almost dropped his cup. '*Here . . . with . . . you?*'

'Well, you'd actually have a room on the top floor in the servants' quarters with Cook and Dora,' she explained. 'I could give you bed and board and a small wage, and we'd have to get you some new clothes. I'm sure we could find enough to keep you busy. Stan does most of the outside work but he'd be glad of a hand in the gardens come the summertime. What do you think?'

'I, er . . .' He was lost for words and shook his head, his eyes full of tears. He could hardly believe what he was hearing. 'If you're quite sure, miss, I'd love to work for you,' he said in a quavering voice.

It was decided as simply as that, although Violet was already dreading what Cook and Dora might think of the idea. Somehow she couldn't see either of them being too happy about it.

She waited for him to drink his second cup of tea and finish off the shortbread before telling him, 'Come along, I'll introduce you to Cook and Dora. I think Stan has gone off on an errand but you can meet him later.'

As she led him along the highly polished tiles in the hallway towards the green baize door that led to the kitchen, his eyes were on stalks. Never in his wildest dreams had he ever imagined himself living and working in a place like this. And for Miss Stroud too.

Dora and Cook looked up when they entered, and just as Dora's had, Cook's nose wrinkled with distaste at the unkempt man standing beside her young mistress.

'I've brought someone to meet you,' Violet told them with a broad smile. 'This is Mr Clegg, or Cleggy as he prefers to be called, and he's going to be joining the staff as our odd-job man.'

Cook's mouth dropped open and Dora gasped.

'You've given me quite a list of little jobs that need doing lately, Cook, so I'm sure Cleggy will be happy to get them done for you. Stan can't be expected to do everything in a house this size.'

'B-but . . .' Cook looked horrified. 'If he's goin' to be stayin' 'ere an' usin' my kitchen he'll 'ave to smarten himself up, miss,' she said indignantly.

'Of course, we're aware of that. I thought Stan might take him shopping for some new clothes this afternoon after lunch. And you, Dora, could perhaps get a bedroom ready for him up in the servants' quarters, if you wouldn't mind. I'm sure he'd welcome a trip to the barber's and a nice hot bath too, wouldn't you, Cleggy?'

He gulped and nodded, not too sure about that, but he didn't want to spoil his chances.

'Good.' Violet smiled round at them; it had gone better than she'd hoped. 'I'll leave you all to get to know each other. Come and see me after lunch, Cleggy, and I'll give you some money for new clothes.' And with that she turned and quickly left the room with a little grin on her face. Cook was clearly dismayed at the thought of Cleggy being there but Violet hoped that once he had smartened himself up and she got to know him a little better that might change.

Left alone with the new arrival Cook glared at him. She wasn't too happy with the new member of staff at all, but Violet was the boss, so who was she to argue? She had no doubt that as soon as the man got his hands on some money for clothes, he'd be off like a shot never to be seen again, which to her mind would be the best outcome for all of them. Meantime she supposed she'd have to feed him. He looked half starved.

She motioned him to the table and after crossing to the stove she measured a good portion of beef stew and dumplings into a dish and slammed it down in front of him.

'Get that down you,' she ordered none too kindly. 'An' while you're eatin' it, I'll lay a few ground rules down. Miss Stroud might be the mistress, but the kitchen is *my* domain!' She glanced around with satisfaction at the spotlessly clean room. Violet often teased her that it was so clean she could have eaten off the floor. 'If you want to be in 'ere you'd best get yourself off to the barber's for a start off an' 'ave that lot chopped off.' She motioned towards his hair and beard with disdain. 'Then you can get yourself to the public baths an' 'ave a good scrub before gettin' rid o' them rags you're wearin' an' gettin' yourself into some clean togs. You'll use this staircase 'ere that leads up to the staff's rooms an' when you get back Dora 'ere will 'ave a room ready for you. An' you *never, ever* enter any other part o' the house unless the young miss asks you to, is that all clear?'

When he nodded, she went on, 'I've a list as long as me arm o' small jobs that need doin', startin' wi' a shelf that's come down in the pantry. You can start on them tomorrer. Idle 'ands make work for the devil, so don't think as you ain't goin' to earn yer keep.'

'I'm 'appy to do anythin' you ask,' Cleggy answered humbly.

Somewhat mollified, Cook nodded and went about her business.

As promised, after lunch Violet gave him some money but he informed Stan that he was quite capable of shopping for himself and set off.

'Hmm, now 'is pocket is full we won't see 'im again, you just mark me words,' Cook told Dora smugly. 'I've no doubt he'll head for the nearest inn an' the money will be gone afore tonight!'

Imagine her surprise when there was a tap on the door later that afternoon and she opened it to find a respectable man standing there.

'Yes?' she said tartly.

'Er, it's me, missus . . . Cleggy.'

She blinked, hardly able to believe her eyes. 'Oh, er . . . right, you'd best come in.' He was clean-shaven and his hair had been neatly trimmed. He was wearing a new shirt and trousers, with a plain warm coat over them, and carrying a bag that she supposed would hold a change of clothes. Even the smelly old boots had been replaced with a pair of sensible black ones.

'I didn't recognise you wi'out all that hair,' she admitted grudgingly. Now that he was clean, she realised that he was nowhere near as old as she had first thought. He was probably somewhere in his late fifties, much the same age as herself.

Once inside he fumbled in his pocket and held out a sum of money to her. 'This is the miss's change. Could you see she gets it, missus? You did say I ain't allowed past that door.'

Cook coughed to clear her throat before handing the change to Dora who went to take it to Violet.

'Could I per'aps take these things up to me room?' he asked politely.

Cook nodded. 'Aye, top o' the stairs, the last door on yer right.'

He nodded and set off to explore his new home as Cook thumped down heavily onto the nearest chair. Dora came back looking amused. 'You got that wrong, didn't you?' she said with a twinkle in her eye.

Cook sniffed and stuck her nose in the air. She hated to be proven wrong about anything. 'Well, at least he came back. But now we'll just wait an' see 'ow useful 'e is about the place. He'll probably idle about all day expectin' to be waited on.'

Dora entered the kitchen the next morning to get the fire going only to find it already burning brightly, and the sound of banging and hammering coming from the pantry. Opening the door, she found Cleggy busily fixing not just the broken shelf, but he was adding a brand new one above it as well.

'You can never 'ave too much storage space in these places,' he told her. 'Oh, an' there's a pot of tea brewin' on the table.'

Dora was surprised and impressed as she went to pour the tea. Cook entered the room shortly after and raised an eyebrow.

'What's all that racket?'

Dora grinned. 'It's Cleggy. He's in the pantry fixing your shelf back up and puttin' up a new one besides. He lit the fire and made a pot of tea before I came down as well.'

'Oh . . . right!' She'd been so sure Cleggy wouldn't stay around, and even if he did, she had doubted he'd be much help. But if he carried on at this rate, she might be forced to eat her words.

Shortly after breakfast, which Violet insisted on eating with them in the kitchen, she asked Cleggy, 'Did you sleep all right?'

His face lit up. 'Oh, I did indeed, miss. Eeh, that bed is so comfortable.' After becoming used to sleeping in shop doorways Cleggy felt as if he had died and gone to heaven.

'Good and has Cook found you any little jobs to do yet?'

Cook answered for him, saying shortly, 'Actually he's already been working in the pantry.'

There was an amused look in Violet's eyes but she said nothing. It was clear Cook hadn't been at all happy about Cleggy joining the household, but if this kept up, she might just be forced to admit that he was a godsend. Dora and Stan already seemed at ease with him so hopefully the arrangement would work out. Cleggy certainly seemed happy enough – like a new man in fact – and she hoped it would last because she had a soft spot for him.

Chapter Thirty-Three

'Are you sure you 'ave everythin' you need?' Edie fussed for at least the tenth time in as many minutes.

'Yes, I'm quite sure,' Violet told her as she tied the ribbons of her bonnet beneath her chin. A cab would be arriving in a few minutes to transport her, Sally and their luggage to the train station and from there they would make their way to London.

It was now mid-February and Violet knew she couldn't delay going away any longer. She had sat in her room for the last few evenings letting out the waists on her gowns and had taken to wearing a shawl to disguise her thickening waistline. The staff had been told she was taking a long vacation abroad and Mr Chapman would handle all the bills in her absence.

'Just promise you'll write regular an' take good care o' yourselves.' Edie wasn't at all happy about them going but could see the sense in it.

'We will,' Sally promised as she too put her bonnet on.

When they heard the cab draw up outside they made their way out of the drawing room where they found Dora, Stan, Cook and Cleggy waiting for them in the hall to wish them goodbye.

'Eeh, I envy you goin' off to France for a bit o' sunshine,' Cook said with a sigh. That was what Violet had chosen to tell them, although she hated to lie. 'You have a wonderful time now, an' you can tell us all about it when you get back.'

'We will,' Violet agreed as she gave them each an affectionate peck on the cheek. Stan and Cleggy went outside to help the driver load their luggage onto the back of the cab and once it was secure, they gave Edie a hug and hurried out to it.

As the carriage drove away, Violet leant out of the window to wave.

'This is it then,' Sally said quietly.

'It is but there's still time to change your mind if you've decided you don't want to come.'

Sally shook her head. There was no way she would have let Violet travel alone, although she was still very concerned about what would happen once the baby was born. Violet just seemed intent on getting out of Oliver's way for now, but they needed to make a plan soon.

An hour later their luggage was loaded into the baggage car at the rear of the train, and they were settled into their compartment, which fortunately they had to themselves. As the train pulled out of the station, Violet stared despondently from the window, thinking about Toby. He had been trying unsuccessfully to see her for weeks and she felt guilty about ignoring him, but she knew it was for the best. What point could there be in letting their relationship develop when there could be no future in it?

'Are you all right, pet?'

Sally's voice brought Violet sharply back to the present. 'Yes. I thought we might find a hotel in Euston to stay in while we look for some rooms to rent.' She had made sure to bring enough money to tide them over comfortably for some months.

Sally nodded and grinned. 'I thought old Cleggy was going to cry when we left. That chap follows you about like a shadow. I think he'd catch the moon for you if you asked him to.'

Violet smiled. 'He's a sweetheart, isn't he? I'm so glad we took him in. He's so grateful. The rest of the staff get on well with him too, especially Cook, which is surprising considering how horrified she was at the thought of him moving in.'

'Hmm, I've noticed. In fact, I wouldn't be a bit surprised if we didn't have a bit of a romance developing there.'

'*Really?*' Violet looked shocked. 'What makes you think that?'

'Cook's got him wrapped around her little finger from what Dora tells me. He even sat last night helping her wind the wool for a jumper she's knitting him.' Sally chuckled. 'And haven't you noticed how Cook has spruced herself up since he arrived?'

'I hadn't really.' Her thoughts had been so taken up with avoiding Oliver and worrying about what would happen when the baby was born that she'd scarcely thought of anything else.

At last the train drew into Euston and Sally hurried away to get a porter to fetch their luggage. They then left the station to hail a cab and once one drew up beside them Violet asked, 'Could you direct us to a hotel please?'

Glancing at her smart clothes he nodded. 'I'd recommend the Great Northern Hotel in King's Cross for you, miss.'

They clambered in and once they were settled Sally slipped the thin gold wedding band from her finger and put it on to Violet's.

'You'd best wear this while we're here, pet,' she advised gently. 'And when you book us in to the hotel, book in as Mrs Stroud.'

Seeing the sense in what she said, Violet nodded, deeply touched that Sally had entrusted her wedding ring to her.

They stared out at the teeming streets as the horse picked its way through the traffic. Sally had thought Hull was busy when she'd first arrived from Nuneaton, but this was even busier.

Eventually they pulled up outside the hotel and a bell boy in a smart uniform ran down the steps to carry their luggage inside for them while a doorman held the door wide and bowed.

'Eeh, I feel like royalty,' Sally whispered as they approached the desk in the enormous foyer. It was very grand and she couldn't help but think it was going to be very expensive.

Violet booked them into adjoining rooms and Sally's mouth dropped open when they stepped into the first one. It was very luxurious and the view across King's Cross from her window was breathtaking.

'King Edward himself wouldn't feel out of place in these rooms,' she said with a grin. Suddenly her sensible clothes felt very out of date. 'But isn't it ridiculously expensive?'

'It is rather but it's only until we can find a couple of rooms to rent.' Even though she was now a woman of means Violet still hated to be extravagant.

They were both tired, so Violet ordered a meal to be sent to their rooms.

'We'll have an early night and start the search for somewhere to stay tomorrow,' she suggested. 'And we can perhaps do a bit of sightseeing at the same time seeing as you've never been to London before.'

The next morning, bright and early, they went down to the hotel dining room for breakfast. It was nice to be waited on and Sally knew she would have enjoyed it under other circumstances. But she was still sick with worry about how Violet would handle the birth of this poor unwanted baby, and she was even more worried about what would become of it after the birth. She could quite understand Violet's reason for not wishing to keep it – the poor girl had had it foisted on her by someone she now detested, but still, none of that was the baby's fault. The poor little soul hadn't asked to be born after all. Still, for now she pushed her concerns aside and concentrated on finding them somewhere to stay. And so after breakfast, Sally posted the letter she'd written to Edie the night before, and they set off.

Some of the small apartments they looked at were ridiculously expensive while others were awful, so by the end of the first day, they were both feeling despondent.

'Everything in London seems to be twice as expensive as back at home,' Violet said as they stopped in a café for an evening meal. Even so, Sally had enjoyed seeing some of the London landmarks as they travelled on the trams. However, she had been rather disappointed at her first glimpse of the River Thames. It had always looked so glamorous in pictures, so the sludgy, slow-moving water had been rather a let-down.

'Cheer up, pet,' she told Violet, who was looking dismal. 'It's only our first day and we're sure to find somewhere suitable soon.'

The following day they visited Spitalfields in East London and wandered around the market where Sally got speaking to a woman when they stopped for a cup of tea at a stall.

'You wouldn't happen to know of any respectable rooms around here to rent, would you?'

The woman, who spoke in a broad cockney accent, grinned, revealing tobacco-stained teeth. 'I would as it 'appens, ducks. My sister runs a respectable establishment in Bell Lane. It ain't far from 'ere. Look, I'll write the address down for yer. Just go an' ask for Cath Bailey an' tell 'er Mary sent yer, an' if she's got any rooms available, she'll put yer right. She ain't cheap mind, but she's reasonable an' she minds who she takes in. Good luck, ducks.' She went on to give them directions and deciding they had nothing to lose Sally and Violet set off.

The house wasn't in the most salubrious of areas but they could see that the lace curtains hanging at the windows were clean, and the front door had a fresh coat of green paint.

'Oh well, we're here now so we may as well try our luck,' Sally said optimistically. 'It can't be any worse than some of the flea pits we've already looked at, can it?'

Stepping up to the door she knocked and soon it was opened by a plump, kindly-looking middle-aged woman with greying hair who was wearing a spotless white apron over a plain grey gown.

'Good day,' Sally introduced themselves to her before telling her about her sister recommending her.

She gave them a friendly smile as she held the door wider. 'You might just be in luck,' she told them. 'I 'ave a young newly-wed couple 'ere at present who're moving into their own little house this week. But the rooms won't be available till then, so I'm afraid I can't show 'em to you.'

'When could we see them?' Sally asked. The woman had led them into a spotlessly clean sitting room.

'They're movin' out on Thursday, so if you find 'em suitable, I could 'ave 'em ready for you by Friday mornin'.' She went on to ask them how long they might be staying.

'Oh, er . . . we're not quite sure yet,' Sally told her. 'At least for a few months.'

'Well, I shall 'ave to tell yer the same as I tell the rest o' me tenants – I don't allow no 'anky-panky in 'ere. I run a respectable place, so no men allowed in the rooms an' no visitors after nine at night.'

'That would be quite acceptable,' Sally answered primly.

'Good. And you'd 'ave to share a bathroom, the rooms I'm thinkin' of are on the first floor an' the privy is in the backyard. The rooms ain't posh, but they're furnished and clean, but you 'ave to supply yer own beddin'. I'll cook you an' evenin' meal each day if you request it for a price, an' I'll do your washin' an' ironin', again for an extra price.' She went on to tell them how much the rooms would cost, which they both thought was reasonable.

'Come back Thursday evenin' when the young couple 'ave gone an' you can look at the rooms an' make your minds up,' Mrs Bailey told them.

'What did you think?' Violet asked as they walked away.

'It seemed all right.' If truth be told, Sally didn't much care where they stayed. Violet had lost her sparkle and she just wanted this whole sorry affair to be over for the girl's sake.

On Thursday evening, as agreed, they returned to Bell Lane and after looking at the two rooms on offer, they agreed the rent and arranged to move in after lunch the following day.

It was mid-afternoon when they arrived at Mrs Bailey's lodging house and she showed them up to their new temporary home. Just as she had promised the rooms were spotlessly clean, if somewhat basic. The first room consisted of a rather sagging but comfortable sofa, a fireplace, with a small fire already burning, over which they could boil a kettle for tea, a small table with two ladder-back chairs at either side of it, and an old sideboard. Faded flowered curtains hung at the window and there were rugs thrown across the floorboards. The second room boasted two single beds, a chest of drawers, a small wardrobe and a washstand.

'It ain't posh, but it's clean an' tidy,' Mrs Bailey informed them. Then narrowing her eyes she asked, 'Mother an' daughter, are you?'

'Yes . . . yes we are,' Sally said before Violet could open her mouth. 'And the rooms will do very nicely, thank you. We'd like to take you up on your offer of an evening meal each night, if we may. We'll eat out the rest of the time. Oh, and also it would be nice if you'd attend to our laundry.'

'As you wish.' The woman was obviously curious about them and why there were there, but when Sally offered no further information, she told them how much the first's month rent plus their extras would be and Violet paid her in advance.

Once the woman had gone, Sally stared round with satisfaction. 'It isn't as fancy as the place we've just come from but I'm sure we'll be comfortable here,' she said cheerily to try and perk Violet up. 'So if you don't mind starting to unpack our things I'll go out and get us some bedding and some tea and sugar. I'll bring us some bread and butter too. We can always toast some bread on the fire for breakfast and we can make sandwiches for snacks. I'll arrange for a bag of coal to be delivered each week as well. I imagine it could be quite cold in here without a fire.'

Violet nodded glumly as she thought of her comfortable home. She was missing Edie and the staff, and Toby too, although she was trying hard not to think of him.

Once Sally left, Violet sank down on the sofa and buried her face in her hands as misery tore through her. This would be her home for the next few months and all she could do now was make the best of it.

Chapter Thirty-Four

They were eating breakfast in their sitting room one morning late in March when a look of shock suddenly passed over Violet's face and her hand dropped to her stomach.

'What's wrong, pet? You're not in pain, are you?' Sally hurried towards her, her face heavy with concern.

'N-no, not pain . . . but something moved,' Violet said shakily. The colour had drained from her face and she looked terrified.

Sally heaved a sigh of relief. 'Phew, you had me worried there.' She patted Violet's hand comfortingly. 'Don't worry, that's just the baby making itself known. You'll have to get used to that now. I remember when I was having . . . my little boy, I felt as if he was playing football inside me sometimes.'

Violet looked amazed as she stared down at her stomach. She had less than four months to go until the baby's birth and it was getting harder by the day to hide her condition. As yet, Mrs Bailey hadn't seemed to notice, but both Sally and Violet wondered how long it would be before she did, and dreaded to think how she might react. She had made it clear this was an adult-only lodging house and that she didn't take in families with children. But this wouldn't be an issue; Violet had no intention of staying there once the baby was born, but she still hadn't decided what to do with it. The only thing she was sure of was that she wouldn't keep it under any circumstances. Just the thought of Oliver's child growing inside her still made her feel physically sick and she knew she would never be able to bond with it.

She glanced at Sally curiously. It was so rare for her to speak of her life before she arrived at the café. 'It must have been very hard to lose him and your husband as you did,' she said softly.

'It was hard to lose my boy but not his father.' Sally's eyes were full of pain as she gazed into space. 'I met my husband when I was on the rebound, you see, and I knew within weeks that I'd made a grave mistake in marrying him, but it was too late. He was a drunkard and a bully. I thought things would get better when Richard was born but he never showed any interest in him. Most of his money went over the bar of the local pub so I was working two jobs to try and pay the rent and the bills. I couldn't rely on him to do it. And then they both got sick and . . . well, the rest you know.'

'Oh Sally, how awful for you.' Violet gripped her hand and squeezed it gently.

Sally forced a smile back to her face. 'There's no use crying over spilt milk. It's you we have to focus on now – you and the child you're carrying.' A closed look came over Violet's face, just as it did every time Sally mentioned the baby, but this time Sally would not be quietened. 'We must start making plans soon,' she urged gently.

Violet rarely ventured out of their rooms but unbeknown to her Sally had already started making enquiries. 'There are a few options open to you.'

Violet stood and walked away to stare from the window, just as she always did when Sally brought up the baby, but this time she wouldn't be put off. 'It's no good burying your head in the sand,' she pointed out. 'We have to start making plans, and soon. The first option is you decide to keep the baby.'

Violet shook her head violently. 'No, that's not going to happen. How could I face them all back at home if I turned up with a baby in my arms? I would be branded a fallen woman and the child would be known as a bastard.'

'All right, don't get all upset,' Sally urged as Violet began to nervously pluck at the material of her skirt. 'The second option is the workhouse.'

This, again, was met with a shake of the head. 'I don't want this baby, but everyone knows the majority of little ones that enter the workhouse don't reach their first birthday.'

'Well, there's a foundling home in Poplar,' Sally went on. 'Or we could find someone to foster the child for a price?'

'I suppose if we have to make a choice the last option is the best one,' Violet said glumly.

Sally nodded. 'In that case I shall start to make enquiries. The second thing we need to do is set up a midwife for you for the birth. I don't think I'm brave enough to deliver the baby by myself.'

Violet hated the very thought of it but could see the sense in what Sally said, so she nodded her agreement. 'Very well, I'll leave it to you.'

One bright sunny day in April, Sally persuaded Violet to go for a stroll with her. 'It'll do you good,' she urged. 'You're as pale as putty and need to get a bit of fresh air.'

Mrs Bailey was still cooking their evening meals but for some weeks now Violet had taken to eating hers up in their rooms rather than going downstairs.

Once outside, Violet had to admit that it was nice to feel the spring breeze on her face. After the long hard winter, it was good to see the flowers springing to life in the park and feel the sun on their faces.

When Violet began to tire, they turned to go back to their rooms. They had just entered the hallway when Mrs Bailey suddenly appeared from the kitchen.

'Afternoon, ladies.' As her eyes settled on Violet, she quickly pulled her shawl about her but not before Mrs Bailey noticed her swollen stomach. Her smile slid away and she looked shocked as she asked, 'Are you . . .'

'If you're asking if she is with child, yes she is.' Sally stepped in quickly as colour flooded into Violet's face. 'Unfortunately, she was widowed shortly before we came here which is why we decided to get away for a while. We had no idea she was with child at that time.'

Mrs Bailey pursed her lips. She clearly didn't believe a word of it. They had only been there for a couple of months at most and judging by the size of Violet's stomach she was much further on than that. 'I see, well I wish I'd known that before I offered you the rooms. I don't accept babies in here. The noise they make upsets the other tenants.'

'As I just explained, we weren't aware that Violet was with child when we arrived but don't worry, as soon as the child is born, we will be returning home.'

Mrs Bailey frowned. Her first instinct was to ask them to leave but then they were very good tenants. They kept themselves to themselves and were never a bit of bother, and if they were planning to leave immediately after the birth, she supposed she could stretch a point just this once.

'In that case I suppose I could allow that,' she said eventually, and Sally sighed with relief. The last thing they needed was to have to start looking for somewhere else to live.

'Thank you.' Sally said sincerely, and taking Violet's elbow she whisked her away up the stairs before the landlady could change her mind.

'Phew, she had me worried for a minute,' Sally admitted when they were in the privacy of their rooms.

Violet was mortified. 'Did you see the look on her face? I don't think she believed a word you said.'

Sally shrugged as she hung her shawl over the back of a chair. 'It doesn't really matter; we won't be here for that much longer. Sit yourself down and I'll go and get a bucket of water so we can make some tea.'

Two days later, Sally told Violet, 'The lady in the corner shop has given me the address of a woman who can assist you during the delivery. She's delivered dozens of babies around here by all accounts.'

Violet shuddered at the thought of the birth. The closer the delivery came the more terrified she was. Even so she trusted Sally implicitly, so she nodded.

By the end of June Violet had forgotten what her feet looked like. If anything, she had lost weight on her body and her hugely swollen stomach looked incongruous on her small frame.

'It won't be long now, pet,' Sally told her encouragingly. 'And then you can return home to Edie and try and put all this behind you.'

Violet nodded despondently as she sat at the open window. There was no relief from the heat in the city and she felt as if she was going to melt. She hadn't been able to sleep properly for days and she had a constant niggling backache that made even walking about the room painful.

Sally was preparing to visit the shop for fresh bread and milk and before she went, she asked, 'Is there anything you fancy? A cream cake perhaps or some fruit?'

Violet shook her head. She didn't know what she would have done without Sally. Nothing was too much trouble for her and they had grown closer than ever. She still missed Edie dreadfully and wrote to her often to keep her updated on what was happening.

'No, I'm fine thanks,' she answered. She had hardly eaten enough to keep a bird alive for days and Sally was forever worrying about her and buying titbits to try and tempt her.

'Right, I'll be off.' Sally put her bonnet on and lifted her basket. 'I shan't be long. Will you be all right until I get back?'

'Of course.' Violet mustered a smile and watched from the window as she strode down the street. Suddenly a pain in the pit of her stomach made her double over and she gasped. Her backache had got worse during the course of the morning but it had been nowhere near as bad as the pain she had just experienced. Standing, she began to cautiously pace the room hoping that a bit of exercise would help. It couldn't be the baby coming, she reasoned. It wasn't due for at least another couple of weeks.

Ten minutes later the pain returned, and once again Violet doubled over as fear swept through her. What if the baby had decided to come early? She was there all alone!

She waited until the pain passed before going to the sideboard and taking out the tiny baby clothes Sally had been buying and making. Violet had said the child wouldn't need them if they weren't going to keep it, but Sally had sensibly pointed out that the baby would still need something to wear when it first arrived. And so for weeks the dear soul had been busily stitching tiny nightgowns and knitting little matinée jackets. There were bootees and bonnets, small blankets and a beautiful shawl that Sally had lovingly laboured over. But it wasn't due for at least a couple of weeks yet and Violet wondered if it did come now would it even survive?

The pains continued to come at regular ten-minute intervals and by the end of another half an hour Violet knew that her fears were founded. This baby was going to be born whether it was premature or not!

She almost cried with relief when Sally stepped into the room sometime later.

Sally saw at a glance what was happening and dropping her basket onto the table she rushed to her. 'How long have the pains been coming and how far apart are they?'

'Th-they started shortly after you left . . . and they're coming about every ten minutes,' Violet gasped as Sally led her into the bedroom.

'All right, there's no need to panic. First babies have a habit of taking their time. You could be hours away from giving birth,' she assured her. 'Even so I'm going to run and fetch Mrs Button to come and have a look at you.' She helped Violet onto her bed and wagging a finger at her she told her, 'Stay there and don't move until I get back. I shall be as quick as I can, I promise.' Then she ran from the room as if the hounds of hell were snapping at her heels as Violet curled up in a ball and began to cry. The day she had both wished for and dreaded had finally arrived and there could be no stopping it now. It was a terrifying thought.

Chapter Thirty-Five

Sally was back within ten minutes and as she rushed into their rooms, Violet could hear someone huffing up the stairs behind her.

A stick-thin, elderly woman with grey hair and sharp features soon appeared in the doorway. Seeing that Violet was in the middle of a contraction she came over and placed her hand heavily on her stomach.

'Hmm, when this pain is over, I want yer to lie on yer back an' draw yer knees up so as I can see what's goin' on.' She shoved the sleeves of her drab dress up to her elbows. Taking off her bonnet, she tossed it onto the chest of drawers. 'You'd best go an' get some water on the go,' she told Sally.

'Already? Is she close then?' Sally said.

'No, yer daft ha'porth, I want some tea, an' I wouldn't mind a drop o' somethin' strong in it.'

Violet flushed with embarrassment as the woman flipped her onto her back and threw her skirts about her waist before bending to examine her most private parts. She inserted a finger and after feeling about, causing Violet to yelp with pain, she straightened and wiped her hands on her apron.

'There's nowt much happenin' yet,' she informed her. 'You could be hours away so I'll 'ave me tea an' leave yer to it fer a while. I've got another woman in the same state in the next street an' she shouldn't be long now.'

Violet groaned as she turned onto her side. She had tried not to think about what it would be like when the time came, but if this was just the beginning she had a terrible feeling it was going to be much worse than she had feared.

Sensing her fear the woman grinned, revealing a set of broken, worn-down teeth. She was never going to win any beauty contests, Violet thought as she hugged her swollen stomach and blinked back tears. Soon after Sally appeared with her tea.

'I've put a bit of brandy in it for you,' she told the woman.

With a nod the old lady took it from her and gulped it down in seconds, despite it being steaming hot. When she had finished, she handed the cup back to Sally and swiped the back of her hand across her mouth. 'She's nowhere near yet,' she informed her. 'So I'll be back later.'

Sally was a little nervous of being left alone with the new mum-to-be but she supposed Mrs Button must know what she was doing, so she raised a wobbly smile and nodded as the woman left.

Minutes later there was a knock on the door and Mrs Bailey appeared looking worried. 'Is the baby comin'? I just saw Mrs Button leavin'.'

Sally nodded. 'Yes, but she's only just started. Mrs Button says it could be hours yet.'

'Well just make sure as she don't go yellin' out,' the landlady said grimly. 'I don't want 'er upsettin' me other tenants.'

Over the next few hours, the contractions grew stronger and closer together and by teatime Violet was exhausted.

'How much longer will it be?' she groaned as Sally mopped her sweating brow.

'Babies have a habit of not coming until they're good and ready, but you're doing really well,' Sally praised. It was breaking her heart to see Violet in so much pain but there was nothing she could do about it. She had already lined a drawer with a blanket, which would serve as the baby's temporary crib, and set out a change of clothes for both the babe and Violet.

'When will Mrs Button be back?'

Sally smoothed a damp curl from Violet's forehead. 'She shouldn't be long now, pet. Just try and rest between the pains.'

Mrs Button finally appeared at ten minutes to eight that evening. 'Me other lady gave birth to a fine 'ealthy girl,' she crowed with satisfaction. 'I just stayed be'ind to 'ave a little tipple to wet the baby's 'ead.' Sally and Violet could well believe it, they could smell the drink on her breath. 'Now flip over onto yer back an' let's 'ave a look at where you're at.'

Once again, she leant down to examine Violet and when she straightened, she smiled with satisfaction. 'She's comin' along nicely, but I reckon it'll be the early hours afore this one puts in an appearance,' she stated matter-of-factly. 'So Sally could yer per'aps make me a sandwich? an' then I'll 'ave a little nap while we're waitin'. I ain't 'ad a bite o' food pass me lips all day long an' me stomach is startin' to feel like me throat's been cut.'

Four doorstep cheese sandwiches later, Mrs Button crossed her arms across her scrawny bosom, leant back in the chair and seconds later her snores were echoing about the room.

'I don't know about you, but I think it will be her disturbing the neighbours with her snoring,' Sally whispered as she sat on the side of the bed with Violet clinging to her hand.

As it grew dark Sally lit some candles and the oil lamp while Mrs Button slept on. Violet had been very brave with barely a whimper but the pains were so strong now that she couldn't help but groan. Sometime later the lamplighter lit the streetlight outside and the crowds on the pavement diminished as people retired to their homes.

As the little clock on the shelf struck twelve, Mrs Button woke and knuckled the sleep from her eyes. Violet was thrashing about on the bed silently praying that death would come and claim her, for surely that would be preferable to this agony.

'Ah, that's better.' The woman yawned and stretched. 'Right, Sally, you go an' put the kettle on again while I check on our young madam 'ere. Me throat's as dry as the bottom of a birdcage.'

While Sally went to do as she was asked, Mrs Button bent to Violet and clucked with satisfaction. 'That's it, duckie,' she chortled, rolling her sleeves up again. 'You're just about there now. So, when I tell yer, I want yer to push as 'ard as ever yer can.'

Strangely, by this stage Violet no longer felt embarrassed. She wouldn't have cared who had looked at her so long as they could end the pain.

Sally came back with the tea, which the woman again downed in a gulp before saying to Violet, 'I want you to put your hands behind your head now an' grip the 'eadboard. Then when the next pain comes, push as 'ard as yer can. Ready?'

Violet nodded and when yet another pain gripped her, she lifted her head and pushed for all she was worth. 'That's it, that's it. A few more o' them an' this baby will be 'ere,' Mrs Button encouraged. 'Come on . . . an' again. Good girl, keep it comin'!'

As the pain abated, Violet flopped back against the pillows. 'I-I can't push anymore,' she whimpered.

Mrs Button was having none of it. 'Oh yes you can. Now 'ere's another one comin' – this could do it, push. Push!'

Violet gritted her teeth and did as she was told, and suddenly a mewling cry echoed around the room and as if by magic the pain stopped and the baby lay between her legs on the bed.

'What is it?' Sally rushed forward and started to cry as she stared down at the tiny new life. 'Oh, Violet, my love,' she said throatily. 'You have a son, a very *beautiful* little son.'

Mrs Button deftly cut the cord and after wrapping the baby in a towel she passed him into Sally's waiting arms. 'Well, 'e might 'ave put in an appearance a bit early but there's certainly nowt wrong wi' 'is lungs,' she commented with a chuckle. 'Go an' give 'im a bit of a clean-up while I deliver this afterbirth, eh? Then my work 'ere will be done an' I won't be sorry, I don't mind tellin' yer. It's been a bloody long day an' I'm ready fer me bed.'

As Mrs Button saw to Violet, Sally carried the infant away to bathe him in a bowl of warm water while Violet lay staring at the ceiling with tears in her eyes.

She had a son. It was a lot to take in and her feelings were mixed. She had never wanted this child, and yet now that he was here and she had heard him cry her thoughts were all over the place. Somehow, she knew that if she saw him, she might want to keep him and so she steeled herself to stay strong. If she kept the child, she would be condemning him to a life where he would be branded a bastard and no child deserved that; he hadn't asked to be born, after all. But one thing was for sure, she knew she couldn't abandon him to a workhouse. Sally had told her some days before that she had found a foster mother who was willing to take him after the birth, and she resolved to speak to her about it as soon as Mrs Button was gone. It would be for the best if he were to go to his new home as soon as possible; there would be no sense in allowing herself to grow fond of him.

The midwife left soon after with a smile on her face and her payment plus a healthy bonus tucked into her pocket.

Sally had washed Violet from head to toe, changed the soiled bedding and put her into a fresh nightgown before she asked tentatively, 'Would you like to feed him? He's growing restless.'

'No, no I don't want to see him. Feed him with the bottle you bought.'

Sally pottered away with a sad shake of her head. She had bought the double-ended glass feeding bottle some days before just in case this happened, and once she had warmed some milk the child sucked on the rubber teat greedily before giving a burp of satisfaction and slipping back to sleep.

'He looks like a little angel,' she sighed as she gently laid him back in his drawer.

'Does . . . does he look like Oliver?' Violet whispered.

Sally shook her head. 'Not at all. He has your colour hair and your eyes. Have you thought of a name for him?'

When Violet shook her head, she nodded before suggesting, 'In that case would you mind if I called him Richard?'

Violet shook her head again. She knew this was the name of the little boy Sally had lost.

'Not at all. But this foster mother you've found – is she reliable? I mean, I remember reading in the newspaper about that baby farmer, Mrs Amelia Dyer, who was hanged for killing the babies that were entrusted to her; I wouldn't like him to go to someone like that.'

'I promise you, the person I have in mind would bring him up as her own and he'd want for nothing.'

There was a knock at the door and Sally went to open it to find their landlady standing there looking none too pleased.

'I just saw Mrs Button leavin'. Does that mean the babe 'as been born.'

'It has indeed. A fine baby boy.'

'I see, so what 'appens now? I told yer from the start I don't allow children 'ere. It wouldn't do to 'ave it disturbin' me other tenants.'

'Don't worry, Mrs Bailey, the baby will be gone first thing in the morning,' Violet assured her weakly. She was worn out and just wanted to sleep.

The woman looked mildly surprised. 'But will you be well enough to go that soon?'

'No, Sally has found someone to care for the baby until I get my strength back and as soon as I have, we'll be on our way too.'

'I see.' Mrs Bailey thought it rather an odd arrangement. She hadn't ever met a mother who would be happy to be parted from her child so soon after giving birth. 'That's fine then. May I see the baby?'

'Of course.' Sally led her to the drawer where the little boy was sleeping with his tiny thumb tucked into his rosebud mouth.

'By 'eck. I 'ave to say he's a 'andsome little chap, ain't he?' She reached down and gently stroked the silky skin on his cheek. Then, straightening, she told them, 'Right, there shouldn't be a problem. Get well soon, m'dear, an' congratulations.'

She slipped away and once the door had closed behind her Violet turned on her side so she wouldn't have to look at the drawer where her child was sleeping, and quietly began to cry. She couldn't wait for the morning to come so that this whole sorry nightmare would be over. How different things might have been if only the child had been Toby's but it was too late for if onlys now.

She slept intermittently that night, aware of the baby's every movement and the fact that Sally rose at three o'clock to give him another bottle.

Sally was up bright and early and made Violet some tea and toast, but Violet couldn't swallow it; there seemed to be a lump in her throat. Next Sally fed baby Richard and changed his binding before asking tentatively, 'Are you still in the same mind now that you've slept on it?'

Violet nodded. 'I'm sorry, but I'm afraid I am, Sally. It will be for the best all round.'

'I'd best get him ready in that case.' Sally lifted the baby and wrapped him warmly in a shawl and one of the tiny matinée coats she had painstakingly knitted for him.

'How much does this person charge to take him?' Violet's voice came out as a croak and when Sally mentioned what to Violet sounded like a ridiculously small amount she frowned.

'That doesn't sound like enough to bring a child up. Are you quite sure about this person?'

'Oh yes. She lost a child, so I think Richard will be loved and will want for nothing.' Violet reached for her reticule and counted out the ten pounds Sally had mentioned, before adding some extra.

She lay back and watched as Sally put her coat and bonnet on. She lifted the child and asked once more, 'Are you quite, *quite* sure you're doing the right thing, pet? Is there nothing I can say to make you change your mind?'

Violet miserably shook her head, tears glistening on her lashes. 'I'm sure, Sally. Please don't make this any harder than it already is. Please . . . j-just take him.'

She turned over and stared at the wall, listening as the door closed. Her son was gone forever; there could be no changing her mind now. And with that knowledge she allowed the tears to flow, hot and salty.

Chapter Thirty-Six

Much to Violet's distress, Sally insisted she stay in bed for the next three days. During that time, she waited on her hand and foot and Violet was more grateful to her than she would ever know. During the time they had known each other they had grown closer and closer and Violet didn't know how she would ever have coped without her.

On the morning of the fourth day, Violet insisted on getting up and although she felt a little weak and wobbly, she told Sally, 'I think I feel well enough to go home now.' Her milk had come in the day before and her breasts were swollen and painful, but Sally had bound her tightly to make the milk dry up all the sooner.

Sally looked horrified. 'But you should be in bed for at least a week. You shouldn't even be up let alone catching trains and travelling.'

But Violet was determined. The room seemed strangely quiet without the baby, even though he had only been with them for one night. She had asked no questions about the foster mother Sally had taken him to; she trusted her implicitly and hoped that the child would be loved and have a good life.

'I shall be fine,' she told Sally as she lifted her clothes and began to get dressed. 'I want to get home and see Edie.'

'I see, then if that's the case there's something I should tell you.' Sally looked upset. 'You see, the thing is, I decided some time ago that once all this was over, I was going to return to the Midlands . . . It's where I belong. I wrote to Edie to tell her so a couple of weeks ago.'

'But you've made a new life with me and Edie in Hull now!' Violet was horrified. 'I don't want you to go, Sally. I'd miss you so much.'

Sally gently shook her head, her eyes heavy with tears. 'And I'll miss you too, and Edie. But the Midlands is where my roots are and I want to go back there, so once I've put you on the train to Hull, I shall be catching a different one. There's no point in coming all that way with you only to have to do another journey. You will be all right on your own, won't you? You can get a cab when you get into Paragon Station at Hull to take you to the house.'

'Oh Sally.' Violet was sobbing unashamedly. 'I don't know how I shall manage without you.'

Sally put her arms about her and gave her a gentle hug. 'You'll be just fine and we can keep in touch,' she pointed out. 'We can write to each other.'

'But it won't be the same as having you there,' Violet sniffled as she mopped her wet cheeks with her handkerchief.

'You'll soon get back into your old routine. Just make sure you keep well away from that Oliver, and if you have any more problems with him go to the police.'

As they packed their belongings, both their hearts were heavy. Soon after Violet went downstairs to inform Mrs Bailey they were leaving and to pay any rent due.

The woman looked shocked. 'But surely you should still be in bed, m'dear,' she frowned. 'The layin'-in period for a new mother is usually a week. But I dare say you're missin' your baby an' are keen to go an' pick him up. I can understand that.' She took the money and smiled. 'I have to say, you an' Mrs Bridges 'ave been grand tenants. I'm sorry to see you go, but good luck for the future. Ta-ra fer now.' When she disappeared off into her room Sally began to carry their luggage downstairs, flatly refusing Violet's help.

Outside they flagged a passing cab and were soon on their way to the station, both in a sombre mood. Once they arrived Sally summoned a porter to put Violet's cases into the luggage van and all too soon it was time to say goodbye.

'Are you quite sure that I can't change your mind and get you to come with me?' Violet implored.

Sally shook her head. 'No, pet, my mind is made up. But you just take care of yourself and tell Edie I'll write to her soon.' She nudged Violet towards the open carriage doors, saying gently, 'Off you go now, the train will be leaving in a minute.'

'Goodbye, Sally . . . and thank you . . . for everything.' Violet's eyes were so full of tears that she could scarcely see where she was going and so after planting a last kiss on Sally's cheek she stumbled aboard and settled in a carriage. She peered out of the window, hoping to catch a final glimpse of the woman who had been so good to her. But it was too late; Sally had been swallowed up by the crowds. Violet flopped back in her seat feeling dead inside. She had come to London a young girl but after the birth of her child, one she would never know, she was going home a woman.

It was late afternoon before the cab pulled up outside Seagull's Roost. The driver lifted Violet's luggage down and took it up the steps to the front door. Then, with a hefty tip in his pocket, he raised his cap and left.

She couldn't be bothered to root through her bag for the key, so she rang the bell, and when Dora answered the door, she beamed at the sight of her.

'Aw, miss, it's so lovely to 'ave you back. We didn't know when to expect yer,' she said as she ushered her inside. 'Just 'old on there a minute an' I'll get Cleggy to come an' lift yer bags in for you.'

She hurried away to fetch him while Violet took her hat and coat off. Cleggy looked just as happy to see her as Dora had and Violet was pleased to note that he still looked as neat and tidy as when she had left. He had gained some weight too and his face no longer looked gaunt. Even his limp didn't seem to be so pronounced.

'Welcome 'ome, miss.'

She gave him a weary smile. 'Thank you, Cleggy.'

'Is there anythin' I can get for you?' Dora enquired as Cleggy began to manhandle the luggage inside.

'Oh, a cup of tea would be wonderful. Then you can tell me all about what's been going on while I've been away.' She saw Cleggy and Dora exchange an anxious glance before they hurried away and she made her way to the drawing room. The house seemed enormous after being used to the tight confines of the two small rooms she and Sally had lived in, and she sighed with relief as she sank down into an easy chair.

Soon after Dora returned with Cook, who was delighted to see her. 'We didn't know you was comin' so I'm afraid I only did a meat pie for the evenin' meal,' Cook apologised.

'Oh, that will be delicious I'm sure, don't go to any unnecessary trouble for me,' Violet told her. As she bustled away, Violet noticed that there seemed to be a spring in her step, and she'd had her hair cut into a more fashionable style as well.

'Now tell me what's been happening here while I've been gone,' Violet encouraged Dora as the girl poured out a cup of tea for her.

Dora frowned. 'Well . . . nothin' much 'as happened 'ere,' she said cautiously. 'But I'm afraid there 'ave been problems at the café.'

Violet sat straighter in her chair. 'What sort of problems? Edie is all right, isn't she?'

'Er . . . not exactly . . .' Dora licked her lips, which had suddenly gone dry. She knew how close her young mistress was to Edie and that what she was about to tell her would cause her distress. 'I hate to have to tell you this but not long after you left, she had a bad turn. The doctor says it was a seizure, a stroke like, an' she's been bedridden ever since. It were touch an' go for a while an' the good Lord only knows what would 'ave 'appened if Lottie hadn't found her when she turned in for work that day. The poor girl is exhausted. She's been tryin' to keep the café goin' as well as runnin' up an' down the stairs all day tryin' to care for Edie. She's been brilliant!'

The colour drained from Violet's face as she bounced out of the chair, the tea forgotten. 'I must go to her,' she said in a wobbly voice, and she flew into the hallway and snatched her bonnet and coat from the hallstand.

'I'll get Stan to drive you there in the carriage,' Dora offered.

Violet shook her head. 'No, it's all right. I don't want to have to wait while he gets the horse harnessed. It'll be quicker if I hail a cab.'

As it happened there wasn't a cab in sight so Violet ran until the stitch in her side made her stop and lean against a wall while she got her breath back, and all the while her heart was beating like a drum. She was still not fully recovered from the birth and now this latest news seemed to have sucked all the stuffing out of her. But wild horses wouldn't have kept her from Edie's side, so after a few minutes she moved on. At last, the café came into sight. The door was wide open to let some of the heat out and Violet burst through it. The place was full of customers and Lottie and her sister were racing about like headless chickens trying to see to them all.

A look of relief flashed across Lottie's face when she saw Violet and she rushed to greet her and draw her towards the kitchen.

'I just got back and heard what's happened to Edie,' Violet burst out. 'How is she, Lottie?'

Lottie shook her head as she rubbed the back of her hand across her sweaty forehead. 'Not good to be honest, but she's a damn sight better than she was,' she said sadly. 'We all thought she was a goner for a while back there, but thank goodness she survived, though I doubt she'll ever be the same again.'

'But what could have brought this on?'

'Ah well, we've got our own theory about that.' Lottie scowled. 'When I got 'ere to start work that mornin' I found the door swingin' open. Someone 'ad broken in an' made off with all the takin's an' I reckon Edie caught 'em at it. She were lyin' at the foot o' the stairs wi' a lump the size of an egg on 'er fore'ead, God love 'er! The doctor said 'ad she been left like that for much longer she'd 'ave died for sure.'

'And have they caught whoever it was who broke in?'

Lottie snorted in disgust. 'Have they bloody 'ell as like! But I've got me own thoughts on who it might 'ave been. Provin' it is the 'ard bit!'

Violet reached across and squeezed her arm gratefully. 'Thank you for all you've done for her, Lottie. And don't worry, I'm back now and I'm going to help you as much as I can.'

'That's a relief. Would you mind goin' up to check on her? I ain't 'ad time for the past hour or so, we've been that busy. This warm weather seems to be drawin' folks out o' the woodwork.'

'Of course.' Violet lifted her skirts and raced up the stairs in a most unladylike manner, and seconds later she was in the little sitting room where she and Edie had spent so many happy hours together.

She passed through it into the bedroom and her first sight of Edie propped up against a mound of pillows brought tears to her eyes. The weight seemed to have fallen from her bones and one side of her face had dropped. Her hands lay uselessly on top of the eiderdown and drool dribbled down her chin, but at the sight of Violet her eyes seemed to come alive and she gave a grim caricature of a smile.

'Oh Edie, I'm so sorry this has happened to you,' Violet said brokenly as she bent to kiss her cheek. 'If I could find who's done this to you, I'd put a knife in their heart, *I swear* I would. But don't worry, I'm back now and I'm going to make sure that you have the very best of care.'

Edie tried to speak but all that came out was a grunt, so after straightening the bedclothes Violet told her, 'I'm going down to the kitchen to get you a drink and something to eat, and when you've had that we'll get you washed and changed into a clean nightdress, shall we?'

She found that Lottie had a large pan of chicken soup ready for Edie and she smiled her approval. It was clear from that the poor soul wasn't going to be able to eat anything solid. Thankfully most of the teatime customers had left by that time and the café was a little quieter.

'Look, you finish up here and I'll stay with Edie tonight,' Violet offered.

'Are you sure you don't mind?' Lottie looked relieved. 'To be honest that would be a great help. Me an' Maisie 'ave been takin' it in turns. She obviously shouldn't be left on 'er own, but the trouble is me an' Frank 'ave been told that our landlord wants to sell the 'ouse we're rentin'. He's only given us till the end o' the month to be out but we ain't had time to look for anywhere else yet.'

'You just get home to Frank,' Violet urged. 'I'll be fine here.'

'Are you sure? After the break in . . .' Lottie's voice trailed away and she looked worried. 'Frank's been comin' round an' checkin' the place at regular intervals.'

'You just tell him to have a night off. And don't worry, if who-ever broke in last time comes back, they'll wonder what's hit them,' Violet said angrily. She ladled some soup into a dish and made her way back upstairs to Edie, but most of it just ran out of the side of her mouth and trickled down her chin, and she only managed to get a couple of spoonfuls into her. Violet could see the frustration and dismay in her eyes. Edie had always been such an independent, active woman, Violet could only imagine that being confined to bed in such a sad condition must be horrifying and humiliating for her.

'Don't worry, we'll try again later.' Violet lovingly wiped her face clean. 'Now, how about trying a few sips of this tea. It's just how you like it, strong and sweet,' she crooned.

When it was evident that Edie had had enough, she told her, 'I'm going to go down and help Lottie close up. Then I'll ask her if Frank can pop round to my house and let them know that I'll be staying here with you tonight.'

A single tear slid down Edie's face and it almost broke Violet's heart. 'I won't be long,' she promised and hurried away to begin what was going to be a very long night. It had certainly not turned out to be the homecoming she had hoped for.

Chapter Thirty-Seven

That night Violet dozed intermittently in the chair beside Edie's bed and woke feeling like she hadn't slept at all. She had just made some tea when Lottie arrived with Maisie.

Violet poured the tea and asked, 'How is your search for somewhere to live going?'

Lottie sighed despondently. The places they liked were way out of their budget and the places they could afford were little more than slums.

It was then that an idea occurred to Violet and she asked, 'How would you and Frank feel about living in the rooms above here?'

Lottie looked surprised. 'But Edie and Sally live up there.'

Violet shook her head. 'Sadly, Sally has gone home to live in the Midlands and I can't see Edie being able to manage here on her own anytime soon, can you?'

'So where will she live?' Lottie looked confused.

'With me,' Violet declared determinedly. Edie had spent most of her life caring for her, and now it was time she returned the favour.

'Well . . . I suppose it would make things a lot easier, and I could keep this place going for her,' Lottie admitted.

Violet nodded in agreement. 'That would take a weight off her mind, I'm sure. She's very proud of this café. And if she's living with me, I'll be able to make sure that myself or someone is with her all the time until she hopefully begins to get better. It can't have been easy for you running up and down the stairs trying to care for Edie and keep this place going.'

'It hasn't been,' Lottie admitted. 'And while I've been busy down here, I've been frettin' about Edie bein' up there all alone. But are you sure?'

'Quite sure,' Violet told her. 'It's the best solution all round. I can't think of anyone more suited to keep this place running smoothly and it will solve your housing problem too.'

'When are you thinkin' o' movin' her?'

'I shall have to ask the doctor if he thinks she's well enough to be moved yet,' Violet answered. 'When is he due to come in and see her again?'

'This mornin' actually. He's been callin' in most days.'

'Then let's see what he thinks when he arrives. Now I'm going to take some porridge and tea up and see if I can get something inside her. I'll tell her what we're planning as well and see what she thinks of it.'

Lottie snorted and grinned. 'Good luck wi' that. You know what an independent old cuss she is.'

Violet was in full agreement but as things stood, she really couldn't see there was another option.

Just as Violet had expected, her idea didn't go down at all well and Edie wagged her head from side to side. Her body was weak from the seizure but it was clear that her brain was still as sharp as ever.

'Now don't go getting yourself all upset. It won't be forever,' Violet soothed her. 'It will be just until you're well enough to come back. And in the meantime, you can rest easy knowing the café is in capable hands. What could be better? Anyway, I'm doing it for purely selfish reasons. I've missed you and it will be nice for us to be back under one roof again, even if it's only for a short time, so stop getting yourself all het up and eat some of this porridge.'

The doctor arrived mid-morning and Violet stood to one side as he gently examined the patient. When he was finished Violet followed him back into the small sitting room where he told her,

'I think she's out of danger now, although obviously she's going to have to take things easy.'

Violet asked him then if Edie was well enough to be moved and told him of her proposal to take her to live with her, and he thought it was an excellent idea, although he warned, 'You must be aware that she will need a lot of nursing and, sad as I am to say it, I doubt she will ever be as strong as she was. If she isn't careful another seizure could be fatal.'

'I understand,' Violet replied solemnly. 'But I'd rather you didn't tell her that. Not yet at least, she'd only fret.'

There was a tap at the door and when it opened Violet felt herself flush and the breath caught in her throat as she saw Toby standing there. He looked almost as surprised to see her as she was to see him.

'Oh, you're back off your holiday.'

Violet nodded as butterflies fluttered to life in her stomach. He was just as handsome as she remembered, but her face gave nothing away as she told him of the conversation she and the doctor had just had, and about taking Edie to live with her. She was very aware that she must be looking somewhat dishevelled. Her hair had escaped its pins and hung loose about her shoulders and her gown was crumpled, although Toby was far too much of a gentleman to comment.

'I think it's an excellent idea,' he agreed. 'When do you think she will be well enough to be moved, Doctor?'

'As soon as you like, providing she's well wrapped up. And she won't be able to tackle the stairs of course.'

'I can help there,' Toby offered. 'I can carry her down to my carriage and we could take her this morning, if that isn't too short notice?'

'Well . . . I'd just need a little time to pack some of her stuff so that she has familiar things about her,' Violet replied. 'Could you give me half an hour?'

'I can give you as long as you like.'

They said their goodbyes to the doctor, who promised to call in at Seagull's Roost to see Edie from then on, and when he had departed, Toby asked, 'Did you have a good holiday?'

'Yes, thank you,' she replied primly. 'And how is the soup kitchen doing?' she went on, hoping to change the subject.

'Busy as ever.' He chuckled. 'Although we've missed having you there.'

'Did you, er . . . come here for a reason?'

He shook his head. 'I've been calling in most days, to check on Edie and see if she needs anything,' he informed her.

'I see. Then I must thank you for that. I have worried about Edie being here alone at night.'

'With good reason.' His face was solemn now. 'There's been another spate of break-ins. Word has it that it's Ned Banks's gang again, although the police haven't managed to catch any of them.' He could have added that it was rumoured that her stepbrother was also a part of the gang, but he thought better of it.

Violet started to collect a few of Edie's things together before going to tell her what they'd planned. She could see Edie was none too happy about leaving her home, but in this instance, Violet knew that it was best for her. She had no doubt Dora would help take care of her and at least there someone could be with her all the time.

'Is there anything I can do to help?' Toby asked.

Violet paused for a moment before nodding. 'Actually, there is, if it's not too much trouble. I'm thinking it would be easier for everyone if Edie was downstairs back at home. That way she'd be able to see people coming and going and it might speed up her recovery, so perhaps you could go to the house and tell them what's been decided and ask Cleggy and Stan if they could bring a bed down from one of the spare bedrooms and put it in the day room – there's a nice view over the docks from there – and by the time you get back I should be able to have her ready to go.'

'Of course.' He left immediately and she paused for a moment to watch him. She had tried so hard not to think of him in the time she had been away but seeing him again had roused all the feelings she had tried so hard to stifle. She sighed. There was no point in thinking of what might have been; she was the mother of an illegitimate child now and she could just imagine the look of disgust on Toby's face if he should ever find out.

Thoughts of the baby brought hot tears stinging behind her eyes. She had thought it would be the easiest thing in the world to give him up, and yet when Sally had taken him to his foster mother she felt as if a little piece of her heart had gone with him. All she could do now was pray that he would be loved and have a happy life.

By the time Toby returned, Violet had packed everything Edie would need.

'I'll put a blanket around her,' she told him as they gently eased Edie to the edge of the bed. Toby lifted her carefully as if she weighed no more than a feather and soon she was propped up in the carriage with Violet's arms protectively about her and a warm blanket tucked about her knees.

'Everyone at Seagull's Roost is very excited about you joining them there,' Toby told Edie kindly. 'I have a feeling you're going to be spoilt.'

Edie grunted and glared at him but he merely smiled as the carriage set off for her new home. On arriving they found Dora busily making up a bed with fresh sheets in the day room and Cleggy, Stan and Cook all waiting in the hallway to greet Edie.

Toby carried Edie in, and Dora and Violet fussed about getting her comfortable in bed. They had placed it so she had a good view of the docks and had rearranged the furniture about it.

'You have been busy,' Violet praised as she looked around with satisfaction. 'I think you'll be really comfortable in here, don't you, Edie? And I can sleep on the sofa at night so you're not on your own.'

Again, Edie shook her head, but Violet wouldn't be swayed. 'I shall stay with you whether you like it or not,' she told her with a tender smile. 'You'd do the same for me if I were ill, wouldn't you?'

'Is there owt I can get for you, miss?' Cleggy asked, as eager to help as always.

'Not at the minute, Cleggy, but thanks for bringing the bed down, you too, Stan.' The two men nodded and took their leave, although Cleggy was back minutes later with a bunch of gladioli he had picked from the garden.

'I, er . . . thought these might cheer you up, Edie,' he said self-consciously.

Violet was touched. 'They're beautiful, Cleggy, and that was really thoughtful of you. Could you perhaps find a vase for them, Dora? We'll stand them on the table by the bed so Edie can see them.'

Toby had started to feel rather uncomfortable. 'Is there anything else I can do, Violet?'

He'd noticed a subtle change in her. Nothing he could put his finger on, she just seemed more grown-up somehow.

'Nothing, but thank you for all your help.'

He lifted his hat and made for the door, where he paused. 'Would you mind if I popped in to see her occasionally?'

'Of course not, I'm sure she'd be glad of the company. And thank you again for your help.'

Seeing his carriage rattle past the window Violet felt strangely disappointed that he'd left. She had been home for less than a day and yet so much had happened that her mind was in a whirl. Seeing Toby again hadn't helped. But now she had the perfect excuse to try and put him from her mind. From now on all her time would be spent caring for Edie and hopefully one day the woman would recover enough to become independent again. Violet wouldn't even allow herself to think of the alternative; Edie had been the only person who had ever shown her any affection – apart from her father and, more recently, Sally. And Toby, of course, but she pushed thoughts of him firmly away.

Chapter Thirty-Eight

Over the next month Violet rarely left Edie's side. Cook spent hours every day preparing tasty treats to try and tempt her to eat, and the doctor was a regular visitor. Thankfully, she was no worse and there had been no further seizures, but recovery was still a long way away. All the staff were devoted to Edie. Every day Cleggy cut her a small bunch of flowers from the garden to brighten her room. Stan came in for an hour every afternoon to read the newspaper to her and Dora helped Violet with bed baths and nursing. At night Violet snuggled down on the sofa so she would be close should Edie need her, but Violet could see the frustration in Edie's eyes. She would become agitated, as if she was trying to tell her something, but all that came out when she opened her mouth was a series of grunts and gasps. It broke Violet's heart to see her this way but she never faltered in her care.

Each day Violet would spend time bending and stretching Edie's useless limbs to try and keep the muscles strong and return some movement to them, but so far her efforts had been futile. Even so, Violet was determined and always tried to be cheerful in front of her, even when she felt like crying. Toby called regularly with gifts of fruit, flowers or chocolates, which Edie couldn't eat, and every time he came Violet left the room. It would have been pointless to spend time with him and grow close again.

Then one fine evening, as it was approaching dusk, she was sitting reading her book as Edie stared out at the street from her window, when Violet noticed her becoming agitated. The one good hand that she still had any movement in was flapping on the bedspread and she was making guttural noises.

301

Violet was at her side in a flash. 'What is it, dear?' She was afraid Edie was about to have another seizure. 'Are you in pain?'

'Ugh, ugh!' Edie's eyes flashed to the window.

As Violet glanced up, she became aware of a figure slouching by with their hands deep in their coat pocket and their head bent. She recognised him immediately and her stomach sank. It was Oliver. But what was he doing loitering about again? Violet had made it more than clear she wanted nothing more to do with him the last time she had seen him. Stepping forward she quickly swished the curtains closed to prevent Edie becoming any more afraid.

'It's all right, he's probably just passing by chance,' she soothed but Edie's eyes said differently and Violet frowned. 'Have you seen him hanging about before?'

'Ugh, ugh!'

Violet took that as a yes and bit her lip. If he was making a nuisance of himself again it could only mean one thing. He was after money. Her stomach started to churn but when she turned back to Edie her face was calm.

'There – he's gone now, look.' She gave Edie a reassuring smile. 'Now you just rest while I go and ask Dora to make us a nice cup of cocoa.'

After seeing Dora, she slipped quietly out of the front door, glancing up and down the street. For a moment she thought Oliver had gone but then she saw him leaning against a wall and she made her way towards him stopping some distance away. She still didn't dare get too close.

'May I ask why you're loitering about again?'

'Huh! And may I ask where you've been for the last few months?'

'I decided to take a long holiday.' She stuck her chin in the air defiantly. 'I wasn't aware that I had to ask your permission!'

He took a step towards her, and she immediately took a step back.

'I'm surprised you could bear to leave your fancy Mr Brabinger,' he spat nastily.

'What?' She looked shocked. 'I'm quite entitled to come and go as I please. And just for the record, Toby isn't my fancy man.'

'So why is he always in and out of your place then?'

Violet's heart skipped a beat. If Oliver knew that Toby was a regular visitor then he must have been watching the house.

'If you must know I've brought Edie to stay with me,' she told him sharply. 'She had a seizure and she's been very ill. Toby has been calling to see her as they're good friends.'

'You must think I'm daft if you think I'll swallow that! An' if he didn't come away with you why did you suddenly go? Was there a reason? Seems strange that you were gone all that time? You arrived back just about nine months after we had a our little get-together if I've done me sums correctly,' he smirked.

Terror pulsed through her veins. Was it possible that he'd discovered she had been carrying his baby?

'Oh, don't be so ridiculous.' Violet had had enough and turned to leave but his next words stopped her in her tracks.

'It'd be a shame if anything were to happen to old Edie to bring on another seizure, wouldn't it? Especially if she's been as ill as you say. Another one could see her off, no doubt. And if anyone were to tell Mr Toby Brabinger what happened between us two, he might wonder why you disappeared off so quickly for so long . . .'

She turned back to him, her hands shaking. 'If you said anything to Toby it would be your word against mine, he'd never believe you. And Edie's receiving the best of care.'

'I've no doubt she is, but I reckon Toby might think there's no smoke without fire, don't you?'

Violet glared at him. She wouldn't allow him to see how terrified she was. But she knew she wouldn't be able to bear it if Toby ever found out about the baby. 'Is that a threat?'

'As if.' He smiled as he stroked his stubbly chin. He looked as if he hadn't shaved in days and his clothes were none too clean either, she noted. 'And if Edie's here then who's looking after the café? Thinks a lot of that place, doesn't she?'

'Lottie and Frank have moved in, and Lottie is running it,' she told him. There was no point in lying, he would only have to go there to see for himself.

He narrowed his eyes. 'Let's hope they're all right as well, eh? Been a lot of fires and break-ins in that neck of the woods lately. The thing is, though, for a moderate fee I could keep my eye on the place and make sure that nothing bad happened to it.'

So that was it. He was trying to blackmail her. Her first instinct was to tell him to go to hell but something told her that if she did and anything happened to Edie, or Lottie and Frank for that matter, she would never forgive herself.

'And what do you call a *moderate* sum?' Her voice was scathing.

He shrugged. 'I dare say twenty pounds would keep the wolf from the door . . . *for now*!'

'*Twenty pounds!*'

'Don't tell me you can't afford it,' he snarled. 'A wealthy young woman like you. Hardly seems fair, does it? Here's you livin' the life of Riley while me and Mother are existing in a slum. Seems only right you should help us out a bit. We are family after all.'

'I *despise* you,' she spat before she could stop herself, angry colour flooding her face. 'And you're not and never have been my family!'

He chuckled. 'You weren't saying that when you were following me about with those puppy dog eyes!'

'That was before I grew up and saw you for what you really are.' She'd had enough now and just wanted him gone. The frightening thing was she knew he was capable of hurting those she loved if she didn't comply with his wishes. He had her over a barrel.

'You can have your damn money. But I don't keep that amount in the house, so you'll have to wait until I can get to the bank tomorrow.'

'Fair enough.' He was all smiles now. 'I'll meet you outside the café at eleven o'clock tomorrow morning. Just make sure you're there.' He thrust his hands into his pockets and marched away, whistling merrily.

Violet watched him go, her hands clenching and unclenching at her sides as she desperately tried to compose herself. Eventually she turned and made her way back to the house. Edie must never learn of this encounter; Violet was determined to keep her from getting upset at all costs.

The following morning Violet was waiting for Oliver outside the café at eleven o'clock sharp.

He swaggered towards her with a grin on his face. 'Good, I'm glad you kept to our arrangement. It'd be a shame if these nice windows were to be put through again, wouldn't it? I dare say they'd cost a pretty penny to replace.'

'Just take your money and get lost,' Violet snapped as she thrust an envelope at him. Then she flounced into the café without giving him so much as a second glance.

'Weren't that Oliver Stroud I just saw you talking to?' Lottie asked, looking concerned.

'Yes, he was just passing.' Violet was keen to change the subject. 'So how is business?'

'Good as ever,' Lottie responded. 'The woman I've taken on to do the cookin' is good at her job, so all in all it's goin' well. How is Edie?'

'I think she's slightly better, although she still isn't able to speak or move her limbs much. She is eating slightly more, though, and the doctor says that's a good sign. The staff are marvellous with her. The next stage will be to get her sitting in a chair for short periods. I don't want her getting bed sores.'

'And what about you? How are you coping?' She thought Violet looked pale and wondered if it had anything to do with Oliver.

Violet shrugged. 'I'm fine. My main priority is getting Edie up and about again.'

'That's all well and good, but you must have a little time to yourself,' Lottie pointed out. 'I'm sure Toby would take you out for a break like a shot if you'd let him.'

'I don't need anyone to take me out, least of all Toby Brabinger,' Violet responded more sharply than she had intended. Then she instantly felt guilty; Lottie was only thinking of her welfare after all. 'Honestly, I'm fine. Now if you're sure there's nothing you need, I should be getting back to Edie. I've left Cleggy and Dora keeping an eye on her.'

'Of course, an' have you 'eard from Sally yet?'

She asked the same question every time Violet visited the shop but there had been no word. Sally had told her that she had written to Edie to inform her of her decision to return to the Midlands while they were still in London, which meant they had probably known about it before she did.

When she arrived back at the house, she found Cleggy sitting at the side of the bed reading the newspaper to Edie and she smiled. He was unrecognisable from the vagrant she had taken in. His face was still clean-shaven and his eyes no longer looked haunted. She couldn't imagine being without him now. Nothing any of them ever asked him to do was too much trouble and he felt like part of the family.

'I'll take over now, Cleggy,' she offered.

'Right y'are, miss. I'll get back to paintin' the spare room. Pop up an' 'ave a look when you get a spare minute. It's lookin' smart.'

'I'm sure it is.' She smiled and once he'd left the room, she turned her attention to Edie. 'And how are you today? Shall we sit you up a bit more so you can see what's going on through the window?'

She was in the process of trying to heave Edie up when the door opened and Toby appeared.

'Let me do that,' he offered and while Violet plumped up the pillows, he gently lifted Edie up onto them.

Dora was the next to appear, waving an envelope and smiling. 'Look what the postman just brought. It's got a Midlands postmark

306

so I reckon it could be from Sally.' They had all missed her, especially Edie. The letter was addressed to Violet.

'Right, let's see what she has to say, eh?' She smiled at Edie and settling onto the chair next to the bed she slit the envelope and took out Sally's letter.

Dear Violet,
   I do hope this letter finds you well and fully recovered.

Toby raised an eyebrow at this, wondering if Violet had been unwell while they had been away, but Violet rushed on.

I'm sorry it's taken so long to write to you, my dear girl. By now I'm sure Edie will have told you why I have come back to my hometown, and I pray that one day you will find it in your heart to forgive me. My address is above. I have found a very nice little cottage to rent and I also have a job in the local corner shop, which is very convenient. I miss you all dreadfully but feel content that I have made the right decision. Perhaps one day you might bring yourself to visit? You will always be so welcome, as any of you would be, but if you choose not to, I will understand. The time I spent with you in Hull and London were the best days of my life and I will never forget them. Be happy my dear girl and try to think kindly of me.
   With fondest love,
   Sally xxx

Violet frowned as she looked at the address on the letter. Sally was staying in Attleborough, a small parish on the outskirts of Nuneaton, but what had she meant when she said that Edie would have told her why Sally had chosen to return home? Of course, Sally could have had no way of knowing about Edie's seizure or the fact that Edie had been unable to speak.

She glanced at Edie who had tears running down her cheeks, and her one good hand was furiously plucking at the eiderdown.

'What does she mean, Edie?' Violet asked. 'What was it you were going to tell me?'

Edie gulped then with a superhuman effort she managed to gasp, 'L-Lot-Lo . . .'

'Are you trying to say Lottie?' Violet questioned.

Edie nodded.

'Does she also know whatever it is you should have told me?'

Again, Edie nodded, and Violet patted her hand. She was burning with curiosity now. 'All right, don't get upset. I'll go and see Lottie,' Violet soothed.

'You could have a lift back to the café with me when I leave, if you like? It wouldn't be out of my way.' Toby offered.

Violet wanted to refuse, but knew it would appear churlish. 'All right, thank you. I'll give you a little time with Edie and be ready to leave when you are.'

She left the room to discuss the menus for the next couple of days with Cook, and half an hour later Dora sought her out to tell her that Toby was ready to leave. Violet went into the day room to peck Edie's cheek and tell her that she wouldn't be gone for long and was sad to see that Edie was still very agitated about something.

In the carriage, Violet stared from the window. Whatever Lottie was about to tell her was clearly important, but she had absolutely no idea what it could be. Still, she consoled herself, she'd know soon enough. She just hoped it wouldn't be something bad.

Chapter Thirty-Nine

Sensing that Violet needed some quiet time, Toby thoughtfully sat back in the carriage and left her to her thoughts. When the carriage pulled up outside the café, he asked, 'Would you like me to come in with you? Or I could wait and take you home after?'

'Thank you, but no, I shall be fine,' she told him primly. She was still keeping him firmly at arm's length, although sometimes it was hard when she remembered back to the night of the ball when he had whirled her about the dance floor and she had melted into his arms.

'As you wish. Good day, Violet.' He politely handed her down from the carriage and she watched it rattle away across the cobblestones, before making her way into the café.

The early evening rush had just started and Lottie looked up in surprise when Violet entered. 'Oh goodness, two visits in one day! Is Edie all right?'

'She's fine,' Violet assured her. 'There's something I need to speak to you about, but I forgot you'd just be starting your busy time. It can wait. Meantime, give me a pinny and I'll help you take the orders.'

It was almost two hours later before the last of the customers left and Lottie turned the sign on the door to closed.

'Thanks fer lendin' a hand.' She smiled as Violet handed back the pinny. 'Now, what did yer want to see me about?'

'Er . . . could we go upstairs where it's a bit more private?'

'O' course we can. Frank won't be in fer a while yet. They're still unloadin' the cargo off one of the ships into a warehouse on the docks. I'll just ask Maisie to make a start on the cleanin' up, an' then I'll be there. You go on up.'

Violet climbed the stairs to the little rooms where she and Edie had spent such happy times together and very shortly after Lottie joined her.

'So, 'ow can I help yer?'

Violet took Sally's letter from her bag and passed it over, and when Lottie had read it, the colour drained from her face and she sat down heavily on the small sofa.

'I've been 'alf expectin' this, seein' as I knew Edie wouldn't be able to talk to you about it.'

'So? Don't keep me in suspense. What is it you have to tell me?' Violet was on the edge of her seat. She and Lottie were close and kept no secrets from each other – she was one of the few people, including the staff at her house, who she felt she could trust with her life, and who Violet had told about the baby before leaving for London.

'I suppose I should start by tellin' you that Sally turnin' up 'ere wasn't quite as coincidental as we all thought at first,' Lottie said quietly, nervously twisting her fingers together. 'Apparently Edie an' her 'ad been writin' to each other for years an' shortly after your dad passed away, Edie asked her to come an' join 'er here.'

Violet frowned. 'But why would she do that? And why did she never tell me that she and Sally already knew each other?'

Lottie licked her lips. 'They didn't tell yer because Sally ain't 'er real name. Her real name is Sadie an' . . . an' she's your birth mother.'

Violet gasped with shock. 'But why did she never tell me?'

'I think she were too afraid that you'd 'old it against 'er – the fact that she left you wi' your dad when you was just a baby, I mean. And that's why Edie an' her always kept in touch, so that Sadie could know you were all right. It wasn't till your dad passed away that Edie realised there'd be no reason why she couldn't be close to yer anymore, an' when she suggested it to Sadie she jumped at the chance. The rest yer know. From day one everyone could see the likeness between you two – an' the bond, if it comes to that. I'm surprised you ain't guessed before. Why do you think she volunteered to go with you when you went off to 'ave the baby? She knew 'ow hard it was goin' to be for you to give it up, an' she wanted to be there for you. She never really got over havin' to let you go, see?'

Violet buried her face in her hands as she pictured Sally's – or Sadie's face, as she would now have to think of her. She had gone searching for her mother and for months she had been right under her nose.

'I-I can't believe that she didn't tell me,' she said with a croak in her voice.

Lottie sighed. 'We tried to persuade her to, but as I explained, she were too afraid o' you rejectin' her cos she'd left you. But it weren't from choice, I can assure you – her family had kicked her out an' she had nowhere to take you. But she never stopped lovin' you, or your dad. That's why she kept in touch wi' Edie so that she could at least know how you were.'

'Oh, the poor thing . . . how awful it must have been for her.' Violet now knew first-hand how hard it was to give up a child, even one that hadn't been planned.

'So, what will you do now?' Lottie asked gently.

Violet took a deep breath. 'I suppose I should go and see her.'

Lottie nodded. 'I reckon you should. She's a good woman an' she deserves a little happiness. After she had to give you up, she had a terrible time wi' the chap she eventually married. Just get used to the idea then go an' put her out of her misery. An' don't get worryin' about leavin' Edie. From what I've seen o' the lot at your house they're more than capable o' takin' care o' her while you're gone.'

Violet nodded. 'I'm sure you're right, but I think I might just write to her for a start and tell her that I have no bad feelings towards her. I can understand perfectly why she did what she did. It must have been terrible for her, but she was thinking of what would be best for me, wasn't she?' A thought occurred to her and she frowned. 'But how shall I address her now that I know the truth?'

Lottie shrugged. 'However you feel comfortable. Sally, Sadie or Mum if you feel ready for that. I really don't think she'd mind; she just wants to know that you forgive her. But there's no rush. You need a bit o' time to get used to the idea first, there's no need to decide just yet.'

Violet nodded and once she had dried her tears and composed herself a little, she set off for home again.

Edie was watching the door for her return and when Violet entered the room, she managed to raise her good hand.

Violet took it and kissed it gently. 'Lottie told me everything,' she said quietly, and Edie nodded.

'I'm so glad I know,' Violet said softly. 'Ever since Papa died, I've wondered what my real mother was like. Now I know and I couldn't be more pleased about it, although I must admit it's come as a bit of a shock.'

For the first time since she had returned from London, she saw Edie give a crooked smile and felt a slight pressure on her hand as Edie's fingers closed around it.

'I shall go and see her when you're a little better,' Violet went on.

Edie shook her head and gestured towards the door. Violet knew she was telling her she could go and see her as soon as she liked, but she still thought it would be best to write to Sadie first.

That night as she lay in bed, she couldn't help but think how sad it was that her father and Sadie couldn't have married. How different her life would have been if he hadn't met Anna. Much like her own life might have been with Toby, she thought, if she hadn't been taken down by Oliver and given birth to an illegitimate child. Again, guilt coursed through her as she thought of the infant. Would the people who were fostering him tell him one day that he had been illegitimate? And would he wonder about her as she had wondered about Sadie? With a sigh she turned over and eventually drifted into sleep.

The next morning, Violet wrote to Sadie to tell her that she understood why she had left her with her father. She assured her that she bore her no ill feelings and said that now she knew the truth, she hoped they would be able to get to know one another even better. She also told her of Edie's seizure but insisted she try not to worry as she was receiving the best of care and was showing slight signs of improvement.

She had decided after a lot of deliberation to address the letter to Sadie. It still didn't feel quite real to address her as Mama or Mum and she hoped Sadie would understand. She was very tempted to also ask if she had received any news of Richard, but thought better of it. It was probably best if she tried to put that part of her life behind her, although it was proving to be easier said than done, and she found herself frequently thinking of the child and wondering if he was being well cared for.

She could think of nothing else to say so she eventually signed the letter and, after making sure that Edie had all she needed and was as comfortable as she could make her, she left her in Dora's capable hands and strolled down to the post office. It was yet another hot, muggy day and she welcomed the breeze from the sea in her hair as she made for home, only to slow her steps as she saw a familiar figure striding towards her. Her stomach sank. It was Oliver, but looking very different from when she had last seen him. He was smartly dressed and his hair had been neatly trimmed. She briefly considered turning and walking the other way but knew it would be pointless as he would simply follow her. As he drew level, she avoided looking at him and made to sail past, but he stepped in front of her and gave her a charming smile.

'Just the person I was hoping to bump into.'

She turned a cold gaze upon him, but he didn't flinch. 'You could at least pretend to be pleased to see me,' he said sarcastically. Then to her consternation he did a little twirl. 'I wanted to thank you for the new togs,' he goaded. 'As you can see, I'm looking much smarter now thanks to your little handout.'

'I thought you said you needed the money for rent and food for you and your mother.'

'I did, and that's exactly where some of it went.' He chuckled. 'But you could hardly expect me to walk about looking like a tramp now, could you? Which leads me to what I wanted to see you about. The thing is, you see, that first payment didn't go as far as I'd hoped, so I could do with another instalment.'

'*What?*' Violet was horrified. 'But you can't have spent it all already? And what do you mean, *another* instalment? I didn't agree to that.'

He shrugged. 'Then you must have misunderstood me. I shall need regular payments if you want to ensure the café and Edie stay safe. And that I don't have a little word in Toby's ear!'

'How regular?' she asked warily, glad there were other people about. Just the thought of being alone with him made her skin crawl.

'Oh, I should think monthly would suffice . . . for now. Unless any unexpected bills crop up.'

Violet shook her head. 'I don't think so.' She was hoping to call his bluff. 'I can run the house and pay all the staff on that amount each month.'

His face set, he drew himself up to his full height and lifted his arm, and for a horrible moment she thought he was going to strike her. But glancing about at the people teeming around them, he seemed to think better of it and lowered his arm.

'I would have thought Edie's and your reputations were worth far more than twenty pounds a month to you.'

Violet gritted her teeth. She would have given her last penny to keep Edie safe but she wouldn't tell him that. 'I'll pay you just once more.' Her eyes flashed as she stared steadily back at him. 'But if you come asking again, I shall have no choice but to inform the police that you're blackmailing me and that you raped me.'

He laughed, an ugly sound that echoed along the street. 'Oh yes, and how would you prove it? There's no evidence that you've given me money, and as regards the rape I would just deny it and say that you were willing. It would be my word against yours and your reputation would be ruined. Is that what you really want – for the whole world to know you're soiled goods?'

'You are a *disgrace*,' she ground out, her temper flaring. 'Don't you have any pride at all? You're young and healthy, so why don't you find a job and earn your *own* money?'

'Why should I when you've had more than you can ever earn handed to you on a plate? So let's get down to business; I think we'll make the next payment twenty-five pounds. When can you have it for me?'

As Violet thought of Edie and the upset this would cause if she ever found out, her shoulders sagged. Another sudden shock could easily bring on another seizure and she was more than aware that in her weakened state Edie might not survive it.

'I'll have it for you tomorrow morning. Meet me outside the café at eleven o'clock, but don't come near the house again.' She turned and walked away, her stomach churning. And to think she had once hero-worshipped Oliver! How could she have been so blind?

Briefly, she thought of going to Toby and telling him what was going on but dismissed the idea almost immediately. She had no doubt he would try to help her but it wasn't right to drag him into this mess and she couldn't bear the thought of him knowing about the baby. She had been far too busy with Edie to help him at the soup kitchen, but even if she hadn't been, she knew deep down that it wouldn't have been wise. It was best for both of them if she kept her distance. She had, however, insisted on making a donation each week towards the cost of running the kitchen. Toby had assured her there was no need, but Violet could afford to do it and wanted to help the homeless in any way she could.

With a sigh she hurried homewards, keen to get back to Edie, but her heart was heavy.

Chapter Forty

'Everythin' all right, miss?' Dora questioned when Violet entered the house.

Violet nodded and plastered a smile on her face, although inside she was crying. 'Everything is fine, Dora.' She took her bonnet off and patted her hair into place. 'How is Edie?'

Dora grinned. 'A bit perkier again today, I reckon. I just got her to 'ave a few sips o' tea an' Cook's made her some more chicken broth fer lunch. She seems to be able to manage that well now. Oh, an' Mr Brabinger called. He bought Edie the most glorious bouquet o' flowers. That room is startin' to look like a florist's shop. I've just put 'em in water for 'er.'

Violet went to check on Edie and found her watching out of the window, but at the sight of Violet she gave a lopsided smile and patted the bed at the side of her.

Violet went to her and after kissing her cheek she read the newspaper to her until Edie dozed off. She was still sleeping a lot but thankfully nowhere near as much as when she had first brought her home.

The doctor called later that day and after examining Edie he smiled at Violet, who was looking anxiously on. 'She's doing really well,' he assured her. 'In fact, I think it's time we started to let her get out of bed for short spells to sit in the chair. We don't want her muscles wasting. Perhaps half an hour each afternoon for a start and we'll see where we go from there.'

Violet was thrilled with the news and that very afternoon she and Dora eased Edie out of bed and into the comfortable chair they had placed ready for her right by the window.

'Didn't I tell you you'd be up and about and back to yourself in no time?' Violet said encouragingly. 'You'll be bossing us all about again soon, so we'd better make the best of it.'

Edie gave her another crooked grin while Violet went off to check how things were doing in the kitchen. Cleggy had just come in from the garden with fresh picked vegetables and with his shirtsleeves rolled up to the elbows to show his suntan. Violet couldn't help but think that if she hadn't known who he was, she wouldn't have recognised him as the poor homeless waif she had first met. She also noticed the slight flush that rose in Cook's cheeks at the sight of him and it did her heart good to see it. Dora had noticed it too and as she caught Violet's eye, she gave her a cheeky wink and a grin.

The next day, Violet was up early to go to the bank before meeting Oliver, who was waiting for her as she approached the café.

'There's a good girl,' he chortled, as, grim-faced, she held out the envelope with the money in. 'I trust I don't need to count it to make sure it's all there?'

She turned away without a word and entered the café and when she glanced out the window a few minutes later, she was relieved to see that he had gone.

'Not havin' trouble wi' that one, are you?' Lottie asked. She had glimpsed Violet speaking to him from the window.

'Er . . . no, not really.' Violet longed to confide in her but was too afraid of how it would affect Edie if word got back to her.

Lottie was wiping the tables and she paused to say in a low voice, 'Apparently there were another night watchman injured in a robbery at the warehouses last night, an' whoever it was got away wi' bales o' silk just come in from China an' worth a fortune. Word has it that it's Ned Banks an' his gang again. Anyway, how is Edie?'

Violet was only too happy to change the conversation. 'She's doing well. Even having short spells out of bed each day. What can I do to help? Dora's watching Edie so I can spare a couple of hours.' She bustled away to take her bonnet off and fetch an apron just in time for the mid-morning rush.

Before they knew it, they were into September and with every day that passed Edie seemed to grow a little stronger. She spent most of her days sitting in a chair now rather than lying in bed, and with Dora and Violet's help she had even managed to take a few steps, although her speech was still very slurred.

'Y-you . . . go see Sad . . . ie,' she sputtered one morning as Violet was helping her to dress. Edie was a proud woman and didn't want to spend a moment longer than was necessary in her nightgown.

Violet paused in the act of putting slippers on Edie's feet and looked up. 'But are you sure you'd be all right here with Dora?' Sadie had replied to her letter expressing relief that she now knew the truth and saying she was longing to see her again. But until recently, Violet wouldn't have dreamed of leaving Edie.

Edie nodded vigorously as her one good hand stroked Violet's cheek. 'D-Dora is . . . good,' she garbled.

Violet smiled. In truth it wasn't just Dora who helped to care for Edie. Cleggy and Cook were devoted to her too and so perhaps she could risk a short time away. The doorbell sounded at that moment and Dora appeared to tell them that Toby Brabinger had arrived.

Edie's face lit up. She always looked forward to Toby's visits and Violet's heart did the strange little jerk that it always did at mention of him.

'Send him in, Dora, Edie is decent now.'

Seconds later Toby appeared with a basket of grapes and oranges. He smiled at Edie and nodded politely towards Violet. She felt a pang of regret that he no longer singled her out or paid her any special attention. Her cool behaviour towards him had made it more than clear that he would be wasting his time and he had finally got the message.

'How are you today, Edie?' He planted a gentle kiss on her cheek as he placed the basket of fruit within reach of her good hand.

Violet meanwhile got on with tidying the room, although try as she might she didn't seem able to stop her eyes from straying towards him. The weather had turned windy and cool, and with his hair slightly windswept he looked so handsome that it was hard to ignore him. Time and time again she had relived how he had swept her around the dance floor at the ball and how for those few shining moments they had felt as if they were the only two people in the room. But then cold reality would hit home and she would realise how useless it was to continue encouraging him. She knew all too well that as soon as he discovered she was the mother of an illegitimate child, albeit one that had been forced upon her, the tender look she had seen in his eyes would turn to one of contempt and she wouldn't be able to bear it.

'I was thinking of going to see Sadie for a few days now that Edie is on the mend,' she told him.

Lottie had told him that Sadie was Violet's birth mother and he smiled. He was pleased they had finally found each other. 'That should be nice. Will you be all right travelling on your own?'

Her voice was prim again as she lifted her chin. 'Of course. Why wouldn't I be? I'm a grown woman.'

'Yes . . . yes of course you are. Forgive me.'

She lifted Edie's dirty clothes and left the room, not returning until she heard the door close behind him a short time later. *Why am I always so mean to him?* she asked herself. He certainly didn't deserve it, but it was the only way she knew of keeping him at arm's length.

When she told them what Edie had said, both Dora and Cleggy thought a visit to Sadie would be wonderful, and so Violet began to wonder when she should go. Should she write to Sadie first to tell her when to expect her or just turn up? She decided she would like to surprise her and there was no time like the present, so that very evening she began to pack her clothes into two large carpet bags. She would leave the next morning.

'How long will you be gone?' Dora asked as she helped fold her clothes.

Violet shrugged. 'I'm not sure. But I shouldn't be longer than a couple of weeks at most. If you can manage without me for that long, that is?'

'O' course we can.' Dora beamed at her. 'A break'll do you the world o' good. An' I've no doubt Sadie will be tickled pink to see yer.'

'I hope so.' Violet put the last-minute bits and pieces into the bags before going down to get Edie ready for bed.

The next morning, after a tearful goodbye to Edie, Violet set off for the station and soon she was on the train on the first part of her journey to Nuneaton. Her mind was in a whirl and she was so taken up with thoughts of the reunion to come that she didn't notice the shady figure that had been following her, nor see him slip into a carriage a couple down from hers.

Her life had changed so much in such a short time and with Edie being ill she hadn't really had a great deal of space to process every-thing. But now a worm of excitement started in her stomach. Today she was going to stay with her birth mother. It was incredible to think that not so long ago she had believed Anna was her mother. Now that she knew the truth it was as if pieces of a jigsaw were all falling into place. A smile twitched at the corners of her mouth as she gazed sightlessly from the train window and wondered how Sadie would react to her turning up so unexpectedly. Hopefully she would be pleased. It wouldn't be long now and they would be able to catch up a little on all the years they had been apart.

It was mid-afternoon when the train finally chugged into Trent Valley Station and once she had found her way out to the road Violet hailed a cab and gave the driver Sadie's address.

'I'll 'ave you there in two shakes of a lamb's tail, miss,' the friendly driver informed her as he swung her bags onto the cab.

A short time later they stopped outside a small cottage, and after the driver had lifted her bags down and she'd paid him, Violet opened the small gate in the picket fence and approached the front door, which was painted a cheery red. Most of the late summer flowers were past their best, but the lace curtains at the window were white as snow, and the place looked cared for. Violet's heart began to thud as she tapped at the door. Perhaps she should have let Sadie know she was coming after all? Still, it was too late to worry about that now.

When Sadie, wearing a large apron tied around her waist, opened the door, her mouth gaped open. '*Violet!*' Tears spurted from her eyes as she stepped forward and embraced her in a bear hug. 'Oh, my *dear* girl. Why didn't you let me know you were coming?'

Violet grinned as she returned the hug. 'I wanted to surprise you, but I didn't want to leave Edie until I felt sure she was on the mend. I hope you don't mind me turning up unannounced?'

'Of course I don't.' Despite what she said Violet noticed Sadie glance anxiously over her shoulder. 'You, er . . . you'd better come in.'

Violet stepped past her into a small, tidy sitting room. There was a fire blazing in a fireplace on either side of which stood two wing chairs with gaily coloured cushions. Matching curtains hung at the tiny leaded windows and everywhere looked cosy.

'Why, this is lovely,' Violet said with a smile.

'Well, I do my best. Now put your bags down while I go and put the kettle on. You must be longing for a hot drink after your long journey.'

'I am,' Violet admitted as Sadie disappeared through a door that led into a tiny kitchen. It was then that a noise to the side of a small dresser caught her attention, and moving towards it, she gasped, the colour draining from her face. Inside a wooden crib lay a chubby baby waving his hands in the air and cooing. Violet knew instantly who it was. This was Richard, her son!

Chapter Forty-One

Violet stood as if rooted to the spot as shock coursed through her. But surely this couldn't be! Sadie had told her that he was with a new family in London.

After a moment she became aware of Sadie standing next to her shamefaced.

'But I-I don't understand. You told me he was with foster parents.'

'I know I did, pet, and I'm sorry.' Sadie was silently crying now. 'I *meant* to find some, I really did, but after I saw him, I knew I had to keep him. I'd already had to give you away as a baby and I couldn't give my grandson away too. But don't worry, no one will ever know he's yours if you don't want them to, and I'll take such good care of him, you have my word.'

Violet thumped down heavily into one of the wing chairs.

Sadie wrung her hands. 'I'm sorry, I *truly* am,' she muttered. 'But I couldn't have lived with myself if I'd let him go too. That's why I left you to go home alone. I had to get Richard back here and find us somewhere to live. And look at him. He's thriving and such a good baby. The only time he ever cries is when he's hungry or needs a clean binding.'

Violet was still too shocked to speak as she turned her eyes back to the little soul in the crib. She had not even allowed herself to look at him after the birth and had wondered time and time again what he looked like. Her fear being that he would look like Oliver. But now she saw with a little flash of relief that he looked nothing like him. He had exactly the same colour eyes and hair as her own and a look of her father about him. She felt a little maternal instinct stirring deep inside. He really was a beautiful, contented baby.

'Would you like to hold him?'

Violet shook her head. It would be wrong to become attached. There was no way she could ever claim him. And yet she so wanted to stroke his downy hair and feel the soft skin of his cheek.

'No . . . I, er . . . no.'

Sadie nodded. She could only imagine what a shock it must have been to find him there. She knew she should have told her and had fully intended to do so when the time was right, but the opportunity hadn't arisen. Violet was so busy caring for Edie and she hadn't wanted to burden her with anything else. And now it was too late; her secret was out and she could only hope that Violet would forgive her.

She went back to the kitchen and returned with steaming mugs of tea and a bottle of milk for Richard. Violet was still looking dazed so after placing her tea within easy reach of her, Sadie lifted the bottle and sat down in the chair opposite, her attention fixed on the child. He grinned gummily up at her and Violet saw the bond between them as Sadie eased the rubber teat between his tiny lips. The baby started to suck greedily and within minutes the bottle was empty and he gave a large burp. Sadie smiled as she lifted him over her shoulder and patted his back. 'He loves his milk. I'm thinking of starting to wean him soon.'

Violet didn't say a word. She was still trying to take in the fact that the baby she had thought she would never see again was here in the room with her. When Sadie was satisfied that Richard had brought his wind up, she gently laid him on the chair and expertly changed his binding and by the time she had finished his eyelids were drooping and within seconds he was fast asleep. Sadie laid him gently back into his crib and pulled the blankets under his chin before giving Violet a tremulous smile.

'That's it for now. He should sleep for at least a couple of hours, so I'll get us something to eat. I've a stew cooking if that's all right for you, then I'll show you where you'll be sleeping.

I have two bedrooms here. One will be Richard's when he's a little bigger but for now he sleeps in my room. It makes it easier for the night feeds.'

Violet nodded numbly, desperately trying to keep her eyes away from the slumbering baby. Throughout the pregnancy she had felt as if she had a monster growing inside her, the product of a rape. But now it hit her that none of what his father had done was Richard's fault. He was the little innocent in all this.

'How have you explained him away?' she asked eventually as she sat at the small table with Sadie eating her meal.

Sadie flushed and lowered her eyes. 'I told everyone that my widowed daughter had died giving birth to him,' she said apologetically. 'I could hardly tell the truth, could I? Luckily my job in the corner shop has been a godsend. The old couple that own it are quite charming and happy for me to take him with me for now. He's no trouble and sleeps in a drawer behind the counter, although I realise I shall have to make other arrangements when he gets bigger. But that's a bridge I'll cross when I come to it.' She sighed, reaching across the table and squeezing Violet's hand. 'I really am *so* sorry for deceiving you, pet. Do you think you can ever forgive me?'

Violet stared back at her for a few moments before nodding solemnly. Strangely enough she could. She could only begin to imagine how hard it must have been for Sadie to leave her with her father all those years ago and after being present at Richard's birth it would have been harder still to abandon her only grandchild.

Sadie's face brightened. She had been so afraid Violet would cut all ties with her when she discovered what she'd done, but it appeared that she would accept it and it was a blessed relief.

'I thought the amount you said the foster family had asked for wasn't enough,' Violet said quietly. 'But now I know that it's you who will be caring for him I want to settle a sum on you that will ensure you don't have to work if you don't want to.' And then as a thought occurred to her, she asked, 'Does anyone back at home know about this?'

Once again, Sadie looked ashamed. 'I wrote and told Edie what I was proposing to do while we were still in London. Then when he was born, I knew I couldn't bear to leave him. He's so little and defenceless and none of this is his fault.'

Violet could only nod in agreement.

Later that evening, when Richard woke for his next feed, Violet watched in fascination as Sadie gently washed him in a tin bowl and put a clean nightshirt on him before feeding him again. Everything about him was fascinating and she could hardly believe she had given birth to something so perfect .

'What will you tell him about where he came from when he gets older?' she asked in a shaky voice.

Sadie looked at her soberly. 'That all depends on what you want him to know, pet.' Her voice was gentle. 'I can stick to the story I've already spread about if that's what you want. Just have a think about it.'

She didn't ask Violet if she wanted to hold him again. She could see that Violet was still wary of him and didn't want to push things.

'Anyway, how is Toby and everyone else back in Hull?' she asked as she settled Richard back into his crib.

A closed look spread across Violet's face. 'They were all well when I left, except Edie of course, but thankfully I think she's turned a corner now.'

'And Toby?'

Violet sniffed and shrugged. 'Fine the last time I saw him. He calls in to see Edie often.'

Sadie sighed. 'Are you quite sure it's Edie he's coming to see? It was as clear as the nose on your face that he had a soft spot for you before we left for London.'

'And do you really think he still would have if he knew about the bastard child I gave birth to?' Violet instantly felt ashamed as she saw the look of hurt flash across Sadie's face. As they had just agreed, none of this was Richard's fault. Not that most men would look at it that way.

'I wish you wouldn't call him that,' Sadie said quietly.

A solitary tear ran down Violet's cheek. 'I-I'm sorry. It's just all been such a shock to find him here.'

'I can understand that. Now let's get some sleep. It's been a long day and I have work tomorrow morning. You'll be all right here on your own for a few hours, won't you?'

Violet nodded and after lifting Richard, Sadie set off up the staircase with Violet following.

Outside, under the cover of darkness, a shadowy figure moved away from the window with a smirk on his face. So his suspicions had been right. He was a father and he intended to use the knowledge to his advantage!

Over the next two days Violet kept herself busy pottering about the cottage while Sadie took Richard to the shop. She did some washing one day, which she pegged out in the little garden at the back of the cottage, and on another day, she made them a steak pie for their dinner with an apple pie to follow. She still hadn't made a move to so much as touch the baby but slowly she began to realise that it was getting harder not to. And then one morning when the rain was hammering down outside and Sadie was getting ready for work, Violet tentatively suggested, 'Why don't you leave Richard here with me today? I'm sure I've watched you feed and change him enough now to know how to do it.'

Sadie paused to stare at her with a question in her eyes. 'Are you sure you want to, pet?'

Violet nodded. 'Quite sure; it isn't fit to take him out in this weather and he'll be perfectly all right with me until lunchtime. It will give me something to do.'

Sadie looked uncertainly down at Richard, who was sleeping peacefully in his crib, before nodding. 'Very well. But if you need me, you know where I am. I shall be back for lunch.'

After Sadie had left, Violet looked down at her son. His long dark eyelashes were curled on his plump little cheeks and with his thumb jammed in his tiny mouth he looked like an angel.

'Oh Richard, I'm so sorry,' Violet muttered as she bent to lift him. He was heavier than she had expected, thanks to the tender loving care he received from Sadie, and she relished the sweet baby smell of him. She was still cuddling him when he suddenly opened his eyes and stared solemnly up at her.

She gave him a reassuring smile. 'It's all right, sweetheart. Sadie will be back soon,' she soothed as she rocked him to and fro. 'I'm your mummy . . .'

Tears burned at the back of her eyes as she went to the kitchen, still holding him in one arm, to warm his milk. He watched her the whole time she was feeding him and she began to wonder: would it really be so terrible if she was to take him home and bring him up herself? Plenty of other young women had had a child out of wedlock and it wasn't as if she couldn't afford to keep him.

She was still pondering when Sadie returned, and she felt hopelessly hurt when Richard's little face lit up at the sight of her. He had been as good as gold for her but not once had he smiled at her as he did at Sadie. The bond between the two of them was plain to see and common sense kicked in. How would she explain him away and what would happen when Oliver heard she had turned up out of the blue with a child? He was bound to guess that he was his, which would only cause yet more problems. Still, she consoled herself, she had plenty of time to think about things before she went home and so she relaxed and enjoyed getting to know Sadie better.

Sadie told her about her upbringing and the grandparents Violet had never met and slowly they grew even closer until, after almost two weeks, Violet knew it was time to go home. She said as much to Sadie as they sat having a cup of cocoa late one evening.

Sadie sighed. She had loved having Violet here but had known this day would come. 'Will you come back and see us?' There was a quiver in her voice.

Violet patted her hand gently. 'Of course I will . . . Mum.'

Sadie blinked. Violet had called her Mum for the first time and she felt as if she had been given a great gift. 'Oh, my darling girl, I'm so sorry that I couldn't keep you all those years ago,' she sobbed.

Violet nodded in understanding. 'It's all right, I was in exactly the same position with Richard, wasn't I?'

'I was afraid you might decide to take him back with you,' Sadie confessed.

Violet sighed. 'I can't pretend I haven't thought about it,' she admitted. 'But I know this arrangement is best for him. For all of us, really. It's more than clear how much he loves you. But I insist you allow me to send you some money so you don't have to work if you don't wish to.'

'Very well,' Sadie agreed reluctantly. Anything was better than losing Richard – she didn't think she could bear that. And so that evening Violet wrote to Edie and Lottie and told them she would be returning the following Saturday.

On the day of her departure both women were tearful as Violet packed her bags. She had decided she would catch the train shortly after lunchtime, which meant she wouldn't arrive back in Hull until later that evening, but she didn't mind. It meant she got to steal a few more precious hours with her mother and Richard.

'Just promise me one thing,' Sadie implored her. 'Don't turn your back on Toby because of what Oliver did to you. I know he wouldn't blame you if he knew what had happened, and good men like him don't come along often – I should know.'

Richard whimpered then and both women rushed to pander to him.

'I think he's been spoilt while you've been here,' Sadie teased as Violet cuddled him and buried her face in his baby curls. She hated to leave him but knew it was the right thing to do. Sadie clearly adored him and her love for him was returned.

Sadie had hired a cab to take Violet to the station and when they heard the horse clip-clopping across the cobblestones Sadie hugged Violet fiercely.

'You take good care of yourself, my girl,' she said in a choked voice. 'Write to us often and come and see us again very soon, promise me.'

'I promise, Mum. Goodbye, and goodbye for now, Richard.' Her own eyes were moist as she tore herself away from them and clambered into the cab. As it pulled away, she leant from the window and waved until Sadie and Richard were lost to sight.

It was time to go home but once again she would be leaving a little part of her heart behind her.

Chapter Forty-Two

Because of problems on the tracks, the journey home involved two changes – one at Leicester and the second at Sheffield – so it was gone ten o'clock at night before they chugged into Paragon Station in Hull. It was raining heavily when Violet emerged from the platform carrying her heavy bags and she was so tired she felt as if she could have slept for a week. There was not a cab in sight and she sighed at the thought of the walk ahead of her. Still, there was nothing else for it, so she gripped her bags and set off. She decided to take the short cut, which would involve passing the café, and when it came into view, she was alarmed to see that the large window to one side of the door was boarded up. Biting her lip, she glanced up to where the rooms above showed chinks of light through the drawn curtains. Lottie and Frank were clearly still up, and she briefly considered knocking them up to find out what had happened. But then she thought better of it. It was very late and she didn't want to disturb them, so she continued through the drizzly rain feeling tired and miserable.

Soon she was in the labyrinth of alleys that bordered the docks. There were no streetlights here and she glanced about nervously wishing she had stuck to the main roads. From the tall, terraced houses she passed, which housed whole families in just one room, she could hear the sound of babies crying and people quarrelling, although luckily because of the rain most people had stayed indoors. She hurried on and as she approached the main road, at last she saw the glimmer of a streetlight. *Not long now and I'll be home*, she thought as she hurried her steps.

Suddenly she heard someone coming up behind her and she turned her head to see who was there, gasping as she saw Oliver loom out of the shadows, an ugly smirk on his face.

'Been somewhere nice, have you?'

For a moment fear rooted her to the spot, but then sticking her chin in the air she glared at him. 'It's none of your business where I go, now step out of my way. I want to get home.'

She was terrified he was going to attack her again but her pride wouldn't let her show it.

'I'll be more than happy to do that,' he said with a sick grin. 'But I reckon we need to have a little chat first.'

'And what could we possibly have to chat about?'

'Our son perhaps? He's a nice little chap, ain't he?'

'Wh-what do you mean?' She was shaking now.

'Let's just say I've seen him. You called him Richard, I believe.'

Violet was lost for words, but it seemed Oliver had plenty to say.

'It's a shame you turned down my offer of marriage. Especially now we have a son,' he smirked. 'We'd have made a nice little family, and it doesn't seem fair that I can't be part of his life, does it?'

Violet realised with a shock that he must have followed her to Sadie's.

'I was thinking,' he went on, 'that it doesn't seem fair to him or me that he can't live with his father. But then it would be a shame to uproot him, wouldn't it? He seems to be perfectly happy with Sadie.'

'What do you want?' she snapped.

He chuckled. A cold sound that turned her blood to water. 'Well, I was thinking that if I'm not going to be allowed to be a part of my son's life I should be compensated.'

Her fear was fast turning to anger now and she dropped her bags and glowered at him. 'Don't you think you've already had more than enough money out of me?'

He shook his head. 'Nowhere near enough. And I'm sure you wouldn't want to disrupt him, so how about you pay me a nice lump sum to forget he exists?'

'How much?' she said through clenched teeth.

'Hmm . . . I was thinking something like a thousand pounds!'

'*A thousand pounds!*' Violet almost choked. 'Are you *mad*? You'll not get another penny out of me.'

His expression changed and he leant menacingly towards her. 'I shouldn't be quite so hasty in making up your mind if I was you,' he threatened. 'What would people say if they knew you were the mother of an illegitimate child? What would Toby Brabinger think?'

'Oh, *tell* who you like,' she spat, lifting her bags. It had begun to rain harder now, and the drops were like needles on her face.

'Fair enough. I'll tell you what I'll do. I'll be outside the café tomorrow at midday. If you're not there with the money . . . well, let's just say you'll live to regret it.' And with that he turned and strode away and was swallowed up by the darkness.

'Eeh, look at the time,' Dora fretted. 'She should 'ave been 'ome hours ago. What do yer think could 'ave 'appened to 'er?'

She was sitting with Cook, Cleggy and Stan in the kitchen drinking cocoa and waiting for Violet's return and they were getting seriously worried.

'I reckon I'll give her another ten minutes then Stan an' me can go along to the train station to see if her train's been delayed,' Cleggy suggested.

Stan nodded in agreement. 'But are yer sure it were today she wrote she was comin' back?'

'O' course we're sure.' Cook lifted the letter Violet had sent. 'It says 'ere look.'

'In that case I reckon we should set off now, Cleggy,' Stan said.

As they started to put on their outdoor clothes the women fussed over them. 'It's comin' down cats an' dogs out there,' Cook fretted. 'Be sure you wrap up warm, mind.' And with a deep breath she added, 'Eeh, what a week it's been one way or another!'

Dora nodded in agreement. 'You can say that again, an' now the miss bein' late. Edie is still wide awake, bless 'er, an' I know she won't sleep till Violet's home safe.'

'Well, you go an' keep her company, pet,' Cleggy advised as he and Stan made for the front door.

They had almost reached it when they heard a key in the lock and Violet spilled into the hallway. She was breathless, having run almost all the way, and her face was ashen.

'Eeh, miss, whatever's happened?' Dora rushed forward to take Violet's elbow and lead her inside.

Violet dropped her bags onto the floor. 'I-it was Oliver,' Violet told them in a shaky voice. 'He followed me home again.'

'Has he hurt you?' Cook was incensed.

'N-no, he was just threatening and demanding money again.'

It was Cleggy who was angry now. 'It's about time that young bugger had his comeuppance,' he ground out, making for the door.

Cook caught his arm and shook her head. 'No, you might make things worse. Let's hear what our miss has to say first.'

They took her into the kitchen and while Violet got her breath back, Cook made a large pot of tea. Violet had calmed down by the time a mug was placed in front of her and told them, 'I'm all right, really, and I don't want Edie to know about this. It might set her back.' She went on to tell them of Oliver's demands for yet more money and they were all disgusted and angry.

'I reckon it's time we went to the police,' Cleggy declared.

Violet shook her head. 'No, Cleggy, that will only make things worse. And don't worry. I told him in no uncertain terms that he wouldn't get another penny out of me so hopefully that's the last I'll see of him.'

'Hmm, we'll see,' he answered, although he very much doubted she was right. Men like Oliver Stroud didn't give up easily. Even so, Violet was the boss, so he didn't feel he could go against her wishes.

When Violet had composed herself, she went to see Edie with a smile plastered on her face and told her all about the visit to Sadie and Richard.

'Sadie told me that you knew she'd decided to keep him, but I suppose she asked you not to tell me, didn't she?'

Edie nodded guiltily, and Violet patted her hand.

'It's all right. I can understand why. And now I've grown used to the fact I think it was for the best all round. Richard is adorable and he's thriving under Sadie's care; she absolutely dotes on him. But tell me, what's been happening here while I've been away?'

Dora had joined them and it was she who told her, 'Lottie an' Frank 'ad the café window put through. They're fumin' an' suspect it were Ned Banks's gang again, although they can't be certain.'

Violet sighed. It felt like they were never going to be free of Oliver and the gang, especially now that he had found out about Richard. Even so, she had decided she was going to brazen it out and stand her ground against him, otherwise where would it all end? He would bleed her dry if she let him.

'I see. Then I'll go and see them in the morning and get it fixed. Meantime I'm shattered. It was a long journey because the trains were delayed and I'm ready for my bed.' She rose and leant across the bed to kiss Edie's cheek then made her way to her room where she stood in the window looking out across the docks, and finally allowed the tears she had held back to fall.

She knew there was very little chance of Toby not finding out about Richard. Oliver was so spiteful he would probably break his neck to tell him. Looking back, she supposed it had always been inevitable the truth would come out someday.

Finally she got into bed and slept fitfully until first light when she got up to get ready to visit the café. Once she had checked on Edie, she set off. However, as the café came into sight, she was shocked to see men there already fitting a new pane of glass with Toby supervising.

'I was coming to organise that,' she told him shortly, flushing with embarrassment.

He smiled a greeting. 'Hello, Violet. I wasn't sure when you'd be back so I thought it best to get it done.'

'That's very kind of you but there's no need now I'm in a position to get it done myself.' Then a thought occurred to her. 'Was it you who paid for it the last time?'

When he looked guilty and bowed his head she had her answer. 'And was it you who sent the flowers and the tables and chairs?'

Again, there was no answer and after a moment she asked, 'But why?'

He shrugged, looking uncomfortable. 'I suppose I felt guilty for what you heard me say in the café that first day – when I told the lady at the next table that the café would be no competition for my restaurant. I didn't mean it to sound as it did, and I could see that I'd offended you. I'm sorry.'

Violet sighed. 'Well, it's water under the bridge now, but I'll pay for the window this time, if you don't mind.'

'Of course. I'm sorry if I've offended you.' Looking uncomfortable, he doffed his cap and left.

Violet bit her lip. She was aware how rude she must have appeared but then, what difference would it make now?

For the rest of the morning, she helped Lottie in the café, and just as he had warned, at midday she glanced out of the window to see Oliver standing across the street.

It was time to make a stand so after collecting her coat she told Lottie, 'I'll be off now,' and slipped away.

Oliver grinned when he saw her walking towards him and led her into the shelter of a ginnel away from sight of passers-by. 'I thought you'd see sense after you'd slept on my request,' he told her with a cocky grin.

'Then you thought wrong,' she said icily. 'Because I came to tell you exactly the same as I did last night. This blackmail stops now; you'll not have another penny piece off me, so do your worst!'

His grin disappeared and his lips set in a grim line. 'If that's your final word on it I should warn you that you're going to rue that decision.'

'I don't think so,' she retaliated, turning about and hurrying away.

Late the following evening she was sitting with Edie in the drawing room when someone started to hammer on the front door.

Edie looked startled. 'Wh-who could . . . that be at this time o' . . . night?'

'I don't know but I'll go and find out,' Violet promised, laying aside the newspaper she had been reading to her.

She swept into the hallway just in time to see Dora open the front door and Sadie fall into the hall, looking dishevelled and almost hysterical.

'Whatever's wrong?' Violet rushed forward to put her arm about Sadie's shoulders and was shocked to feel her shaking like a leaf in the wind.

'I-it's Richard,' Sadie sobbed. 'I put him outside in his pram for a bit of fresh air this morning while I got ready to go to the shop and when I went outside again he was *gone*! Somebody has taken him!'

Chapter Forty-Three

Violet gasped. 'What do you mean, someone's taken him?'

'Just what I say.' Sadie was beside herself with despair. 'I only left him for a few minutes, I swear I did . . . but when I went back outside there was no sign of him!'

Hearing the ruckus, the rest of the staff had rushed into the hall and they were all shocked.

It was Cleggy who took control of the situation, for it seemed no one else was able to. 'Right, let's get a stiff drink inside you – you look like you need one,' he told Sadie. 'And then we'll decide what's to be done!'

'Done!' Sadie wailed. 'We have to find him. He's so little and vulnerable. What if someone has hurt him or—'

'Now, now, let's not let our imaginations run away wi' ourselves,' Cleggy said sternly as he led her past the drawing room towards the day room. 'It's my guess that if someone has taken him they're goin' to want money for us to get him back.'

Violet visibly paled. '*It's Oliver*,' she stated flatly, remembering his threat. 'I'd stake my life on it! He demanded money off me and I refused him and he said I'd live to regret it.'

'So let's go and get him back then.' Sadie grasped her arm. 'There's not a minute to lose. He might hurt him.'

Cleggy shook his head. 'From what I've 'eard of him, if it's Oliver that's got him he won't harm him while he thinks he's worth somethin',' he said sensibly. 'Trouble is, no one seems to know where he's livin' now an' it's too late to start askin' round this evenin'. I reckon we're gonna have to wait till mornin' to start the search.'

'But shouldn't we go to the police?' Violet asked with a tremble in her voice.

Cleggy shook his head again. 'Not yet. We don't want to do anythin' to upset 'im. An' I'll guarantee if it is him that 'as him he'll be makin' it known sooner rather than later. We've just got to sit tight an' wait to see what happens.'

There followed a restless night and although everyone except Cleggy eventually retired to bed, none of them slept much. Early the next morning they gathered in the kitchen looking pale and sick with worry. Cleggy had chosen to stay up to keep watch in case Oliver decided to pay them a visit but there hadn't been a sign of him.

'I shall never forgive myself if anything has happened to him,' Sadie sobbed. Her eyes were swollen and red-rimmed and they could all see how much the little boy meant to her.

'You mustn't say that,' Violet soothed her. 'If Oliver was out to get him, he would have found a way sooner or later. Let's just concentrate on getting him back safe and sound.'

At that moment the doorbell rang and Dora raced to answer it. She came back with Toby, and Violet paled. He was about to find out what had happened to her, and shame made her bow her head.

However, no one had time to say anything as Dora held an envelope out. 'This were on the doormat; it's addressed to Miss Violet.'

Cleggy grimaced and punched his fist into his hand. *'Damn it!'* he ground out. 'He must 'ave come an' put it through while we've been in 'ere. I would 'ave seen him if he'd come during the night!'

Toby looked bemused as he stared around at the sea of tired faces. 'Would someone please tell me what's going on? Is Edie all right?'

'Oh yes, sir,' Dora assured him. 'It ain't Edie . . . it's little Richard.'

'Richard?' Toby looked more confused than ever.

Dora handed Violet the envelope while Sadie falteringly told him the sad story from start to finish, omitting nothing.

When the tale was told he looked shocked, but it was Violet who broke the silence when she told them, 'We were right. It was Oliver who took him and he's demanding a thousand pounds for his safe return.' She couldn't even bring herself to look at Toby, she was so ashamed.

'May I see the letter?' He held his hand out and she gave him the scribbled message.

'Hmm,' he said when he'd read it through three times. Then he read it out.

Violet,

Didn't I tell you you'd live to regret it if you didn't comply with my request? You have only yourself to blame for this. However, I am willing to return the baby to you in good health providing you do as I say. Be outside the café this evening, alone, at ten o'clock with the money in full or you can forget ever seeing the child again. I hope it won't come to that.

Oliver

'The *lousy* bastard!' Cleggy blurted out, then glanced apologetically around at the women. 'Sorry!'

'I think you can be forgiven under the circumstances. In fact, I couldn't agree with you more,' Toby said through gritted teeth. 'Now, here's what we're going to do. Cleggy and Stan come with me, and, ladies, I want you to stay here.'

Sadie opened her mouth to object, but Violet squeezed her hand and she clamped her lips shut.

'Where're we goin'?' Cleggy asked.

'There's a certain chappie, Billy Boy Mellor, who works for Ned Banks who I know would sell his soul to the devil for half a crown,' Toby told them. 'I've got no doubt if we find him, he'll know where Oliver is staying and once we know that it'll be plain sailing. But in the meantime, Violet, I want you to go to the bank and get out the money, just in case.'

She nodded numbly, still unable to meet his eye.

Soon after the men departed and after a brief discussion in which they agreed to meet outside the café at midday if they'd had no luck, they split up to search for Banks or his crony.

For the women left back at the house the morning seemed endless, each minute feeling like an hour, and by the time the men reassembled at the café, they'd had no luck whatsoever.

'I've got an idea where Billy Boy might be,' Lottie told them when they went into the café to grab a quick cup of tea before resuming the search. 'He's usually in the Crown and Anchor down by the docks most dinnertimes. An' I'll tell you somethin' else – there were a couple o' shady-lookin' blokes in here earlier on, and when I went to take 'em their breakfast it sounded like they were discussin' another break-in that's goin' to happen tonight in the big warehouse down by the docks. They should be horsewhipped. The last poor sod they attacked has died. O' course they clammed up when I got close but I heard enough.'

'I see,' said Toby thoughtfully. 'In that case I'll try the inn first and if we have any success I think it's time we gave the police a tip-off, but I want to make sure the baby is safe first.'

The three men set off for the Crown and Anchor. It was a very run-down place, frequented by the dockhands and sailors, with dirty sawdust on the floors and nicotine-stained walls, and as they walked in they received more than a few curious stares.

They glanced around and sure enough there was Billy Boy Mellor with a jug of ale in his hand speaking to another chap at a table by the fire.

'Go and get us all a drink,' Toby instructed. 'And leave this to me.'

Billy Boy Mellor stared at him suspiciously as Toby approached him with a smile. 'What d'yer want?' he snapped as the chap he was with sidled away.

Toby slipped into his seat. 'Actually, I wanted to give you a chance to earn a bit of money,' he said pleasantly.

Billy scowled. 'Oh arr, doin' what?'

'All I want is Oliver Stroud's address. Can you help me?'

The man shook his head, but Toby wasn't done. Money talked and he knew there was no honour amongst thieves.

'I only want to talk to him,' Toby went on, drawing a wad of notes out of his pocket. He saw the greed in Billy's eyes as he caught sight of them. 'And I would, of course, pay for the information.'

'How much?'

'Shall we say ten pounds? . . . No, let's make it twenty.'

Billy thoughtfully stroked his stubbly chin. Oliver was a much more recent member of the gang, so he didn't really feel any loyalty towards him. And twenty pounds was an awful lot of money.

Seeing him waver Toby rushed on, 'He need never know it was you who told me where he lives. But if you're not interested . . .' Deciding to call his bluff he made to rise.

Billy quickly reached out to grab his arm. 'Hold yer 'orses. What do yer want him for anyway?'

'Just a chat.'

'Hmm . . . Right y'are then. But I want the money in me 'and first.'

Toby peeled off two ten-pound notes and slapped them on the table, keeping his hand on them till Billy said, 'Far as I know him an' his ma took a room at old Mrs Craddock's place in Dock Square. First floor, I reckon.'

'Thank you.' Toby pushed the money over to him and indicated towards Stan and Cleggy that they should leave.

Cleggy knew the area well and after passing through a labyrinth of stinking alleys they reached the house.

'What do we do now?' Cleggy asked as he stared at the dilapidated building.

Toby took a deep breath. 'I think we've got to hold fire before we do anything. But first I'm going to go in and see if I can determine whether the baby is there or not. If it is, the next stop is the police station to warn them what's going to happen at the warehouse this evening. It's high time this gang were taken off the streets once and for all, but they mustn't have any idea that we know.'

Cleggy and Stan stood back while Toby made for the door, which was hanging off its hinges. He quickly climbed the staircase to the first floor, stopping at each door to listen. Soon he was rewarded with the sound of a baby crying. His first instinct was to break the door down and rescue the poor little mite, but common sense told him to bide his time, so he slunk down the stairs again.

'I think he's in there,' he told Cleggy and Stan. 'Can you two stay here and look for any sign of Oliver? I'm going to tell the police what's going on and tip them off about tonight. Hopefully one of them will come back with me and help us rescue Richard.'

After Toby had left, the two men went to stand behind an old tumbledown latrine out of sight. If Oliver did appear, it wouldn't do for him to see them.

Sure enough, almost an hour later, Oliver slunk towards the house and disappeared inside.

'Perfect!' Cleggy grinned. 'If the cops come back with Toby they'll catch the lousy bugger with the baby red-handed, an' they'll 'ave him bang to rights for blackmail an' kidnap.'

Another half an hour passed before Toby appeared with two burly police officers.

'Right, let's go in,' Toby said as some barefoot children scarpered, wide-eyed, at the sight of the police officers.

When they reached the first floor, Toby pointed to a door. 'If I'm right they're in there,' he told them.

The larger of the officers rapped on it. 'Open the door. It's the police.'

The room suddenly became quiet save for the sound of a baby crying so the policeman tried the door only to find it was locked.

'Right, stand back,' he warned. 'I'm going to break it down.' Seconds later there was the sound of splintering wood as he jammed his shoulder against it and the lock snapped, sending the door banging back against the wall.

Someone screamed and Toby saw it was Anna, looking terrified and wild-eyed. Oliver was heading for the window, intent on escape but the second policeman rushed forward and tackled him to the ground before he could reach it.

'Get off me, *you swine*,' Oliver cursed as the policeman snapped handcuffs onto him. Anna meanwhile was crying louder than the baby.

'It wasn't *me*,' she cried. 'It was Oliver's idea. I told him he shouldn't.' The first policeman stepped forward and cuffed her too as Toby hurried across to the drawer where Richard was lying and gently picked him up. He was red in the face and whimpering, his little hands balled into fists of rage, but thankfully he looked unharmed.

'All right, little chap,' Toby crooned. 'Let's get you home to your mum, eh?' Turning to Cleggy, he asked, 'Could you go back to the main road and flag a cab? Goodness knows when this poor little soul was last fed.'

Cleggy hurried away as the police led Anna, kicking and fighting, towards the door.

'You get him back to his mother,' one of the policemen told Toby. 'We'll get these two to the station then someone will be round to take statements later this afternoon. And don't worry, sir, I doubt these two will be able to get up to any more mischief for some time to come.'

Chapter Forty-Four

The minute the cab pulled up outside Seagull's Roost the women rushed out to greet them and Richard was handed into Sadie's arms.

'I-I can never thank you enough,' she sobbed as Violet looked on with tears streaming down her cheeks.

They carried the baby inside and Dora went to warm some milk for him. Because Sadie had arrived with nothing, Cook had had the foresight to send Dora shopping for anything Richard might need that morning.

'Oh, I've been *so* worried about you,' Cook told Cleggy, and crossing the room, he planted a gentle kiss on her cheek. She blushed prettily. Although the feelings between them had been steadily growing, it was the first time he had publicly shown her affection and she hoped it wouldn't be the last.

The men went on to tell them all that had happened, and on hearing that Anna and Oliver were now safely locked up a sigh of relief echoed around the room. Everyone was fussing over the baby, who thankfully seemed no worse for his ordeal, which was a blessed relief, when they considered what might have happened.

'Thank you, Toby,' Violet said quietly.

Looking embarrassed he shrugged. 'I only did what anyone would have done.'

Sadie took Richard away to give him his bottle before taking him in to Edie, who had guessed that something was amiss. She was getting better by the day and they had all been worried that this might set her back.

'What will happen now?' Cook asked.

'Well, hopefully if what Lottie heard turns out to be the truth, the coppers will be lyin' in wait fer Ned Banks's gang this evenin' an' they'll catch 'em red-handed,' Cleggy told her.

'Let's just hope they do, an' once they've locked the cruel buggers up they should throw away the key. There's two families wi'out a dad thanks to them buggers. Now, I'd best get some dinner on. We ain't been able to do nothin' fer worryin' all day.'

Toby left soon after and later that evening, the police came to interview Sadie about the kidnapping, and she cried as she relived how terrified she had been when she found Richard's empty pram.

Early the next morning, the same policeman appeared to tell them they had caught Ned Banks and two of his gang during the break-in at the warehouse.

'One of them, Billy Boy Mellor, squealed like a pig when questioned,' he told them. 'And it was him that confirmed it was your stepbrother, Oliver Stroud, who murdered the first night watchman.'

Violet gasped. She knew Oliver was bad, but she had never realised he would sink to those depths.

'I see.' Her voice was quaking. 'And where are he and my stepmother now?'

'They're being held in the cells at the station until they go to court,' the policeman informed her solemnly.

'Would it be possible to see my stepmother?'

Cook looked at her askance. '*What?* Why would yer want to do that?' she growled.

'I just feel I should. She was a part of my life for many years, after all.'

'Huh! Leave her where she is an' let her rot, that's what I say,' Cook snapped.

The policeman, however, nodded. 'I should think you'd be allowed a few minutes with her, miss, if you're quite sure that's what you want?'

'It is.'

'Then perhaps you could call into the police station at three o'clock this afternoon and I'll tell the desk to expect you.'

After he left, Cook glared at her, but nothing she said would change Violet's mind. She felt it was something she had to do.

Toby agreed with Cook when he called in later that morning but when he saw Violet was determined to do it, he said, 'Then at least let me come with you. Take you there, I mean.'

'Very well, thank you.'

And so at the agreed time Toby's carriage pulled up outside the police station.

'Would you like me to come in with you?' he offered.

She shook her head. 'Thank you but no, I think this is something I have to do by myself.'

She made her way into the station and the same young policeman who had visited the house led her down a steep concrete staircase, worn with time, to the cells below.

Thankfully Anna was in the first one she came to, so she didn't have to set eyes on Oliver.

The woman was pacing up and down the cell like a caged animal but on seeing Violet she approached the bars and leant so close that Violet could almost taste her fetid breath.

'They're going to hang my boy, you know,' Anna spat. 'And all because he was forced to steal to make enough money for us to exist in a filthy hovel while you lived like a lady.'

'Wh-what do you mean he's going to hang?'

'It wasn't his fault,' Anna ranted agitatedly. 'If that silly old night watchman hadn't gone for him, he wouldn't have had to stab him, would he?'

'So Oliver did stab him?' Violet was horrified. She hadn't wanted to believe it.

Anna shrugged as she started to pace again. 'The police caught Ned Banks and two of his cronies but the rest of the gang got clean away. How can that be fair? My boy and Ned are for the noose and the others are all walking about scot-free.'

She seemed to come to herself then and turned on Violet with such a look of hatred on her face that Violet involuntarily took a step back. 'And now I pray that *you're* going to die too. Slowly and painfully for all the years of pain and heartache you caused me. Can you imagine what it was like having a little bastard foisted on me and having to bring it up as my own?'

Suddenly Violet could stand no more and turning she lifted her skirts and stumbled back up the staircase with tears streaming down her face. She wasn't sure what she had hoped to achieve by coming to see Anna, but if anything she had only made things worse, and now she knew that she never wanted to set eyes on her again.

She was subdued and upset when she climbed back into the carriage and Toby sensed that she didn't want to speak, so they made the journey back to the house in silence.

Over the rest of the week, they managed to fall back into something of a routine until one day Sadie told them, 'I think it's time I went back home.'

'You don't have to,' Violet assured her. She'd loved having Richard close at hand. 'You could both stay here.'

Sadie shook her head. 'Thanks for the offer, love. But all Richard's things are back in Nuneaton and I don't have to worry about it happening again now that Oliver's locked up.'

And so the following day Violet accompanied her to the train station and they said their tearful goodbyes and once the train had pulled away Violet turned and sadly made her way home. Somehow life had to go on as normal. Toby hadn't visited since the day they had gone to the police station, and she had missed him more than she liked to admit. And she felt ill – so ill. Everything that had happened since her father's death finally caught up with her, and she hadn't been able to eat or sleep.

'You should see the doctor,' Cook told her as she watched her slowly decline. Since she'd taken Sadie to the station, she'd refused to even set foot out of the door, and would sit in the chair for hours at a time rocking to and fro, locked in a world of her own.

Violet shook her head, insisting she was fine.

And then one morning when she hadn't put in an appearance by lunchtime Dora was sent to her room to find her collapsed on the floor. While Cook and Dora lifted her into bed, Stan ran to fetch the doctor.

'She has a fever so she must have caught a chill, and she seems to be in shock,' the doctor informed them. 'From what you've told me I think she's had some sort of mental breakdown. Poor thing, it's hardly surprising really.'

'What can we do fer her?' Cook was almost beside herself with worry.

'Just keep her cool and let her rest and hopefully when she wakes up, she'll start to mend. Meantime I'll pop back in tomorrow to check on her.'

Someone was talking to Violet from a long way away, but she fought to stay in the dark. There was no fear in the dark, but the voice was so loving and gentle that she blearily opened her eyes and blinked towards it.

Someone was holding her hand, and turning her head ever so slightly, she saw that it was Toby. His head was resting on the bed at the side of her and he seemed to have no idea she was awake as he softly spoke to her.

'Come on, my love. Wake up, *please*. You can't leave me now. What would I do without you?' Some slight movement must have alerted him to the fact something had changed and as his head snapped up and he saw her watching him his face lit up. Springing up he raced towards the door. '*Dora, Cleggy*, come quickly and send for the doctor. She's awake!'

Footsteps and then Dora and Cleggy were hanging over her, looks of wonder on their faces.

'Oh, Violet, you gave us a rare gliff, I don't mind tellin' yer, pet.' Tears were chasing down Dora's plump cheeks. 'We didn't think you were ever goin' to wake up, but thank God you've proved us wrong! Now just lie still. Stan's run for the doctor to come an' check you over.'

Violet managed to turn her head enough to find that she was at Seagull's Roost in her own bed. The last she remembered was standing in her bedroom.

Dora gently lifted her head and helped her to sip some water, and nothing had ever felt so good as it slid past her cracked, dry lips. She felt too weak to lift her hand so she just lay there and allowed them to fuss over her until soon she slipped back into a peaceful sleep.

'She was awake,' Dora told the doctor when he arrived shortly after. 'But then she went back to sleep again!' She sounded worried but when the doctor examined her, he was smiling.

'Don't worry, the fever has broken and she's in a peaceful sleep. I think she's suffered some sort of a mental breakdown from sheer exhaustion. She'll probably be like this for a few more days but sleep is the best cure now, although she had me worried for a time.' She had been so ill that he hadn't thought she was well enough even to be transferred to the hospital, but it appeared that Violet was going to recover against all the odds.

Dora and Toby sighed with relief; they had barely left her side apart from to look after Edie.

'Just try and get as much fluid into her as you can and start her on a light diet, little and often,' the doctor went on as he snapped his bag shut. 'And remember, you can send for me at any time of the day or night should you have any concerns.'

Once he had gone, Dora rubbed her eyes. She looked worn out, as did Toby.

'How about I make us both a nice cup o' tea while she's restin', eh?'

'That sounds just what the doctor ordered,' Toby answered, smiling for the first time since the terrible day he had heard of Violet's collapse, and after a glance at the patient they both quietly left the room.

The next time Violet woke she was immediately aware of the scent of flowers and glancing towards the table at the side of the bed she saw a huge bowl full of red roses.

She still felt a little disorientated as she tried to process everything that had happened. Anna had verbally attacked her, and what was it she had said about Oliver? Something about him going to hang? Slowly it all began to come back to her and she felt a tear slide down her cheek.

When Toby came back into the room and saw she was awake he beamed from ear to ear. He was unshaven and dishevelled and didn't look much better than she felt.

'How are you feeling now?' he asked, hurrying over to the bed, although he didn't try to touch her.

'Better, I think. But I can't seem to grasp what's gone on or why.'

He sighed as he took a seat at the side of her. 'Your body went into shock after you went to see Anna. Do you remember? I believe she is in a mental asylum and from what I've heard it's doubtful she'll ever come out, and Oliver is safely locked up so you've no need to be afraid. You're quite safe.'

Violet shook her head as she tried to take it all in.

'Anyway.' Toby rose again and grinned as he touched his bristly chin. 'Now that I know you're over the worst I'm going to get myself back home and have a bath.'

He turned and left, still making no attempt to touch her and for some reason that irked her as she suddenly remembered what she had heard him saying as she had come out of her unconscious state. *Come on, my love. Wake up, please. You can't leave me now. What would I do without you?*

When Dora came back with a bowl of water to give her a wash, Violet asked cautiously, 'Has Toby been here for long? How long was I asleep?'

'You were all but dead to the world for four days.' Dora sighed. 'And never once did he leave the room apart from to eat and go to the toilet, bless him. He's a good man. It's just a pity you can't see it.'

Violet scowled. 'What do you mean?'

'Why, it's as plain as the nose on yer face, ain't it? A blind man on a gallopin' donkey can see how much he loves yer, but you've kept him at arm's length for that long I think he's given up hope of you ever changin' towards 'im. But that's enough o' that. Let's get you spruced up an' into a clean nightgown, eh? Then you can 'ave some chicken broth wi' Edie.'

Over the next three days Violet grew steadily stronger until she was well enough to sit in a chair by Edie for a short time each day. Edie was also very much on the mend and able to take a few steps at a time on crutches, so all in all everything was looking up.

Chapter Forty-Five

One morning, when Dora came to bring Violet some breakfast, she was beaming. 'You'll never guess what?' She was bursting to share her good news. 'Cleggy an' Cook 'ave just informed me that they're gettin' wed! Ain't that marvellous news?'

Violet was thrilled to hear it, although it didn't come as a complete surprise. She had watched their relationship blossom and couldn't have been happier for them.

'They just want a quiet do,' Dora went on happily. 'Cleggy is goin' to ask Mr Brabinger if he'll be 'is best man. She wants Stan to walk her down the aisle an' you to be her matron of honour.'

'And when is all this going to happen?' Violet asked happily.

'Just as soon as they can arrange it. I reckon they're goin' to see the vicar today and once the banns 'ave been read there's nothin' to stop 'em, so you 'ave to hurry up an' get properly better now.'

'It's certainly something to look forward to,' Violet agreed as she started to think of what she could buy them for a wedding present.

When Toby called later that afternoon, laden with yet more flowers, he was as thrilled with the news as the rest of them.

'It's marvellous,' he said enthusiastically. 'I insist on throwing a little reception at the restaurant for them after the service as my wedding gift to them.'

A week later Violet sent Dora with Cook to help her choose her wedding outfit, and Toby took Cleggy to be fitted for a new suit. It was Violet's wedding gift to them.

Cook chose a smart two-piece costume in blue velvet with a very ostentatious hat sporting peacock feathers to go with it, while Cleggy insisted on a more conservative grey pinstriped suit and a white shirt.

The wedding was set for the end of October, which they all hoped would give Edie and Violet time to get even better, and with this occasion to look forward to they both did. Toby continued to call each day, but he and Violet were back to being polite but cool with each other, which concerned Violet more than she cared to admit. She began to think that she must have imagined the words she had heard him utter, for he never so much as touched her. There were regular letters from Sadie, who reported that Richard had cut his first tooth and continued to thrive, and Violet knew she had made the right decision in allowing him to stay with her, although she thought of him often.

They had heard that Oliver had been sentenced in late September. He had been charged with manslaughter because the jury had decided that he hadn't intended to kill the night watchman, and so he would escape the noose, but would spend the rest of his life in prison. Violet could only feel relief that she would never have to see him again.

Finally the day of the wedding dawned and the wedding party, including Sadie and Richard, set off for the church in a carriage that Toby had sent for them. Once they arrived, Cleggy and Toby hurried inside to take their places and the women followed at a more leisurely pace.

'I feel a bit daft havin' all the palaver at my age,' Cook muttered as Violet straightened her skirt for her, but despite what she said she was glowing and Violet was sure she and Cleggy would be happy together.

Toby had bought Edie a wheeled bathchair and she was beaming too as Dora pushed her into the church. And then Cook and

Stan took their positions and solemnly marched down the aisle with Violet close behind them as the 'Wedding March' echoed around the beautiful old church.

As the couple made their vows the light from the stained-glass windows shone down on them, as if the heavens outside were giving them their blessing, and once the service was over, they left the church to be showered with rice while the autumn leaves blew down from the trees.

It was a very happy party that arrived at Toby's restaurant where he had organised a slap-up meal with as much champagne as they could all drink. Later in the day, when everyone had eaten their fill, Cleggy and Cook cut the cake and the speeches were made.

When it came time to leave, Cook said, 'But first I must throw my bouquet.' Giggling like a girl, she turned her back on the guests and tossed her posy of cream freesias and white rose buds over her shoulder. It landed squarely in Violet's arms and she blushed as everyone began to cheer.

'Looks like you're next, pet,' Lottie laughed. She'd had more than a few glasses of champagne and was in a merry mood.

They all followed Cook and Cleggy outside to the waiting carriage that would take them to the best hotel in town, another wedding present from Toby, and Cleggy proudly helped his new wife into it. Everyone cheered as they drove away and slowly the guests began to leave. Dora and Stan had already taken Edie home some time before when she had started to tire, and once Lottie and Frank had left for their rooms above the café, there was just Toby and Violet left.

'That's that then,' she said quietly, smiling at him. 'It went rather well, don't you think?'

'It's been a wonderful day,' he agreed. 'Now will you let me give you a lift home, Violet? I really don't like the thought of you walking home alone.' They were both thinking of the night Oliver had attacked her.

'Well, I, er . . .' Violet felt embarrassed. It was the first time they had been completely alone since she had been ill, and she didn't know what to say to him. But she knew it would be rude to turn him down, so she nodded.

'I hope you won't mind me saying this, but I thought you looked beautiful today,' he said as he helped her into the carriage.

She lowered her eyes as a flush stained her cheeks.

'Actually, you were by far the most beautiful girl there,' he said softly.

It was then she decided there were things that needed to be said and there might never be a better opportunity, so before she could change her mind she rushed on, 'Toby . . . I'm sorry if I've seemed standoffish to you. It's just that . . . I'm not pure anymore.'

'Are you talking about what happened with Oliver?' he questioned gently, and she nodded miserably.

'But none of that was your fault!'

Violet cringed with shame. 'But it made me feel . . . dirty. That's why I kept you at arm's length,' she said eventually in a tear-choked voice. 'I knew that no decent man would ever want me after that, especially since I had a child.'

He frowned. 'And what makes you think that? Any decent man would know that you had the child forced upon you. But what surprises me is the fact that you didn't bring him back with you after visiting Sadie the first time.'

'I-I wanted to,' she confessed. 'But after seeing how much Sadie adored him and how much he loved her I couldn't separate them. She had already been forced to give me up when I was a baby and I couldn't put her through any more pain. Instead, I've made sure she has enough money to ensure that both she and Richard will never want for anything. And . . .' She paused before going on, 'I haven't told anyone yet, but I've also instructed Mr Chapman to put the house into Edie's name. She'll be able to live there comfortably on the money she makes from the café and I'll have more than enough with the boatyard business. She's doing really well now, thank goodness, but I think both you and I know she'll never be able to work again, and I want her to spend what time she has left in comfort.'

'That's a very admirable thing to do,' he murmured as he reached to take her hand. 'And what you've done for Sadie is very selfless too. But what will you do now?'

She shrugged. 'I suppose I shall stay at the house to help with Edie.'

'Or you could come and stay at mine.'

She raised her head to stare at him. 'Stay at yours? What do you mean?'

'Exactly what I said. You could stay at mine. You are without doubt the most stubborn, contradictory, kind and caring woman I have ever known, and you must know how much I love you. I always have, and I can think of no one else I'd rather share my life with than you.'

Suddenly all the feelings she had for him bubbled to the surface and she smiled. 'I might consider it but only on one condition.'

'And that is?' He went to sit beside her and slid a hand about her shoulders, turning her towards him.

'That you make an honest woman of me and marry me first.'

'Is that a proposal?' he asked with a twinkle in his eye.

She grinned. 'I suppose it is.'

And suddenly it was as if they were the only two people in the whole world again as he stared at her with all the love he felt shining in his eyes. 'I think that could be arranged. And as far as I'm concerned, the sooner the better. But tell me, does this mean that we are now officially engaged to be married?'

There were stars in her eyes as she stared at him. 'I suppose it does.'

'In that case I demand my right to kiss the bride-to-be.'

Violet was only too happy to give in to his demand as she melted into his arms.

Epilogue

Four Years Later

'Oh, for goodness' sake, lad. Sit down, can't yer? You'll wear a hole in the carpet at this rate, marchin' up an' down!' Edie snapped.

They were all sitting in the lovely drawing room of Toby and Violet's home, while upstairs the midwife and doctor waited to bring their first baby into the world. Violet's pains had started early that morning and she had insisted on Toby fetching Edie, who had turned up in no time with Cleggy. They had been there anxiously waiting ever since, and over the last hour the cries that sometimes echoed down from the bedroom had been more and more agonised.

'*Surely* the baby should have come by now,' Toby groaned, running his hand through his thick thatch of hair yet again. It was almost standing on end now and he was a bag of nerves.

'Now don't start that again,' Edie told him. 'You said the same to the doctor two hours since, an' didn't he tell you babies don't come till they're good an' ready!'

Their little maid, Dolly, entered the room, bearing yet another tray of tea. They felt as if all they had done that day was drink tea!

After glancing around at the sea of nervous faces, Dolly started to strain the tea into the cups. Just then a sudden silence settled on the room and she stopped abruptly. As one they all looked towards the ceiling. And at last, they heard what they had been waiting for: the wail of a newborn baby.

'Thank God.' Tears started to stream from Toby's eyes as Cleggy rushed over to pump his hand.

'Congratulations! Sounds like you're a dad, son.'

Edie was openly crying with relief as she added her good wishes to Cleggy's. Back at Seagull's Roost, Sadie was anxiously waiting for news. She and Richard had finally been persuaded to move in with Edie the year before and they had lived happily together ever since. Overall, the last few years had been good to them. Dora was now walking out with a young man, and they sensed a wedding on the horizon. Stan was still happily single and anxious to stay that way, and Lottie and Frank were now the parents of a two-year-old daughter called Primrose, and still contentedly living above the café, which Edie had made them partners in some two years ago. After all, as she had pointed out, what did she need it for now? She was very comfortably settled in Seagull's Roost and when anything happened to her it would go to Sadie.

The only dark spot on the horizon had come the year before when Violet had suffered a stillbirth, which had almost broken her heart. She had been convinced it was punishment from God for giving birth to an illegitimate child, and for some time she had sworn she would never try again. But then nature had taken its course and the result was now yelling lustily in the room above.

They were still laughing and celebrating when the midwife stuck her head round the door. 'It's a girl,' she informed them.

Toby rushed towards her. 'Thank you, nurse. Are she and my wife both all right? Can I come up and see them now?'

'In answer to your first question, they are both fine, the baby is quite beautiful. And in answer to your second question, no, you can't see her just yet. I'll call you when you can come up.'

Toby started to pace again, while Dolly brought in the bottle of champagne that Toby had had chilling ready for this occasion.

'Well, here's to your lovely new daughter, Toby,' Edie said, raising her crystal champagne flute high. 'May she live a long, healthy, happy life.'

'Here, here!' They chinked their glasses together and drank a toast to the new arrival just as the midwife reappeared with a tiny bundle wrapped in a pink shawl.

'Would you like to meet your daughter, Mr Brabinger?' she asked with a sparkle in her eye.

Toby stared down at the baby in awe, wondering how he and Violet had managed to make someone quite so beautiful. She looked remarkably like her mother and Toby fell in love with her at first sight. They were all cooing over her when the doctor appeared and in his arms was yet another bundle, this one wrapped in a blue shawl.

'And when you've finished saying hello to her, perhaps you'd like to say hello to your son too, Mr Brabinger?'

'*What? Twins!*' Toby could hardly believe what he was seeing. He was now the father of two children and his son looked just like him, with the same colour hair and eyes.

'Dolly, I reckon you're gonna have to go an' get another bottle o' champagne,' Edie chuckled, and Dolly was only too happy to rush away and do just that.

'And now, Mr Brabinger, I suggest you go upstairs. Your wife is eager to see you,' the doctor said.

Toby tore himself away from the babies and took the stairs two at a time. He found Violet propped up against a mound of pillows in their room looking tired but unbelievably contented. In fact, she seemed to be glowing.

'So, what do you think of them?' she asked, holding her hand out to him.

Gripping it he kissed her fingers. 'I think you are by far the bravest, cleverest woman I ever knew, and the babies are just *adorable*. No wonder you were so big, eh?'

She giggled as he stroked the damp hair from her face. 'The trouble is, we'll need another crib now and—'

He held his hand up. 'Don't you get worrying about things like that. Edie has it all in hand and first thing in the morning she and Sadie will be going shopping to get us everything else we need. I thought we ought to perhaps think of getting a nanny too. It's going to be hard for you with twins. What do you think?'

'I think it's a *terrible* idea,' she told him bluntly, although she was smiling. 'They're my babies and I'll look after them. If I need help, I'm sure Edie and Sadie would be more than happy to step in.'

He chuckled and nodded. 'You're quite right. I hadn't thought of that. But now I suppose we should think of names. Have you anything in mind?'

'I have, actually. I thought William for him and Lucy for her?'

If it were possible his smile stretched even wider. '*Perfect!*' he declared. 'And we'll have to start thinking about a christening. Who will we have for godparents?'

'I rather think they're all downstairs making themselves known to our children, don't you?'

He became serious as he stared at her for a moment. 'Have I told you recently how very much I love you, Mrs Brabinger?'

'Not since this morning,' she giggled.

Their eyes locked and they both fell silent as they thought of the life that lay before them. This would be the start of their happily ever after.

Acknowledgements

As I found out very early on in my writing career there are a lot of people involved in getting a book ready for publication besides the author. A whole team of people, in fact!

So, first of all my thanks go to my wonderful agent Sheila Crowley for all her encouragement and support.

Thanks also to my brilliant editors, Sarah Benton and Claire Johnson-Creek, who are always the first to read my efforts and offer advice that will make the books even better. To Holly, Natalia, Beth and the whole of my publicity, marketing and sales team, who always go the extra mile for me. Not forgetting my copy-editor and proofreader and of course the brilliant graphic designer, Jenny, who always manages to come up with such beautiful book covers.

There are far too many people in my Rosie team to mention here but you all know who you are and I want each of you to know how very much your hard work on my behalf and your support means to me. You are all stars, thank you so much. xx

Rosie GOODWIN

Want to keep up to date with the latest from Rosie Goodwin?

With exclusive content from the author herself, book updates, competitions and more, the Rosie Goodwin newsletter is the place to be if you can't get enough of Britain's best-loved saga author.

To sign up, you can scan the QR code or type the link below into your browser

https://geni.us/RosieGoodwin

Hi everyone,

Once again Christmas seems a long way away. I hope it was a good one for all of you. As always for me, and probably most of you as well, it was a fairly manic time. All that shopping, wrapping, delivering of presents and suddenly it's all over in the blink of an eye, isn't it? As usual the house was grottoed up to please the littlies and that's another job in itself, getting the tree and all the decorations out and putting them all away again. Still, it's all worth it to spend time with the ones we love most.

I always find after Christmas and the New Year a little bit of an anti-climax when all the hustle and bustle is over, but still, we have the spring to look forward to now and hopefully some nicer weather. I've really missed being able to get out into the garden, although I do find I tend to write a lot more in the winter when I can't do anything outside, so that's something.

And now here we are with the third book in my Flower Girls Collection on the shelf – *Our Sweet Violet*. This has been such a lovely series to write. I was almost sad when I finished telling you all about our Violet but I do hope you'll love reading it as much as I loved writing it. Poor girl, as usual I gave her a pretty hard time but like all of my main characters, she's a strong girl.

Your reviews on the first two books in the collection and the lovely comments I've received have been amazing so thank you so much for all your support. And of course, last year I attended many events where I got to meet some of you, which was lovely. Most of an author's life is spent locked away with our imaginary characters so being able to get out of the office to meet readers is a real treat! Last year we also introduced my newsletter, which is another lovely way of getting to speak to my readers and let you all know what I'm up to. You can see the link to sign up in the page ahead of this one. And for those of you who haven't done so already please do go over to The Memory Lane Book Club group and sign up there as well.

Later in the year I can promise you all something a little different with my brand-new series, and I really hope you'll enjoy that as well.

Meantime, I'm busily tapping away at the keyboard and trying to keep ahead so I have time to get out into the garden when we finally have some sunshine!

Do stay safe everyone, I shall very much look forward to hearing what you think of *Our Sweet Violet*.

Take care.

Much love,
Rosie x

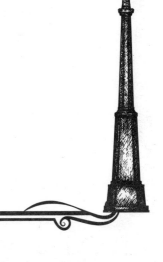

Our Fair Lily

Meet Lily Moon: miner's daughter, parlour maid, determined dreamer and the first of the Flower Girls in a brand-new Rosie Goodwin collection.

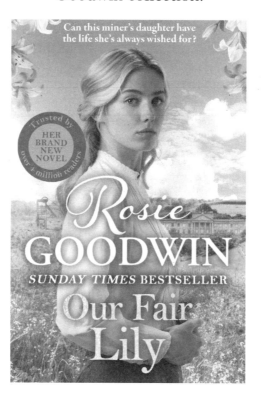

Available now

Our Dear Daisy

Meet Daisy Armstrong: a hope-filled, strong-willed young woman determined to make the best of life and the second of Rosie Goodwin's Flower Girls.

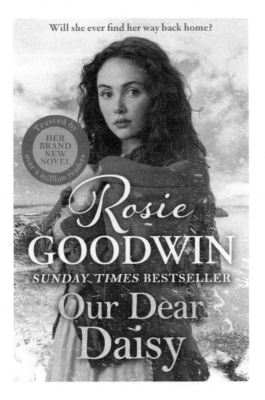

Available now

The Lost Girl

Can Esme lay the ghosts to rest to save
herself and find the life she deserves?

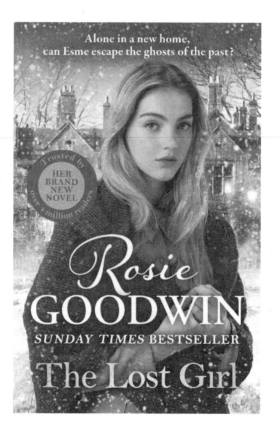

Available now

The Days of the Week Collection

Have you read Rosie's collection of
novels inspired by the 'Days of the week'
Victorian rhyme?

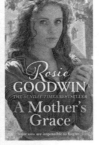

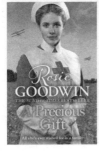

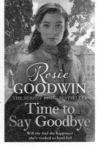

Available now

The Precious Stones Collection

Get to know Opal, Pearl, Ruby, Emerald, Amber and Saffie in Rosie's Precious Stones series.

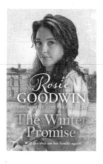  

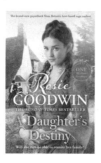  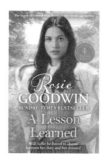

Available now

· MEMORY LANE ·

Introducing the place for story lovers – a welcoming home for all readers who love heartwarming tales of wartime, family and romance. Join us to discuss your favourite stories with other readers, plus get book recommendations, book giveaways and behind-the-scenes writing moments from your favourite authors.

· MEMORY LANE ·

www.MemoryLane.Club

www.facebook.com/groups/memorylanebookgroup